Devilish Details

Lynn Emery

Chapter 1

Jazz stood outside leaning against the police cruiser watching the festivities. Nine o'clock on a Thursday night, the start to the weekend when she made sixty-percent of her profit. Candy Girls didn't have "exotic dance interpretation" every night like some clubs. Instead Jazz opted to have two quality dancers rather than a stable of hard looking girls that she could pay less money.

She tamped down the urge to cuss out the police officers strutting around on her property. At least they'd turned off those damn flashing blue and red lights on top of the three cruisers. After years of working in broken down clubs as first, a waitress, then a bartender, and last a dancer, Jazz had managed to pull together money to buy her own club. Okay, so Candy Girls wasn't the classy place she wanted, but it was a start. Now these damn cops...

The three waitresses working that night stood in a huddle with the weekend bartender, Tyretta. Two smoked cigarettes as they sneered at one uniformed officer in particular. He kept glancing at them. Dressed in the requisite tight, sexy red body suits and shiny black shoes with red bows, Jazz had to smile with pride. All three had figures that made men stare. Chyna, a petite twenty-year-old Chinese-American, crossed her arms over her enhanced breasts. Her given name was Hua, but she never used it. Chyna eyed the police officer as though keeping him in sight would ward him off. Jazz walked over to them.

"Y'all just be cool. This should be over in a minute," Jazz said. When Tyretta snorted, Jazz moved closer to her. "I mean it, Ty. Don't let your smart mouth write a check I have to cash. There is nothing for them to find."

"You better hope none of your customers are holding," Tyretta muttered and sucked in more smoke from her cigarette. Holding was her way of saying they had drugs on them.

"Then that's on them." Jazz frowned when Tyretta gave another snort and added a grunt at the end for emphasis.

"They'll take us all in, girl. Why you think they showed up? Cops don't care about loud music in this hood," Tyretta replied and went back to work making her long cigarette shorter.

"What? I-I can't be arrested. My parents can't find out I'm working here," Chyna blurted out as her eyelids fluttered.

The police officer that had been eyeing the waitresses up and down popped out of nowhere it seemed. His hands rested on his duty belt. "Don't worry about it, Miss..."

Silence stretched as he waited for Chyna to fill in her name for him. She inched closer to Jazz and mumbled, "Thanks."

"What I mean is we're just here enforcing the noise ordinance. Two of your customers were fighting in the parking lot when I pulled up. Another one has an outstanding warrant." He spoke in an officious tone, trying to convey that he was somehow in charge of something. "I'm Officer Tim Mathis by the way."

"Thanks for the information Officer Mathis," Jazz said with a smile. She moved a little to partially block his line of sight on Chyna. "The other officers over there patrol here often, so they know my club is usually no problem."

"Yeah, right," Officer Mathis said gruffly. He was about to go on when the supervising officer on the scene called to him. He walked away, but looked over his shoulder before leaving.

"He keeps staring at me in a way I don't like," Chyna whispered.

"What you expect with them twin volleyballs you got?" Tyretta retorted, once again baiting Chyna about her breast implants. "Besides, guys stare at all of us all night. Hell, you oughta be grinning right back at that cop. We always could use a friend in on the po-po squad in this part of town."

Chyna ignored the dig about her newly acquired "C" cups. She didn't get any bigger implants because of her slender frame. Still, because she was so tiny and just under five feet five, even in heels, she looked voluptuous. She grabbed Tyretta's cigarette and took a puff.

"Yeah, you could be right. He's not bad looking either," Chyna said. She looked at the brown-haired man with interest. "For a white guy and all."

"You gonna go for it?" Rochelle, the third waitress, nudged Chyna with an elbow.

"I don't want no cops, on duty or off, hanging around my place," Jazz cut in shortly. She tapped Chyna's arm to pull her attention away from the officer in question. "Hey, you heard me?"

"Yeah," Chyna replied, still looking at him. Her tone said she wasn't listening. She'd given the policeman a slight smile, and he'd smiled back.

"Damn it," Jazz started but broke off the beginning of her lecture when a familiar tall, dark frame came toward them.

"Well, looky here," Tyretta whispered. "Humph, now that's what I call a nice chunk of change right there."

"Another cop," Rochelle spoke low through tensed lips.

"I'll be happy to be nice to this one." Tyretta stood straight to give him the full effect of her almost six feet of curvy girl appeal.

Jazz sighed and wished she had one of her smooth smoking, slender cigarillos. Then she remembered that she was trying to quit. Detective Don Addison looked at ease despite being built like a professional wrestler ready to deliver a beat down. He wore a dark leather jacket over a sweater against the cool, late, last April night air. Jazz figured he had to be at least six feet four inches tall. Not that she was measuring him up or anything. Detective Addison didn't like her. She didn't like him either, not one bit. Okay, so maybe he looked good, but like one of her former foster mothers used to say, "Everything that looks good ain't good for ya." She must have been talking about Detective Donald Ray Addison for sure.

"Evening ladies. Another exciting night at Candy Girls I see," Detective Addison said in his silky baritone.

"Yeah, we always have something fresh over here," Tyretta said. She smirked when Jazz shot a heated look in her direction. With a jerk of her head, she led the other two women away. They joined the dancer on duty.

"I was in the neighborhood and just dropped by to say hello," Detective Addison quipped. He crossed his arms and watched his colleagues.

"Yeah, right. You moved from homicide to the loud noise patrol."

Addison's solid milk chocolate face moved closer to a smile, but it faded. "Nah, dude got killed over on Dalton Ave."

"I knew it. You showing up ain't a coincidence. Anybody I know?" Jazz's heart sped up despite the casual way she asked the question. "Or you can't talk 'cuz it's an on-going investigation like y'all tell reporters."

"It's already been on at least one news show. Some guy name of Brandon Wilks. Got shot tryin' to rob another drug dealer. Do you know him?" Addison went from watching the cops searching Candy Girls to studying Jazz.

"I don't associate with drug dealers, Detective Addison. At least not anymore," Jazz added when his left eyebrow inched up. "That kind of crap is bad for business."

"This," Addison swept a hand at the nightclub. "This is not a business for you to be in. Not if you want to stay away from bad things, Jazzmonetta."

Jazz sucked in air and let it hiss out. She bristled at his presuming he knew her well enough to use her full name, and lecture her. "Well, thank you for that inspiring mini-sermon, Deacon Addison, but my club is legitimate. I have security, and I can take care of myself."

"I'm not a deacon," he replied mildly. "You sure didn't mind getting spiritual guidance from that slick Reverend Fisher. Y'all still dating? I'm surprised his congregation didn't toss him out of that big fancy church."

"Lawrence, *Reverend Fisher,* is respectful and discreet." Jazz tossed a section of her dark red weave over one shoulder. She noted with satisfaction that Addison looked at her with less than professional interest.

"So you didn't answer the question," Addison said.

"No, I'm not seeing Reverend Fisher anymore. Not that it's anybody's business," Jazz said, putting enough sass in her tone to irritate him, she hoped.

"Humph, interesting. I meant you didn't say if you knew Brandon Wilks, the dead robber," Addison said dryly and gave a soft chuckle.

Jazz spun to face him. The twinkle in his eyes inspired an urge to slap him. "You think I'm hooked up to any crime within ten miles, huh?"

"Now, honey, don't make me call out your rap sheet." Addison took a step back and held up two huge hands, palm out. "Calm down now. You don't want my fellow officers to come storming over here."

"You- you..." Jazz no longer saw a tall, handsome, thirty-something man with the kind of muscles she liked. No, he was another tool of the system looking to have fun messing with other people's lives.

"I'm just teasing you. I already know you don't. I've tracked down Wilks' known associates in the last twelve hours since they carted off his sorry carcass." Addison titled his head to one side. "Okay, so bad joke."

"Humph."

Jazz spun until her back was to him. She pushed down the anger bubbling in her gut. She'd spent a big part of her youth having people play head games on her. First, her mother. Vivienne had no business giving birth. Apparently God, Allah, Buddha, or whatever deity in charge at that moment didn't give a shit about the poor kids she pushed out. Then a succession of social workers, unfit adult relatives, and foster parents had their turns. At sixteen Jazz decided she was done with people screwing with her. In the twelve years since, she'd kept that promise to herself.

"Bullshit. You wouldn't be here if you didn't think he, or maybe the dealer that shot him, was connected to me." Jazz flipped back to street smart mode. "Well?"

"Just so happens the guy that shot Wilks, Cleavon Bennett, goes with a woman that used to perform with you. She works for your old boss now. But that's not why..."

"Uh-huh, I knew you didn't end up over here cuz you took the scenic route on your day off. I haven't seen Kyeisha in almost a year since she took her thieving butt off my property." Jazz scowled at him and looked away again.

"You and Lorraine still have bad blood about you buying Candy Girls out from under her, huh? Then Kyeisha pretended to be your friend, but was spying for Lorraine." Addison shook his head. "Yeah, you got a right to still be pissed."

Jazz clapped her hands slowly. "Give the man credit. His investigation skills are still sharp. So now you're going to say I set up her man to get revenge. Like I've got time for that kind of petty shit."

"Hmm, you know, I hadn't thought of that angle.

The case may be solved. Let me make a note," Addison said and pretended to write with an invisible pen on an invisible note pad.

"Keep working the cop thing. Your comedy is stank," Jazz retorted.

Addison dropped his hands. "Okay, look. Let's call a ceasefire"

Jazz felt the heat go out of her animosity, but she wasn't ready to give much ground. She had to let him know she wasn't going to just melt because of his overgrown boyish charm. And, he was still a cop.

"Whatever. Go on and ask your questions." Jazz crossed her arms and stared him down.

"I didn't know there was a call over here," Addison said. He sighed when her expression didn't change. "So, have you talked to Kyeisha in the last twelve to twenty-four hours?"

"I haven't seen her in almost a year *like I told you*. Let me save you some time. Yeah, I knew Cleavon was her boyfriend, and yeah, along with everybody else in the 70805 zip code, I knew he was a dealer. No, I don't know where she is, and I sure as hell don't know where Cleavon is. If they got sense, they're miles away, 'cuz the guy either has a gang or family looking for them. Probably both." Jazz finished by letting out a hiss of boredom. She sure needed that cigarillo.

As if on cue, the uniformed officer acting as the supervisor strolled over. "I'm Sgt. Patrick Evans, ma'am. I hear you're the owner of this establishment?"

"Yes, and I'd like to get back to business. Wednesdays are a big day for me. I'm losing money out here while y'all arrest some folks for misdemeanor possession," Jazz replied crisply.

"We've allowed your employees to go on inside.

But are you saying you knew some of your customers were carrying illegal substances?" Sgt. Evans glanced at Addison with both of his blonde eyebrows raised. Addison said nothing, but nodded.

"Oh please. I run a night club serving liquor while girls dance around poles in one of the rough spots of Baton Rouge."

Jazz pointed to a rectangular board painted white with bold black letters next to the double front doors. The rules were spelled out. "No loitering, no guns, and no drugs allowed on the

Sgt. Evans tapped on the screen of a small tablet. "Okay, just keep the music and the noise on the parking lot to a minimum as best you can." He walked off.

"Whatever to you, too," Jazz mumbled low. She swung around to face Addison. "You done questioning me?"

"I wasn't formally questioning you, Ms. Vaughn. I just happened to see the flashing lights and decided to... Okay, fine. You don't believe me. If you see your friend Kyeisha, tell her to give me a call. You've got my number."

"Humph, I sure do. And Kyeisha is *not* a friend of mine. Don't expect me to call you," Jazz said. "Goodnight Detective Addison."

"You could call me Don every once in a while you know," he replied.

Jazz had already turned and was walking to the club. "No, I don't think so."

"See you around," he called back, and gave a throaty chuckle.

She didn't look over her shoulder. Instead she flipped a hand in the air and kept going. Once inside the club again, she checked with the bartender, cook, and the tall local man she'd hired as security. Jazz looked around. None of the tables, fixtures, or anything else was obviously damaged. She'd check again in the daylight to be sure.

Byron, her security guy on duty, approached. "Hey Jazz, Lilly sayin' she's too shook up to finish tonight. She wants to go home. I figure with the smell of cop still around here, might as well let her." He shrugged his hulky shoulders.

Jazz glanced around at the dark interior of the club. Already, three guys had come in to sit at the round tables scattered around the floor. One was alone. The other two took a separate table about five feet from the stage. Rochelle got busy taking their drink orders. Tyretta was behind the bar. She wiped a spill from the counter top that looked like marble, a cheap laminate surface, obvious even with the lights low. The door swung open and a guy stuck his head in. After looking around for several seconds, he eased inside as though still on guard.

"Y'all want to give up getting paid?" Jazz grunted when Byron didn't answer right away. "I'm running a business to make money. Get the music ready."

"Okay boss," Byron replied. He dutifully headed for the small booth set off to the side that contained a sound system hooked up to three speakers, each attached to a wall in the club.

"Cops asked her maybe one question, if that, and she's shook up," Jazz mumbled to herself as she strode across the floor.

Another door like the one that led to her office was on the opposite side of the bar. She pushed through it. A short walk down a hall brought her to the dressing room door, which she entered without knocking. Lilly sat in one of four chairs at a table. A mirror stretched the length of the wall above the table. She half turned when Jazz came in, but went back to stuffing make-up into a worn imitation leather tote bag. Only six two months past twenty years old, she had smooth dewy skin that needed little make-up. Jazz hired her because she saw not just talent, but a chance to keep Lilly from slipping into an even worse kind of profession. The signs were clear to Jazz. Lilly had had to grow up fast and hard, so Jazz made allowances. She considered Jazz old at twenty-seven, but had the good sense not to make that opinion too obvious. Jazz had survived her own tough childhood by learning to read people. She knew exactly what Lilly thought of her.

Lilly was the youngest employee and the one with the snappiest attitude. Cutting some slack was one thing. But bottom line, Jazz had a business to run, and nobody would be allowed to mess with her hustle.

"Byron told you I'm not feeling well," Lilly said flatly. "I can't perform when I'm upset. I'll be stumbling all over the stage. Mama always said I was born with bad nerves."

"So you don't need your paycheck tonight?" Jazz replied.

Lilly looked up at Jazz's reflection in the mirror, a frown on her smooth honey brown face. "Well I did one set before the police showed up and got our customers all jumpy. I should at least get half my pay," Lilly protested. She turned around on the swivel stool and then stood to face Jazz. She put both hands on her hips. At five eight, Lilly seemed to loom over Jazz, who stood five-feet-five if she had on one inch heels.

"Customers expect to see dancing. I sell more liquor and food when I have a show. You work the full night like I hired you to do, or this will be your last night." Jazz didn't raise her voice but returned Lilly's glare with one of her own.

"Damn, betcha only three old dudes out there," Lilly shot back. But she turned around and started unpacking her make-up.

Jazz watched for a few seconds as she applied dark red lipstick. Then she brushed out the long, thick black hair that was mostly an expensive weave. Lilly shimmied out of the cotton jumpsuit to reveal she still wore her costume. The shiny neon red halter and matching thong made her honey brown skin seem to glow. Customers flocked to Candy Girls to watch Lilly wrap her long legs around the dancer's pole. Still Jazz was beginning to look for a replacement. Lilly got on her damn high horse too often. Jazz was sure one night she wouldn't show, would walk out in a huff, or Jazz would throw her out. The last possibility might be the first to happen. No employee would dictate to Jazz or give her attitude for long.

"Consider that visit from the police a long break. It's almost nine o'clock. You perform between eight and midnight. I'll pay the same." Jazz turned around to leave.

"Gee, thanks."

Lilly went on applying make-up. She dusted sparkly body powder across her generous cleavage and then the rest of her body, paying special attention between her thighs. The glitter was her signature. Guys lapped it up. Jazz was about to set her straight when Tyretta pushed through the dressing room door.

"Child, you better get your glittering rear in gear. The natives are gettin' restless. You got some good tips comin' your way. Guess who just slid in all undercover?

Lil' Bit," Tyretta blurted out before anyone could take a stab at it. "Girl, you know he got some fifties with your name on 'em. I've been keepin' him hydrated for ya."

"Just as long as he keeps his sticky hands offa me. He be tryin' to sneak a feel when he passes a tip." Lilly made a face, but began to primp with quicker movements. The sound system kicked in, playing a raunchy song by a local female rapper.

"Them bills gonna spend the same, girl. Sticky or not," Tyretta quipped.

"You ain't even lyin'," Lilly tossed back with a chuckle. She shook her butt as if warming up, humming along with the music. "Later."

Jazz nodded at her as she walked by. "You have trouble, just signal Byron. These dudes know I don't play that touchy feely crap with my employees."

"Okay," Lilly said. Her tone and attitude were less salty. She dipped and swayed her hips to the music as she pranced out.

"And why are you in here instead of getting guys to spend money on drinks and food?" Jazz snapped at Tyretta once Lilly exited.

"I came in here to save her silly ass from a whippin', and *you* from getting arrested," Tyretta replied and pointed a forefinger at Jazz.

"Humph. I think you just delayed what is eventually going to happen anyway. Lilly is on my nerves every chance she gets." Jazz glanced around the dressing room. "And she better straighten up the mess, too."

"Oh c'mon, relax boss lady. She's not the only one that junks this room up. What's got you in such a bad mood?" Tyretta picked up scarves on the floor and draped them on hooks attached to the walls as she talked.

"You mean losing almost three hours of income, a smaller than usual crowd because of the cops, and being linked to a murder isn't a clue?" Jazz shot back.

Tyretta dropped a hairbrush on the table and stared wide-eyed at Jazz. "Wait, a murder? Who said anything about a murder? I thought the cops came around because of loud music and noise out on the parking lot."

"Yeah, they always use some lame-ass excuse to make trouble. Some lil' dude got shot up by Kyeisha's thug boyfriend. Addison naturally hauls his long, tall self over here to harass me," Jazz grumbled. "And, Lilly sure as hell better clean up before she leaves."

"Right, I'll tell her," Tyretta replied. She followed Jazz out, a frown twisting her chocolate brown face.

Jazz headed down a hallway behind the stage out front taking the back route to her office on the opposite side of the club. She turned right at another shorter hallway that ended in her office. Tyretta followed on her heels asking questions about the murder.

"Look, you think I'm CNN or Fox News?" Jazz retorted over her shoulder. "All I know is some dude is dead and they looking for Cleavon. That's all I want to know. Why in the hell he think Kyeisha is a friend of mine?" She muttered another curse at the ringing cell phone on her cluttered desk. "Well at least nobody stole my cell while I was out there."

"Detective Addison uses excuses to hang around 'cuz he's sweet on you." Tyretta took a melodramatic step back when Jazz spun around and scowled at her. "I'm so scared, but I gotta tell the truth."

"Humph." Jazz sat down at the desk. She found the box of cigarillos, pulled one out, and lit up. She inhaled the sweet smoke and let it out.

Tyretta had become the closest anyone had ever come to being Jazz's best friend. They'd met at a group home after both had been kicked out of separate foster homes. Despite appearances, their bickering never amounted to more than their unique way of communicating. In some ways they were closer than Jazz was to her older sister, Willa. She thought of her sister because the caller ID on her phone showed Willa was calling. The phone played a popular R&B tune again. Jazz grunted and picked up.

"Yeah, Willa. The cops must call you when they come around here, huh? Get out of my business. I'm grown." Jazz rolled her eyes to the ceiling. She sucked in more smoke, and let it trail from her open lips. "Yes, I'm fine. Hell no, I don't need bail money. I'm at the club. I'll talk to you later. I'll let you know 'bout dinner on Sunday. Bye."

"She cares about you. That's something. More than I can say for my jacked-up family," Tyretta mumbled.

"Willa is a control junkie, all right? Not enough she got them two crumb snatchers to take care of, but she gotta be in my face asking questions." Jazz dropped her cell phone into the pocket of her leather jacket. Then she took it out again and sent a text to Byron. "See if Lilly is out there workin' her butt to make me some money."

"I think it's wonderful that she invites you over for Sunday dinner."

"You wouldn't think it was so *wonderful* if you had to deal with her holy-roller Aunt Ametrine preaching at you over mashed potatoes and meatloaf. Sister Ametrine will all but hit you over the head with her Bible. Talks about how Christians need to 'smite the demons out of misguided folks'."

Willa and Jazz had grown up in foster care thanks to Vivienne, their troubled, neglectful mother. They'd been separated six times. Jazz being younger had stayed with Vivienne almost four years after she was born. Willa had been removed by child welfare by then. Willa's fourth set of foster parents adopted her. Through them she gained three aunts and six uncles, "holy-roller" Aunt Ametrine being one of her adoptive mother's two sisters. Jazz didn't call them her family, because in her mind they weren't. No matter what they tried to say.

"Is it good meatloaf? I love me some good meatloaf and gravy. Umf!" Tyretta nodded.

"You're not listening to a damn thing I say. I..." Jazz stopped when her phone signaled a text. "Damn right she better be dancing. I got bills to pay."

"Who'd you say got killed tonight?" Tyretta said, switching gears back to the murder.

"It was yesterday or last night. Some guy named Brandon Wilks." Jazz waved a hand and turned her attention to the invoices on her desk.

"I know that name," Tyretta said frowning. "I wanna say he ran with the South Side of Town boys, you know that gang from the bottom."

"You mean one of the four or five gangs in the bottom," Jazz replied dryly.

"The Bottom" was the nickname for a south Baton Rouge neighborhood. Starting in the forties and fifties, many middle-class and stable blue collar African-American families moved there. The area boasted the first Black high school offering a diploma. Two of the city's first African-American doctors had offices there and so did a black dentist. Small businesses flourished as well, with upholstery shops, various repairs shops, and more that catered to black customers. Black Baton Rougeans avoided the demeaning experience of being forced to enter through a back door or being called "boy" and "girl". And like many black neighborhoods, the passage of time brought change that wasn't for the better. The downward slide began in the mid-1970s. When crack hit in the eighties, the slide became a speedy tumble down into a crime infested "hood".

"I think they hooked up with some of those Spanish dudes that started movin' south of LSU. Off GSRI Road, you know where I'm talkin' about. Or maybe they got into a turf fight with 'em. I don't know. That was three years ago maybe." Tyretta sat back and warmed to her subject. "Yeah, I heard they kissed and made up, started doing deals together. Or something."

"Nice history lesson, Tyretta. Now get back to..." Jazz's head snapped up. "What did you say about Spanish dudes?"

"You know I was livin' in Atlanta back in the day, moved there in 2005 for a minute. When I came back in 2007, I dated this guy named Rasheed. Damn, he was fine but he--"

Jazz cut her off to redirect her back. "Right, Rasheed was all that. But what about the Spanish dudes?"

"Some crazy gangsters from Houston and Cali I remember. Rasheed used to party with them. Wonder where he is now?" Tyretta brushed her long locks as though expecting handsome Rasheed to walk through the office door.

"In prison. Got thirty years for stabbing his girlfriend. She almost died. You remember the names of any of those Hispanic gangsters?" Jazz got up and came around the desk.

"Damn, he didn't even kill the girl and he got thirty years," Tyretta said.

"She was the third person he attacked in four years, and he had a record for other stuff. That dude is a violent psycho with a nice body and charming smile. Good thing y'all broke up."

Jazz leaned against her desk and crossed her arms. She'd rattled off Rasheed's fate, but her mind was on another handsome gangbanger, one from her own past and with a sexy, silky Spanish accent. Filipe Perez had been her lover of the moment four years earlier, but Jazz didn't remember Brandon Wilks. Not that she knew all of his thug life associates. Like Rasheed, Filipe was in prison. Jazz hadn't kept in touch, mainly because she'd helped put him there.

"Damn, Rasheed. You crazier than I thought you was," Tyretta said and stood up.

Chyna knocked though the door was halfway open. "Hey, I wanna take a break, Ty. Not many guys out there, so you won't be running your legs off. Sorry, Jazz."

"We'll pick up by Friday or Saturday," Jazz said, her thoughts not on the small crowd or weekend.

"Okay, I'm comin'", Tyretta replied and waved to her. When Chyna left, Tyretta turned back to Jazz. "So you know that guy what got shot after all?"

"I'm not sure. Maybe I can find out though. Bet my pain in the ass sister can tell me but not before I have to hear a long lecture. Guess I'm going to put up with her smart mouth kids and crazy aunts."

"Quit frontin', 'cuz you love those kids." Tyretta had a distracted expression as though her thoughts were elsewhere. "You're lucky to have a place where you're welcome."

"Yeah, whatever," Jazz retorted with snort. She sent a text message to Willa accepting the Sunday dinner invitation and asking for a favor. Then she plotted out making time to do some of her own research.

Chapter 2

"Well at least she closes that den of iniquity on Sundays," Aunt Ametrine said in her usual judgmental stage whisper, knowing full well the subject of her criticism could hear her. She looked at Willa's daughter Mikayla. "Pass me the peas, baby."

"Yes, ma'am." Mikayla complied and then glanced at her seventeen-year-old brother. "What's a den of iniquity?"

Anthony lost his look of bored distraction, the expression he used around his elders. His brown eyes twinkled. "That means Aunt Jazz operates a place where it ain't nothin' but a part-ee, part-ee. Get down and part-ee," he sang the words while bobbing his head.

"Hey! Ain't nothin' but a part-ee," Mikayla joined in with gusto. She dropped her fork and waved her hands in the air like the popular hip hop artists her mother disliked.

"Heh-heh," Papa Elton grinned at their antics but wiped it from his face at the dirty looks from his wife and Willa.

"Stop that," Mama Ruby said, her voice sharper than a steak knife.

"Ahem, yes ma'am," Anthony replied and shushed

his baby sister. Still, he wore the remnant of a smirk.

"Yes, Mama Ruby," Mikayla answered dutifully.

Willa spread her squint of disapproval from her adoptive father to her son. "Daddy, don't encourage them. Y'all have been watching those old blaxploitation movies from the seventies too much."

"I like the funk," Anthony offered. He smothered a laugh when Aunt Ametrine slapped a hand on her chest.

"Lord have mercy, the things these young people say," Aunt Ametrine huffed in true church lady fashion.

Papa Elton cocked a thick black eyebrow at her. "Oh calm down, Ametrine. Funk is a music genre from back in the day. You ought to know. You was on the dance floor with the rest of us at The Spot back in the seventies. Remember? Yeah, your favorite group was the P-Funk All Stars. You was dating that guy Junior Patin and--"

"Yes, and I changed my life around for the better," Aunt Ametrine cut him off. She patted her face with a napkin. "Praise Jesus for his grace and mercy. Beryl, wasn't the choir in fine form at worship this morning?"

Willa's Aunt Beryl blinked at her sister in surprise. "Um, yes indeed. Sister Carter's niece has a beautiful voice."

The conversation shifted to topics more comfortable for Aunt Ametrine. Willa's kids joked as they helped her clear the table. At Willa's urging, the older adults agreed to have dessert in her living room. Jazz picked up a couple of serving platters and trailed after her sister from the dining room to the spacious kitchen. Once saucers of cake and a silver pot of hot coffee were loaded on a wheeled tray, the kids went off to serve their elders. The sound of their voices in spirited discussion floated in. When they were alone,

Willa faced Jazz.

"You know Aunt Ametrine is just... being herself. She doesn't mean any harm." Willa shrugged at the look Jazz gave her. Then she finished loading the dishwasher.

"Yeah, she's holier than everybody to let her tell it. But Mr. Elton got her good though." Jazz barked a laugh. "He was about to yank some skeletons out her closet, and them bones still had meat on 'em."

Willa suppressed a giggle by pursing her lips. "Mama Ruby is going to get on him I bet."

"I don't think so. Miss Ruby didn't say a peep. She was trying too hard not to laugh. I'm getting a picture of Sister Ametrine getting funky on the dance floor." Jazz grabbed a dish towel and waved it in the air as she shook her hips. She did her imitation of Aunt Ametrine's generous butt sticking out as she moved.

"You got Aunt Ametrine down. Like Papa Elton said, bet she got loose and real funky," Anthony said from the archway that led to the dining room. He cut a couple of moves too while making the sounds of a beat.

"Stop it, Anthony. Show some respect for your great-aunt," Willa said, forcing a stern expression.

"Yes, ma'am." Anthony stopped dancing. He shot a glance at Jazz and grinned.

"What did you come in here for anyway?" Willa asked.

"Grandmamma wants ice cream." Anthony cleared his throat and shifted from one foot to the other.

"Okay, then get busy." Willa got out a tray and piled bowls on it with spoons. Anthony got a container of ice cream from the freezer and left with the tray. "You see what you started? He'll be imitating his Aunt Ametrine for days."

"You mean like this?" Jazz struck another pose with

her butt in the air and shimmied across the tile floor.

"Stop it," Willa said. She lost the battle to be disapproving and burst into loud laughter until tears came down her nut brown cheeks. She got control. "Girl, you too crazy."

"Hey, somebody gotta lighten up these Sunday-come-to meetings," Jazz wisecracked. "Anyway, thanks for including me."

"Of course you're included. Always," Willa said and gave Jazz a hug.

Jazz cleared her throat and moved away. Sentimental moments had been few and far between in her life. Willa had more experience with that sort of thing. Somehow Willa had come out with fewer scars from Vivienne and a succession of foster homes. But then, she hadn't suffered the same kind of trauma Jazz had gone through. The memory of abuse tried to push through Jazz's defenses. Sometimes a touch or a scent set off flashbacks to that night and... Jazz started to get a cigarillo from her purse in the pantry, then she remembered Willa's strict no smoking policy. *Do something with your hands, move.* Jazz strode back to the dining room with the dish towel. She gathered up the table cloth, put the lovely centerpiece back on the polished wood table, and went to the laundry room. Once she'd started the wash cycle, Jazz went back to the kitchen and started cleaning the granite countertops.

"Hey, you don't have to do all that," Willa said over her shoulder as she scrubbed a ceramic serving bowl she didn't want to put in the dishwasher.

"You don't want stains to set in the tablecloth." Jazz kept moving around the kitchen, looking for other things to do.

"Hey, hey. Slow it down, girl. Remember I've got household help. Why else would anybody have kids, right?" Willa quipped. Her smile faded as she looked at Jazz. "You okay? I mean the other night..."

"Yeah, oh right. The cop thing at my club. That was nothin'. Unless..." Jazz felt the anxiety ease its grip on her chest. She breathed easier as she sat down on a stool. Propping her elbows on the long breakfast bar, she studied her big sister. "You didn't happen to do a little digging. Mighty strange you were on the phone calling to see if I was alright. How'd you know anyway?"

"Ahem, one of my friends is a reporter at WKXL. She was listening to her police scanner and heard Candy Girls mentioned." Willa swiped the bowl dry and started washing a second matching one.

"So you got eyes and ears around town. Humph, that's damn smart."

Jazz had to admit she was impressed. Like most, Jazz had been skeptical that her bourgie sister could handle the rough and tumble of a security and protection business in the 'hood. Willa had inherited Crown Protection when her ex-husband was murdered. Before he died, Willa had moved into being a solidly middle-class soccer mom, complete with pearls and twinsets.

"Thanks, but just so you know, I'm not keeping tabs on you," Willa added.

"Sure, sure. I believe you." Jazz watched Willa continue her routine of everything in its place and a place for everything. Wheels turned as Jazz crossed one leg over the other.

Willa put away her matching serving pieces in the cabinet with glass doors that displayed them. Then she joined Jazz at the breakfast bar. She gazed at Jazz's three inch heel red leather boots. "I love those. They are gorgeous."

"These? Hey, you can borrow them anytime." Jazz stretched out one leg. The black velvet leggings were neatly tucked into the boots. "I got another pair like this in black. Girl, got these on one of those sites online with designer clothes cheap. Here, try 'em on."

"Okay, hold it," Willa blurted out and waved a hand in the air. "Now I know you've got something up your slick little sleeve. C'mon, out with it."

Jazz stopped in the act of unzipping one boot. "What? We wear the same shoe size I think, and I know you don't have nothin' hot like this. That sexy Cedric would sit up and beg if you stepped into the office tomorrow wearing these."

"Cedric and I, I mean we... How many times I have to say he's my employee?" Willa stammered. Then she scowled at Jazz. "And don't try to fake me out by changing the subject to Cedric and me, not that there is a 'Cedric and me'."

"Well there *would* be a 'Cedric and you' if you stopped dressing like a Black Barbie Goes to the Office doll. Those boring suits and..." Jazz broke off when Willa planted a fist on one hip. "Just sayin'."

"Are you in some kind of trouble?" Willa demanded.

"Me? Why certainly not, dear sister. I've been walking a straight line ever since Reverend Fisher set me down the path of redemption." Jazz stared back at Willa. "I don't appreciate that look of skepticism."

"Two words about your path, Candy Girls. You could have opened a restaurant, a clothing boutique, or even a manicure shop. A bar with girls dancing naked?" Willa crossed her arms.

"I have a restaurant," Jazz shot back. "And my dancers are not naked. It's against city ordinance. Your mama operates a bar."

"Mama Ruby's place is a full service cafe. Her bar features some of the best bands around south Louisiana, and her waitresses are fully clothed," Willa countered, ticking her points off on the fingers of one hand.

"Yeah, well she'd triple her net receipts if she took some of those clothes off her waitresses," Jazz quipped and laughed at the squinty-eyed look Willa gave her.

"Such a smart-ass," Willa retorted and hopped off the stool. She put two slices of red velvet cake on dessert plates and came back to sit down.

"Careful, Aunt Ametrine will throw some of that anointed oil on you for cussin' like a backslider. By the way, Mama Ruby gave me business advice. Pretty good advice, too."

"Yeah, you just didn't mention the naked dancing girls in your business plan." Willa stuck cake in her mouth and chewed.

"Half-naked, thank you." Jazz grinned and winked at Willa. When her sister rolled her eyes, Jazz sighed. "Okay, I'm still the foster kid Mama Ruby couldn't get to straighten up. Too many rules for me. I'm more like Vivienne than you."

"No, you're not like *her*," Willa said. For years she'd avoided calling Vivienne mother. "Biology is not destiny. We all consider you family. Dion and Shaun included. They're our brothers even though we don't share birth parents. We're here for you. Always."

Jazz shifted on the stool, uneasy with the emotional drift of their conversation. As a child she fought leaving Vivienne, which was against all logic since their mother cared way more about herself than anyone. Mama Ruby tried, but Jazz rebelled and ran away to Houston, Texas at fifteen. She'd found Vivienne, and a whole new education in hard knocks. Still there was no going back. Jazz had grown up too fast to be mothered Mama Ruby style. When Jazz accepted that Vivienne would never offer any kind of warmth or refuge, she'd hit the road on her own at sixteen.

With a sly smile, Jazz changed the subject. "Since you're here for me, how's about the 411 on two dudes, name of Brandon Wilks and Cleavon Bennett."

Willa dropped her fork leaving half the cake on her plate. "I just *knew* you were in some kind of trouble. One dead drug dealer and another one on the run. The police are looking for Bennett, but they think he's-- Wait a minute, tell me what you've done first."

"Nothing, I swear." Jazz hissed a sigh. "The police came out claiming neighbors had complained about noise. Okay, some customers did get rowdy on the parking lot. Some dude's wife showed up mad about his being at the club. Then his side woman showed up, too. The wife went off. The guy's friends tried to calm things down, but it didn't work."

"You left off the part about the drugs," Willa cracked and arched her perfect eyebrows.

"Two customers had several ounces of weed, one had warrants. The usual stuff." Jazz dug into her cake. "Hey, this is good."

"The dead dealer, Jazz?" Willa poked Jazz's arm with a forefinger.

"Yeah, yeah. So the cops are interrogating my innocent customers and using the bad apples as an excuse to search my place. Addison shows up while I'm outside. Acts like he was just in the neighborhood. I didn't buy it." Jazz savored another piece of cake. The butter cream icing melted on her tongue. "Hmm, umph."

Willa pursed her lips for a moment before she spoke. "You know Brandon Wilks and Cleavon Bennett?"

"Nah, not really. I know his triflin' girlfriend with her lyin' ass self. You met her a couple of times. Kyeisha Lathers," Jazz replied and twisted her lips as if tasting something sour.

"The same Kyeisha that you slapped so hard her earrings came out, that Kyeisha? Good Lord, Jazz. Please tell me you didn't have a beef with her boyfriend, too. You can't be going around beating up people you don't like," Willa lectured.

"That no good heffa called the city on me twice and the health inspectors four times, her and that lowdown Lorraine. They wanted to ruin my business all because I snapped up a good deal on Candy Girls. Not my fault Lorraine wouldn't pay her property and business taxes," Jazz scowled at her sister.

"I'll ask again, did you get into it with her boyfriend? I mean there's got to be a reason Addison came looking for you."

"The answer is no, I didn't get into it with Cleavon. I only met him two or three times. Hardly said more than hello to the dude." Jazz finished her cake while Willa sat in thought for several moments. "So what did you find out?"

"Cleavon has the usual small time thug profile. He's been arrested twice for domestic battery, possession of weed, and four times for theft. So far, nothing major, not that what he's been picked up for isn't bad enough," Willa said with a frown.

"He's done worse, but the police haven't caught him yet," Jazz added.

"Good point. Or he had more serious charges that got plead down, or the district attorney's office didn't have enough evidence."

"Well I'm betting they won't have that problem this go round, which is why he's hiding out. Claiming self-defense to protect your dope won't impress the judge or a jury," Jazz said with a laugh.

"Unless..." Willa drummed the granite countertop with her fingertips as she thought.

"What? You know something," Jazz said and slapped Willa's shoulder lightly to get her attention.

"Cleavon seems to get a new Get-Out-Of-Jail-Card a lot. Cedric's theory is he's giving up some people. Not that Cedric knows anything solid." Willa shrugged when Jazz looked skeptical. "I know it's not much."

"Look, jails stay full. I know at least ten dudes and girls that have records like Cleavon. They go in, get out. Get picked up for one charge, do a plea to a lesser charge. It happens," Jazz replied. She got up and poured herself a cup of coffee from the coffee pot.

"You need a new set of friends, Jazz," Willa retorted.

Jazz spooned sugar into the coffee and came back to sit again. "Whatever. I'm just sayin'. The streets don't automatically think 'snitch' just cuz somebody is in and out of jail. Please tell me Kyeisha is in trouble, too."

"She got out on bond, but even though she was in the house with drugs, Cedric's source doesn't think she'll be charged. She's gone underground, too," Willa said and nodded when Jazz's eyebrows shot up.

"You think she's helping Cleavon hide? That would be a stupid move. Oh wait, I forgot. Kyeisha got there late when they were passing out smarts," Jazz wisecracked.

"Helping Cleavon hide will make her an accessory." Willa stopped talking when Mikayla came into the kitchen.

"Hmm, I just came to see what y'all doing." Mikayla sidled up to her mother and placed an arm around Willa's waist.

Willa kissed the top of her thick, curly hair. "We're talking. Go help Anthony serve Mama Ruby and them."

"He already did. You look so pretty, Auntie Jazz." Mikayla flashed a smile at Jazz.

"Thank you, short and beautiful. Are you still amazing your teachers at that fancy private school?"

"No, ma'am. I go to Cedarcrest now. It's pretty okay for a public school." Mikayla wrinkled her nose as if a bad smell had seeped in.

"Go on back to the living room," Willa said firmly, avoiding Jazz's look.

Mikayla took a deep breath to launch into a rebuttal. "But--"

"Your grandparents don't get to see you as often as when you were little. *Go*." Willa pointed toward the living room.

"Yes ma'am." Mikayla gave Jazz a sad look and then walked out with heavy steps. "But I don't get to see Auntie Jazz either, and she's stuck in here."

"We'll be there in a minute," Willa shot back, still pointing. Once she was gone, Willa turned her focus back to Jazz.

"Mikayla don't wanna listen to boring church talk or about your Aunt Beryl's flower garden," Jazz joked and sipped more coffee.

Willa laughed. "Yes, I wouldn't be surprised if she

decides to become a private investigator. She loves snooping around. Speaking of which, I'm sure you've done some street level research."

"I didn't learn much more than what you've told me. Cleavon has a mean streak and a bad temper. Much as I despise Kyeisha, I hate guys who beat up women even more. Lucky for him nobody mentioned him being a snitch. If they did, Cleavon would have a lot more to worry about than getting arrested."

"But that could be another reason he's running, Jazz. Think about it. If he gets caught on this serious charge and takes a deal folks might start going, 'Hmmm'." Willa finished up her slice of cake.

"Okay, that makes sense. I still don't get why Addison would come to Candy Girls behind Cleavon or even me knowing Kyeisha. My gut is telling there's more. And I hate surprises." Jazz sighed. "Well maybe with Kyeisha having her own problems, she'll stop messin' with me. I've got half a mind to pay Lorraine a little visit."

"Jazz..."

"I'm not going to beat up the woman, unless she swings on me first," Jazz added. She laughed at Willa's dramatic groan in reaction.

"Don't call me if you end up in the city jail," Willa blurted out. "Seriously, Jazz, think about changing your life. Mikayla and Anthony would love to see more of you. If you had a nice, quiet business they could visit..."

"I'm not trying to be a bourgie role model. That's *your* job and their Black American Princess pretend aunt. I'm surprised MiMi isn't here by the way," Jazz said.

"She's having dinner with her parents." Willa grinned when Jazz looked at her in surprise. "Yeah, I know. I'm sure we're going to get some good gossip."

"Damn, those fancy rich people fight more than the fools in the hood. What is up with that?" Jazz eyed the red velvet cake, considered a second slice, and then resisted.

"Much as she runs her mouth, MiMi doesn't go into detail about her family business. She just keeps saying they're 'very dysfunctional'.. She keeps her visits few and spaced out. Says it's just too toxic for the baby." Willa got up with the two empty plates. "Sure you don't want more cake? I saw you staring at it."

"No, thanks. I stuffed myself on fried fish last night. Got to watch the meals even though I'm not dancing these days. I've got plans," Jazz replied.

Willa spun around in the act of rinsing a plate. "You mean performing?"

"Don't look all scandalized. No, I'm not going on the pole again. But I'd like a bigger and better version of Candy Girls. If I'm going to offer quality adult nightlife I need to look the part for marketing purposes. My business advisors say it makes a difference." Jazz smiled.

"Quality adult nightlife," Willa echoed. She finished rinsing the plates and dried them. "I see."

"Relax. I'm not talking about live porno shows or anything. I want a larger club with some of the top bands in the region. Another section will be a Chinese restaurant and of course lounge area." Jazz nodded when Willa turned around again to gape at her.

"Chinese food?"

"You know my waitress Chyna, right? Well I didn't just hire her to sling drinks. When I interviewed her she talked about having worked in her grandmother's takeout place. That was before she fell out with her parents. But I'm going to help her make up with them." Jazz bounced one boot covered foot as she talked.

"You've always got a Plan B all right," Willa said.

Jazz grinned at the trace of admiration in her big sister's voice. "Plans B, C, D and E, girl."

"Always thinking." Willa leaned against the counter.

"We were born poor, Black, and female. Toss in a mother like Vivienne and the one thing I learned is help ain't comin'. You got to learn how to make it." Jazz stopped smiling.

"Since you mentioned our mama, have you talked to her lately?" Willa asked.

"No."

Willa walked back and sat down again. "Me neither."

"Hey, that's some fancy silver coffee server you got. Years ago Vivienne gave me one like it, but it's got more pieces. Well, she left it when she took off. Running from a bad check charge," Jazz added with a snort.

"Be sure it's not stolen goods," Willa put in.

"Shoot, I'm sure that silver is stolen goods. She snatched it from some rich family she was working for years ago. I'm betting that the statute of limitations has run out," Jazz quipped.

"That's so not funny, the memories we have of our mother," Willa said as she struggled to keep a frown on her face. Then they both burst into laughter.

Jazz spoke when she could breathe. "Whew, at least she's good for a laugh every now and then. So, can you keep checking for me?"

Willa dabbed at her eyes with a paper napkin and nodded. Then she looked at Jazz. "You're not keeping anything from me are you? Wait, I don't know why I'm asking. Of course you are."

"No, I wouldn't hold out on you." Jazz gave her a wide-eyed expression of innocence. "Seriously, I didn't find out anything else. You know I only keep stuff from you to avoid those lectures and to keep y'all out of danger." She waved a hand toward the sound of family enjoying each other's company.

"Uh-huh. Or so I won't blow a hole in one of your crazy schemes," Willa retorted. "I'll keep looking for another week."

"Girl, thanks a lot. I owe you on this for real," Jazz cut her off before one of those lectures started.

Willa pointed a finger at Jazz. "If you have anything to do with those thugs or that murder--"

"Mama, everybody wants more cake and ice cream," Mikayla sang out as she bounced into the kitchen. She skidded to a halt as her little snoop sensors picked up something more interesting. "What's going on?"

"You're right on time, Kay-Kay. We were just sayin' we should ask if anybody wanted more cake or coffee. Right, sis?" Jazz glanced at Willa with a grin.

"Sure. I already made slices," Willa said with a squint at Jazz.

Anthony and Papa Elton bustled in soon after, engaged in a loud debate over sports. Willa's mother and aunts soon followed. The kitchen overflowed with family chatter as everyone joined in. The warmth didn't come from the oven or stove. Mama Ruby teased Aunt Beryl about her latest boyfriend. The youngest at fifty-eight, Beryl was the only single sister. Pearl, the fourth sister, lived with her second husband in Atlanta. Aunt Beryl took their ribbing with good humor. Papa Elton admonished them to lay off Beryl in between arguing with Anthony, and playing with Mikayla. Willa joined in at times, but kept an eye on Jazz. "You better not be messing around with more gangsters. I'm not visiting you in jail *again*," Willa hissed low so the others wouldn't hear.

"Don't worry, girl. I'm being my usual careful self," Jazz whispered back. She giggled at the heated glare Willa gave her in response.

Chapter 3

The next morning Jazz sat in her living room with her feet up on the sofa, smoking and reading. She'd converted the half story upstairs space in a small building behind the club into a living area. A stone path from the sidewalk ran along the west side of her building. The path ended at the stairway that ended at her small porch. Although at first Jazz had seen it as a step down, living on the property hadn't been so bad after all. Plus she was saving money on rent. She was about to start making notes on the pad in her lap when the doorbell chimed. She stabbed her cigarillo out and stomped to the door.

"This better be the delivery man bringing food for the kitchen. Comin' here at..." Jazz broke off and glanced at the digital clock on her wall. "Damn, it's eight o'clock."

MiMi Landry mugged at Jazz from behind large designer sunglasses at the peephole. " When Jazz yanked open the door, she gave her an air kiss as she breezed past to cross the open floor plan to the kitchen."I brought breakfast, so don't shoot me." I'll make some fresh coffee."

"I had breakfast, and have you ever heard of calling people *before* poppin' up at their house?" Jazz slammed her door hard.

"Breakfast is not three cups of coffee and a cig," MiMi said. She looked around at the room. "I kinda like it. But don't you think spice orange, tan, and brown are more masculine colors?"

"I think you should mind your own business. Please don't come up in here telling me how to live," Jazz shot back. Despite her smart comebacks, she opened the large paper bag. The smell of sausages floated up and Jazz breathed in.

"Uh-huh, I knew you'd dig in once you got a whiff. I got it at Mama Blue's Kitchen on N. 22nd Street." MiMi's voice echoed as she stuck her head into a cabinet to reach dishes.

"You went deep in the hood? Well cut off my legs and call me Shorty," Jazz joked.

"Hey, I figured you'd want some home cooking like you're used to over in this part of town," MiMi replied.

"With your snobbish self. I've eaten in fancy restaurants just like you, for your damn information."

MiMi eyed the plates and cups. Then she went to the sink and washed them. "You got dust on these things like you never use them."

"I don't need plates to eat take out from those handy containers they give you. Or I grab something from the kitchen downstairs. Willa's Aunt Beryl got me those fru-fru plates with flowers all over 'em anyway," Jazz said with a snort.

"They consider you family. That's why. We're all family in fact. Look how they've adopted Sage and me, "Mimi replied.

Jazz sat on a barstool at her breakfast counter separating the living room from the kitchen. She watched as MiMi bustled around. "Look at you all domesticated and shit," Jazz quipped.

"With a baby I had to learn some domestic skills, but trust me, I'm no little homemaker yet. Girl, between the baby and working, I'm too tired for that mess. I just wish I could hire a housekeeper. Money is tight." MiMi removed the small sausage links and eggs and put them on a large plate. Then she put it in the microwave oven, turned to Jazz, and gave a dramatic sigh.

Jazz raised an eyebrow. "So what happened to what's his name, that rich boyfriend you were grooming to support you in style?"

Just then, the microwave timer bell dinged. MiMi busied herself with the plates. She fussed over pouring the coffee. "Landon Connor Matthews, III. You know, I'm not sure he's father material. Here, have these delicious biscuits."

"Thanks," Jazz said and eyed her.

"Hmm, these are so, so good. I'm going to check out their donuts for our next office meeting." MiMi gave her lips a dainty dab after chewing a tiny portion of sausage. "I stick to vegetarian dishes. My favorite health food grocery store has veggie patties on low glycemic bread. But a treat every now and then won't hurt."

"Don't bring that mess up in here," Jazz retorted. Then she sipped coffee as she studied MiMi. "So Mr. Big Stuff, *Landon,* dumped you, huh?"

"We're taking a break, you know, to examine our relationship," MiMi said. She sniffed. "It was my suggestion."

"Drop the act. For months it's been 'Landon says

this' and 'Landon does that'. You were looking at China and silverware designs. What happened?" Jazz stared at MiMi until she squirmed on the barstool.

"I told him we needed to take our relationship to the next level. Sage had gotten used to him being around, and..."

"You'd been freakin' him long enough so he needed to do the right thing," Jazz cut in.

MiMi winced. "Don't be crude."

Jazz smothered a smirk. "Sorry, tell it your way."

MiMi brushed her long hair back. "I opened myself up to that man for months. I cooked meals for him, even introduced him to my family a couple of weeks ago."

"Wow, serious stuff." Jazz thought, *no wonder the guy started backing off.*

"Okay, so maybe he wasn't quite ready for the whole 'meet the family' scene. He kept giving excuses why I couldn't meet his family. You're saying I pushed too fast?" MiMi gulped down coffee, the food on her plate forgotten.

"Well it's been almost four months and--"

"Four months and two weeks," MiMi put in. She broke off a corner of a biscuit but only toyed with it.

Jazz raised an eyebrow. "All righty then. It's not like you were being too intense about it, huh?" "Okay, okay. You're saying I was too pushy. Hell, I'm not getting any younger and I've got expenses. Sage needs a private school. She's gifted, I can tell already," MiMi blurted out.

"Y'all had an argument and you told him that?" Jazz barked a laugh. "No wonder he's gone."

"I'm not stupid. I told him we I'd be the perfect wife to help build his business. My mother trained my sister and me to be assets to the right kind of husband." MiMi lifted her chin and sat straight.

Jazz started to be blunt and say Mrs. Landry raised her girls to be gold diggers, but decided against it. Instead she cleared her throat and said, "I'm guessing he didn't take the 'put a ring on it' speech very well."

MiMi glowered as though Landon stood across from them in the living room. "He'd be lucky to have me, the stumpy little jerk."

"Well that plan is a wrap. What's your back-up?"

"Landon was my back-up after Mario Deschamps turned out to be a creep. Remind me not to listen to my family again about who to date," MiMi retorted. She dropped her head. "I'm tired of being poor."

Jazz gave a grunt. She got up and poured herself another cup of coffee, dumped five teaspoons of sugar into the cup, and sat down again. "Trust me, I've been poor and you ain't even close."

"I'm *poor*. I've been wearing the same spring clothes for the last two years. Look at these shoes, just look. Gino Valachi pumps from three years ago," MiMi whined. "I can't take Sage to her interview dressed last year's fashions."

"Damn, so you're so desperate you gonna put the baby to work?" Jazz clapped a hand to her forehead in mock horror. "Now that's bad."

"Don't be ridiculous. I have her on the list for an exclusive day school, Magnolia Woods Academy. People practically sell their homes just to get the tuition for that place. They expect a certain kind of background and family. We both have to attend an interview as the final step in the selection process." MiMi tapped a lacquered fingernail on the faux marble countertop as she spoke.

"Speaking of ridiculous," Jazz mumbled as she gulped more coffee.

"Hey, getting into the right kindergarten means getting into the right private schools on up to college. My Sage is going to have the best, damn it."

"Well thank you for the latest episode of As-The-Drama-Queen-Turns, but I've got things to do before the club opens." Jazz stood and drained the last coffee from her cup. "Thanks for the breakfast, and have a great day."

MiMi grabbed the cup from Jazz's hand and pulled her back down on the stool. "Which brings me to why we need to find that money."

"What money?" Jazz pulled away.

"Don't play with me, Jazz. You know what money I'm talking about. Before Jack was murdered, he hid money overseas. I'll bet he used connections Filipe had to launder his drug money," MiMi said, eyes shining at the thought of tracking down a boatload of cash.

"In case you forgot, I broke up with Filipe when he went to prison. Not to mention I helped put him away. So before you even ask, hell no. I'm not going to visit him and ask about money." Jazz leaned in and stabbed a forefinger at MiMi's nose to punctuate her last statement.

"Ahem, so you don't think trying to make up with him would..."

"You're bat-shit crazy, MiMi, you know that?" Jazz shot back.

"Yeah, yeah... I was just thinking out loud for a minute. Don't get all hostile," MiMi snapped.

"I have to get to work. Lock my door on your way out," Jazz said.

"Wait, now that you mention the club, I saw those

articles in the newspaper. Not good for business." MiMi raised a perfectly arched eyebrow.

"What articles in the newspaper?"

"See, this is why you need to get up early and pay attention to the news."

MiMi reached into her leather hobo purse and pulled out a copy the Baton Rouge Daily News and handed it to Jazz. The paper was already folded to the "Crime Beat" section. One short article talked about the mayor's efforts to clean up neighborhoods. Bars and smoke shops were targeted for closure, said to be "ground zero for unsavory activities". Candy Girls was given as an example, with mention of frequent complaints from law-abiding neighbors of loud noise and rowdy behavior.

"Damn," Jazz said and clenched her teeth.

"Read the other one." MiMi pointed to another article.

"Police answered a call of shots fired to find a man dead in a house on Dalton Ave. They are searching for Cleavon Bennett and Kyeisha Lathers in connection with the murder. Both have a connection to the nightclub Candy Girls where several gang members are known to hang out." Jazz let out a red hot string of expletives. She worked to calm her breathing and read on.

"Uh-huh, Candy Girls mentioned twice in connection to crimes. Not good." MiMi sipped coffee daintily.

"Damn," Jazz repeated with more force. She threw the newspaper across the room.

"We both need cash, sweetie. Unless you have a pot of money to open another place once the mayor and his clean-up-Baton Rouge folks close down Candy Girls." MiMi lifted a shoulder when Jazz glared at her.

"I'm just sayin'."

"They're a long way from closing my business, and if they try..." Jazz huffed out several jagged breaths.

"I hear you, but the thing is we all need money. Willa does, too, if she stops being so hard-headed and admit it. Poor Mikayla is in a *public school*, "

"Which is not the end of the world."

"Crown Protection is operating on a thin margin, very thin. They need to upgrade their computer systems to keep pace with the competition," MiMi said.

She spoke with more authority about the security business than Jazz knew she had. Jazz squinted at her. "You got that from Cedric."

"My point is we're *owed* a substantial amount of money that's sitting somewhere in a foreign country. That's just un-American," MiMi said and crossed her arms.

"So Willa is on board with your plan to find the money her late husband hid away?"

"Jack was Willa's soon-to-be *ex-husband*, and my fiancé let me remind you. And the father of my child. Which brings up another point, Jack would want his children to be taken care of. You know he loved Mikayla and thought of Anthony as his son." MiMi pressed home her points.

Anthony was almost five years old when Willa and Jack married. They developed a close bond because Anthony's biological father faded from the picture. Jazz hadn't cared for Jack, with his silky upper-class charm and snooty family. Still he'd been an attentive father to both kids, and hadn't treated Anthony differently after Mikayla was born.

"I notice you didn't answer my question. Tell me about the conversation you had with Willa." Jazz sat back to wait for the answer she had already guessed.

MiMi cleared her throat. Then jumped off the stool and started cleaning up the remains of breakfast. She spoke with her back to Jazz as she washed the two plates. "How do you function without a dishwasher, girl? I haven't had a chance to call her. I've been so busy with work and all, but she'll benefit just like us."

"In other words, you're scared she's going to refuse. As I recall, she's still the executor of Jack's estate."

MiMi swiped the plates dry with angry motions. "You know how she is! Sometimes I could just chew nails in frustration at the way that woman... I know she's your sister, but--"

Jazz waved a hand. "Oh you don't have to hold back with me. We've gone more rounds than a couple of professional wrestlers."

"Willa has to send a request as executor to the bank Jack used, and they'll help us track the wire transfers." MiMi huffed and rinsed out the coffee cups.

"But she won't," Jazz prompted.

MiMi assumed a sour face and mimicked Willa's voice. "We don't have any proof there was money, much less where it went. Jack traveled to three foreign countries in the two years before he was murdered."

"There it is then. Nothing we can do," Jazz replied dryly. She looked at the newspaper again and frowned. "Assholes."

"Look, we need to show Willa she's writing off a big chunk of money. We could be talking about close to a million dollars." MiMi marched back to sit across from Jazz again. "Filipe owes you, too. We might get a line on his stash since he was in business with Jack and Ryan. I've got a plan."

"I better get some more caffeine." Jazz got up and poured more coffee into one of the clean cups. She turned back to face MiMi, leaning against the counter. "Okay, go."

"These two drug dealers in the article, they both ran with Filipe's guys. Yes, they were getting their supplies from Filipe. Since you're friends with his girlfriend you can find out more.""

"I sure as hell don't get why everybody thinks we're friends. Let me throw a big load of cold water on your scheme. The last person she'll want to help is *me*. I hardly know Cleavon, and that's just fine since he's on the run, and I don't need trouble with the cops. I'm lucky those gangstas that hung with Filipe ain't looking to put me in a body bag. Enough reasons for you?" Jazz cocked an eyebrow at MiMi. Then she frowned. "How do you know all this anyway?"

"Cedric and I got to talking while I was waiting for your stubborn sister to make time for me Friday. Girl, Willa had me out in the lobby for almost an hour. Can you believe it? We're family," MiMi complained. "I'm like an aunt, no wait make that step-mother, to Anthony and Mikayla."

"Riiight," Jazz drawled as she peered over her cup. Only MiMi would look over the fact that she'd been sleeping with Willa's husband before the divorce was quite final, and became his "Baby mama".

"On the bright side though, I had time to chat up Cedric. You think they've slept together yet? Dang, Willa must have ice in her panties if she can be around that fine man every day and..."

"Will you get back to the subject of tracking down a big load of money?" Jazz cut in.

"Oh, yeah. We'll talk about those two later," MiMi

replied and went on without missing a beat. "Anyway, I told them my friend Jason says the mayor's office is on a big push to clean up bad neighborhoods. Jason works in the city services division, and he said Candy Girls is one place they've gotten complaints about. He remembered it being mentioned after we cracked Jack's murder investigation."

Jazz laughed. "We?"

MiMi ignored the dig. "So I mentioned it to Cedric, you know giving him some inside gossip. That's when he told me that those two drug dealers used to do business with Filipe. Somebody has taken over being the main supplier since Filipe went to prison. Cedric has his sources. Did you know?"

"As a matter of fact I've got sources myself," Jazz tossed back.

"Reach out to Kyeisha through mutual acquaintances and offer help. She might come to you and then you can get a bit more information." MiMi nodded like a bobble-head doll.

"Kyeisha went to work in Lorraine's little dive on Forty-Sixth Street after she tried to stab me in the back. She's evil and not too bright, but she's got sense enough to stay outta my way." Jazz slid from the stool and poured out the now cold coffee left in her cup.

MiMi followed by washing it out, and then washing the coffee pot. ". Now she's in a tight spot she might need you. What did you tell me about Lorraine? She's not one for loyalty. Now that Kyeisha is in trouble, Lorraine won't help, right?"

Jazz looked at the clock and saw it was closing in on nine thirty. "I've got to get ready to open."

"But wait a minute," MiMi protested, wiping her hands dry on a dish towel.

"Monday through Wednesday we depend on the lunch crowd to make money. My cooks should be coming in another thirty minutes." Jazz's cell phone played a popular tune at that moment. She found it on the sofa and hit the speaker.

"Morning' boss lady! I'm here. Got Pizzolato Bros. delivering some food," Rochelle said.

"I'm coming down to let you in." Jazz ended the call and walked to her bedroom down a short hallway. "I don't have time to be playing around with you."

MiMi followed her. " Trust me, I'm serious."

"Uh-huh." Jazz grabbed a pair of leggings draped over a chair and pulled them on. Then she dropped the robe, grabbed a t-shirt from her closet and pulled it over her head. She smoothed out the reddish blonde weave pulled into a long pony-tail. She spun to face MiMi waving a forefinger in the air. "Look, give up on that money. I'm staying away from trouble. That's it. Now will you get outta my way? Runnin' in my bedroom like you live here or something."

MiMi jumped out of her path when Jazz marched out of the bedroom. Then she trailed after Jazz still making her case. "We can't just wave bye-bye to that kind of money. It belongs to me... us I mean."

"Uh-huh. Go to work selling lipsticks and let me get back to my grind," Jazz said over her shoulder without looking back. MiMi followed out, waiting patiently as Jazz locked her door and went down the stairs.

"I'm the regional cosmetics and accessories buyer. I supervise one employee, thank God, so I don't have to travel as much," MiMi snapped. She chattered on.

"Yeah, whateva," Jazz said. She jingled the keys as a greeting to Rochelle and opened the door, still tuning out MiMi's litany of complaints. "Hey Ro-Ro."

"Good mornin'," Rochelle said with a grin and looked at MiMi. "I said *good mornin'*."

MiMi broke off in the middle of a sentence and blinked at her. Then she smiled. "Excuse me, ma'am. How are you?"

"I'm fine, thanks for askin'." Rochelle rolled her eyes when she turned her back to MiMi, and went into the club.

"Goodbye, MiMi." Jazz waved at her as a cue to leave.

"At least promise to talk to Willa, girl. Please. I'll bet Filipe has millions stashed away."

Jazz smacked her lips and then sighed as she gazed off as if considering. She managed to keep from laughing while MiMi stood holding her breath. MiMi had made good points about tracking down the money. "Okay, I'll talk to her. But let me do it my way, and don't be calling me every day asking about it." Jazz glared at her in warning.

"No, no, I won't bother you. Oh thank you, thank you." MiMi grabbed Jazz in a hug.

"I'm serious, MiMi. Start stalking me and I won't say one word."

MiMi made a cross on her chest. "I swear, girl. I'm going to let you totally handle it. I better go. Look, I'll call you, no; you call me when you know something. Thank you."

"Yeah," Jazz retorted.

"I gotta go. We have a sales meeting in fifteen minutes. I'm going to get you samples of quality make-up from some of the best brands, so you won't have to keep wearing that cheap stuff." MiMi blew a kiss.

"What the hell you mean cheap?"

MiMi had already rushed off, balancing expertly on

three inch heels. She grinned and waved gaily once inside her shiny Buick Enclave. "Bye, girl."

"That heffa," Jazz muttered and went upstairs again.

Chapter 4

Hours later, Jazz sat on a small patio area outside the club smoking and sipping from a can of cola. She needed a break from the smell of fried chicken, fish, and fried onion rings. A cooler with more soda and bottled water sat against the wall for employees. Jazz kept it stocked by way of a small perk for them. Cheap but solid lawn chairs and a couple of tables were arranged under the awning.

With help from Chyna, Rochelle had served a steady string of lunch customers from eleven thirty that morning straight through to well after two o'clock. Shift workers from local hospitals and plants got off from work to get food. Rochelle had been right to convince Jazz that serving food was a good idea. Jazz thought back to MiMi's revelations about the Mayor going after 'nuisance' businesses. Having a strong customer base for a restaurant would come in handy. Maybe she should be one-up on the local politicians and close Candy Girls first. A new name and a new start might work. Jazz smiled as she added another fall back to her growing list of options. The sound of a powerful car engine rumbled down the alley. Minutes later, she heard the solid thunk of a car door shutting. Detective Addison strolled into view. She watched him approach through the smoke from her cigarillo. When Addison was two or three feet away, Jazz raised an eyebrow.

"I was waiting to see if you was a drug dealer or a cop," she said.

"Say what?" Addison eased his solid body onto one of two wooden barstools.

"You got a 340 hp 5.7 liter Hemi V8. Am I right? Two kinds of drivers need that kind of power to move fast; folks trying to get away quick, and the folks trying to catch 'em."

Jazz crossed her legs and gazed up at him. She tried to ignore her physical attraction to the nice hunk of manhood before her. Detective Don Addison had the body of a well-toned pro wrestler. Dimples gave him a killer smile. She glanced off to blunt the double whammy effect. It helped, but the tingle down her spine didn't stop.

"Have a cola or some water," Jazz said and pointed to the cooler.

"Believe I will, thank you ma'am. You know cars, too? Now if you tell me you follow football, I'm going to arrest you for being the perfect woman," he replied.

"I knew you'd find a trumped up charge to put handcuffs on me," Jazz said. She gave him a crooked smile.

"Nah, I'd never try to tie you up in any way. Unless you like that kinda thing," he said softly with a twinkle in his coffee brown eyes.

"My, my, Detective Addison, the way you talk. You're going to make me blush." Jazz couldn't help but laugh with him.

"When you let that ten foot high wall down, we enjoy each other."

"Yeah, well I've never had much luck with authority figures, particularly cops. We didn't meet the first time under the best conditions," Jazz said.

Addison's expression turned serious as he nodded. "You did the right thing helping us put Filipe Perez away."

"If you say so." Jazz looked away when his intense gaze unsettled her. "Thanks for listening when we told you my nephew didn't kill his step-daddy."

"You're welcome, Jazzmonetta," Detective Addison said.

A flash of pleasant heat joined the tingling at the way his baritone voice made her full first name sound. Jazz shifted in the chair as a familiar ache shot through her pelvis. Damn cops always starting some kind of trouble, she thought. She pushed away lustful images of Addison without his shirt, and every other stitch of clothing. Jazz pulled smoke from the cigarillo and let it out to calm her nerves.

"Of course, y'all made him a suspect in the first place," she wisecracked. "I can't thank you for that shit."

Addison rolled with it and grinned at her. "Hey, give us some credit. We put away the real murderer"

" "So long to the asshole."

"I'll drink to that one," Addison said. He raised his can of iced tea and tapped it against Jazz's can of cola.

"So did another coincidence bring you this way again?" Jazz emptied the last of her soda and tossed it into the trash basket nearby.

"I talked to your former boss. Lorraine Taylor

would like nothing better than to see you go down. Doesn't matter what for, she just has you on her list. What'd you do to her?" He cocked a dark eyebrow at her.

"She swears I stole Candy Girls out from under her. Lorraine hating my guts is not breaking news, Detective. She's been telling the world for the last two years. I'd like to see her hook me up to Kyeisha's trouble." "Oh believe me she tried. She mentioned Cleavon and Brandon had done business with Filipe. Dropped a few hints that maybe you were in business with them, and you put Brandon up to robbing Cleavon."Addison chuckled at Jazz's string of expletives in response. "I'm just telling you what she said."

"Let me guess. I'm trouble, don't have a loyal bone in my body, and would stab anybody in the back."

"Yeah, with a few cuss words thrown in," he replied. "It's obvious she's doesn't have any real info to track their supplier."

"Don't be so fast. If Kyeisha keeps in touch with anybody it would be Lorraine. They're thick as thieves. Hell, they are thieves. Lorraine knows more than she's telling." Jazz smashed the smoldering remains of her cigarillo.

"We agree on that angle. I'm keeping a close eye on Ms. Lorraine for sure. Be careful though. You're building up quite a mean collection of enemies. Filipe will be out in about four years." Addison rested his elbows on his thighs.

"Filipe thinks I didn't stick by him, and for that he's pissed. He doesn't think I turned him though. His pal talking his head off helped me on that one. I knew he would," Jazz said, referring to the thug Addison and his partner arrested before they caught Filipe.

"Just don't keep walking so close to the edge. These people you've been hanging with don't play."

"Yes, mother," Jazz wisecracked. "Hey, you'll find Cleavon soon enough. He doesn't have much money or many places to hide. Tracking his dumb ass should be easy."

"Truth, except we're not even sure Cleavon was the shooter now. There were at least seven people in the house, and most of them were armed. We found five handguns and an automatic rifle." Addison heaved a sigh. "At least we got all those killing machines off the street."

"Good luck getting any of 'em to talk." Jazz said, and started to go on but stopped short of thinking out loud.

She gazed down the alley that gave her a view of the neighborhood. In other circumstances she might have given dark, handsome and sizzling hot a nudge. Addison had brains to go with that nice brawn. All he needed was a few "what ifs" or sly hints that sounded like offhand conversation. But she had more of an interest in where her tips might lead.

"We'll see," he replied and finished his tea.

Jazz glanced at him sharply. "You be careful on them mean streets."

"Thank you, ma'am. I'll do that." Addison smiled at her. "Back to Lorraine..."

"Lorraine's great-uncle left his place to her mama. When she died Lorraine took over, but she didn't have any business sense. She didn't pay her property taxes or payroll taxes. Name a mistake, she made it. I tried to tell her, but she wouldn't listen. So I paid up the taxes and got the buildings and land."

"Not every day you can find solid real estate. Plus

the neighborhood is turning around. Smart move," he said with a nod.

"Hey, I pay attention. Lorraine thought I dropped the cash so she could have the business back, and I'd have a job." Jazz barked a laugh. "Ain't that crazy? Why would I pay Lorraine's debt to be her underpaid employee? C'mon now."

"I'm guessing she didn't offer you any money then." Addison laughed hard when Jazz glared at him. "Gotcha."

Jazz crossed her arms. "Kyeisha came to work for me. Come to find out she's snitchin' to Lorraine. Not only that, Kyeisha leaving the kitchen dirty, putting dead bugs around the place, and then Lorraine would call the health inspectors. I bounced her lyin' ass outta here hard."

"Don't be telling an officer of the law you committed battery," Addison said. When she grunted, he hissed out a noisy breath. "I'm trying to keep you out of jail, Jazz. You can't be swinging fists on folks."

"Did Kyeisha file charges? No," Jazz said mildly. "Not every disagreement requires police intervention. Besides, I wouldn't be surprised if she has warrants."

"Right now the stakes are high, so watch yourself. Well, let me get to it." Addison stood and rolled his shoulders. "Got a long night ahead."

"Especially if you're gonna be searching roach motels looking for Kyeisha and her new boyfriend," Jazz joked. She gazed up at him in appreciation, but worked not to let him notice. His sexy deep laugh made it hard.

"Gotta love that smart mouth," he replied.

"Some might call it a great sense of humor." Jazz winked at him, and was rewarded with more musical laughter. She could get addicted to the sound.

"Have a good evening. By that I mean no trouble," he rejoined and pointed at her.

"Hey, wouldn't dream of it. See ya later." Jazz stood.

"You will," Addison promised. With a wave, he strode back to his unmarked cruiser.

"Uh-huh, that might not be bad at all," Jazz murmured, watching the graceful power of his stride.

* * *

Two days later, Jazz had another early morning outside her routine. At eight o'clock she was up and moving. This time it was by choice. The sunny April day didn't seem to improve the mood of drivers. Baton Rouge deserved its reputation for horrible traffic. By the time she got to the offices of Crown Protection, Jazz had more reasons not to end up with the usual kind of job. MiMi had it right. Jazz needed a big cushion of cash so she wouldn't have to work for anyone else. Or worse, end up working a regular gig like the miserable commuters.

She pulled into the five level parking garage next to Willa's office building and found a space after circling for three minutes. Then she took the elevator down again with more morose looking people. More proof living a conventional life sucked. She needed to have her best persuasive game face on with her big sister. After a flirty grin at the security guard, Jazz got off on the fourth floor. Glass doors with bold gold lettering straight ahead informed potential clients they'd reached Crown Protection Services, LLC. When Jazz pushed through to the lobby, a loud female voice greeted her. She glanced around but didn't see anyone.

A young female receptionist kept talking on the phone despite her worried expression. Kay, Willa's office administrator, made frantic gestures at her to continue business as usual.

"Take a message if you can," Kay whispered frantically. "I'll go check on Willa."

"Hey, what the hell is goin' on up in here?" Jazz said.

"Some lady came in and said she wanted to discuss a contract. That's all I know," Kay replied.

She scurried down the hall leading to Willa's office with Jazz close behind. Despite her three inch e Italian leather boots, Jazz overtook Kay and beat her to the office. When Kay knocked on the door and paused, Jazz pulled her aside.

"Knock my ass." Jazz jerked the door open and marched in.

A tall woman dressed in an expensive dark green wool suit and tan cape shook her purse in the air. "I want to know where that slut is right now. Is she here? I'll bet she's in one of these offices."

"Excuse me, but you best calm the hell down; screaming at my sister like you've lost your damn mind." Jazz was just getting wound up.

Willa came from behind her large polished oak desk. "Everybody calm down. Mrs. Netterville, MiMi doesn't work here. So aside from causing more problems for yourself, staking out my office won't do you any good."

Mrs. Netterville squared her shoulders. "Are you threatening me? I know important people in this city, including a top police official. From what I've read about you and your *associations* the last thing you want is a lawsuit or criminal charges filed. Let me tell you one thing..."

Jazz stepped between Mrs. Netterville and Willa. "Uh-huh, let me tell you something first."

"Jazz, don't," Willa muttered through tight lips though she kept a strained smile.

"I'm Mrs. Crown's sister, and a friend of Ms. Landry. I happen to know running around with someone, and his name isn't Netterville. Between you and me," Jazz said. She dropped her voice low enough that Mrs. Netterville craned her neck to listen. "Well, she's my friend true enough. But MiMi has a problem sticking to one man longer than a minute. Know what I mean?"

Mrs. Netterville blinked at the sharp turn of the conversation. "Well I..."

"You've been on your feet and stressed out. Have a seat, ma'am. You want a glass of water? Kay can get you a bottle." Jazz pointed to one of the deep red leather chairs facing Willa's desk.

"What?" Willa whispered, but broke off when Jazz shot her a warning look.

To both Willa and Kay's surprise, Mrs. Netterville sat down. "You must think I'm horrible, acting so..."

"Ghetto? Nah, men can push you." Jazz nodded with a sympathetic expression.

"I'm just so upset at the way John has been acting."

"Look, ma'am. I'll save you some time and say it straight out. MiMi moved on to a guy with more money than Mr. Netterville." Jazz flipped a hand in the air. "Girl, MiMi can flirt with ten men, and then take off with number eleven. Let me ask you something. Has he been gone on weekends or overnight trips lately?"

"No, but..." Mrs. Netterville's eyebrows pulled

together in concentration.

"MiMi has been seeing this other guy for long weekends. Now he's single, but since he's engaged to another woman I won't stir up mess by dropping his name. Anyway, she tells me all this stuff. So I can promise you she's just flirting with your hubby. If I was you, I'd put the fear of God and a divorce lawyer into him. Know what I mean?"

"Yes, I do," Mrs. Netterville said softly and nodded.

"Where did he meet MiMi anyway, girl?" Jazz glanced at Kay. "You mind getting me a cup of coffee?"

"If you don't mind, I'd like a cup, too," Mrs. Netterville asked, much of the steam gone from her mood.

"Uh, I have a fresh pot right over here," Willa broke in. She headed to the long table on the wall near an alcove and seating area of her office.

"I'll do it. Danesha has everything under control out front," Kay said.

Kay's gaze was glued to the scene playing out. Before Willa could react she got busy with cups and filling them. Willa pulled a third chair from the small conference table nearby and sat down. She seemed on alert for another meltdown from the volatile matron.

"So you were about to tell us where they met," Jazz prompted.

"There was a business mixer sponsored by the Baton Rouge Chamber of Commerce. You know a chance for business owners to network. Those things are dry and boring, or so I thought before now. Apparently MiMi Landry made quite an impression. Oh I know the whole story, and she did more than flirt," Mrs. Netterville said with a huff. "They've met for lunch at least twice that I know about. So don't try to tell me it was nothing. I'm no fool."

"Obviously we don't take you for stupid, ma'am. You've been with him long enough to know his tricks, I mean, how he behaves," Jazz added.

"Not recently. I suppose turning fifty has him wanting to prove he's still got it," Mrs. Netterville replied and bit her lower lip. Her society manners kicked in when Kay offered her a cup. "Thank you, dear."

"Appreciate you, girl." Jazz took a cup, sipped, and winked at Kay.

Willa waved away an offer of coffee from Kay and faced the older woman. "Mrs. Netterville, I understand you're upset, but Jazz is right. You may be jumping the gun. Even two lunches might just be business. MiMi has done consulting on the side. She's had experience with managing cash flow and property control."

Jazz coughed hard. She cleared her throat loudly. "Goodness, I drank too fast and it went down the wrong way."

"Are you okay?" Mrs. Netterville handed Jazz a napkin.

"Um-hum." Jazz avoided Willa's pointed glance.

"Anyway, I'm sure you'd do better discussing this with Mr. Netterville," Willa finished.

Mrs. Netterville took a dainty sip from her cup, put it down and then stood. "I apologize for making a scene. But f Ms. Landry thinks she can take my husband, she's in for a hot mess of trouble. She doesn't deserve such loyal friends. You girls should consider if she's worth your time."

"Oh I have, trust me," Willa mumbled low as she stood. "By the way, why did you think MiMi would be here?"

"I Googled her and read news stories, you know when her fiancé was murdered over a year ago. They mentioned you and her, how you helped solve the case. The stories made it sound like you were sisters almost, and that she helped in other investigations at Crown Protection."

"Yeah," Willa said dryly. "MiMi gave some colorful interviews."

"Goodness, I'm hosting the alumni chapter of my sorority for lunch. I should get going. I apologize for causing a commotion at your place of business." Mrs. Netterville walked to the door.

Willa and Kay followed her. They kept up a steady stream of niceties as they guided Mrs. Netterville on her way. Both were eager to get her out before her mood swung back to Mrs. Screaming Jealous Wife Threatening Legal Action. When they returned, Jazz sat calmly finishing off the smooth expensive blend Willa preferred. When her sister came back and shut the door, Jazz put down her empty cup.

"You need to cut expenses and stop paying fifteen dollars for a bag of Colombia Supremo. MiMi says this place is bleeding cash." Jazz leaned back in the chair.

"That was a gift from a client, and I seldom give a crap about what MiMi says. We're not bleeding cash if it's any of your business, or hers; which it isn't." Willa gazed at Jazz with one eyebrow lifted. "You dragged yourself out of bed and got all made up this early for nothing."

"I had errands to run, and I just happened to be..." Jazz's voiced trailed off at the look on Willa's face. "Oh hell, why even try. Look, MiMi isn't a complete idiot when it comes to money. She's right. Some of that money is mine, hers, and yours. We earned it."

"I'm not chasing after laundered drug money," Willa broke in before Jazz could go on. "I'm not following any advice from MiMi. Did you just see what kind of trouble she causes? She shows up and shit hits the fan.."

"Just listen a minute."

"Okay." Willa moved the tray of cups back to the side table. Then she poured a fresh serving of the gourmet brew and sat down in her leather executive chair. "I need a good laugh."

"That's the spirit, sis. Keep an open mind," Jazz drawled. She heaved a sigh. "Okay, so MiMi has, let's call them challenges."

Willa snorted. "Yeah, let's."

"But in this case she's on the target. My place is doing okay. I break even and pay myself a small amount every month. Lucky I don't pay a mortgage or rent." Jazz slumped back in her chair. "Owning a business is a butt whipping every damn day."

"Who you tellin'?" Willa retorted. "Have a donut. One of my employees brought them in fresh this morning."

Jazz looked at the open box of glazed fried temptation. "No, thanks. I better keep my figure in case I end up dancing at somebody else's club soon."

"Wait, are you holding back?" Willa frowned at Jazz and put down her cup. "I've got savings, so if you're about to have serious money problems--"

"You know I don't roll like that. I've been taking care of me one way or the other for a long time. Besides, you've got kids." Jazz looked away from the sadness that flittered across Willa's face. "Anyway, I'm not saying I'm about to be on the street"

"Are you sure?" Willa went into mother hen mode

as she left her chair and sat next to Jazz.

"Yeah, it's just... I need the cash. Maybe I'll ditch the dancers, and just have the restaurant. Or I could buy in a nicer part of town. I don't know. Do something different like open a coffee shop." Jazz brushed a hand over her eyes. Silence stretched between them.

"Nice try."

"What you mean?" Jazz replied.

"You love the craziness, the wild night life of a club. You were doing good until you dropped that 'open a coffee shop' bit at the end." "Hey, I love coffee. It could work," Jazz wisecracked with a crooked grin.

"I'm not getting caught up in another MiMi scheme. Between the kids and Crown Protection, my hands are full. If you've got any sense, you'll ignore her attempts to suck you in as well." Willa got up, walked around her desk and got back to being the boss again. She opened a folder.

"Didn't you say that about $250,000 was unaccounted for after Jack died? I'll bet there's more and..." Jazz stopped when Willa looked up sharply.

"I'm close to sealing the deal on two major contracts. A huge company with three warehouses at the Baton Rouge Port is looking over our proposal. We've bid on another contract with the port itself. Who would do business with Crown Protection if I'm connected to drug trafficking and money laundering? No." Willa's expression and tone said the discussion was closed. She went back to signing papers and flipping pages.

Jazz savored the last drops of the delicious coffee and put the cup down. "You're right. Damn it."

Willa sighed and looked at Jazz again. "Honestly, I'm sympathetic to MiMi's logic. Hitting that lottery would do wonders for our cash flow and our ability to expand, but the stakes are too high."

"I hate it when you make me agree with you," Jazz retorted. She brushed her long weave over one shoulder.

"Hey, let's talk about the risks to you. Filipe will definitely start to thinking if he gets wind that you're looking for his money. Plus the city considers Candy Girls a nuisance. Get involved in more trouble and you'll play right into their hands, and Lorraine's." Willa rocked back in her executive chair. "We need to convince MiMi to let this thing go, or she'll cause us both problems."

"We'll have to threaten to whip her little spoiled ass. You know how the girl is about money," Jazz replied mildly.

"There you go getting street again. We most certainly will not threaten her" Willa frowned at Jazz like a displeased school principal. She rocked back and forth for a few seconds. "But yes, we'll have a girlfriend lunch. She'll see the logic once we explain the risks for us all, including her."

Jazz gazed at her older sister. Willa was serious. MiMi and logic when a big pile of money was involved..? Jazz gave a short laugh. "Yeah, okay. If you say so."

Chapter 5

Two nights later, Jazz was too busy with a Friday night crowd at Candy Girls to think much about MiMi or missing dirty cash. Both the lounge and the tiny dining room she generously called a restaurant were packed. Jazz helped out waiting tables and ringing up take-out orders. Music blared all night. With hardly a minute to take a breath, by just after midnight, everyone was exhausted. Food orders dwindled. The serious party people danced to a disc jockey duo Jazz had hired.

Tyretta and Jazz sat outside on the patio. Rochelle, serious about cleaning since the health inspections, continued sanitizing every utensil insight. They listened to the clang-bang of her working in the kitchen with help from her older brother Yancey. He helped out for cash to supplement his disability income and feed his gambling problem as well. Tyretta noisily sucked more beer from the can she held.

"Damn, guess everybody decided not to be scared of the cops showing up," she said.

"Folks forget about that stuff in this neighborhood.

Who hasn't had the police at their house, ya know?" Jazz replied. She coughed a bit after blowing out smoke. "I need to quit these things."

"Yeah, while you're young," Tyretta agreed. "I've had my share of sins, but smoking ain't been one of 'em. Watched my granddaddy die of emphysema. Now that's a slow horrible way to go, with your lungs burnt black and gasping for air. Damn." She shook herself as though willing away bad memories.

"Humph." Jazz winced as she crushed the remains of her cigarillo. "Thanks for the pep talk."

"For your own good." Tyretta used the pinky finger of the hand holding her beer to point at Jazz.

Rochelle came to the screen door leading to the kitchen. "Hey, my brother Yancey took off on me. I told you not to give him that money so quick, Jazz. Now I need help."

"Woman, you've scrubbed every damn inch of the place." Tyretta stood despite her protest.

"And we had no violations at the last inspection. Plus they could show up for a pop inspection any time. Now come help me move this big pot." Rochelle fanned her face with one hand.

"Oh, well if that's all." Tyretta pulled the screen door open.

"Then we'll scrub the cook top, wipe down the counters with disinfectant, and mop," Rochelle said with a crisp nod. "Now c'mon."

"Damn," Tyretta grumbled as she followed her inside.

Jazz laughed at the loud complaints as Rochelle barked orders that floated through the open door. Heat from the kitchen kept her warm in the cool April night air. Headlights flashed by as cars passed on the streets.

Across a vacant lot east of the club, a bright green "Open" sign blinked off. The Keep It Clean Laundromat had extended hours to midnight on Fridays and Saturdays. The owners, a Korean couple, loaded up their Toyota SUV. The wife waved at Jazz and she waved back. Jazz loved their "live and let live" attitude, and so they'd become friends.

Soon most of the noise came from Candy Girls. Single family homes stretched down the blocks around the scattered small businesses. Lights glowed through cheap curtains or blinds showing the mostly blue collar residents were home from work. Jazz stood up to go inside when a voice stopped her cold.

"Hey, girl. Look, don't yell or anything. I just wanna talk to you, okay?" Kyeisha's raspy words came out jagged from nervous energy.

Jazz glanced to her left into the dark void between the back wall of a vacant store and her building. The clamor of customers having a good time sounded too far away. Rochelle had pushed the solid door to the kitchen shut as she mopped the floor. Kyeisha stayed in the shadows, just beyond the soft glow of the single bulb illuminating the patio. Jazz strained to get a clearer look, but couldn't. She made no sudden moves. Kyeisha could be armed. In fact she most likely was carrying a weapon of some kind.

"Sure. What's up?" Jazz said, hoping her voice sounded calmer than she felt.

Kyeisha hissed a laugh. "You and all of Baton Rouge know what's up. I didn't shoot that guy."

"Okay, you might wanna tell the police cuz I'm not the one lookin' for ya. Running from 'em won't help. Trust me cause I know," Jazz replied.

"Shit, the police and DA don't care who go to

prison. The more they send up, the better for them. You know what I'm sayin'."

"What about your friends or family? They can talk to the police for you," Jazz offered.

The harsh sizzle of curse words sliced through the darkness. Too late Jazz remembered Kyeisha's family situation, both parents in prison. Her combination of half and whole siblings were spread out between Baton Rouge and Houston, Texas. They were just as likely to claim any reward offered by the authorities for turning her in.

"Lorraine won't call me back. The rest of those bitches showin' me they ain't no friend of mine. The only brother that might talk to me is on the road in his truck. I'm not gonna tell you what his wife said when I tried to explain." Kyeisha's footsteps shuffled in the darkness, a habit she had when stressed.

"Yeah, tough spot," Jazz said, working hard to think her way out of her own tough spot.

"Can't trust nobody," Kyeisha blurted out.

"You got something to offer the DA., right? Get a deal." Jazz hoped her security guard would take a break and show up. The desperation in Kyeisha's voice worried her.

"I grabbed a bag of cash from the place when the shootin' started. Been stayin' in a motel across the river," Kyeisha muttered low as though talking more to herself than to Jazz. "Ain't safe being out here."

"Cleavon got any ideas on your next move?" Jazz replied.

"Let's go in your apartment. You first. Don't yell or nothin'. I'm just sayin' keep it quiet." Kyeisha took one step to the edge of the yellow light, enough to let Jazz see she held a gun. She kept it pointed at the ground.

Small comfort.

Jazz didn't move. "Is Cleavon with you?"

"Just get up," Kyeisha snapped.

"Okay, okay. Keep it cool," Jazz replied evenly. Her anxiety turned to anger, but she worked on controlling her temper.

She glanced at the rear entrance to the club. The door had swung shut. Jazz tried sending psychic signals to Tyretta or Byron, since it was his night to work security. Surely one or both would come looking for her soon. She tried walking slow, but Kyeisha hissed at her back.

"Don't try nothin' cute, Jazz."

"I don't know what you talkin' about, Kee. I'm doing what you asked. Damn," Jazz replied in a casual way. "I've got to get my key out and stuff. You need to relax."

"You try relaxin' with cops and thugs on your ass," Kyeisha shot back. "Now move it."

"I'm movin'," Jazz said.

With Jazz in the lead, they climbed the stairwell to Jazz's apartment. Still none of her employees came outside. The loud thumping beat of bass from speakers and muffled raucous laughter told her they were busy. Kyeisha had picked the perfect night to show up. No doubt she'd been keeping watch somehow. Jazz didn't believe her talk about having no friends. Kyeisha had a cunning streak.

When Jazz opened the two bolt locks and pushed the door open, Kyeisha shoved her through. Kyeisha kicked the door to shut it, but only succeeded in causing it to bounce back hard. The sturdy fiberglass and steel door slapped against Kyeisha back throwing her off balance. Jazz punched her in the face twice with as much force as she could.

"I'ma kill you," Kyeisha huffed in rage as she staggered to one side.

Jazz concentrated on twisting the gun out of Kyeisha's right hand. They s they fought for control of the gun. Jazz let out a string of profane threats. Adrenaline and anger pushed her on. She managed to jam one knee into Kyeisha's side. The shout of pain sounded like sweet music. Then a shot from the revolver exploded in the room. Kyeisha still held on cursing. She braced the heels of her athletic shoes on the carpet to keep Jazz from moving her. Forever seemed to go by until heavy steps sounded on the stairs.

"Get your ass off me," Jazz managed to get out, though breathless and not as loud as she wanted.

"Hey, Jazz," Byron yelled. "You okay?"

"Hell no, she's got a gun," Jazz screamed. As if to prove her point, another shot went off. "Damn it, Kyeisha. The cops are on their way. Give it up."

"Bitch, I just wanted to talk to you. This shit is all your fault," Kyeisha wheezed.

Jazz brought her head up and butted Kyeisha's chin hard. The squeal of agony gave her great satisfaction. At the same time she managed to twist Kyeisha's wrist. The handgun fell to the floor. Then she landed a solid kick in to Kyeisha's left shin.

"Ow, shit. Owwee." Kyeisha went to her knees then rolled onto her side holding her face.

Just then Byron and another man stumbled through the door. The lights switched on. The other guy, a rough looking local from the neighborhood, held his own gun. Both men looked around the room wildly.

"Damn, how many of 'em in here?" Byron burst

out.

"I got this one," the other man said, pointing his pistol at Kyeisha.

Jazz supported herself with one hand on the sofa back nearby. She gasped for air to regulate her breathing and get her shattered nerves under control. "Check my bedroom and the bathroom just in case."

Byron nodded. He went down the hall past Jazz's kitchen and came back seconds later. "Naw, ain't nobody got in."

"Okay." Jazz sat down on the sofa arm. "The police?"

"Not unless some of the neighbors called. I only heard because I was out in the parking lot. Some woman got too drunk and too loud. I was helping her friends get her into the car. Ray-Ray came along 'bout that time. Thanks, man." Byron nodded at Ray-Ray.

"Hey, y'all helped me out one time," he rumbled, referring to the alibi Jazz gave him less than a year before. He was indeed at the club when a 'business rival' was assaulted. "Who the fuck this?"

"A friend," Kyeisha spat and then grunted in pain.

"Ain't no pals of mine come visiting with a gun," Ray-Ray shot back. He seemed perfectly at ease holding someone at gunpoint.

"Hold up," Jazz broke in. Sirens keened but then faded. "Well that's one advantage of being in the hood. People hear gunshots and keep cookin' supper."

"Nearest houses at least two blocks away. You got some good insulation up in here, remember?" Byron looked more at ease as well. Knowing he wasn't up against an armed gang no doubt helped. "Ray-Ray, go tell Lil' Eric all clear."

"Right. See ya lata." Ray-Ray gave them both a nod.

He stared at Kyeisha as he made a wide circle around her to the door.

"You need me to stay here?" Byron kept his gaze on Kyeisha as he directed his question to Jazz.

"I got the two way radio. I'll leave it on Channel three. Help me tie her up first."

Jazz went to the small desk in a corner of her open floor plan, her office. She retrieved another two way radio. She'd gotten them for her security staff to use during large parties at the club. Then she pulled a chair from her dining table to the middle of her living room. She jogged to her bedroom and came back with a long scarf.

"Uh-huh." Byron pulled plastic handcuffs from a back pocket of his jeans as Jazz came back and held Kyeisha down.

"What the fu--" Kyeisha twisted around on the floor and batted away his big arms, or tried to. "Y'all ain't gonna throw me in the swamp somewhere. Get off me, mutha..."

"Shut up. We been nice considerin'," Byron boomed at her.

"Nice hell! I came by here to talk and this crazy..."

Jazz stood back once Kyeisha's wrists were bound behind her. She hooked a hand under one arm while Byron grabbed the other. They lifted Kyeisha to a standing position and marched her to the chair. Before she realized what was happening, Byron had tied one of her ankles to a chair leg. Kyeisha kicked out at him. Jazz slapped her hard until her head bounced.

"Bitch, you gonna be so sorry," Kyeisha shouted.

"You're lucky I didn't shoot you." Jazz leaned down and spoke close into her ear. "You want more of that, keep kicking."

Kyeisha glared at her, but kept her leg still as Byron secured it. "This ain't even called for, Jazz."

"I'll check in with you once I'm downstairs," Byron said. He left with one last scowl at Kyeisha.

Jazz wiped the sweat from her forehead and fanned herself. The ringing in her ears from the gunshots made her feel disoriented. Still she forced herself to move around. Kyeisha's furious gaze followed Jazz's movements around the apartment. Jazz checked all the windows to make sure they were locked. She made sure Kyeisha could not move, then Jazz went into the bathroom. She leaned against the sink, a wet towel pressed against her throat. When Jazz went back to the living room, Kyeisha blinked at her. She sat still but her gaze darted around as though searching for a way out. Jazz got a matching chair from the table. Before she sat down, she got two bottles of water from her refrigerator. Twenty minutes had ticked by. Jazz's nerves and hands were less shaky. She still felt like she had cotton balls stuffed in her ears. Jazz studied Kyeisha for another ten minutes as she sipped water. Then she uncapped the second bottle and extended it.

"Go on. I'm not trying to poison you, fool. I broke the seal," Jazz said mildly. She let Kyeisha down a third of the half-pint then put the bottle down. "Well?"

"Well what?"

"You came to talk, so talk," Jazz said.

She talked alright. A stream of curse words came out like hot lava from a volcano. Kyeisha used up her store of profanity to describe Jazz, and then started inventing new words. Eventually she ran down like a doll whose battery had run low. She puffed out short breaths.

"Now that you got that out your system, let's chat.

I'm assuming Cleavon is close by, or was. If I know your taste in men, I'll bet he took off faster than the bullet from that first shot," Jazz said and grunted a laugh.

"You don't know shit about him. He gonna bust in here any second and--" Kyeisha bit off the words when Jazz lifted the two way radio.

"Hey Byron, get some of your boys to sweep the alleys and side streets. Cleavon might be nearby," Jazz said when he answered. His voice came through saying he would. Jazz hit the button breaking the transmission. "Thanks for being so helpful."

"Fuck you," Kyeisha spat.

"Tsk, tsk. You came to me for information or you thought I had something you needed. Such language, pointing a gun at me and insults. I'm not feeling real sociable toward you or your man right now." Jazz lounged against the back of the chair, waiting. She sipped more water.

Kyeisha seemed to mentally weight her options. Then she hissed out a slow breath. "Okay, look, I didn't come to you right. I had the gun cuz we don't know who's for us or who's ready to shoot us and claim the reward. And I didn't point it at you. You didn't have to freak out and shit."

"Uh-huh. Skip to the point of this little visit," Jazz replied. Kyeisha scowled in silence. "I could call the cops."

Kyeisha smiled slyly. "You won't do that. The city wants to shut you down. Oh yeah, I been watchin' the news. That detective came over here, too."

Jazz decided not to mention that Kyeisha was filling her in on useful information. So Cleavon had one of his people watching Candy Girls. She would let her keep talking. The reason might come out soon enough.

"I could earn brownie points turning you in. Show the mayor I'm a good citizen and shit," Jazz replied in a tone as cool as the April evening outside.

"Damn." Kyeisha licked her lips. "We can help each other. Filipe's old gang want some money they think he owes them. They don't get it from him, they might come looking for you."

"Even locked up they'd be smart not to screw with Filipe. He's got more first, second, and third cousins in gangs than I've got hairs in my weave. Girl, you better warn Cleavon not to stir up that nest of avispas," Jazz replied.

"Nest of what?" Kyeisha frowned at her.

"Spanish for wasps," Jazz said with a wave of her hand.

"Oh. Cleavon ain't tryin' to say it's you. He don't know Filipe trusted you that close, and I haven't told nobody, not even Cleavon... yet." Kyeisha wore a sly expression again.

Jazz planted her elbows on both knees. She rolled the plastic water bottle between her hands. "Go on."

"Me and you could split the cash, sell the drugs, and keep the money."

"What about your true love Cleavon? Don't tell me you'd leave him out of our big payday." Jazz said dryly.

"Well you know how it goes. Besides, he's slapped me around one too many times. I was just shootin' bullshit a minute ago. He don't know I'm here, and I don't have to tell him," Kyeisha replied.

"So you were lying about Cleavon being close by; and, you didn't tell anybody about me knowing where Filipe hid his stuff?" Jazz said.

"Just between you and me, girl. Your boys will tell you nobody is out there watchin'." Kyeisha smiled.

Jazz nodded and smiled back at her. "I gotcha. So if I kill you now, and keep all the money for me, I'm safe."

"Lorraine knows," Kyeisha blurted out, spit flying everywhere. Her eyes went wide as dinner plates.

"Humph, you ain't as dumb as I thought," Jazz murmured and sat back again.

Chapter 6

For the entire weekend Jazz went on with business as usual. She waited until Sunday evening to arrange a meet up with Willa and MiMi. Jazz got a headache with both women chattering at top speed on a three way call. Willa had agreed after an intense debate. On the other hand, MiMi squealed with delight at the suggestion. Willa insisted she wasn't going to spend any time during regular business hours discussing "dumb schemes to get non-existent drug money". The meeting was set for Monday evening. MiMi volunteered to play hostess. When Jazz texted Willa to let her know, the reply text was a curt, "OMG here we go."

Since Mondays were the slowest day at the club, Jazz left Byron in charge. He'd earned her trust, he had good sense, and he could stand up to Tyretta. Most of the money came from lunch and dinner take-out orders anyway.

By seven o'clock, Jazz sat in was at MiMi's. They looked at each other across the totally not child friendly glass top table in MiMi's breakfast nook. Jazz would have loved a smoke, but wouldn't only because of the baby. Sage sat in her lap sucking on a pacifier looking at the adults with interest. She seemed to know a show was about to start. It did.

"You drugged her?" Willa jumped to her feet. "See this is why I didn't want to get hooked up with you two."

"It was just one of those over the counter cold pills, and only a couple or three capsules. Kyeisha slept like a baby, didn't she Sagey-boo?" Jazz gave the eighteen month old a gentle pinch on her plump cheek. Sage giggled as if she got the joke on Kyeisha.

"Jazz..." Willa hissed out air like a hot air balloon losing inflation. She waved both hands as though at a loss for more words.

"That was kind of risky, girl," MiMi ventured. "I mean, what if she was allergic or something?"

"Well she ain't. Byron's pals say she woke up with nothing more than a stiff neck," Jazz said with a grin. "I'm just sorry I wasn't inside Lorraine's dump to watch both their expressions."

"How in the world did you get her there?" Willa said, her arms doing more dramatic arcs as she spoke.

"A wheelchair, one of my customers was getting a lap dance. Mr. Billie is always more comfortable in one of our leather chairs. I mean, the girls can't get too close in the wheelchair anyway." Jazz breathed in the scent of baby lotion as she kissed the top of Sage's head. She bounced Sage on her knee. "Sweet baby girl."

"Well at least she's not discriminating against the disabled," MiMi said when Willa looked to her for support.

"You've both lost your damn minds," Willa blurted out.

"Not in front of the baby," MiMi admonished.

"You need to stop being so high strung, Willa. Kyeisha wasn't knocked out all the way. We got her down the stairs, slipped her butt into the wheelchair and had some dudes drive her to Lorraine's place across town. Mr. Billie didn't even miss his wheelchair, trust me. Monique kept him happy," Jazz said, referring to the second dancer who worked for her part-time.

"Now I'll have to live with that image in my head for days," Willa muttered. "Skip to the part why I should give a flying sh--"

"Watch your mouth," MiMi snapped and placed both palms over Sage's ears. The toddler happily sucked the pacifier unaware of the drama.

"Bad Auntie Willa is a terrible role model," Jazz said and rocked gently from side to side. She smothered a giggle when Willa gave her a look hot enough to set off the fire alarm.

"Come to mommy. There's my sweet girl."

MiMi took the baby in her arms and hummed a tune. Sage's eyes drifted closed. Motioning for them to be quiet, MiMi continued humming as she took Sage to the nursery.

Willa gave Jazz another dirty look and went to the stove. She put more pasta and shrimp on a small plate and sat down again. "Humph, I'm the bad role model. Un-freaking-believable."

"Yeah, I have to say that was funny." Jazz winked at her.

MiMi returned and sat down between them before Willa could reply. "Now let's develop a strategy."

"From purring nursery music to running after drug money. Real nice," Willa shot back. She speared a shrimp and pasta with her fork. Once she'd stuffed it in her mouth, Willa blinked in surprise. "Hmmm, not bad at all."

"Thanks," MiMi replied and frowned at her. "We don't have any evidence that it's drug money. Jack was going to invest in what he thought was a legitimate business expansion. He trusted Ryan. It's not our fault, but at least we could do some good with it. ."

"Hell, all money spends," Jazz grabbed a forked and ate off Willa's plate.

"I've read that the drug business is so big, any money you test will show traces of cocaine. You could be walking around with so-called 'drug money' in your purse right now for all you know." MiMi tossed her thick hair over one shoulder. "So now what do you say?"

Jazz stared at her genuinely impressed. "Damn, MiMi. You could be a lawyer."

Willa put down her fork. She closed her eyes and rubbed her forehead. "Just tell me why I'm here instead of watching Mikayla at dance practice. And make it quick, because then we have to pick up Anthony from his film academy lab."

"What about his car?" MiMi said, getting off the subject.

"It's in the shop right now," Willa said in a tight voice. She turned to Jazz. "Get to the damn point. That way I can say refuse and be on my way."

"See? His car is in the shop *again*. Tell me you don't need money. My nephew needs a car. He's earned it the way he turned around his grades and..." MiMi's words trailed off at the dark glance from Willa.

"MiMi, you slept with my husband. You're not Anthony's aunt by any stretch," Willa hissed her voice getting louder.

"Your ex-husband that you didn't even like, much less love anymore. More than a couple of people thought *you* murdered him," Jazz put in. She raised both palms when her sister turned back to her. "I'm stating facts."

"Jazz, don't keep testing me," Willa warned in a soft yet deadly tone.

"But you're right. MiMi, you're like his step-mother. Except you didn't marry Jack. So technically you're the baby mama," Jazz said with a grin.

MiMi glared at Jazz. "We were engaged."

"My point is technically, I don't think either of you has a strong claim to any of Jack's money on moral grounds. I on the other hand was in business with Filipe. But, I'm generously including you two. We're family." Jazz smiled at them sweetly.

"Bullshit," Willa and MiMi blurted in unison.

"You need my investigative resources to track the money in the legitimate world the way your thug buddies can't," Willa said and crossed her arms.

"I can sniff out information from our upper class social circle. You know they won't talk to you, or your *colorful* friends. Remember the economy hit bottom in 2008. I'll bet Jack wasn't the only frat boy to lower his standards when it came to financing business." MiMi arched an eyebrow.

Jazz shrugged. "Okay, so it takes a village."

Willa barked a laugh empty of humor. "Now she's a philosopher."

"You two need me to crawl under the rocks for clues on the street. The big point is we all need each other," Jazz snapped.

"But *you two* forget something. I don't give a frig about the money. Crown protection may be operating on a thin margin, but we're not anywhere near being broke. Anthony just earned a scholarship, so I don't need the money for his college tuition," Willa put in before MiMi could interrupt. "As for him not having a car? Two words - bus system. By the way, I raised Anthony to take care of himself. He doesn't expect to get handed everything on a silver tray."

"I don't see why Anthony should do without because you're hard-headed," MiMi shot back.

Willa stood and looped her oversized satchel purse over one shoulder. "We both know you're thinking of the designer clothes you want to buy. I'm out. Don't bother calling me to another of these crazy conferences. The answer will still be 'Hell no'."

Jazz stood and faced her. "You haven't heard what Kyeisha told me yet."

"Doesn't matter what hot clue Kyeisha dropped, or even if she knows which psycho drug dealer we can talk to about Filipe's banking habit. I. Don't. Care. Bye." Willa started for the door.

"She threatened me," Jazz said.

Willa stopped and turned around. "You could whip Kyeisha's ass any day of the week and twice on Sunday."

"Kyeisha made it clear. She's more than ready to tell Filipe and his old gang boys that I put him in prison. To make it better she'll tell them I took the money," Jazz said.

"Shit," MiMi spluttered and then covered her mouth with a hand.

* * *

Two hours later, Jazz settled back in the leather

seat of her Ford Explorer. She wheeled the black SUV through MiMi's upper-class enclave, through the solid working-class part of town, and then to more familiar territory.

Poor people who worked hard had no choice, not enough money to leave the hood. They lived jammed up against drug dealers, dope heads, and prostitutes in an uneasy mutual existence. Good citizens and lowlifes kept a close eye on each other: one to keep from being victimized, the other to detect anyone reporting them to the police—and to retaliate. Neat, though old houses with trimmed tiny front yards were next to abandoned urban shacks. Well, no neighborhood is perfect. This was Jazz's world, and she understood it all too well.

Jazz smiled as she drove and took a drag from her cigarette. Her favorite Wyclef Jean album blasted from the speakers. Guilt is a wonderful thing. Her big sister had a powerful protective streak and family loyalty off the scale. W Jazz had pushed both of those buttons at once. Now they were a team. Finding that sweet cash would be no biggie.

"Yeah baby," Jazz sang out, bobbing her head to the beat. "Damn, Willa is right. I need to quit. I can't have my baby smelling like stale smoke."

She tossed the half-smoked cigarette from the rolled down window. The traffic light turned red at the corner of East Boulevard and Terrace Street. A couple of urban entrepreneurs, a fancy name for street hustlers, waved to her. Drae and a dude known only as Ja'Blow grinned at her, but didn't slow their roll. No doubt they had places to go and people to rip-off.

"Hey, y'all on the way to grandma's for cookies?" Jazz shouted as at them.

Ja'Blow tugged on his sagging jeans. "Yah, I got

some cookies for you fine woman."

"That's what's up," Drae added with a grin. "Comin' to get me a private dance, girl."

"Yeah, yeah. Y'all got talk, but if your money ain't right, won't be no action tonight," Jazz wisecracked.

She laughed out loud when the men pretended they'd been shot, staggering along the sidewalk. Jazz hooted at them and honked her horn. A group of young men hanging on another corner joined in with catcalls.

Her playful mood almost made her miss the signs. Even so, her reflexes kicked in too late. Jazz saw another black SUV, this one a Land Rover, pull up behind her. She'd noticed it about six blocks back because she wanted one. Too pricey for her, but not for a successful gangster. Hoping she was being paranoid for nothing, Jazz cut the steering wheel sharply and screeched off before the light changed. She barreled down narrow Alice Street. The Land Rover followed, lights flashing in her rearview mirror.

"Damn, damn."

Jazz didn't hang much in south Baton Rouge, so she guessed at the next move. She shot around a corner. The Explorer leaned like it would rollover and her heart jumped. The big tires held to the pavement. Before she could breathe out her relief, a metal road barrier rushed at her and she slammed on the breaks. Boxed in.

"Shit, shit, shit."

Jazz fumbled with the sliding top of the console at her elbow. The .380 Smith and Wesson played tag. Her fingers scraped against more junk than she should have had in there with it. By the time she pulled it out the Land Rover had pulled up on her bumper. One dark figure crouched behind the open passenger door.

"You messed up my woman, bitch. I don't much

care, but it's the principle. Know what I'm sayin'?" The familiar voice called.

"Cleavon? Ain't you got enough trouble without this? You need to be keeping a low profile, dude," Jazz shouted back. In the small house to her left an elderly woman sat on her screened in porch, her profile outlined by the lit window behind her.

"Y'all better stop all that cussin' and mess out here," the lady called out.

"Woman, get in here and shut the damn door," a man, most likely her husband, called out.

"Ma'am, go inside before bullets start flyin'," Jazz said in a harsh whisper, not sure the woman would hear.

"They better not shoot at you," the woman came back in a feisty tone.

"I'm gone start shooting at them," Jazz replied.

"Lawd have mercy. Take care of business, baby." The woman scrambled from her chair and a door slammed shut a second later. The light in the window went out.

"Nobody better call the fuckin' police," a deep voice shouted to the houses on the small dead end street.

"Just us now, girl. You ready to talk?" Cleavon called.

"Don't be stupid, the police will show up. I hit 911 fool. I know you've heard of hands-free calling."

Cleavon barked a laugh. "You ain't called cuz you got your own problems. Besides, I'm off the hook. The police got nuthin' on me."

"The police need to do their damn jobs better," Jazz muttered. Sweat stung her eyes as she blinked hard. "You know they got forensics these days, so don't get too comfortable. Now go on 'bout your business, and I'll go on 'bout mine."

"You gonna help your Filipe's boys to take me out. I can't sit around waiting for trouble to come to me," Cleavon replied. The driver's side door and a rear door of the Land Rover swung open at the same time. "Now join me for a little chat. I got a bar in here, some smooth scotch and good sounds on the system."

"Yeah, sure. Give me a minute to fix my make-up," Jazz yelled.

In a quick motion she stuck the .380 out of the car window, aimed, and fired straight ahead at the dead end. Gun still in her right hand, Jazz jammed into reverse gear and hit the accelerator. Her rear bumper crashed into the front grill of the Land Rover even as it screeched in reverse seconds later. Shouts came from both sides of the Land Rover. A scream of pain echoed in the night air as one open door of the big SUV thudded against a thug's tender parts. Jazz braked but fired a second shot as more incentive for them to get out of her way. The tat-tat of gunfire blasted behind her. Glass pelted her as the back window of her Explorer shattered.

"Hell, I'm gonna die on a dead end street for something I haven't even done yet."

Jazz fired again out of frustration. Then trees, shotgun houses, and her Explorer lit up with blue flashes. Another crash sounded as the Land Rover tried to ram past a police cruiser. When that didn't work everybody bailed out of it. The sounds of feet hitting pavement came as cops went after Cleavon and his buddies. Bright white spotlights turned dark into artificial daytime.

"Show your hands," a female cop boomed from a

loudspeaker. When Jazz complied, the woman continued. "Now exit the vehicle. Keep your hands visible, get on your knees and then lie on your stomach with your arms out. Do it now."

Jazz knew when to hit the mute button on her smart-ass mouth—this being one such situation. Jittery cops circled all around the area chasing thugs. Not the time to pop off. Without saying a word, Jazz followed instructions. Sweat made gravel and dirt stick to her face, yet she said nothing. The hard pavement smelled sour. Jazz still held her tongue.

"You got anything sharp on you that might stick me like needles or razors, a knife?" the female cop asked.

"Nothing like that," Jazz replied.

A pair of hands roughly pulled down her body to make sure. "Arms behind your back, ma'am," a male cop said.

Now they decided to be polite? Jazz gasped when hands jerked her wrists together and plastic cuffs snapped on. Seconds later she was yanked upright by a cop on either side lifting her by the armpits. Jazz grunted, but didn't complain. First leaning against it, and then seated in the back seat of a police cruiser, she answered questions for an hour. People who lived in the houses stood on their front steps or porches watching. After a while, only a couple stayed. No doubt observing police action had lost its novelty in that part of Baton Rouge.

"This your gun, Ms. Vaughn?" The female cop held up the .380.

"Yeah, and I obviously need it in this crime infested city. I happen to have a permit for it, too. You'll find it in the console." Jazz struggled to keep heat out of her tone. She had a serious problem with authority, thanks to her mother. No time to act out her mama issues though.

"Humph." The officer walked off as she spoke to another officer.

Jazz sighed and rested her forehead on the steel mesh cage designed to protect officers in the front seat. The heat, hard vinyl seat, and lack of head room combined to make Jazz feel miserable. At this rate, she would be begging for them to take her in for booking. After too long a time, the female cop returned. Without speaking, she checked to make sure Jazz had no arms or legs sticking out. Then she slammed the door shut. Moments later, they were on their way.

At the police station, Jazz got her first full on look at Cleavon. Jazz sat on a long bench waiting to be interviewed. A brawny male officer with blonde hair pulled Cleavon along. Cleavon kept his head down. He shot a sideways glare at Jazz for a second before the officer not so gently urged him not to dawdle. Jazz sighed when they disappeared around a corner. A tall shadow blocked out the florescent lighting.

"Why doesn't seeing you here surprise me?" A deep voice rumbled.

Detective Armand Miller, once Addison's partner and now the head of the Homicide Division, looked down at her. He wore the same disapproving expression Jazz had seen from dozens of authority figures in her short twenty-seven years. And he got the same reaction.

"I don't know. Cause maybe you're a damn fortune teller or something? I'm a victim, and by the way, I know my rights. If they ain't gonna charge me..." Jazz was just getting warmed up when Miller raised a hand the size of Texas.

"Settle down and come with me. Officer Thomas, do the honors." Miller nodded to the female uniformed officer who'd been at the scene.

"Yes, sir." Officer Thomas had a blank expression as she went about following his orders. Minutes later, the thick plastic had been cut off.

"This way," Miller said before Jazz could comment again.

The female officer walked closely beside Jazz but didn't touch her. They walked past desks covered by papers. Officers moved around with purpose. No drinking coffee and eating donuts in this place, no time. Baton Rouge had not only grown economically, but the crime had kept pace with more PR worthy milestones. The murder rate was one such nasty flow chart that kept going up. Jazz had no interest in contributing to those numbers, at least not as a victim. Kyeisha was another thing. She'd no doubt sent her crazy lover to take a bite out of Jazz. She'd have to pay.

Jazz let out a hiss when they entered an interview room. " Great, I get shot at and now I'm being harassed."

"Don't start before you find out what's goin' down," Miller rumbled. He nodded and the officer left.

"What's up?" Jazz rubbed the indentations on her wrists caused by the thick, hard plastic cuffs.

"You tell me." Miller leaned back against the chair as though he had all kinds of time and patience.

Though she knew the game, Jazz was still unnerved by his impassive stare. She heaved a sigh. "Okay, you want the truth?"

"I come to work every day hoping to hear the truth, Ms. Vaughn," Miller replied evenly.

"Bet you get disappointed a lot around this place."

"So lighten my load and give me hope in humanity again. Tell me *all* of the truth. Not just the parts you want to tell," Miller added when Jazz opened her mouth.

Jazz studied him. Miller sat calmly allowing Jazz to size him up. "Why are you talking to me? Okay, okay." She held up a hand before he answered. "You're asking the questions, I'm supplying the answers. I got it."

"I'm interested in why a murder suspect was chasing you down like you're a witness that could get him convicted," Miller said, dropping a bomb with precision.

"I don't know anything about Brandon's murder. And don't pretend to be surprised. You've talked to Don, Detective Addison," Jazz added when Miller's black coffee eyes widened. "You already know I'm acquainted with the players in this tragic story of love gone bad."

"Come again?" Miller blinked at her and sat up straight.

"Well I heard Kyeisha was doing Brandon behind Cleavon's back, and I mean these dudes ain't romantic or anything, but they do take having their pride stepped on pretty seriously." Jazz tossed in this nugget to get his attention back on Cleavon and away from Don. She didn't want to mess up the man's career.

"A love triangle?" Miller's skepticism came through loud and clear.

"Kyeisha ain't big on loyalty. If a new guy throws a little money around, that's all it takes. She's also not too smart. Everybody knows Brandon had a big mouth and liked to brag. I'm sure he had plans to move on Cleavon's drug business along with taking his woman."

Miller nodded solemnly and rubbed his strong jaw. He gazed out through the glass windows of the interview room at the bustle of the squad room. "Hmm. Could be. But why would Cleavon come after you? Unless you were at the house that night and managed to get out before the trouble started."

"No way. I've got sense enough not to hang out in stank drug shacks with a bunch of gun toting idiots. Besides, ain't none of that crew my runnin' buddies. You already know that, too." Jazz relaxed against the back of the chair. Miller knew she wasn't involved in Brandon's murder. So she'd wait for him to get to the point.

"The truth about why he came after you," Miller said mildly. He leaned back in his chair.

"Damn it." Jazz hated being caged up, and any police station was her second least favorite place in the world. The first would always be foster care. "Kyeisha came to me with some wild ass story about Cleavon and Brandon fighting to become king of the thugs. They think I know about Filipe's connections to get serious drug shipments."

"Do you?" Miller asked as he tapped a large forefinger on the table top.

"Do I look like I've totally lost my damn mind?" Jazz shot back without thinking. She took in a breath and exhaled. "Sorry. Listen, I'm a former exotic dancer turned *legitimate* business woman. Even on my worse day, I never got involved in Filipe's business. Never."

"You know more about Filipe's enterprise than you're willing to admit, even to my former partner," Miller shot back. "We both know that's why you've got characters like Cleavon coming at you. He won't be the last either. If you're straight with me, maybe I can help."

"My only crime was I partied with Filipe and other friends who got into some seriously illegal mess. Now you in my face accusing me of crap I didn't do." Jazz glared at him.

"This is the price you pay for hanging with a bad crowd, Ms. Vaughn," Detective Miller replied dryly.

"I had that lecture at least a dozen times when I was a kid, so let's skip it," Jazz retorted. She brushed off his Sunday School Teacher scolding. She focused like a laser on his lack of reaction to Filipe's name. "So you've connected Filipe to Brandon's murder."

"Is that why Kyeisha came to see you? They think you know where he has inventory and cash stored? I seem to recall something about warehouses on Interline Ave. back when we were investigating Jack Crown's murder." Miller lifted one dark eyebrow at her.

He was getting too close for comfort. Jazz shifted in her seat. She needed a story to steer him to another angle. She had visions of a press conference with him and the district attorney standing next to a table piled with cash. Her cash.

"Detective Miller, I swear, I don't know anything I told Kyeisha what I'm telling you, except louder. I don't know anything about Filipe having money floating around."

"You emphasized the point to her," Miller said.

"Yeah, but she didn't believe me," Jazz replied with heat.

"Did this emphasis get physical by any chance?" "She understood my position by the time we parted company," Jazz said. She doubted Kyeisha had complained to the police. "You need to be asking Kyeisha all these questions. She talked like she knew a lot about Cleavon's connections and how Filipe's gang tied in to it all."

"Interesting." Miller continued to gaze at Jazz in

silence, waiting again.

"She's thick with Lorraine Taylor. Try looking for her over at Lorraine's place, The Sweet Spot. Kyeisha had one of those low rent duplex apartments over on McClelland Drive. Well, if she kept paying rent she'd be over there. She gets evicted a lot. Then she ends up at her mama's house over on West Garfield in old South Baton Rouge." Jazz shrugged. "I'm trying to tell you all I know."

"She's moved to a place on Concord. In fact, she upgraded to a three bedroom unit. Been paying her bills on time and she got a car," Miller replied.

"Kyeisha rarely held on to a job or money for long, so that's a clue she's getting paid on the regular. Why you wasting time on me? Drag her ass in for questioning," Jazz shot back.

"We did find her, just not all of her."

Jazz shivered at the way he'd said those words. Miller's brows pulled together as he continued to nod; waiting for her to ask. She didn't want to, but the words tumbled out. "What you mean not all of her?"

"Fingers, three fingers. Identified them from prints we have from her previous arrests. They're hers alright. Lots of blood in her apartment, too." Miller continued to nod like a bobble-head doll.

"Just her fingers," Jazz replied weakly.

"You got something more you wanna tell me, Ms. Vaughn?" Detective Miller wasn't big on melodramatics or beating home a point once made. He sat watching as the full effect of his disclosure did the work for him.

Chapter 7

The next morning, Jazz sat in Willa's office at Crown Protection. Tyretta had come along to. She felt a little better surrounded by people she trusted. Not to mention the five trained security staff that happened to be in that day. They were meeting with Willa's handsome chief of operations in a large conference room on the west side of their office suite. Cedric Robinson really wanted to wanted to trade that one in for "Willa's man". Protective as ever of Willa, Cedric stuck his head in the office twice to update them that he would join them soon.

MiMi showed up after dropping Sage off at the fancy daycare paid for with granddaddy's money. Willa kept sitting down and then popping up to pace around the office. She shot questions at Jazz and Tyretta. Sipping gourmet brew and eating her second donut, Tyretta seemed quite content. She kept glancing around Willa's office in appreciation. MiMi was uncharacteristically quiet. The mention of severed body parts apparently had dampened her enthusiasm for the money chase.

Willa pointed a finger with a soft pink polish on the nail. "So tell me again what Miller said, and don't roll your eyes. I want to know his exact words."

Jazz rolled her eyes anyway and started from the beginning. Trying to put on her best streetwise bravado had been a defense mechanism for years. Still, Miller had done a great job quite rattling Jazz down to her bones. As Willa suspected, Jazz could reconstruct Miller's words down to his non-verbal cues. She didn't just replay what he'd said, but the way he'd said it. Willa and Jazz had learned that survival skill living with their unpredictable mother, her string of boyfriends, and bouncing around in foster care.

Willa sat on the edge of her large oak desk. "He waited until the very end to mention the fingers. Then he refused to give you more details."

"Said the investigation is on-going. They hope to find more evidence, they're interviewing witnesses. Blah, blah, blah." Jazz rubbed her eyes. She'd been unable to sleep the night before.

"You know he won't tell you much more. You a suspect," Tyretta piped up and licked icing from one thumb. "Yeah, you whipped her ass and then drugged her."

"Oh my God." MiMi blinked like she'd just been slapped.

Jazz hissed in frustration. "I defended myself and tied her up, sure. But I didn't put a beating on that fool, much as she deserved it."

"We got to find that heffa and figure out what's what," Tyretta replied and gazed steadily at Jazz.

"Uh-huh, I know what you're saying," Jazz said softly.

"No," Willa said and slapped a palm on the desk. "You two are crazy if you're thinking of going after Kyeisha. Cleavon is waiting for you, or did you forget?"

"How the hell I'm gonna forget after he jammed me up on a dead end street? But Cleavon got more problems of his own. He's sweatin' to find money and take over Filipe's business." Jazz looked at Tyretta again.

Tyretta took Jazz's cue and began her street level report. "Filipe has a sharp new lawyer. He's got a good shot at his appeal, so he could be getting out. I mean they didn't tie him directly to the whole drug deal smuggling ring. That deacon at Abundant Love, the one over the prison and ex-offender 'ministry', he got most of the blame."

"He won't be talking or hiring an attorney since somebody killed him before Filipe was charged," Jazz retorted. "And one of Filipe's boys got the blame for killing the shady deacon, and then *he* turned up dead."

"All excellent reasons we should let the police do their dirty work and get back to our lives," Willa put in firmly. "Filipe finds out you're sniffing the trail of what belongs to him, he's going to start thinking."

"She's makin' sense," Tyretta said. "If Filipe ain't suspicious you snitched, he will be if one of his gang says you're after his money. Or anything he owns. I agree with your sister. Leave this mess the hell alone."

"Wait a minute. We're looking for *Jack's money*," MiMi blurted out. "We'll make that clear. No asking around his gang or any of the ghetto fabulous folks. No offense, Tyretta."

"None taken," Tyretta replied and poured more coffee into her cup. She gave Jazz the side eye though.

"We have a legitimate need to settle his estate. Searching for assets is part of the legal process. No need to involve Jazz at all." MiMi's tone became more confident the longer she talked. "You have a responsibility to account for property, cash, investments or whatever as the executor."

Jazz looked at Willa. "She's makes a good argument. If you happen to find out there's more money than might be Jack's then... some of it is mine."

"Hmm, that could work. Keep the search in the bourgie world, the civil courts. No mention of Jazz. Might be ticklish for a minute or two, but it could work." Tyretta sipped coffee. She might have been a corporate type considering a business strategy. Of course the orange braids, matching nail polish, and skin tight zebra leggings didn't fit the image.

"Forget that idea," Cedric's deep voice seemed like a thunder clap. All four women jumped.

"Damn, got coffee on my new leggings!" Tyretta protested. She grabbed a napkin and took angry swipes at the offending wet brown spot. "Who the hell..."

"Sorry ladies. I came in after my other meeting ended," Cedric replied and nodded to everyone as a greeting.

Tyretta's mouth hung open as she looked at him. Her gaze drifted from his face down to his feet. "I'll get some of that stain remover and these will be good as new. Can I get you anything?"

"He moves around real smooth and quiet," Jazz said with a grin.

"He's good at that," Willa replied.

"I'm gonna want details later," Jazz whispered back with a wink.

Willa blushed. Looking away, she became fascinated with an ink pen on her desk. "I meant he's good at blending in when he investigates."

"Yeah," Jazz wisecracked. When Willa buttoned up her navy blue blazer, Jazz's smirk widened.

"Filipe has eyes and ears everywhere. He'll make the connection. He's a lot of things, but stupid isn't one of them," Cedric said.

"He's right. The minute there is anything on record about me searching for money outside the United States he'll know." Willa nodded in agreement.

"Not to mention the media might get interested. Jack's murder investigation played big in the news," Cedric added.

MiMi winced. "Jerk reporters."

"Reverend Fisher had a fine old time giving a couple of interviews. All that stuff about the sin of envy and the wickedness caused by the love of money." Willa gazed at Jazz.

"Don't give me a look. I didn't tell him what to say." Jazz lifted her nose in the air. "He was my spiritual adviser. He didn't ask me to write his sermons or anything."

"Yeah, well your 'spiritual adviser' sure didn't succeed at putting you on the road to righteousness," Willa retorted. "And he didn't stop passing the collection plate at Abundant Love Ministries either."

"He didn't stop lovin' the Lord or money," Tyretta chimed in and cackled. "Nice church though. I attend service there once in a while. Lot of members."

"Amazing," MiMi said. "The fact that gangsters were using his ministry to run a drug and gun operation didn't damage his reputation or the church's either. He came off looking like a saint because he forgave them, and visited some in jail."

"Reverend Fisher is a survivor," Jazz replied with a smile. Then her amusement withered as she considered

Cedric's argument. "So you're saying we should back off."

"Crown Protection is doing a little better than breaking even. I have three appointments this week alone to get long-term contracts," Cedric said to Willa.

Willa stared at Jazz. "Thank you. Please tell them we're not about to close our doors." "Far from it," Cedric replied. He turned to MiMi. "I know you'd like a richer lifestyle, but you're doing just fine. You have a job, a very nice house, and income from Jack's investments..."

"Very modest income," MiMi protested.

"Aunt Ametrine would say you're blessed and don't have sense enough to know it," Willa said. She ignored the dirty look MiMi shot her way. "Bottom line is he's right. Jazz, the last thing you should want is anything to do with thugs. Go back to just running your club. Let the police keep the heat on Cleavon, and eventually he'll lose interest in you."

"I have no doubt Filipe has eyes on Cleavon, which means bad news for Cleavon. Let's not get caught in the crossfire," Cedric said.

"Hell, no. Drive-bys with bullets flying everywhere is bad for my health. We better let them fight it out and stay low," Tyretta said. She flashed a smile at Cedric, who blushed and cleared his throat.

Jazz frowned at Tyretta. "A minute ago you agreed with me."

"I'm willing to consider new information and stay *flexible*," Tyretta replied, her gaze still on Cedric. "I'm real *flexible*."

Cedric blinked hard and looked at Willa. "I've got calls to make, but stay far away from anything that involves Filipe Perez."

Tyretta sprang to block his exit as he started for the door. She stuck out her hand. "It was a pleasure meeting you."

"Um, same here. Bye." Cedric left as if he had urgent matters elsewhere.

"He's got a serious thing for Willa, so stop wasting your time sweetie," Jazz drawled.

"Hey," Willa blurted out and stood straight.

MiMi waved a hand. "Oh everybody knows you two are hot for each other."

"I don't know what the hell everybody thinks they know, but they need to stay out of my business," Willa said. The heat in her tone threatened to melt anything within twenty feet.

MiMi ignored Willa. "Let's get back to the money. We all know Cedric is conservative, and while I appreciate his sense of caution..."

"Hey, you ever been on the wrong end of a straight mean thug? The more I think about it, Jazz, the more I agree with Mr. Sexy," Tyretta said.

"But, but." MiMi's mouth worked as she tried to marshal another argument

Jazz hissed out a long sigh and stood. She looped her leather hobo bag over one shoulder. "MiMi, just stop. We both know damn well Cedric is right. Those fingers missing the rest of Kyeisha? That's the kind of stuff Latino drug gangs do to people who cross them. I'm sentimental about all of my body parts, so that's a wrap for me on the money chase."

"Now you're talking sense," Willa said. "MiMi, you have Sage to consider. This isn't a game."

"Of course I'd never put Sage in any danger. We're trying to settle her father's estate. Filipe or any of those gang members won't care about..." MiMi's voice died away when Jazz and Tyretta headed for the door.

"I'll meet you outside," Tyretta said. She waved goodbye to Willa and MiMi before scurrying out.

Jazz rolled her eyes and faced Willa. "You know she's hoping to accidently bump into your man."

"He's not my man," Willa snapped loudly.

"All I'm sayin' is give him what he wants before some other woman is all over that good stuff. You keep playing hard to get and you'll end up playing all by yourself." Jazz raised both arched eyebrows at her. "Tell her, MiMi. You're the expert on getting a man."

"Hmm." MiMi wore a deep frown of concentration.

Jazz lightly tapped MiMi on the shoulder as she walked past where she sat. "Take some wise advice and learn how to live within the means you got, girl."

"Not that I care, but Tyretta isn't Cedric's type. But hey, he's free and grown. It's none of my business," Willa replied. She made it a point not to look at the open door that led to her office lobby.

"How much you want to bet Tyretta is making up an excuse to look for the ladies restroom? She's going to hunt him down if it's the last thing she does," Jazz teased. She suppressed a chuckle when Willa's nostrils flared.

"Don't be so obvious, baby sister. I'm not going to take the bait." Willa walked around her desk and sat down. "So you're not going after the drug money? We're clear?"

Jazz grew serious again. "Kyeisha and Cleavon messed with the wrong pack of pit bulls. Let them rip into each other. I'm staying out of it."

MiMi heaved a dramatic sigh. "How sweet. You two pick now to be on the same page, and we'll lose close to a million dollars. I'm sure interest has accrued."

"Yeah, and I'm sure you want all of your fingers, toes, and both eyes," Jazz shot back. When MiMi squeaked at the image, Jazz nodded. "Bye sis."

"Bye," Willa replied. She grinned at a shaken MiMi.

Jazz found Tyretta in the lobby trying to pump Kay for information on Cedric's whereabouts. Kay mouthed a relieved "Thank you" when Jazz collected her persistent buddy and marched her out the glass exit doors.

"So you're sure Cedric and Willa are solid?" Tyretta said the minute they were in the elevator. The doors swished shut and she hit the button to the first floor.

"Positive. Besides, Cedric would bore you into a coma. He likes going to art exhibits and classic jazz."

"Humph, how do you know I'm not into art and classic jazz?" Tyretta tossed her head making the orange blond tresses bounce.

"So you're an Art Tatum fan?" Jazz checked for texts on her smart phone.

"Who?"

"Yeah," Jazz retorted and walked ahead of her when the elevator doors slid open.

"Umph." Tyretta followed her to Jazz's car parked in the lot. "Were you blowin' smoke in there with your sister?"

"No way. Bloody body parts are a sign to leave well enough the hell alone." Jazz looked at Tyretta.

* * *

Jazz stuck to her word. She knew Filipe, his crazy gang members, and his even crazier cousins enough to know when she was well off. They weren't coming directly to her. She'd be a fool to go looking for them.

The next day, a different kind of trouble showed up at the front door of Candy Girls. Literally.

Jazz went down to air the place out and get ready for the lunch crowd. As usual she'd gone in through the back doors first. She was inside when she heard a noise out front. Cautious, Jazz went to the double front entrance doors. Two diamond shaped windows with double-pane shatterproof smoky glass allowed in muted light. She peered outside. Her heart raced when she saw the top of a man's head. He was intent on something. Then moments later he walked off tapping on a tablet computer. Jazz rushed through the process of opening four sets of heavy locks. She swung open the door only to see a car with the city seal pull from the parking lot and go down the street. Only when she turned did Jazz notice the thick paper taped to the door. A plastic bag contained another form. She pulled it out, read one word in red at the top and shivered. She still sat at the bar staring at the papers two hours later. First Byron and then Tyretta arrived to find her there. An ashtray spilled over with cigarette butts. Her fifth cup of coffee had gotten cold.

"Close the place down," Byron said. His words rolling out like the voice of doom. "I got to find another gig. Damn."

"Yeah, Byron cause it's all about you," Tyretta snapped. "Jazz put every cent she had into the place. This is her dream. Freedom from shakin' her ass to somebody else's beat."

Byron bobbed his large head in appreciation. "Hey, that's almost poetic. And I wasn't meaning to just think about me, but I got four kids at the house. Ya know?"

"He's right. This does affect him, and the rest of you," Jazz said. She fingered the papers for a second before pushing them away. Not that getting them out of sight made a difference.

"You need to get a lawyer. The city can't just push us around. We got a legal business. All the right permits and everything. I got a good mind to go downtown put some of those SOBs on notice." Tyretta let loose with a string of curse words that made even big Byron blink.

"That ain't gonna do nothin' but make it worse. Show em they're right to call this place a 'nuisance property'," Byron said sternly. "Jazz got enough trouble without you givin' them evidence."

"Just stop all the noise, Tyretta."

Jazz felt tears pushing at her eyelids. She hated crying, or the weakness that made her tearful. When she was five, Jazz realized crying didn't get her mother's attention. In fact, in the wrong situation, crying just invited more mistreatment. Her childish high pitched squealing further enraged her unpredictable mother or her latest boyfriend. In her nightmare journey through the foster care system, Jazz had met truly sadistic people who enjoyed watching kids suffer. Pleading for help or mercy only assured the abuse would continue— or get worse. So she not only shut down, she learned to get even. But right now, she couldn't work up the energy to feel angry. All she felt was defeated.

Tyretta sat on the bar stool next to her. She put a hand on Jazz's shoulder. "Listen girl, you take some time to rest. Hell, you've been working sixteen hour days for months runnin' this place. Go up to your place and take a nap. We'll open for lunch."

"But the notice," Byron protested as he pointed at the papers.

"Let me see this shit again." Tyretta grabbed the papers and read them. "This is a notice that there's gonna be a hearing in fifteen working days. She's got to prepare to answer charges that Candy Girls, LLC is promoting crime and a general decay of... Dutton Estates? What the hell is Dutton Estates?"

"The city is made up of subdivisions that were named back when neighborhoods were established," Jazz said in a monotone. "Back in 1939 some guy name Dutton owned land around here. It's on all the papers for this property. Nobody even remembers that far back."

"Well, anyway, we're going to fight. Get a lawyer," Tyretta said.

"Hey, she's got a good point. What about that guy on television, Marty something? He's got those commercials saying, 'I'll make them pay!'" Byron said.

"Him? He's only interested in accidents with big rigs. Makes his money getting settlements from insurance companies," Jazz replied. "I gave him lap dances when I worked at Gentleman's Pleasure across town. Good tipper though."

"Then maybe he'll take your case since y'all are friends," Byron replied.

Jazz looked at him and planted a fist on one hip. "You must be joking. How you think Mr. Jewish Family Man would react to his former pole dancer showing up asking for a favor?"

Byron scratched his jaw. "Well, it's business so I don't think..."

"The city is making me an example. Candy Girls has already been in the newspapers. Some sharp reporter will dig up my past for sure. Marty will figure out real quick that he wants nothing to do with me." Jazz sniffed. She jumped down from the bar stool and stomped over to grab a paper napkin. As she dabbed at her eyes, Tyretta made soothing noises while patting her back.

"So like I said, I got to find another job." Byron grunted. "Not that I won't try to help you, too, Jazz. I got a friend owns a string of quick stop shops. Maybe he can find something for all of us."

"Great. Just what we always dreamed about," Tyretta snapped. "Wearing an ugly shirt with a logo on it selling beef jerky, and hoping we don't get robbed by some crack head."

"It ain't like that," Byron replied. "My friend has six nice stores. Well, five now. The cops shut down one after they found some pipes and illegal bath salts in it."

"Oh, that sounds even more exciting, Byron." Tyretta threw up both hands. "Five bucks says your buddy is next on the city's hit list."

"Larry is a nice guy. He's married to my cousin," Byron said, as if that proved Larry's goodness.

"Well unless your cousin got elected mayor last night, that don't mean diddly-shit," Tyretta replied and turned her back to a grumbling Byron. "Look, girl. My friend knows a lawyer who can advise you. He's taken on the city before and won."

"I appreciate the help, Tyretta, but I don't know." Jazz picked up the cup again. She sipped and grimaced at the taste of tepid coffee. "I don't have money to pay a lawyer charging over a hundred bucks an hour while we sit in court."

"His first consultation is free. I think it is anyway. At least let me call and find out. This guy says those city ordinances are weak as dish water." Tyretta nodded when Jazz glanced at her.

"He's had this type of case before?" Jazz pushed away the heavy blanket of self-pity that had settled on her shoulders.

"Yep. Don't let them push you around. They want you to just pack up and run for cover. Hell, Lorraine might be behind this mess." Tyretta waved her arms in outrage. "She needs to get over it and quit hatin' on you."

Jazz felt the flames of anger come alive in her gut. Lorraine. Wouldn't she love to see Candy Girls boarded up and Jazz back dancing on a pole? "Get me that lawyer's name."

* * *

A tall man in a dark gray suit came through the door of the attorney's office suite. Jazz watched him walk through the waiting room, speak to the cute secretary and then disappear through one of three doors. The nut brown young woman continued clicking away on the keyboard of her desktop computer. Her name, Shamekia Thompson, was on a small plaque on her desk. She flashed a brief professional smile at Jazz.

"Mr. Nelson knows you're waiting, ma'am. He just got back from court. He shouldn't be long."

"Thanks."

The phone on Shamekia's desk rang and she picked it up. "Law offices of Higgins, Nelson and Wilson, how may I help you?"

Jazz picked up a magazine from the end table. She settled down figuring the "few minutes" meant she'd be hanging out for at least a half hour. Bored looking supermodels stared back at her from the glossy pages of a fashion magazine. Jazz flipped through articles on make-up, jewelry, and clothes few women she knew could afford. She started feeling as bored as the supermodels when raised voices made her look up. The secretary gave her a tight smile, but remained at her desk. Two male voices rumbled behind closed doors. A loud thud made the secretary and Jazz flinch at the same time. The voices were lower but not by much. Then silence that stretched on for several minutes seemed ominous.

"You maybe better check on your boss?" Jazz offered.

"I'm sure he's okay," the young woman said. Her fidgeting betrayed her attempt to sound unconcerned. When a door banged open she hunched her shoulders and gasped.

"Don't count on this being over, Godfrey. You no good..." The tall man stood in the open office door pointing as he spoke.

"This is a place of business, Ronald. Show some self-control," a calm deep voice flowed, though its owner didn't emerge.

"After what you did, you've got the balls to lecture me on proper behavior?" The tall man thundered back. "One of these days, Godfrey... One of these days..."

The man whirled around and stormed out of the office. Window glass rattled and both table lamps trembled when he slammed the heavy front door. Jazz looked around to find the secretary gone from her desk. All she could see was Shamekia's head. The young woman peeped around a corner of wall leading down a corridor to other offices. A third man appeared. He whispered something to her. She nodded as he gave her a pat on her arm. Then he went into the open door and closed it. If more shouting started, Jazz was prepared to make a run for it herself. Shamekia smoothed down her blouse in a game attempt to regain some dignity.

"Would you like some coffee or a soft drink," she stammered. Her gaze darted to the front door at least three times.

"Umm, no thanks," Jazz said and crossed over to her. "You look like you need a drink worse than me, girl."

"No, no, I'm okay," Shamekia replied with a smile.

"Uh-huh." Jazz went to a spring water cooler in the waiting room. She filled a paper cup and gave it to Shamekia. "Here, you better steady your nerves."

Shamekia nodded and gulped down the water. "Thank you."

"Sure. I guess lawyers get used to unsatisfied clients, huh?" Jazz took the empty paper cup from Shamekia. She handed the young woman a napkin. Then she picked up several papers that had fallen to the floor.

"That was Mr. Nelson," Shamekia blurted out.

"The guy who's supposed to be my new lawyer just had a meltdown and blew outta here? Damn," Jazz said.

"Oh, well... I guess we need to get you another appointment. I mean..." The young woman stammered as she rushed to her desk.

"I came here to get out of drama, not step into more," Jazz retorted. She swung her leather purse over one shoulder. "Nah, sweetie, I'm on my way."

Two men emerged from the office that had been a storm center only minutes before. The man who had tried to comfort Shamekia nodded at Jazz and disappeared back down a hallway. The taller man, the color of honey, strode over to Jazz with a hand extended. Without thinking she shook it.

"I'm so sorry you had to suffer through that unsettling scene, Ms.--" The good-looking man glanced at Shamekia.

"Ms. Jazzmonetta Vaughn, Mr. Higgins. She had a two o'clock appointment with Mr. Nelson, but he..." Shamekia glanced at the front door.

"I'll see you right away, Ms. Vaughn. Shamekia, get Ms. Vaughn a soft drink. Or maybe get one of those small bottles of organic honey infused iced herbal tea. You have one as well. Right this way Ms. Vaughn." Mr. Higgins deftly guided Jazz into his office with a firm hand under her elbow while he gave instructions to Shamekia and offered more apologies.

Before she knew how or when it happened, Jazz had been settled into a comfortable deep green leather chair. A thick napkin had been placed in her hand and she held a crystal goblet, as promised. In ten minutes she told him about her club and the notice from the city of Baton Rouge. She gave him a copy of it to examine as well. And damned if she didn't like the honey infused herbal tea crap Shamekia had practically begged her to try.

Godfrey Higgins, Esq. leaned back in his leather executive chair. He had let her talk without interruption. After ten seconds of silence he tapped on the keyboard of his all-in-one desktop computer. As he worked, Jazz took time to size him up. Higgins looked to be maybe in his early forties. He took care of himself. Jazz surmised he was more than a bit vain about his looks. From time to time he'd brush the sleeve of his shirt or straighten his Kelly green tie. A padded hanger held his wool and silk blend black suit jacket on a rack in one corner. His office was neat. Jazz didn't doubt that the guy had a mirror in a drawer of his desk.

"I pulled up a copy of the ordinances they cited. The pertinent one, by that I mean--"

"I know what pertinent means. Big words were in the English section of my GED test," Jazz quipped.

Higgins glanced at her. A slow smile pulled up his full lips at both ends. "I won't underestimate you again, Ms. Vaughn. Anyway, the nuisance city ordinance referenced states police files are used. Citizen complaints are included by the city as well. Have you requested copies of the files used as a basis for this action?"

"No. I can do that?"

"Definitely, it's your right as part of due process. Your request must be in writing. I suggest you do that ASAP. Many small business owners represent themselves at these hearings. I can give you some guidance for a fixed fee of $300 dollars," Higgins said.

"Okay," Jazz replied. A lawyer trying to save her money? She waited for the catch.

"But word your request to make sure you cover all possible documents. They could use sanitation inspections and any information on record related to your occupational license. They could use information on your building permits, liquor license, and any number of things." Higgins tapped his keys again as he spoke.

"Sounds tricky to me," Jazz said. She raised an eyebrow. "I knew you lawyers would have a way to make more than pocket change off us."

Higgins appeared not the least bit offended. "The law is complicated, Ms. Vaughn. That's why we're still around. People find out they need us the hard way. I can give you a detailed schedule of fees to represent you in this particular matter."

"You've represented a nightclub before with a notice?" Jazz asked.

"An upscale gentlemen's club in Gonzales hired me in 2011 to fight city hall. We won, and it was within five miles of a middle-school. You can imagine emotions ran high." Higgins smoothed down his tie.

"And?"

"The Louisiana state Attorney General's office issued an opinion that their hastily passed ordinance was illegal. The city backed down. The club's previous attorney had taken a different approach. I don't hold back." Higgins gazed at her with determination in his dark eyes. His predatory smile indicated he enjoyed taking on a legal fight.

"Then you're hired. What's next? I mean after I write you a check," Jazz added with a knowing grin.

"We take debit and credit cards," Higgins replied without missing a beat, his handsome smile still in place. "I'll immediately file for a continuance of the hearing date to give us more time, and an expedited request for all discoverable files associated with the notice. Then I'll find the weak points in their case."

Jazz didn't make a move to pull out her wallet. "I've done a bit of research on your law firm. You handle mostly large liability cases. Some personal injury, but only against pretty big companies. Every once in a while you take on a criminal case, mostly white collar. Why would you want my itty bitty case? You won't rack up hefty legal fees repping me."

Higgins sat back in his chair again. "I have a confession."

"Look out, a lawyer fessing up to something. This should be good," Jazz wisecracked.

"I saw the articles about your night club in the newspaper. I also knew Jack Crown. I followed that case as well. You played a role as I appreciate it, right? You were arrested, but later cleared. Sounds like a David versus Goliath kind of fight. I don't like seeing city hall pushing citizens around," Higgins said.

"In other words, you could get some sweet publicity mileage out of defending me. That way you'll possibly attract clients with deep pockets who've gotten themselves in deep shit." Jazz waved a hand to cut off his reply. "Everybody has their reasons. My friend says you're a shark, and I like sharp teeth."

Higgins smiled. "I really like you, Ms. Vaughn."

"I'm ready to pay, so you'll officially be *my* shark," Jazz replied with her most winning smile.

Chapter 8

Two days later, Jazz suffered through another meeting with her big sister. Okay, that wasn't fair. Willa had good intentions, but the road to hell is what Jazz thought when Willa started being "helpful." Listening to Willa preach could be as torturous as roasting on hot coals.

Willa sat across from Jazz in her office, arms crossed and a frown on her face. Cedric fidgeted as though he would find an excuse to bolt any minute. Her office manager, Kay, kept thinking of reasons she needed to pop into the conference room. MiMi sat at the other end of the conference table arguing into her cell phone with her mother, who was awful at babysitting little Sage. The snooty socialite hadn't been much into her own children. Jazz wondered why MiMi kept thinking Mrs. Ora Bertrand Landry would magically become a doting, cookie baking grandmother.

"So this lawyer is willing to represent you, but he's not going after some big time settlement. Something ain't right." Willa looked at Cedric.

"Higgins has a reputation for being what folks used to call an ambulance chaser is what Willa means. He bought an RV to use as a mobile law office. When there was a plant accident, he'd park in the closest neighborhood and sign up clients." Cedric laughed.

"Sounds like an enterprising businessman if you ask me," Jazz replied with a shrug.

"You would see shady moves as thinking out of the box," Willa retorted.

"Drop the snob act. You've been hanging around those sorority sisters of yours too damn long." Jazz crossed her legs and folded her arms like Willa.

"You could learn from my sorors at Delta, like proper manners," Willa mumbled.

"You mean like your esteemed buddy Loren Grady. She got three years supervised probation last year. She was dumb enough to get caught gambling with her company's money," Jazz snapped.

"Hey, Loren isn't my buddy," Willa protested.

"Humph, such golden role models. You're right. I've got a lot to learn from your crew."

Cedric raised a palm when both sisters faced each other to take their spat to the next level. "We're here to talk about the city's notice of closure and Higgins. Remember?"

MiMi dropped her smart phone in the sky blue leather purse and joined in. "I missed some good stuff. Hit the replay button so I can know what's going on."

"Willa and Jazz don't agree..." Cedric started.

"Tell me something I don't already know," MiMi wisecracked and started laughing. She sobered up when the two women glared at her. "Ahem, so what is the issue at hand?"

"Willa thinks Godfrey Higgins is shady," Jazz said in

a clipped tone.

"Well let's see." MiMi whipped out her seven inch tablet computer. "I made some notes. He's been reprimanded twice by the Attorney Disciplinary Board in the past eight years. Both times letters of censure only."

"How'd you do that so fast?" Willa craned her neck to stare at the tablet's screen.

"Public record, girl. All actions taken by the Louisiana Supreme Court are searchable on their website. I learned watching Cedric." MiMi beamed proudly at them all.

"She's right. Even those instances were minor charges. He got busy when his practice took off. The board said he failed to communicate with two clients in a timely way on their cases; it's behavior covered under their professional code of conduct," Cedric added.

"Yes, what he said," MiMi replied.

"Okay, so he hasn't gotten caught yet," Willa said, stubbornly suspicious.

"Some may not like his tactics, but he hasn't broken any laws or violated professional standards. He's a top earning attorney in southeastern Louisiana. He may dance on the line a bit, but then so have *we*, Willa." Cedric raised both his dark eyebrows at his boss/business partner. More than once he'd played the role of policing the three women when they wanted to cross that line.

Willa gave a hiss of annoyance at his inconvenient truth. "You've still got to be wondering why he's taking this case though."

"He gets to fight for the underdog and silence his critics that he just goes after the big money?" MiMi said and looked at the other three.

"Nah, I doubt Higgins gives a shit about his critics.

Willa has a point. I thought of the same thing, but he loves being before the cameras. I've been high profile once or twice." Jazz grinned at the memory of her exploits.

"He gets media attention. Free advertising is one thing all business people love." Willa nodded. "But he loves money even more. I'm thinking he's looking down the road. He wins this hearing and sues the city."

"Damn, I hadn't thought about suing the city. I must be slipping," Jazz joked. Cedric and MiMi laughed with her.

"Lord have mercy. Cedric, I can't believe you're encouraging these two." Willa gave him a side glance and turned to Jazz. "You get to sue the city *if* you win."

"Worth a try. I sure as hell can't sit back and let them take what's mine," Jazz replied.

"I agree with you there. You'd think the city would have better things to do than go after one hood nightclub. There are at least twenty around the city, more even," Willa said.

"Hey, Candy Girls isn't a ghetto hang out. We have working people who get lunch at my place, even families. Don't be comparing my place to major dens of iniquity," Jazz protested with heat.

"Hmm, den of iniquity. You were listening to Reverend Fisher's sermons I see." Willa grinned when Jazz scowled at her.

"You two stop with the sibling rivalry for one minute." MiMi scolded. She sighed. "Now Jazz, do you need help with your legal fund?"

"I'm good for now." Jazz looked down at her peep-toe red pepper sandals.

Willa stood and strode to her desk. She pulled out her checkbook. "You need my help."

"No I don't," Jazz shot back and stood. "I've got it covered, okay."

"This is a loan." Willa wrote the check while ignoring Jazz's angry huffing and puffing. She extended it to her. "I'll go to Higgins and make one out to him if you don't take it."

"Legal cases have a way of stretching on for months and draining bank accounts, Jazz," Cedric said.

"You can take care of yourself, we get it. But don't be stupid. Take the money," MiMi urged.

Jazz stared at Willa for fifteen seconds. They both knew her savings were running low. Candy Girls had pretty much drained what Jazz called her war fund. Jazz also knew Willa would never ask to be repaid. Still she didn't reach for the money. "You've got two kids. Can you afford this 'loan'?"

Cedric answered. "We signed two huge contracts in the last few days. One of our current accounts paid invoices of quite a hefty amount. That overdue bill had me sweating for a minute. Crown Protection is doing fine."

"Okay."

Jazz pushed down the urge to hug her sister. Though she'd find it hard to admit, Jazz worried about Willa and the kids. Sentimentality didn't come easy for her. Instead Jazz shrugged, took the check, and put it in her matching red pepper leather hobo bag. "But I'm going to pay you back."

"You sure as hell better," Willa clipped.

Jazz frowned as Cedric and MiMi exchanged a look. "What?"

"You two," was all MiMi said with a sigh. "Okay, so since we all need money..."

"No," Jazz, Willa and Cedric chimed in sync.

"You just said even if Higgins files a lawsuit against the city of Baton Rouge it could be months, years even," MiMi argued.

"Higgins says he might find an investor for Candy Girls. Why is that funny?" Jazz spat when Willa barked a skeptical laugh.

"Who is going to invest in a small strip joint in a seedy part of town? I'm sorry," Willa said raising a hand. "But we all know it's true."

"Real estate in mid-city is going up in value. You might have noticed that more trendy businesses are opening in the area," Cedric replied. He nodded when the other three looked at him in surprise. "Looks can be deceiving. The city has demolished over a dozen houses that were being used by drug dealers. The police are using high tech methods to track crime and target gang activity. I have a couple of friends who are buying property at the city auctions."

"City auctions?" MiMi blinked at him.

"When folks don't pay their property taxes, the city has an auction. You pay the taxes, and the property becomes yours. The previous owners have twelve months to offer a settlement or appeal. I got Candy Girls and the building behind it where I live when Lorraine owed taxes and couldn't pay up." Jazz grinned when her friends gazed at her with appreciation. "I was paying attention when she complained about her bills. Lorraine kept saying she wasn't going to give the city a dime until she got ready. By the time she got ready, the fines and interest had grown."

"What a dumb move," Willa said.

"Lorraine ran her business into the ground, and still blames me for it. Now she's got a shack on the last piece of property she owns. She got sense enough to hurry up and pay those taxes after she lost Candy Girls." Jazz sighed. "But now I've got new problems."

"Well at least we can deal with the legal system. What about Cleavon and Kyeisha?" Willa asked. She glanced around at Cedric.

"He's still locked up. The guy has outstanding warrants, and other charges," Cedric said.

"Yeah, he's not going anywhere any time soon," Jazz added. "Plus, witnesses saw him with Kyeisha, so now the police know he was the last person to have seen her. So he's a 'person of interest' in her disappearance. I hear Lorraine is scared spitless. Those two heffas were up to something."

"Which is now *their* problem. So we're not going to look for any of Filipe's missing money. My lawyer hit a dead end tracing money Jack might have moved offshore. I don't know how he did, but somehow he left no trail," Willa put in.

"Yes, let's get back to the normal world with no gang leaders, laundered drug money, or dead bodies," Cedric said with a deep sigh.

MiMi gave a deep sigh as well, of despair instead of relief. She stood, picked up her designer purse and stomped to the door. "Crap. I'll have to keep my job and hope that jerk comes through with an engagement ring."

Jazz exchanged an amused look with the other two as they watched her march out. "Life is so hard for a frustrated gold digger."

* * *

Two days later, Theodor T. Ames arrived. The tall man with gray hair was dressed casually, but Jazz could tell his clothes were expensive. He spent an hour quizzing Jazz on how she operated the bar. His list of questions weren't that long, but he covered a lot. Ames spent a good thirty minutes looking at the inside of Candy Girls. Then he walked around the perimeter of her property in the right morning sunshine examining the exterior of both buildings. It was ten o'clock and the Louisiana temperature felt like high noon. Despite the muggy mid-May heat, Theodor T. Ames looked cool. Mentally she called him by his full name because that's the way he'd introduced himself. First to Jazz in a rush of words making sure he emphasized the "T" for some odd reason, then he repeated the ritual when Byron pulled up. Both times he stuck out a meaty hand to pump theirs as he said his name. Jazz watched him from the doorway. When he walked out of view, Jazz and Byron glanced at each other and shrugged. They went back inside Candy Girls. Jazz sat at the bar. She read his business card and flipped through a glossy brochure describing his corporation. Byron grabbed himself a bottle of cola from the fridge behind the bar.

Byron arranged glasses in preparation for the night business. "White guy pulls up in a Benz. Hops out wearing pricey clothes and a seven thousand dollar watch. One of three things goin' on: He's crazy. He's brave cause he got a gun, or he's got a death wish."

"I need him to hurry up. Fridays start being busy around here early," Jazz muttered.

"Hey, you told me he was going to be what they call an 'angel investor'. Sounds like you're having second thoughts," Byron said.

"Second, third, and fourth." Jazz sighed. The fancy brochure made a slapping sound as she dropped it on the bar surface. "I've always gone it alone. I'm not sure about giving up part of my business to anybody."

"Feels like selling your dream, huh? I know what you mean." Byron nodded.

Jazz looked at him with interest. She hadn't seen the philosophical side of him before. "Yeah, sort of like that."

"On the other hand, if you keep tryin' to go it alone you could lose everything. Either way is a risk. Gotta ask yourself which one you're willing to take. What's his contract look like?" Byron switched from lining up glasses to checking which bottles were getting low.

"Bunch of legal crap that Higgins says it's standard language. Ames becomes my business advisor. I'm going to get some work done around here. Fix the place up. I won't spend much. I figure my new investor's money can pay for major renovations," Jazz said with a grin at the prospect of spending a rich man's cash. "Higgins says the smart entrepreneur always uses other people's money. I kinda like that way of thinking."

"Damn, you better be careful. On the other hand, if you don't get some money to help run this place, you got nothin' anyway. Tough spot." Byron squatted to check out the shelf of bottles beneath the bar.

"Gee, thanks for being Mr. Sunshine," Jazz retorted. She picked up the brochure again.

"I'm just sayin'," Byron responded with another shrug.

Detective Don Addison pushed through the front door. Despite the dark interior of the bar, he kept his sunglasses on. Jazz couldn't help but notice how nice he looked in a tan cotton knit shirt and faded blue jeans. He gave Byron a friendly nod as a greeting. Byron nodded back in silent man to man "We cool" fashion. Seconds later, Byron discreetly faded down the hallway leading to the club's storeroom and offices.

"Morning. Who's the suit pacing out front, from the city?" Don sat down as if he belonged right next to her.

From any other guy Jazz would have begun to set him straight. Instead she smiled. Despite his annoying attempts to protect her, Jazz liked knowing he wanted to help. She needed friends she could count on; but a small voice reminded her this cute cop was just that, a cop.

"Nah, he's a potential investor. My lawyer introduced us. I want to do more than serve up drinks and barbecue ribs to sweaty men." Jazz hopped from her perch and went around the bar. Without asking, she got him a tall dark brown bottle of root beer.

Don smiled broadly when she poured the soda into a frosted mug. He took off his sunglasses. "Thanks, just the way I like it."

Jazz ignored the smoky look in his sexy eyes, and the perfect cue for her to get sexy right back. "You're welcome. Anyway, I've got a business plan. I need capital to put that plan in motion."

"You don't have to front with me, Jazz. You're under some pressure with the bad publicity and now the city is trying to shut you down. I've got some savings," Don began but stopped when Jazz raised a hand.

"First, police officers don't make much money, and you've got bills. Second, have you lost your damn mind? Your job would be in serious trouble if your bosses found out you invested in this place. No, there isn't a way for you to secretly 'loan' me some money," Jazz pressed on when he opened his mouth to respond. "This is a legitimate investor with the deep pocket I need."

"Yeah, but just how legit? Have you checked him out?" Don took a swig of root beer.

"Stop talking to me like I have no sense, please. My sister checked out his company. No indictments. His company has no history of investigations by the SEC or the Better Business Bureau, and Ames doesn't have a criminal record." Jazz ticked off the points on four fingers.

Don's eyebrows went up. "Doing your homework. That's good. Who is this lawyer you got?"

As if he'd been conjured up by Addison's questions, Godfrey Higgins strolled in. He wore another expensive suit. "Whew, I'm glad your A/C is working. It's ten in the morning and already eighty-three degrees outside. I'm not looking forward to July and August. Nice to meet you officer."

"How'd you..." Jazz's voice trailed off and she glanced at Don.

"I know an unmarked police car when I see one. No trouble I hope?" Higgins stood as though he wasn't ready to get comfortable around Don.

"Just friends visiting," Don clipped. "Detective Don Addison."

"Godfrey Higgins. I have a general law practice. Nice to meet you." Higgins turned his attention to Jazz. "I was in the area. I called Ted's cell. Since he was still here, I thought I'd stop by. How's it going?"

"I don't know. He's hasn't said much," Jazz replied.

"Don't worry. I looked over his contract. I didn't see any worrisome clauses. I'll go out and talk to him and then set up a meeting. Sound good?"

"Fine with me," Jazz said.

Higgins gave Don a cordial nod. "Y'all have a good

one."

"You do the same," Don replied in a dry tone empty of sincerity. When the door closed behind Higgins, he gave a grunt of disapproval. "I hope you checked him out, too. He's got sleazy lawyer stamped all over him in neon letters."

"Why are you so cynical? Oh right, you're a cop," Jazz retorted in answer to her own question. "Yes, and he came highly recommended by a friend."

"I sure hope you're not planning on trying something dicey with that guy's help."

"Such as?" Jazz said, more amused than irritated. Clearly he knew her well.

"I'm not kidding around here, Jazz. Walking the line, or crossing it, is a favorite sport of yours. One day you'll get in too deep." Don frowned at her. "Like with Filipe."

"We're through. The prison record isn't romantic," Jazz wisecracked.

"His hobby of killing people he even thinks crossed him isn't all that charming either," Don shot back without cracking a smile.

Jazz sobered at his intense words of truth. "I know. Look, I've got a kind of shady background myself, so I don't judge. But I'm done with Filipe. I'm not even in touch with his boys. I hear he's got two boo thangs visiting him on opposite Sundays. He's moved on from me, too."

"I'm glad to hear it," Don said, his voice a deep alluring burr.

"I know," Jazz said and pressed her lips together. Damn her big mouth.

Don laughed softly. "You checked me out while you were at it, huh? I don't blame you. So you know I pay child support for two sons, ages ten and thirteen. My ex-wife refused alimony, but you know that, too."

"Hmm." Jazz concentrated on wiping the condensation from their soft drinks from the bar top.

"I'm not offended you ran a check on me. Saves us time. We don't have to play the usual games." Don relaxed against the bar.

Jazz gave him a head to toe look as she rested her elbows on the bar as well. "Oh I don't play bruh. I'm always serious as can be when..."

"Me again," Higgins called from the door.

"How many exits you gonna take?" Don muttered without looking around at him.

"Shush," Jazz whispered. She pushed away from the bar and walked to him. "Yeah, what's up?"

"Ted finished his assessment. I told him there was no need to come in," Higgins replied. His gaze remained on Don's broad back as he spoke. "I'll let you know about that meeting. Can we talk outside a minute?"

"Sure." Jazz followed him through the door without glancing back at Don.

"Your boyfriend must be jealous, huh? Not too happy to see me show up," Higgins said, his voice low and confidential.

"I'm guessing Ames had something more to say you wanna tell me," Jazz replied mildly. She tilted her head to one side as they stood in the one square of shade available.

Higgins gave a short laugh of appreciation. "I do like your style, Ms. Vaughn. Ahem, yes. Ted likes the potential of this property. You're not far from a major intersection. The lots behind you could become a nice retail area in the next few years. He didn't go into details, but I'm betting he'll help you build up your business and buy you out for a healthy sum, enough cash to start another business."

"Hey, I like the sound of that. I'm not losing money now, but my margin is still slim." Jazz stared off at the neighborhood looking for the same potential Ames saw.

"Like I told you, this area is developing. It may not look like it today, but soon you'll notice. Two major construction projects are about to start within a couple of miles from here. Hard working guys looking to relax after work, some of them from out of town."

"Hard working guys with money to spend," Jazz said with a grin. "Guys who appreciate pretty women serving those drinks, too. I could make a sweet profit and then sell the property."

"I can even put you in touch with a top real estate broker who can find you a suitable commercial property."

Jazz turned to face him. "So you're the man with a plan, all the bases covered."

"I look ahead and have the right contacts." Higgins took out a pair of designer sunglasses and put them on.

"All sounds wonderful for me *if* the city doesn't shut me down and nail the doors shut," Jazz said.

"The city won't be shutting you down, Ms. Vaughn. Concentrate on your business and leave those clowns downtown to me. I'll be in touch." Higgins flashed the same cocky smile he used for his television commercials before he strolled to his black BMW coup.

Jazz watched him drive off and then turned around. She almost bumped into Don. "Set off some warning beeps, man. I almost got knocked out against this chest of steel."

Don looked past her without smiling at her combination joke and compliment. "He's up to something. I can smell it on him like cheap cologne.

"I can assure you, Godfrey Higgins doesn't wear cheap anything. Let's get out of the heat." Jazz spun around and went back inside.

"Watch him," Don said insistently.

"Damn, I'm gonna be too exhausted watching my back to do any-damn-thing. Lorraine, Kyeisha, Cleavon, and according to you, even Filipe is plotting something from prison. Folks who want a piece of me will need to take a number." Jazz gave a laugh as she led the way back to the bar. She went to the fridge and got a bottle of ginger ale.

"This ain't no joke, Jazzmonetta," Don replied. His sober police officer tone was meant to get Jazz to straighten up.

"Yeah, yeah." Jazz waved a hand and drank some of the soda. Then she looked at him. "Wait a minute. You heard anything about Cleavon or Kyeisha?"

"They found blood in her apartment. Somebody tried using bleach to clean it up. Doesn't look good for us finding her alive."

"Or in one piece," Jazz said. Her stomach did a flip-flop as she winced. She looked at Don intently. "Her blood?"

"Too degraded. I'm no fan of foster care, but in this case, I'm glad her kids had been taken away a year ago. They would have witnessed something bad, or even become victims," Don said.

"Yeah well take it from me, the same stuff and worse happens in those places." Jazz couldn't think of one good thing about foster care.

"Listen if you ever want to talk--"

Jazz flipped a switch on the sound system and Erykah Badu's voice flowed from speakers set in the walls. "Sing it girl. Anyway, I promise to eat my veggies, get plenty of rest, and shoot first, then ask questions."

"Very funny. I'm going to be checking on you, starting tonight," Don said. His deep voice asked a question and issued an invitation at once.

She studied him for a long beat as Erykah's signature sassy lyrics surrounded them. Going it alone had worn thin as a stripper's thong. She needed rest alright: rest from loneliness and from hot guys who turned into killers in a blink. What she needed was a good long rest from her okey-doke life. Is that what he promised? Hearts and flowers?

"I'm not a pie baking, cute house in the suburbs kind of woman. You better be careful," Jazz warned.

"I'm ready." Don leaned his tall frame down to kiss her on the forehead. "See you around midnight."

He strode out before Jazz could think of anything smart to say. A first in a long time, she mused. She tried not to tag after him like a puppy, but his exit yanked at her like a magnet. He never looked back but kept walking to his car. When Don got in and saw her standing in the door, he blew a kiss. Then he drove off all casual like he hadn't just caused a tiny earthquake in her world.

"So romantic," Lilly blurted out over Jazz's shoulder. "Now you're doing cops? Girl, half your customers gone be scared to set foot up in here." She spun around and flounced back inside the club.

"What the hell are you doing here so early? You should be at your day job serving chicken tenders and lemonade to college students," Jazz snapped. She went back inside and pushed the door shut with one foot. She locked it.

"I'm going to debut my new dance moves, and I

want my costume to be ready. I'll be in my dressing room." Lilly flipped her multi-colored acrylic covered fingertips at Jazz as she kept going.

"Of course your highness," Jazz said and gave a snort.

"Hey, why you closed that door? The lunch crowd will be comin' in soon. I done took six take-out orders on the phone already," Rochelle yelled from the back of the club. She handed off a box of frozen onion rings to Byron.

"I got the side door open. Made a sign with arrows pointing this way and put it out front," Byron said. His voice faded as he went to the kitchen.

"You thinkin' more than I give you credit," Rochelle said. She looked genuinely surprised as she headed behind him in the same direction.

Jazz blinked in surprise as well but at the rise of emotion that came over her. She owed it to these people to save her business. Byron wouldn't have it easy finding another job with his record. Rochelle hadn't even finished high school, though Jazz had talked her into working on the GED. Lilly felt more comfortable here than anywhere, though she'd eat glass before she'd admit it. Each one in their own way worked hard to make her nightclub and restaurant a success. She would not give up. Maybe city officials and other people saw Candy Girls as a skanky dive, but this place meant a lot more to them. Jazz would not let them down.

Chapter 9

A man of his word, Don showed up at midnight. And, he showed out. He wore a dark blue shirt with the sleeves rolled up and light blue distressed jeans. He stood in Jazz's living room looking all kinds of good. She allowed him to play the gentleman for all of ten minutes before things got hot. Jazz dispensed with the courtship nonsense he tried on her. They were on the floor and naked in short order. Not even a break to get condoms spoiled the moment. He rocked her to the beat of loud music from Candy Girls. And thank goodness for the wall shaking sound. Don had Jazz screaming. Jazz gave as good as she got. After a while, she didn't care if anyone heard them and from his performance, neither did Don. Even after so much satisfying strenuous exercise, neither fell asleep. They lay side by side on Jazz's expensive carpet without speaking for a good twenty minutes—mostly because they were still finding it hard to breathe.

"When you creep at midnight Officer Addison you don't mess around," Jazz said. A first she resisted Don's attempt to pull her into his arms. Soon she relented and rested her cheek against his chest. His rumble of laughter sent warmth through her body again.

"You blew out some of my brain cells, girl," Don replied.

"Good, then we're even." Jazz nudged him playfully.

Don lifted her chin so their gazes met. "I'm not much into creepin' these days. I want more."

Jazz looked away. "Let me take a nap and eat some protein, man. I can't do much more right now."

"You know what I mean."

"Yeah, I know."

Jazz scrambled out of his reach before he could stop her. She went down the hallway. The spacious bathroom next to her bedroom was one of her splurges. The waterfall showerhead set in the ceiling was another. Soon she stood under the stream of warm water covered in foaming multicolor bubbles. When the glass shower door slid open, Jazz didn't speak. Don lathered his body, and they stood under the water together. He put his arms around her and nuzzled her neck. Jazz felt sad, terribly sad. Still she said nothing. They exited the shower. Neither spoke as they toweled themselves dry. She went into the small closet and silently held out a pair of men's cotton draw string pants. Don didn't react. He put on his underwear and the pants. Then he followed her out of the bathroom. Once back in the living room, soft music came from her sound system. The digital clock on it said it was three in the morning. Candy Girls had closed two hours before in keeping with city ordinances.

"You want anything? I can scramble eggs or make coffee." Jazz started for the kitchen but he pulled her back by the hand.

"In a minute. Come here." Don led her from the kitchen to the sofa in her living room. He sat down bringing her along. "I'm guessing you don't want more. And before you answer, let me say I'm not rushing you. You need room to breathe, I got that."

"So we can see other people?" Jazz raised an eyebrow at him.

Don pulled a large hand over his face, sighed, and looked at her. "You ain't gonna make this easy on me, huh?"

"I'm not trying to make it anything for *you*. I'm telling you what I need. You're right, I need room to breathe, but that means more to me than just, I don't have to check in with you daily. Look, I've been through some serious shit. I don't feel all tingly and want some guy buying me roses. One therapist says I have attachment issues. Whatever. I decide who I see and when I see him."

Jazz spoke matter-of-factly, and mostly she believed the speech. Except resting her body against his solid muscles did make her feel... sheltered. Still she had to think through what was happening. He was one of the few good men she'd met. Willa's adopted father, and her foster brothers made it four. Not good considering the number of men she'd known, including her lousy no-show father. So she steadied herself for his anger, disgust, and a heated exit from her life. Don held her hand without speaking for five minutes.

"Good enough."

"Wait, what did you just say?" Jazz stared at him in shock.

"I just want you to loosen up with me, tell me anything. Know that no matter what drops in your life, you can call on me," he said, his deep voice calm and steady.

"Nah, that was too damn easy. I'm sayin' if I want to be with another guy..."

"Yeah, just be safe and I'll do the same. I won't put you at risk."

"Uh, yeah, I mean, goes without saying. I..." Jazz stammered. "Damn."

"And Filipe?" Don said.

"Always used condoms, he..."

"Great, but that's not what I meant. Are you over him?" Don gazed at her steadily.

Jazz didn't try to lie. Don somehow knew that despite what she might have told others, Filipe had a rough edge sexiness that fed her more than any other guy. She hadn't fallen in sloppy romance novel love, yet Filipe's combination of being rough and then talking sweetly in that smooth Latino accented English... did something to her.. She also remembered his cold, deadly way of making enemies suffer. Jazz shivered at the memory.

"Done and over. Took a minute, but Filipe is a dangerous guy. "

"I I played it so Filipe won't think I snitched on him."

"Unless Kyeisha and Cleavon decide to tell him different," Don said..

"I had sense enough not to confide in Kyeisha. I knew she couldn't be trusted with secrets." Jazz gave a hiss of contempt. Despite her dislike of the woman, Jazz felt a chill when she remembered the bloody finger found in her house. "Kyeisha may not be talking to anybody ever again."

"Yeah, but that leaves Cleavon. He needs to be dealt with fast." Don's deep voice sounded like a contained thunder of doom.

Jazz twisted to face him. "Hell no to what you're thinking."

"S'cuse me?" Don's dark eyebrows went up as he gazed back at Jazz.

"Don't be trying to play the handsome prince protecting me. I'm not one of those wimpy chicks you see in the movies. You know, being so stupid somebody has to save her ass all the time," Jazz said.

"You think I'm handsome, huh?" Don put his large left hand on her thigh.

Jazz shook free of his touch. Heat from his flesh seeped through the silk fabric of her robe. Combined with his voice, and smoky dark eyes, Don seemed to weave a spell clouding her mind.

"Stay out of this shit with Cleavon unless the case is yours. And I don't think it will be even if he's charged with murder. Your old partner is trying to bullet-proof your career." Jazz stood up and walked to the kitchen. She glanced at the clock. Almost four in the morning. It would soon be time for breakfast.

Don followed her. "So Armand talked to you the other night. He's my pal, but he needs to mind his damn business. Word for word, what did he say?"

"He talked some serious sense. I'm under a spotlight, and my history ain't squeaky clean. Oh, he didn't have to tell me outright. Look, the man has your best interest at heart."

"Your speech about wanting to be free and easy was bullshit. You're trying to protect my career, is that it?" Don crossed his arms. "I wish y'all would recognize that I'm a grown-ass man. I got this far on my own. And no, I don't think with my dick. I like being a cop."

"All I'm sayin'--"

"No," Don cut her off. "You think I'm all muscle and no damn brains? Cleavon is a drive-by shooting waiting to happen. I want him off the streets for more than one reason."

"If your bosses think I'm hooked up with Cleavon or any of those drug dealing gang-bangers, and they find out your doing me, they'll have the excuse they need to block another Black man from rising to the top." Jazz picked up the glass coffee pot to fill it with water. Then she stopped and turned to him with a sigh. "Don, much as we complain about the police, decent Black folks want y'all on the job. And they need more good guys like *you*."

"Damn." Don blinked at Jazz. He leaned against the granite countertop for support.

"Yeah, I said something nice about the authorities. If you tell anybody, I'll call you a lie," Jazz wisecracked. She became serious again. "I'm guessing Miller will try to keep you far away from any case involving Cleavon. All you have to do is let Miller help you."

"Okay," Don said softly.

The way Don looked at her made Jazz feel something she hadn't felt in years, self-conscious. She turned her back to him and started making coffee again. "Unless you don't care about having your career turn to shit. Up to you. I'm used to having my reputation in the toilet."

"You know something?" Don said, his voice still gentle.

"I know a whole lot more than you apparently," Jazz retorted, not daring to look at him. The affection in his eyes and tone put a scare into her that a gang of thugs couldn't. She jumped and almost dropped the coffee grounds when his lips brushed the back of her neck.

"I've found something rare in you," he whispered. Then he stepped back. His voice returned to its normal timbre. "I hope you offer me breakfast. You wore me out, girl. The least you can do is fix me a slice of toast or something."

Jazz had to recover before she found her voice. "Don't come up in here expecting to be fed on the regular, Detective Addison. I'm hungry; otherwise you'd be shit out of luck today."

"I'll get three hours of sleep before I have to report for work," Don shot back. "I need nourishment to handle them mean streets."

"Humph, then you better keep your damn kitchen stocked."

Jazz giggled when he gave her backside a playful swat. The charged emotional atmosphere between them eased. She relaxed into the laid-back back and forth teasing. After scrambled eggs, bacon, toast and coffee, Don got dressed and went home. But not without a lingering kiss that left Jazz troubled again. Jazz had to get it across to him. She didn't want his career hurt; that was true. Don would make a positive difference as a cop. More truth. But Jazz meant what she'd told him. She didn't have it in her emotionally to be tied up in some deep love affair. Once he woke up to the fact that something inside her was broken, Don would pull away. For good. She knew it would happen without having a psychic tell her. What Don wanted, needed, was the whole hearts and flowers package, complete with sappy wedding vows and kids. And Jazz couldn't give him any of those things. Later when she was about to get in bed, she noticed the cotton drawstring pants. He'd left them neatly folded on the chair.

"Damn," she murmured and headed to the kitchen for more coffee. This time with a healthy shot of bourbon added to it.

* * *

She dreamed of being in at Crestworth Middle again. She wore the school uniform. A bell went off and she sprinted for the door at the signal of freedom, ignoring the teacher yelling at her to slow down. Fourteen year old Jazzmonetta Vaughn flipped Mrs. Peterson a middle fingers and kept going. Another trip to the vice principal's office for sure. The jingle went on and on until Jazz woke up in the present and then stopped. The annoying sound was replaced by pounding that grew louder. Jazz mumbled curse words into her pillow. She rolled over and grabbed the second pistol she owned from the nightstand.

"If that damn carpenter is up this early, he's going to need a doctor." Jazz stomped across the bedroom floor as the pounding continued. Then she stopped in her tracks and looked down at her nakedness. She muttered more profanity as she pulled on panties, a pair of blue jeans and a loose sweatshirt.

"Jazz, come on," came a gruff voice.

"You in trouble whoever you are, cause I don't smell smoke. If my house ain't on fire, waking me up ain't gonna be good for you," Jazz shouted.

Pain thudded at her temples so that she could hardly think straight, increasing her rage. She marched to the door and flung it open. Byron put a finger over his lips. He seemed not to even notice the small semiautomatic pistol she held.

"Shhh, keep it down. I got Kyeisha downstairs. Found her on your steps." Byron looked around nervously. "I got Doc patchin' her up."

"Wait, what the hell you talking about? What time is it?" Jazz squinted. Shadows fell across the landing of her apartment.

"It's almost five o'clock." Byron tugged at her free hand.

"In the damn morning?" Still gripping the gun in one hand, Jazz stumbled down the short flight of stairs behind him.

Byron panted as he urged her on. "In the evening. We cleaned up and locked the place tight last night. I came over to get the place ready and…"

"Wait minute. Slow the hell down. I'm getting queasy." Jazz pulled against his momentum.

"C'mon. I told Doc I wouldn't be gone long. He's scared shitless as it is and…"

"You got to let me have a minute here, Byron. Damn." Jazz rubbed her forehead with the hand holding her pistol.

"Damn, girl. Don't wave that piece around at me," Byron whispered.

"Huh? Oh, yeah." Jazz made sure the safety was back on. Then she stuck the pistol under the back waistband of her jeans. No sense in scaring Doc even more.

"It's Saturday. Our big night. We got to figure something out before Lilly and Tyretta get here. They can't keep their mouths shut. Chyna is working tonight. She's high-strung, will scream her head off if she sees the blood." Byron's words tumbled out as his panic rose.

"I'm surprised Doc agreed to come over here." Jazz leaned against the brick wall of Candy Girls.

"He's my friend," Byron replied simply. For him that explained it all. "Ready?"

"Yeah, I guess."

Jazz followed him through the back door, down the hall, and into the smaller of two store rooms. Neat rows of boxes showed how much care Byron and Rochelle took with the merchandise. A desk sat in one corner of the room. Invoices covered the gray metal top. An air mattress sat in another corner, used in cases when a customer was too intoxicated to drive. Since Byron and Tyretta kept an eye out for those getting wasted, it wasn't in use often. Still Byron kept it clean, or at least it had been.

Jazz took deep breaths to settle her nerves and stomach at the dark red blotches as Kyeisha lay there, eyes closed. Doc straightened up and rubbed his back. He wore dusty Army green slacks. The long sleeves of his plaid shirt were rolled up. Disposal rubber gloves covered both hands.

Doc's full name was Herman Bailey. The non-practicing general practitioner had a shady history, just like many people who ended up in that part of town. Doc had practiced in the neighborhood since the late sixties when most other residents were white like him. He still lived in his brick home three blocks away. As whites moved out and the population changed, Doc stayed on. Doc's prescription drug habit resulted in early retirement. In fact, it was the Louisiana State Medical Examiners strong invitation that he take a rest. Doc didn't learn. He tried practicing part-time and he went back to using. Or maybe he never stopped. Losing his license two years later meant his exit from the healing profession became complete. At three years clean, he realized a new profession was a great idea. He made custom hardwood furniture.

"Took you long enough to get back here."

"Sorry, Doc, but Jazz was sleep and..."

Doc waved a hand wearily. "You called 911? I don't know how she made it here. If she managed to walk, then she's one tough cookie. But I don't think so."

"Let's call one of your buddies to drop her off at the nearest emergency room," Jazz whispered to Byron.

"You got no time for making phone calls. She won't last much longer; dehydration, blood loss, shock. Not to mention she could have internal injuries. This unfortunate young woman has been beaten within an inch of her life." Doc looked down at his "patient".

"He's right. She didn't get here by herself." Jazz rubbed her head in an attempt to clear her thinking.

"I'll call 911, say I found her up the block and brought her here," Byron said as he gazed at Jazz. He seemed to know what she was thinking.

"I can't stay. Judge Price said he'd find a way to toss my rear end in prison if I got into more trouble. I cleaned up her wounds. Put proper bandages on 'em, the best I had in my car." Doc headed for the door, but paused to look at Byron. The older man nodded and then slipped out.

"Thanks, Doc," Byron said at his disappearing shadow.

"Why didn't you take her someplace else? Damn." Jazz pressed both palms on the sides of her head.

Byron pulled out his cell phone. "She needed help fast. I'm calling 911 like Doc said."

Jazz grabbed his hands. "Wait, just wait. Maybe we could put a sheet in your car and drop her outside Mid-

City General Hospital and--"

"You heard Doc. She needs a paramedic and..."

Jazz and Byron froze as sirens whined in the distance. Both hoped the sound would fade away. The pulsating scream at other vehicles to get out of the way grew closer. Footsteps signaled someone coming—several someones. Jazz gripped Byron's forearm, but before she could speak, a policewoman entered the room, gun drawn. She assumed the standard shooting position.

"Drop whatever is in your hands. Put your arms up. Now," she shouted, her voice bouncing from the walls.

A second officer stepped around her to aim as well. "Do it."

"Cell phone," Byron croaked in. He dropped the bright blue device.

The officers got Jazz and Byron out of the storeroom, careful to keep distance between them. The female officer turned on lights along the way. Rochelle came out of the kitchen with a knife in one hand and a large onion in the other. She squeaked when a male officer spun to confront her, his gun pointed.

"Drop the damn knife," he yelled.

"Ye-es, yessir. I'm cooking. Don't kill me. Oh Lord, please don't shoot me."

Rochelle threw the knife far from her. She flung the onion in a different direction. Crying and pleading, she got to her knees. Moments later, Lt. Armand Miller came in with Lorraine of all people. She looked around the nightclub before focusing a hostile gaze at Jazz.

"What did I say? I been telling y'all that no-good bitch is evil. I knew she had Kyeisha up in here," Lorraine spat.

"I'm going to kick your ass, Lorraine, and it's long

overdue." Jazz lunged toward her, but the policewoman moved fast. And she was strong.

Don came in. He took in the scene with a deep frown on his handsome face. Miller gave him a warning glare, jerked his head toward the exit. A muscular white officer with red hair stepped forward. He spoke close to Don's ear. Even so, Don didn't move. The man dropped an arm around Don's shoulder. Don shrugged free with a sharp movement. Still he left the nightclub ahead of the man.

Miller turned to Jazz and Byron. "Somebody better start explaining why a missing woman is here half dead."

"She..." Byron stopped when Miller raised a hand.

"Crawford, talk to the man," Miller said to another uniformed officer.

"Got it. This way, sir," the brawny police office pointed to the side entrance.

"Don't want us to get our stories together, so you interview us apart. Going to be a long night." Jazz tried not to sound as shook up as she felt.

"You got that right. Well?" Miller stood legs apart, a stylus poised over his four inch wide smart phone.

"I was asleep when Byron woke me up, dead to the world." Jazz stopped when the poor choice of words rang too loud in the club.

"Hmm," was Miller's only reply. Still his dark eyebrows twitched up."He said Kyeisha was lying in the alley or something. No, I don't know how she got here. No, I don't know where she's been. I have no idea who beat her or cut off her fingers--or why. That should cover all of your questions. Since I didn't get my full hours of sleep, I'd like to go back to bed." Jazz tucked a couple of stray tendrils that kept falling across her eyes behind her left ear. Miller nodded as he scribbled on the touch screen with the stylus. "Uh-huh. So you were up late last night."

"I was not torturing Kyeisha," Jazz snapped. "I left the club and went to my apartment."

"What time did you leave the club?"

"About eleven. Byron and my other employees had things under control." Jazz chewed on her lower lip. When Miller glanced at her, she stopped. He was looking for a sign she was lying. *Get it together, girl.*

"So you went to your apartment at around eleven. How do you know the time?"

Jazz sighed. "I looked at my cell phone to check for messages as I was leaving."

"I see. Did you go straight home?"

"It's less than two yards out back. I decided not to drive," Jazz replied. When Miller squinted at her, Jazz sighed again. "Yes, I went straight to my apartment."

"You were home alone?" Miller went back to scribbling.

"Yes."

Miller looked up briefly and then down again. "Did you leave?"

"No."

"Anyone come over?" Miller looked at her again.

"I did paperwork and went to bed. Running a business means long hours. I don't have time to party," Jazz shot back with heat.

"So you were alone... all night?" Miller pressed.

"Yes," Jazz hissed at him.

"Which means we can't confirm you didn't leave home," Miller said mildly. He tucked the phone into his jacket pocket. "We're going to the station."

Her heart went from zero to sixty. "Wait a minute;

you can't arrest me with no evidence."

"We have so much probable cause to hold you for questioning it ain't even worth arguing about. C'mon."

Miller marched Jazz to a marked patrol car. The female police officer put plastic handcuffs on her wrists and helped Jazz into the back seat. Jazz shivered at the sensation of being trapped even before the door closed. A bright light flashed causing Jazz to blink.

"Did you have anything to do with the murder of the injured woman's boyfriend?" a reporter shouted as a video camera was aimed at her face.

"Has she been charged yet, Lt. Miller?" A tall Black female reporter stuck a microphone out toward Miller's face.

"This is an on-going investigation. Back up and let us do our jobs," Miller grumbled.

The police officer strode up as if on cue and slammed the door shut. Between the noise and solid glass of the cruiser's windows, Jazz couldn't make out what was being said. She stretched her neck to look for Byron.

Jazz leaned toward the metal grill that separated the rear passenger section from the police officer sitting up front. "What about my friends? They didn't do anything."

"Everybody gets a free ride downtown tonight, Miss," the woman replied. She tapped entries in the laptop, spoke into the radio, and put the car in gear with efficient movements.

* * *

"Four hours of hell," Jazz muttered. She dropped her forehead onto her folded arms on top of the cold metal table in the interview room. "That's going to be the title of my book when I get out of this mess."

Miller sat on one side of Jazz. A female detective, Audra Crawford, sat next to Jazz. She wore a brown suit with an orange handkerchief in the pocket of her jacket. Det. Crawford had done most of the talking since they'd brought Jazz in after processing, which didn't take long. They hadn't booked her though. Which Jazz interpreted as they didn't have enough—yet. The song and dance they performed had the aim of getting a confession, but they were also waiting. Jazz figured they hoped forensics would come in with more information, or Byron would give her up.

"Tell us the truth and we can wrap this thing up," Miller replied abruptly.

"I'm tired," Jazz said without raising her head.

"You've had a rough night," Det. Crawford said.

Miller pushed back his chair, stood, and unbuttoned his jacket. "You're making this harder than it needs to be, Ms. Vaughn." With that he strode out.

When the door bumped shut, Det. Crawford put a hand on Jazz's shoulder. "Look, we're just trying to get at what happened. I'm not after you or anyone who's innocent. I want to help you."

Jazz kept her head down. Her first instinct was to call Crawford on her bullshit approach. The old "show empathy" interviewing tactic. But smarting off would likely only result in more hours in this room. So she sat up, brushed her hair back and tried a different tactic.

"I got it. Y'all have to do your jobs. Hell, in your shoes I'd think I was guilty, but I'm not. Anyone who knows me would tell you I'm not stupid." Jazz kept her voice soft. She put as much weariness into her performance as possible.

Crawford leaned in, as if sure she was about to crack the case. "I don't think you're stupid at all. You've gone from swinging on a pole to owning a business."

She's good. Jazz looked into Det. Crawford's green eyes, bright with anticipation. She guessed her to be in her early forties. Lines fanned out from her eyes. Her reddish blonde hair had streaks of grey. Jazz also figured she used a self-tanner on her skin. Working long hours, this woman didn't take time for sunbathing.

"Exactly what I'm trying to tell y'all," Jazz said dramatically. When Det. Crawford nodded with a sympathetic expression, Jazz went on. "Kyeisha and I had a beef about the way she tried to stab me in the back. Not for real, I mean her and Lorraine keep trying to ruin my business. But I was going to work it out. I wouldn't slice the girl up because of it though."

"It must have been awful to know you faced losing everything you'd earned because of lies. With the city trying to shut you down is what I mean. Lorraine was happy to tell us she'd called the health inspectors and the city on Candy Girls." Det. Crawford sat back. "Hell, she lost the place without any help from me," Jazz spat.

"Yeah, we know about her tax problems."

"So you know Lorraine and Kyeisha dug themselves into holes and more than once. You better go through the long list of other folks they both pissed off." Jazz sat back. "Okay, listen. Kyeisha came by my place a couple of weeks ago maybe. She had the nerve to ask *me* for a favor. See, from what I heard, her boyfriend, that Brandon dude--"

"Yeah, he got shot in a drug house. Then Kyeisha went on the run," Det. Crawford replied.

"This is just street talk because I don't hang with dealers now. If I find 'em hanging out in my club? Out they go. Anyway, I heard Brandon got killed, but Cleavon, Kyeisha's other man, was the real target. Some kind of gang beef." Jazz shrugged as though that's all she knew.

"Filipe Perez's boys think maybe Cleavon and Brandon helped him get put away. To add insult to injury, Cleavon might have taken his last big drug shipment and his cash. You used to run with Filipe." Det. Crawford let the last sentence hang in the air between them.

Jazz blinked at her. Sticking close to the truth made sense. As Jazz read her, Det. Crawford had the same limited view as most police officers; the obvious explanation most likely always turned out to be true. Crawford also seemed to think criminals were simple and not as bright as they thought. The "you're not stupid" speech didn't ring true. Jazz cleared her throat.

"Right, right. Kyeisha thinks I'm still in touch with Filipe, but I'm *not*. I wish everybody would get over that bullshit theory," Jazz said and stared at a corner of the wall. The small camera almost blended in, but she knew it was there.

"So Kyeisha wanted what from you?" Det. Crawford said with force to draw Jazz's attention away from the camera.

"The girl practically got on her knees begging me to visit Filipe in prison and convince him she wasn't hooked up with Brandon or Cleavon. Everybody knows different. Those three go way back. I told her no. Filipe is a way bigger bag of trouble than Kyeisha and Lorraine."

"Agreed," Crawford said with a stoic expression. "So things got physical between you two that night because Kyeisha wouldn't listen."

"I don't care what Lorraine told you. I didn't beat up Kyeisha," Jazz snapped.

"Kyeisha told several people, not just Lorraine. She had bruises on her arms they said."

"Not from me. I shoved her after she jumped me, but then she got some sense and started begging for help. Kyeisha will lie at first, but she ain't the sharpest tool in the shed. Keep questioning her and she'll tell the truth after a while. Ask her."

Miller swung the door wide before Crawford could answer. "Kyeisha can't speak up for you, Ms. Vaughn. She died one hour ago."

Jazz gulped in air to keep from screaming. She gripped the edge of the metal table until her fingers ached. "I want a lawyer."

Chapter 10

The next day Higgins sat across from Jazz in the visiting area of the East Baton Rouge Parish Prison. The DA had agreed with the police that she could be arrested for Kyeisha's murder. She'd been moved from the police station lock-up two days later. Jail wasn't so bad. At least she'd been here before. Except this time Jazz had too much time to think about how she could spend years in a cell.

"How are you holding up? Yeah, stupid question. Sorry." Higgins glanced around at the bleak setting.

"At least none of these other women are trying to mess with me. Once they find out you're suspected of two murders, folks tend to leave you alone. I didn't have to fight over my dessert or which bed was mine." Jazz gave a grim laugh. "So if you gotta be locked up, get charged with murder is my advice."

"Uh, okay," Higgins said and cleared his throat. "You got a big problem."

Jazz eased against the metal back of the chair. She crossed her arms as she gazed at him. "Shit, you're damn smart. What was your first clue?"

Higgins spit out a laugh before he could stop it. "We have to get together socially when this is all over."

"Yeah, when I'm not killing people, I'm a fun girl."

He laughed again, and then lowered his voice. "Your sisters are hiring a top criminal defense attorney."

"Sisters?" Jazz blinked at him.

"Yes, Mrs. Crown and Ms. Landry," Higgins replied as he opened a slim leather folder.

"MiMi is telling people we're sisters? That crazy lil' heffa," Jazz said with a grin.

"Your sisters care about you, Ms. Vaughn. That means a lot under these circumstances."

Jazz's smile faded. "Yeah, they're..." Emotion choked her throat. "So who is this criminal attorney?"

"Keith Phillips. He's represented several high profile clients in the past ten years, including that rapper David Saunders, aka Fast Dawg." Higgins slapped papers on the table top.

"Oh right. I remember. Dawg performed at Candy Girls way back when Lorraine still owned it. I wanna say 2006, maybe 2007. That was before he blew up." Jazz frowned.

"Keith got him off on the murder charge, but Mr. Saunders didn't follow his advice to stay out of trouble. He ended up with a twenty-five year sentence on drug charges," Higgins replied. "Keith has a solid record of winning."

"Y'all on a first name basis?" Jazz looked at him.

"We know each other from Bar Association events and seminars. He's one of the best. If they'd asked me, I would have put his name at the top of a short list. Tells me your sisters are doing their homework." Higgins nodded with appreciation.

"I'm thinking Dion and Shawn helped. My foster brothers," Jazz said when his gaze questioned her. "Naturally they'd tell you they're my brothers, period."

"Not many people can say family run toward them once they get in serious legal trouble. I can assure you of that fact. You're lucky." Higgins gazed at Jazz as if he had to revise his view of her.

If he mentioned Willa's adoptive parents rushing to help she might not be able to stop a crying fit. She could just imagine Mama Ruby and Papa Elton ready to pitch in. Jazz shrugged off another fit of emotion.

"Yeah, they're awright people most of the time," she said.

"When I said you had a big problem, I didn't mean the charges. I'm not Keith, but this case has reasonable doubt by the truckload." Higgins held up a finger. "First, the conspiracy to murder this guy Wilks, flimsy is a kind description. Nothing links you to him; there's no physical evidence and no motive."

"I think Miller threw that in just to scare me," Jazz replied. It worked.

"Yeah, they're hoping Wilks' murder is leverage and will make you talk provide information on Bennett's gang. The murder charge is more substantial, but it has holes. A good attorney could make them even bigger. Keith isn't just a good attorney, brilliant. The guy can twist up a DA's case and toss it in the nearest trashcan."

"Finally some good news," Jazz drawled. "I hear the bad news about to come outta your mouth."

"Second degree murder means your bail could be set at one million, or more. But I'm thinking once Keith starts working the DA will back down to manslaughter. Even so, the bail could be $60,000 minimum. But that means he's got to get to work fast and hard." Higgins' dark eyebrows pulled together in a grave expression. "His retainer is fifty thousand up front. If the trial lasts longer than four months, then he charges by the hour. That's the problem."

Jazz nodded. "I'll get a top attorney if I sell everything I own, but still have to sit in jail."

"You don't look shocked. Most clients, including men, would be wailing right about now." Higgins seemed fascinated with Jazz.

"I grew up knowing how many strikes I had against me. Poor *and* black? You get introduced to the correctional system real quick. Even a public defender needs money to hire investigators and experts. So no, Mr. Higgins, I'm not shocked." Jazz stared at him to get her point across. "What I am is very pissed off. I want a lawyer who is going to go after the DA's case like a drug dealer's meanest pit bull."

Higgins stared back. "Your sisters are planning to mortgage everything they own--"

"Stop them," Jazz said loudly. "Willa and MiMi got no damn business getting into debt because of me."

A sheriff's deputy came into view. "Everything okay in there?"

Higgins raised a hand. "We're fine."

"Fifteen minutes," the man said and walked away.

"Sell the club, the building with my apartment, everything in them both. Do it." Jazz fought to keep her voice from shaking.

"No need. Your investor is willing to give you a cash infusion of two hundred fifty thousand dollars. You heard right," Higgins added.

Jazz squinted at him. "Why?"

"The mayor had a press conference the other day. Two major corporations are locating downtown. That's a mere fifteen minute drive from Candy Girls, Ms. Vaughn. The city has also cleared six lots that were vacant or had abandoned houses on them. Developers are lining up to acquire them. With a name change and some renovations..."

"My place could be a trendy bar," Jazz finished his thought.

"The city would lose interest in shutting down your place. Ames has high powered contacts." Higgins slid the papers to Jazz. "Here's the contract."

Jazz glanced down. Only two paragraphs in and the legalese got heavy. "I'll need time to read this."

"I've highlighted clauses with notes explaining what they mean in laymen's terms," Higgins replied. He pulled out a duplicate of the contract with highlighted text in orange.

"Okay, you get points for thinking ahead. I still plan to look it over." Jazz raised an eyebrow at him.

Higgins nodded. "I wouldn't advise you to do anything less. Besides, your bond hearing isn't for another day or so. Expect it to be high because of the seriousness of the charge. But..."

"Yeah, I knew that word was coming," Jazz muttered as she continued to scan the contract.

"You can use a court appointed attorney, but Keith would do a much better job. So I wouldn't wait too long to sign. Mr. Ames is eager to invest. He's ready to write that check, Ms. Vaughn. I'll keep the original. Call me any time. I'll get over here and get the money in my escrow account, pay Keith, and hold the balance for you." Higgins slipped the original contract back in his leather portfolio as he talked.

"What balance?" Jazz retorted and grimaced. "By the time I pay salaries and expenses with what's left..."

Jazz blinked hard against the tears that formed at the thought of people who depended on her. She'd never considered it before now, but her decisions affected them as well. Byron would struggle to find another job. So would Tyretta and the others. No employees might make her business less attractive to Ames, no matter what Higgins said. Unoccupied and untended buildings deteriorated fast in the rough side of town.

"Ames does want the business to keep bringing in cash. With his corporation's reputation, I think the city might even back off. But that's if--" Higgins broke off as though searching for way to frame his words just right.

"If the city thinks I'm no longer in control," Jazz said.

"Exactly".

Jazz tapped a finger on the metal table top. "Give me a couple of hours to read over the contract and then come back."

"Are you sure?"

"I want this brilliant lawyer's name on record so they call him for the bond hearing. You and I both know they could schedule it any time. The DA might want to move faster to keep me in here." Jazz folded the contract.

"Good thinking. I'll be back in two and a half hours. They'll let you keep the contract because it's from me." Higgins stood and called to the guard.

As Jazz was led back to her cell, she wondered why she should even waste time reading the contract. They both knew she had no good choices but to sign away her business for now. Still, she wouldn't trust Higgins to have her back. No doubt she'd find at least one decent jailhouse lawyer to help her decode the thing.

* * *

Two days later Jazz sat in the courtroom next to her new lawyer. Keith Phillips looked as she'd expected him to given his reputation. His black hair was perfectly in place, his black suit and dark red tie were immaculate. She'd grown more and more confident the longer he talked to her before the bond hearing. He had a sonorous voice that Jazz felt sure would be used to good effect. Her only worry was he'd come across as too over the top dramatic, like a slick attorney from a television drama. She soon realized that Phillips had complete control of how his performance. Jazz figured he saved his drama for juries, where it counted.

Willa sat with her adopted parents in the gallery. Her older sister's gaze darted around at the players, taking their measure. Jazz knew Willa was both scared and furious. She'd gone on a tirade upon learning Jazz had signed a contract to avoid having Willa raise her bail money. MiMi had worked to calm her down. They were in serious trouble if MiMi had become the voice of reason, Jazz mused with a smile. Phillips patted her hand, misreading the reason she was amused.

"Good. Reassure your family that this will turn out fine, because it will," Phillips said with poise, obviously at ease.

"Psst, Jazz. I'm here."

"Ma'am, take a seat." A tall deputy the color of ebony pointed to a bench.

Jazz turned around to see MiMi at work trying to charm the man, and failing. She sat down and grimaced at his back when he walked away. Then she waved at and mouthed something Jazz didn't understand. Willa's father, Papa Elton, gestured to MiMi. With a wide smile of recognition, MiMi popped up again. MiMi asked a couple to move over which allowed her to sit next to him and Willa's mother. Willa sighed and rolled her eyes before looking at Jazz again. The question in her sister's gaze came across clearly. Jazz nodded and turned back around. Looking at the stern judge gave Jazz no hope that her lawyer could fast talk her out of jail.

"The State versus Jazzmonetta Raye Vaughn," the court clerk read in a bland tone. "On the matter of bail."

The assistant DA, a fresh faced young white woman stood. "We're asking that bond be set at 1.5 million dollars, Judge Davis. Ms. Vaughn has known international criminal ties, can liquidate assets and also has an arrest record."

"Mr. Phillips, I'm sure you have a response," Judge Davis said. He sat back as if to say, "It better be damn good, too."

"Yes, your honor. Ms. Vaughn has strong family and social ties to Baton Rouge, and she's lived here all of her life. The assets Ms. Thompson refers to consist of a business she saved for years to buy. As for arrests, the assistant DA knows very well Ms. Vaughn has never been to trial much less convicted of any crime. In fact, she helped the police in a high profile murder investigation. As for the reference to 'international criminal ties', that is ludicrous." Phillip raised a dark eyebrow at the ADA, a silent gesture of admonishment. "Based on her lack of previous convictions and her ties to this city, Ms. Vaughn should be released on her own recognizance."

"Save the fancy flourishes for later, Mr. Phillips," Judge Anderson said dryly.

ADA Thompson's red lips twitched as she worked not to smirk. "Your honor, Ms. Vaughn has documented ties to one Filipe Perez, a convicted felon with dual citizenship in the U.S. and Bolivia."

"Mr. Perez is in prison for drug possession with intent to distribute. Ms. Vaughn was not charged or even questioned in relation to his arrest and conviction. Please provide us with solid evidence of this international connection, Ms. Thompson," Phillips clipped.

"They were intimately involved for a year at least," ADA Thompson replied sharply. "They were close associates. She continues to communicate with his gang."

"What?" Jazz blurted out. Phillips put a hand on her shoulder as a message to show restraint.

"No outburst, Ms. Vaughn. This is not a reality TV courtroom," Judge Anderson rumbled at her.

"Yes sir," Jazz forced out.

"Again, I'm hearing gossip but no evidence. Ms. Vaughn vehemently denies any kind of relationship with gang members," Phillips said.

Jazz relaxed. She had to give it to him, Phillips was sharp. He didn't claim Jazz never had associates with criminal records. ADA Thompson would have a fun time bringing up a list of her friends, including Byron. He least of all deserved to have his past waved like a flag, not after the way he'd turned his life around. Naturally ADA Thompson didn't care about collateral damage done to make her point.

"As for the business she worked so hard to get, the city is trying to shut down her strip club, a nuisance property. We have good reason to believe Ms. Vaughn would just as soon cut her losses, sell the place, and get out of town. She's courting so-called investors as we speak," Thompson smirked at her opponent when Phillips huffed in outrage.

"Damn, how does she know?" Jazz whispered as she looked up at Phillips.

He faced the ADA without glancing down at Jazz. "Ms. Thompson is correct, but the contract Ms. Vaughn signed is hardly enough to do more than pay her mounting legal fees to fight this weak criminal case. In other words, the money is almost spent."

"Then give the court an accounting of those funds. Otherwise we have no way of knowing how much money she has to finance a life on the run," the ADA shot back with heat.

Phillips faced Judge Anderson with a frown of incredulity. "Your honor, we're being asked to prove a negative because the DA's office has no other substantial support for such a high bail amount."

"Ms. Thompson, I have to agree. Your argument about international ties seem to be a reach. Poor dating choices would put a lot of people on the spot." Judge Anderson frowned when laugher came from the court audience.

"Quiet during court," the deputy warned.

"Judge Anderson, Ms. Vaughn's known associations and her history of violence, not to mention the seriousness of the charges..."

"Excuse me? What history are you talking about?" Phillips cut her off.

"She may not have been convicted, but assault with a deadly weapon after a childhood filled with instances of aggressive behavior show a clear pattern," Thompson said, facing the judge.

"May I have a moment with my client," Phillips

said.

"Five minutes," Judge Anderson replied, a look of interest stamped on his ruddy face.

Phillips sat down and leaned close to Jazz. "What is she talking about?"

Jazz felt a familiar queasiness in the pit of her gut. Shame and terror crept up her spine like a clammy hand. She swallowed hard, took a deep breath and closed her eyes. Then she looked over her shoulder. Willa pulled against the restraining hands of both her parents. MiMi blinked in confusion. Jazz jerked her head back to face Phillips.

"I stabbed my third foster father when I was fourteen. He'd, he'd molested me and I couldn't... I couldn't take it again. He almost died cause I cut an artery. I shut down, wouldn't talk., but my sister told them why. His wife, a nurse swore I was lying." Jazz tried to go on, but flashbacks of blood and the sweaty smell of the man's skin made her feel faint.

Phillips gripped her hand and then let go. He poured water in a paper cup from one of two pitchers on the table "Hold on, just hang in there."

"Uh-huh," Jazz managed to get out with a weak nod.

He shot to his feet. "You honor, this is too much. ADA Thompson is trying to be sly and skirt the law that prohibits bringing up closed juvenile court issues. Ms. Vaughn was a vulnerable child, a victim failed by the system and the adults who should have protected her from a predator."

Judge Anderson's face flushed pink even more. "The court will take a ten minute recess. I'll see both sides in my chambers. Now."

"Come on, you have a right to be present," Phillips

said.

"Okay," Jazz replied, unsure she could walk.

Still, she managed to stand when the deputy nodded at her. The soft buzz of whispers from the court audience rose at her back. Jazz had no time to look around at her sister. They were ushered through a side door to the left of the judge's raised dais. A short walk down a hallway, a left and a right brought them to the judge's office. Judge Anderson didn't invite anyone to take a seat. Instead he marched behind his desk, but remained standing.

"I want specifics, Ms. Thompson. Don't leave anything out," Judge Anderson rumbled.

"It's on record that a court considered charging Ms. Vaughn as an adult. Due to the nature of that crime, I believe it's relevant to these charges. In both instances a knife was used as a weapon of vengeance," ADA Thompson said without hesitation.

"She struck out after being abused," Phillips broke in.

"I was raped," Jazz spat out. "Stop using fixed up phrases. I couldn't stand up the first time. See, he liked it rough. I was ten years old."

Phillips hovered close to Jazz, a hand under her elbow. "Thanks for traumatizing my client all over again, Ms. Thompson."

"Your honor..." The ADA raised a forefinger ready to make another point.

"That's enough," Judge Anderson thundered. Both attorneys winced in the face of a judge's wrath. He sat down. "Ms. Vaughn, have a seat.

"Okay." Jazz took a dark red leather chair closest to her.

"Can you tell me about this case, not that I won't

look at the record myself," Judge Anderson added with a dark glance at ADA Thompson and Phillips.

"My foster father raped me. I fought back one night. I had a history of fighting, so the first thing everybody thought was I just lost it. My foster mother told me no one would believe a crack baby hood rat. He was an assistant principal and they had lots of big time friends. My foster care case worker even spoke against me, about how I had attacked other kids before. My sister found out. She tracked down a couple of girls that had been placed in that home, older than me; already on their own. Only one of them agreed to back up my story. They kept the case in juvenile court to protect him, not me," Jazz said and grimaced at the ugly truth. "Like I said, they had plenty of friends."

"Judge Anderson," ADA Thompson started but stopped when the judge held up one large hand.

"Due to the seriousness of this crime, bail will be set at one hundred fifty thousand dollars. Mr. Phillips, to request that your client be released on her own recognizance for a murder charge audacious even for you." Judge Anderson's thick grey eyebrows pulled together.

"We thank your honor for a more reasonable bail amount," Phillips replied with a nod to show respect. Then he cast a dark glance at the ADA.

"In that case, your honor, the DA's office feels Ms. Vaughn should at least wear a monitor because of her history." ADA Thompson was about to continue when Judge Anderson stood.

"You're pressing your luck with me, Ms. Thompson. Your backdoor attempt at introducing the defendant's juvenile record won't work," Judge Anderson said, turning his frown on her.

"The court hearings on whether she would be tried as an adult…"

"I said we won't refer to juvenile court matters. You know very well all such decisions are sealed, and for good reason. Besides which, I happen to agree with Mr. Phillips. From the limited facts it appears Ms. Vaughn was a vulnerable minor child and a victim."

"Thank you again, Judge Anderson." Phillips stood straighter than before and smoothed down his expensive suit jacket.

"Me agreeing with you is not likely to happen again before I retire, Mr. Phillips. Let's go back into session, five minutes." The judge nodded to the court deputy, who in turn directed everyone out of the office.

Ten minutes later the bail hearing was over. Jazz, still wearing the street clothes Chyna had brought her, sat with the rest of the female prisoners. At least she would be out of lock up soon. Not that her troubles were anywhere close to being over.

* * *

The next day, Jazz should have been sleeping late in her own bed. Anyone else would have been too scared or too worn out from nerves to do anything but hide. Jazz felt adrenaline pumping, but the energy that kept her awake was determination to get at the truth. When Willa called a meeting, Jazz didn't argue. She sat in Willa's office watching her pace. MiMi held a sleeping Sage in her lap. The baby was oblivious to the chaos swirling around the adults in the room. MiMi wore an anxious expression. She kept tapping one foot and rocking the baby.

"Put Sage in her carriage before you get her upset," Jazz said.

Without waiting for MiMi to act, Jazz rose and gently took Sage from her. She eased her into the red and white lace cushioned seat, MiMi's sorority colors. Jazz needn't have worried about the baby. Sage continued to wear a blissful expression. Her only reaction was a brief wiggle, a tiny yawn, and then she grew still again.

"I can't believe you signed this," Willa blurted out for the third time. She rattled the contract copy in her hand.

"I haven't lost Candy Girls or my apartment. You can't afford to write a check for $15,000 dollars," Jazz replied mildly. She brushed one of the baby's down curls, and then faced Willa. "You want a second mortgage?"

"Stop counting my money and let me handle my own business," Willa said with a scowl.

"I could say the same thing to you." Jazz heaved a sigh and sat down in a chair. "Look, I appreciate what y'all tried to do. But Higgins looked over the clauses and options."

Willa grunted and sat on the edge of her desk. "That sleaze ball Higgins."

"Don't knock my legal advisor," Jazz said with a crooked grin. Then she grew serious. "You don't honestly think I'm stupid, right? I know what the risks are with this deal. But the city is trying to shut me down. I still owe seventy-five thousand dollars mortgage for all the repairs I did to Candy Girls and making my house livable. Damn Lorraine was a slob."

"I see your point, Jazz, but still..." MiMi tapped her foot nervously again. "I mean, somebody could end up owning what you worked so hard to get. What do we know about this Ames person and his company anyway?"

"I've got Cedric working on it," Willa said. "You may not be able to un-sign that contract, but we should get every scrap of information we can on these people."

"There is a clause that says his company would have to hire me as manager at a minimum salary of fifty thousand a year. Or didn't you get that far?" Jazz raised an eyebrow at her sister.

Willa nodded. "I read every word, every punctuation mark. I know you didn't shake your booty from the age of seventeen to twenty-six so you'd be working for someone else."

"I'm still young enough to start from the ground up if I have to. But hell, who says I'll have to?

"Well, you'll need something to live on for the next few months. Maybe you could work for me. Yeah, I have a vacant position." Willa perked up at the prospect to taking some action to help Jazz.

"Hey, Jazz has style. We've got two positions at the department store. Of course the pay is only twelve dollars an hour, but you get employee discounts." MiMi bobbed her head with enthusiasm.

"The hell y'all talking about?" I can't take no part-time job. I've got a business to run." Jazz waved a hand brushing off their suggestions. "Besides, I'm not selling lipstick all day or filing papers."

"I know you're not talking about opening Candy Girls," Willa sputtered. "Shush before you wake the baby," Jazz said.

"Sage sucked down a whole bottle of milk. Once she's fed, a tornado wouldn't wake her up," MiMi said with a grin of affection at her offspring.

"You damn right I'm going back to running Candy Girls. The city can't stop me, not before the hearing. If I want to hold onto my property, I need to show Ames I can bring in cash. I've got customers who want to show up just to support me." Jazz smiled at Willa and MiMi. "That's right. Some of them are curious, too. Doesn't matter. All money spends the same way."

"Unbelievable." Willa stared back at Jazz shaking her head.

"Listen, his investor group says the publicity has thrill seekers curious. I'm the underdog; a poor young girl who goes from stripping to owning her own business. Just as she's trying to turn her life around, the system turns against her." Jazz spread her arms out dramatically, a solemn martyr-like expression of sorrow on her face. Then she smiled. "You like it? Higgins and Phillips came up with that spin. I say it's fucking brilliant."

"Oh my God." Willa massaged her temples.

"I told y'all not to curse in front of the baby," MiMi whispered for no reason. Then she grinned and stood next to Jazz. "I have to agree. Brilliant."

"You're a murder suspect," Willa spluttered. "You can't be selling liquor and having strippers in your club."

"Our legal system says I'm innocent until proven guilty. They can't yank my license for being accused of a crime. Plus even if they tried, I'd still have the right to a hearing. Higgins already checked." Jazz brushed aside Willa's objection with a shrug. "Oh calm down."

"They're watching every move you make. One fight, one drunk customer causing trouble, or getting behind the wheel and you've given them ammunition. You need to keep a low profile. I'm telling you, Jazz. Don't open Candy Girls," Willa insisted.

"I'm *not* gonna be pushed around. Lorraine is behind them trying to take my place. We both know closing is what she wants. She ain't gonna beat me at this game. No." Jazz stabbed a forefinger at Willa as if she was talking to Lorraine.

"I see Willa's point, Jazz. This is a bold move for sure, but you're open to a set up," MiMi put in. She chewed off the soft pink lipstick she wore. "Maybe you should..."

"I've already passed out flyers for Friday night. Two days from now, Candy Girls is going to have a DJ rockin' the house," Jazz broke in.

"The police are watching," Willa said.

"Which means Cleavon or Lorraine won't make a move on me. Being under surveillance has its advantages." Jazz smiled when both women blinked as her logic sank in.

Willa's smooth brown face became pinched with concern. "I hope you know what you're doing."

"I got this," Jazz replied with more bravado than she felt.

Chapter 11

Friday night Candy Girls did indeed rock. The boom from powerful speakers caused the walls to vibrate. Lilly and Chyna took turns dancing for the customers. For once there were as many females as males packed in the club section. Rochelle was kept busy cooking as the small dining area hummed with people eating nachos, chicken wings, fried catfish, and onion rings. One of Chyna's younger brothers had been hired to help out in the kitchen. Between the two of them, food orders were being served with precision.

Tired from making the rounds to pump up the crowd, by eleven that night, Jazz sat in her office. Byron knocked and came in with an android tablet Jazz had given him. Music and smoke blew in with him when the door opened. Both dissipated when it closed with a thump.

"Had to make a run for more fish earlier before the seafood store shut down. Rochelle said no way would our regular supply last, not tonight. Crazy how many people crammed in the place."

"Yeah, about half of 'em wanna be players that think I'm a cold gangsta." Jazz gave a hard laugh. "That's the streets for you. No wonder the good folks complaining."

Byron handed Jazz the tablet. She clicked on the app and approved the payment. The store would take a direct deposit that night. Byron nodded and tapped the app again so that a receipt would be e-mailed to JV Entertainment, LLC, Jazz's company. The LLC was another one of Godfrey Higgins' ideas. Byron approved, though he still didn't like him. Once business was handled, Byron took a seat. He watched jazz sip from a glass of brandy.

"I need to make some changes, Byron," Jazz said. "I know you and my sister think signing that contract was a bad idea, but..." Her voice died away.

"Hey, I didn't say it was outright a bad idea. Just that it was a tricky situation," Byron rumbled.

Jazz continued to gaze at the television mounted on the wall of her office. A closed circuit camera showed her the inside of the club from four angles. With the click of the remote she could see the kitchen, parking lot, and the front of her apartment out back. The new system was Byron's idea. Jazz agreed. They needed to ramp up security with Cleavon and his gang circling like a pack of feral dogs. Jazz looked at but didn't truly see the action before her. Byron however studied the screen. Satisfied, he settled in to wait for his boss to talk.

"I know, I know. The fine print can screw you. But I was low on options. I paid attention, so don't worry about your job or anything." Jazz transferred her gaze from the television screen to Byron. The big guy had as much philosopher in him as muscle. "I'm gonna do right by my employees."

Byron gave a nod and stood. He put the tablet on her desk. "I know. J I'll be watching your back." With that he walked out. No sloppy sentiment, just fact.

"Thanks," Jazz murmured with a smile as tears wet her eyes. She swiped them away with a grunt. "No time to get all stupid."

The office door swung open without a knock. Don stood looking at her. "Evening. Mind if I come in?"

"Uh, since you didn't knock and you're halfway in anyway, come on. Drink?" Jazz held up the bottle of fine brandy.

"No, officially on duty. You need to tell them you have an alibi for the night Kyeisha was killed. I…"

"Close the damn door before half the block hears all our business, Detective Addison," Jazz cut in.

Don slammed the door hard. "I told Armand we were together, and you told him I was lying for you."

Jazz heaved a sighed. "Yeah, I sure as hell did because--"

"What is wrong with you, huh? Jeez." Don walked in a circle. "You're so hung up on doing it your way, some female street version of the lone wolf. If you don't want me around, just say so. Fine. I'll be on my way. But this going to prison because you're hard-headed is…" Don broke off as though he'd run out of steam.

"What? Nuts, dumb? You don't believe I'm either one. What will happen if you play the damn hero?" Jazz gazed at him. She stood when Don didn't answer. "Hey, I'm talkin' to you."

"Ah, to hell with it," Don burst out. He waved a hand at her and looked away.

"No, you came bustin' up in my place with your drama. So now you're gonna listen to me," she shouted back, pointing a finger at him.

Jazz breathed hard as she reigned in her own hot temper. Then she studied him again. His tormented expression was all for her. Few people had stood for her like he was trying to do. No men in her life. Well, except for Willa's father. Papa Elton made attempts over the years and Jazz always pushed him away.

"My bosses might throw some crap around about poor judgment, but I'm not dumping twelve years as a cop. But I will if it comes down to it. You can't go to prison for a murder you didn't do." Don grimaced. "Life without parole."

Jazz walked over to him and wrapped her arms around his solid chest. The top of her head brushed the bottom of his chin. She breathed in the smell of his clean cotton shirt. Tension left his body as he hugged her back. They didn't speak for a long time.

"You smell like sandalwood with hints of cedar," Jazz murmured.

"So now you're a cologne expert?" Don's voice was muffled as he pressed his face into her mass of hair.

"MiMi, the cosmetics and fine goods expert, schooled me on the better things in life. She's trying to make me as bourgie as her and Willa," Jazz joked. She let go, stepped back, and looked up into his dark eyes. "You ready to listen now?"

Don pulled her to him again. He kissed her long and hard, until both panted from the heat. Then he pushed her away. "Now I'm ready."

"Damn. I need to jump in a tub of ice to get my thoughts together." Jazz gulped in air to clear her head of thoughts about what she wanted to do to him.

"I like throwing you off your game," Don quipped with a sexy grin. Then his smile faded. "We got real trouble, girl."

His reminder of what she was up against did the trick. Jazz blinked back to the subject at hand, murder charges. "Not we, me."

"I'm in no matter what you say," Don started to go on, but stopped when Jazz stabbed a finger into his broad chest.

"You're supposed to listen," Jazz snapped. When he stayed quiet, Jazz sighed. "Miller did what I thought he'd do if you tried to alibi me. He didn't believe a word, which was perfect. I don't want you involved."

"Jazz, you're not being..."

"Listen," Jazz yelled, stomping a foot.

Don raised both hands. "Okay, okay. Shutting up."

"*Thank you*. So I'm guessing Miller hasn't told anyone else on the job what you told him, definitely not your boss." Jazz tilted her head to one side as she gazed at him.

"No, and he made me promise to give him at least forty-eight hours before I said anything. He's been there for me, even pretty much saved my rookie behind during a drug raid once. So I gave him my word."

"Good. You're going to let that deadline pass and keep your mouth shut. Here's why," Jazz said when Don's mouth flew open. "Your bosses would suspend you, and possibly have you watched. If you don't think so then you are dumber than I thought. Don't give me that big bad cop evil eye."

"Humph," Don replied.

"They'll say *you're* involved in Kyeisha's killing. You'd be giving yourself an alibi as much as me." Jazz paused in her rapid fire explanation to take a breath. His expression tightened as her theories hit home. "You know I'm right."

"Yeah, but they could be thinking that anyway," Don said.

"We both know Miller hasn't talked. If you do, they'll have more than station gossip." Jazz nodded as she processed her own theories.

"You're facing a murder charge, Jazz. I don't see how me keeping quiet helps you," Don said, his baritone voice grim.

"Phillips is one of the best criminal lawyers around. Not just in Louisiana, but in the southeast," Jazz replied.

"Which is why cops don't like him," Don retorted. "He specializes in putting scum we clean up back on the streets."

"I'm counting on his skills at freeing scum."

"You're probably the only innocent client the guy's represented in a decade," Don said.

"Look at it this way, he gets to use his powers for good in my case," Jazz quipped. "Phillips is right. The circumstantial case against me is weak, at least for now. I have a feeling somebody is going make it more solid. Expect anonymous tips and maybe some 'evidence' to show up."

"Any idea who?" Don switched into detective mode.

"Cleavon is obvious, but you know something's not adding up. He's no planner, no big picture kind of strategy dude." Jazz frowned as she tried to rearrange the puzzle pieces in her mind.

"Yeah, I see what you mean. He's a mid-level player at best. Could be Filipe is still working his game from prison. It happens," Don said. He sat down.

"None of his gang members left have the nerve or brains to hold his operation together. The one or two that might have are dead." Jazz ran through the list of men left in Filipe's crew. She mentally eliminated each one.

"Which means you need my help," Don insisted.

"Yeah, but still on the force and able to use the resources of the police department. Miller doesn't like or trust me one bit." Jazz snorted.

"Armand is an honest cop," Don said with confidence.

"Maybe. But he's got his theory of what's going on, and me being innocent ain't part of it. Tell me I'm wrong." Jazz gazed at him hard. When Don shrugged, Jazz snorted again. "Uh-huh."

"Okay, but still..."

"You can't help me if nobody downtown trusts you, sweetie. Worse, we're in the same boat if *you* become a suspect. It could happen." Jazz held up a hand when Don started to speak again. "Put some distance between us. Date somebody else even, and make sure Miller knows it. Don't make a big show of trashing me. He'll see right through the act."

"The way you're bossing me around it might not be an act.," .

"Ha-ha funny man. You're single, employed, and good-looking. I'll bet at least two women would be dressed and ready if you called last minute for a date."

"Emm..." Don brushed invisible dust from the leg of his blue jeans.

Jazz sat up, eyes wide. She snapped her fingers. "I'll bet Miller and his wife even introduced you to one of 'em."

"How do you know so damn much?" Don muttered.

"Call her up. When Miller mentions it, and he will, just play it off like you don't wanna talk about your personal business."

Don crossed his arms. "You already know Armand is going to ask me about Shelia."

Jazz nodded with a smile. "I know women. She'll tell his wife, her good friend. The wife will tell Miller."

"Whatever."

"Look, Detective." Jazz rose and crossed to him. She pushed him down on the red leather sofa against the wall of her office. When Don didn't look at her, Jazz straddled his lap. "We had our talk. You're free. I'm free. So don't lie and say you weren't thinking up calling up this lady anyway."

He placed his hands on her thighs. "Who were you thinking of calling?"

Instead of answering, Jazz pulled the purple knit t-shirt over her head. As Don watched, she unfastened the front of her passion purple bra. She kissed him hard as she guided his hands to her breasts. Before long Don wasn't interested in the answer to his question. The fact that the office door wasn't locked made their desire even more intense. If anyone had thought to knock or enter, the noise they made no doubt tipped them off that Jazz didn't want to be disturbed.

One hour and a quick shower later, Jazz sat in her office again going over the receipts for the night. At almost one thirty in the morning the good times were winding down. She didn't even look up when the door opened. She assumed it was Tyretta calling it a night.

"Be sure to help Rochelle fix up the kitchen and dining area before you go. I know you hate housework, but that's why I pay you extra."

Jazz glanced up prepared for an argument from Tyretta. The one person she didn't expect to see strolled in. Lorraine looked around the office. She picked up carved wooden African sculptures on a wall shelf, examined each, shrugged, and put them down again. The forty-five year old woman was dressed in a red tight knit sweater, black slim jeans and spike-heeled black boots with silver studs. Her blonde weave made a bold contrast to her chocolate brown skin.

"Humph. You painted and went all fancy on a room hardly anybody will see," she said.

"Returning to the scene of the crime as they say," Jazz drawled. She relaxed against the leather executive chair back and picked up her glass of brandy.

Lorraine laughed. "Yeah, *your* crimes according to the news and the DA."

Jazz put the tumbler down with a thump. "Nah, the scene where you set me up by bringing Kyeisha here. She was supposed to be your friend."

"I don't have friends, only business partners," Lorraine replied with a casual wave of one hand. "Speaking of business, yours seems to be doing okay considering all your troubles."

"Praise the Lord for loyal customers and good management. So let's clear the air, Lorraine. You lost this property because of carelessness. Stop grinding a grudge that I stole it from you," Jazz said with blunt force. "Not my fault the city caught on you weren't paying enough sales taxes. Then you got behind on property taxes, too."

"Instead of helping me, you jumped on the chance to twist the knife in deeper," Lorraine said. The good humored facade slipped as she glared at Jazz. Then she smiled. "But that's all in the past. You're so right about the city being keeping an eye on nightclubs. I kinda like how they're doing their jobs these days. When is your hearing by the way?"

"What do you want," Jazz snapped, tired of the game.

"Maybe I'm just nostalgic and want to see the old place." Lorraine walked around the room. "Or maybe I'm here to help you out."

"Oh really? I'm gone run outside and look up, because pigs must be flyin'."

Lorraine grinned. She sat down in the chair facing Jazz's desk. "Still got jokes. But I've got a serious business proposition that you oughta listen to, Jazzed up."

"I hate it when you call me that," Jazz clipped.

"I know. Anyway, like I was saying, I've got a solution to your problems," Lorraine continued. She rested both arms on the sides of the chair.

"Glad to hear it. What time do you plan to see the DA and tell him who killed Kyeisha?" Jazz retorted.

Lorraine gave a short laugh. "Okay, not *all* of your problems. I said business remember. Defense lawyers cost big money, and you got a pricey one. Sign my property back over to me. I'll give you twenty thousand in cash, plus all the taxes and fees you paid."

"So generous."

"That was the value when you snatched it out from under me," Lorraine shot back, her smile gone. "We both know you need the money."

"I have money, from an investor. So thanks, but no thanks. I'm good. See yourself out." Jazz lifted the tumbler of brandy in a mock salute and drank from it.

"That white dude won't be so happy to do a deal when all kinds of negative publicity keep hitting the streets. How long will he want to be hooked up with a gangsta tied to a murder and drug dealing? Not long I bet." Lorraine pointed a bright green lacquered nail at

Jazz. "He'll change his mind quick."

"Normally, I'd agree with you, Lorraine, except he sees a big payday ahead. See, if I get off, we'll make Candy Girls a high end entertainment lounge. He knows I have the management skills to get the job done. But if I'm convicted, he gets his hands on the property. Lots of development in this area. He's hedging his bets. This dude is from out of state and has foreign investors. They don't give a shit about bad publicity. They ain't gotta live here." Jazz lifted her tumbler of brandy again. "To cold-hearted business."

Lorraine stared hard as Jazz drained the last of the brandy. "Smart ass bitch. Think you got it all figured out, huh?"

Jazz slammed the tumbler onto the desk and stood. "I did until you framed me for Kyeisha's murder."

"You hope that pricey lawyer can keep you out of prison. I hear it doesn't look too good though." Lorraine stood. She patted the pile of blonde hair twisted up on her head. "Maybe that white guy from out of state will need a new manager soon. Yeah, could be."

"Get out," Jazz spat.

"Listen, things might turn around if you cancel that deal and sell my place back to me. With all these new forensics and cops investigating so hard, new evidence could pop up any day. Think about it before you cash that guy's check." Lorraine gave Jazz a nasty smile. "You know how to get in touch."

"Don't wait on it," Jazz said as she walked around the desk.

"Oh by the way, that fine ass police detective is a nice touch. Screwing his brains out, huh? Wonder why you don't let him alibi you outta trouble?" Lorraine smiled as she studied Jazz for a reaction.

"You don't know what the hell you're talking about." Jazz struggled not to say more or lunge at her in attack mode.

"Yeah I do, and you know it. He left here walking crooked and wearing a satisfied look. You did him in here tonight I bet." Lorraine shrugged. "Hey, two star-crossed lovers ain't my business. I'm offering you both a way out. If you go down, so does Detective Addison. I'll make sure his bosses will find out he's been protecting you."

Jazz strode across the room. Lorraine backed up to the door as Jazz got closer. "I told you to get your triflin', funky old ass out of my damn office. If you threaten my friends or family..."

"Hey, I forgot about that bourgie sister of yours. Her business might not do so well if she's tied to you," Lorraine snarled.

Jazz screamed something unintelligible at the same time she grabbed the front of Lorraine's sweater. Caught off guard, the older woman swung a fist at Jazz's head. The glancing blow made Jazz blink, but rage kept her from feeling pain. Jazz punched Lorraine in the chest. She worked on getting her hands around Lorraine's throat, but a force yanked her away.

Byron put his brawny frame between them. "What the hell..."

"Shit," Tyretta yelled. She dragged Lorraine out of the office and into the hallway.

Chyna and Lilly came running from the club, both shouting in excitement. They helped Tyretta subdue a thrashing Lorraine. The three women pinned her against the wall, all talking at once and telling her to calm down.

"I'm going to finish you off," Lorraine gasped. "You

hear me, bitch?"

Jazz tried to twist free of Byron's iron grip. "Yeah, I'll k--"

"Boss, shut the fuck up," Byron boomed. He shook Jazz by both shoulders until she blinked hard and looked at him. "We can't have this shit, not now!"

Chyna made a wide circle around Tyretta and Lilly who had Lorraine pinned against the hallway wall. Eyes wide, Chyna rushed up to Jazz and placed a hand on her shoulder. "You threaten, she turn up dead, bad news."

"Stay with her," Byron ordered Chyna. He pushed both of them into the office and banged the door shut.

Jazz kicked it and spun around. Marching to a small bar at the other end of the sofa, Jazz grabbed the squat round bottle of brandy. She poured herself a generous portion. After taking a sip, she remembered Chyna and held up her glass.

"You want some?"

Chyna nodded. "I'll fix. You sit and get calm."

"Going to take more liquor and a couple of days. The nerve of her coming in here." Jazz broke off at the muffled angry voices through the door.

"So, we had a good night for business." Chyna casually walked to the door and stood so that she blocked Jazz's view. "After all that's happened you have plenty of customers. Competitors get jealous. My father faced the same thing when he first opened his business."

"Uh-huh." Jazz leaned against the edge of her desk.

"Success is the best revenge." Chyna gazed at Jazz as if looking for signs she'd bolt for the door. "I don't hear voices now. She must be gone."

"Yeah." Jazz lost her taste for the brandy. Instead she pulled a slim cigar from the pack on her desk.

Lilly came in first. She blew out a breath noisily and fanned her face. "Damn, that old heffa got some fight in her. I don't get it. She's got her own place in Easy Town. Everybody says she does good business."

"She still wants payback. First thing I'm going to do is change that damn name." Jazz stabbed the glowing red end of the cigar like it was a pointer.

"Okay." Lilly exchanged a glance with Chyna, who shrugged in response. "At least I don't hear sirens headed this way."

"Lorraine won't call the police. I don't care what she said," Jazz replied.

Byron pushed through the door. "Tyretta, put Lorraine in her car and got her to leave."

"Humph," Jazz grunted with a nod.

The others talked off their adrenaline rush from the fight scene. Jazz said nothing, but continued to puff on the small cigar. She studied the swirls of smoke floating away. The patterns were interesting, like the pattern of events spinning around her. If you watched long enough you began to see shapes and meaning.

"Lorraine didn't come over here just to gloat. That was just a bonus. No, she came over here for another reason," Jazz said softly. The others stopped talking and turned to her.

"What you thinkin', boss?" Byron said.

"I don't know. Right now the whole picture isn't together. But Lorraine wasn't all that attached to this place. Her mother used to get drunk and treat her like dirt. She told me the same stories at least a hundred times once she got to drinking and smoking weed." Jazz looked around.

Tyretta snorted a laugh as she slumped into a chair. "One time she threatened to burn the place down. Said she was gone bring her mama from the nursing and make her watch it go up."

"Real nice," Byron muttered. He wiped his brow with a wad of paper towels.

"You should have seen this office when I got in here. Papers piled everywhere, stained with beer and grease. The bookkeeping tablets were a joke." Jazz wrinkled her nose in distaste at the memory of how smelly the whole place had been.

Chyna jumped and grabbed onto Byron, eyes wide. "What was that noise?"

"I didn't hear nuthin'." Tyretta started to say more when a loud thump sounded. "Oh shit."

"Stay here and lock the door," Byron rumbled.

"No, don't go. Lorraine's gang might be out there waiting for you, for all of us," Chyna cried too late.

"Hey!" Tyretta added reaching out to pull him back..

"Don't come out unless you hear from me." Byron's long legs had taken him out of the room before either of them could protest.

"He's actin' a fool," Tyretta said when the door closed in her face. Where's your pistol, Jazz?" She spun around to find Jazz no longer standing next to her.

"The police took all her guns," Chyna whispered back.

Jazz stood with a 9mm pistol in one hand. "I got his back. You hear any yelling, a shot, or anything dial 911."

"Oh shit. Y'all got to be crazy. Lorraine ain't playing anytime she show to call you out," Tyretta argued.

"Yeah. So she gonna get the fight she wants," Jazz retorted.

She gave a curt nod, a signal for them to get out of her way. The two women parted to either side. Tyretta hissed, her mouth hanging open. Chyna's wide-eyed stare turned glassy with fear. Though her lips moved, no sound came out. Jazz stepped out into the hall. She gently, yet firmly closed the door behind her. Then she moved with caution down the hallway. She heard more soft thumps. A shadow seemed to move to her right. Jazz caught herself before calling out to Byron. If someone had surprised and overcome the big man, she'd only give away her position. But seconds later a yelp and grunt of pain propelled her on. Jazz shoved aside several chairs as she ran across the open floor and around tables. Another shout, this time curse words, came from her left. She raced past the kitchen and adjacent small dining room, down a hallway and to the back. Byron leaned against the steel rear door leading, a palm pressed to his jaw.

"What happened? You okay?" Jazz gasped when she got close, looking for blood.

"I'm alright. Some dude was up in here. Tried to hold him, but he got in a couple good punches upside my head. He hit the door running and took off." Byron seemed more angry than physically harmed.

Jazz glanced outside. "Get in here. No telling what he might have done if you'd cornered him. Now I'm glad the fire marshal made me install this door."

City fire code required at least two exit doors be the push bar type. They locked when closed, but opened when the bar was pushed from inside. The doors provided the security Jazz required, yet if a fire or other emergency happened inside, people could get out fast. The big doors had been expensive, and Jazz complained loudly about them during renovations. At this moment, she wanted to kiss them.

"How'd he get in?" Byron flinched when he moved

one shoulder.

"I don't think it's a coincidence some guy was hiding in here the same time Lorraine came to visit," Jazz replied. "Let's check the rest of the club."

Minutes later they returned to Jazz's office. It took a good thirty seconds of convincing Chyna it wasn't a trap, and she could let them in. Tyretta let loose with a string of profanity, yelling at Chyna to stop being a "crazy-ass wimp." Byron grinned at Jazz.

"Things already gettin' back to normal," he said.

Tyretta yanked the door open. "What did I tell you? Ain't nobody holding a gun on 'em. Damn, the way she kept snivelin' made me want to take the risk just to get outta here. Y'all awright?"

"You didn't know," Chyna replied defensively as she wiped tears from her cheeks.

"Ah, leave the kid alone. She's not hard core like you," Byron said. "You want, I'll follow you all the way home."

Chyna clapped her hands together. "Yes!"

"Oh please. They're after Jazz, not *you*," Tyretta blurted out.

All three gazed at Jazz steadily in silence. Jazz nodded. "Yeah."

Chapter 12

The next day at five thirty in the evening, Willa, MiMi, and Cedric came to Candy Girls. Willa and MiMi sat at the bar drinking soda while Cedric got the grand tour from Byron. As customers drifted in and the music started, they all moved to Jazz's office. Saturdays got busy fast, and Rochelle had been cooking non-stop since eleven that morning. Once settled in with their various beverages of choice, Jazz gave an account of her adventures.

"I called y'all over here because I know who the killer is," Jazz said as she glanced around at a set of startled expressions. Then she laughed loudly. "Okay, I'm bullshitting around. I love old movies where they do that."

"You play too much," Willa snapped.

MiMi giggled. "Girl, you had me going."

"Damn boss. Give me a heart attack like I ain't had enough excitement this week." Byron exhaled noisily. "I'm going out on the floor. Rochelle ain't had a break since two o'clock. Chyna came in to help her cook."

"How is she going to dance and cook?" Willa asked, looking at Jazz.

"She's not gonna dance anymore. I hired another girl to dance with Lilly tonight. Not that I need to explain how I run things," Jazz wisecracked. She turned to Byron. "Fine. We're going to have a normal night. Follow the usual routine."

Byron nodded. "Gotcha."

"Thanks again, man," Cedric called out to him and waved.

"No problem. If I don't see y'all before you leave, everybody have a good evening." Byron waved to everyone and left.

"I may not be leaving. Mama Ruby and Aunt Beryl are spoiling Sage rotten tonight so I can shake my thang." MiMi bobbed her head to the muted beat of music coming from the club.

"You'll shake it home to pick up your baby," Willa said with a frown.

"Yes, mother." MiMi snorted to punctuate her sarcasm.

"Sure, stay and party, girl," Jazz put in to egg her on, but more to annoy her big sister.

Cedric grinned at them and cleared his throat. "I like the security surveillance system. Impressive." He looked at the two flat screen televisions set on the wall.

"Thanks. I can turn on the sound, too." Jazz went to her PC and hit a key. A throbbing neo soul tune flooded the office.

"That's what I'm talkin' 'bout." MiMi jumped to her feet and danced across the floor, hips swaying.

" On Saturday nights jumps old school baby boomers come in around eight. They leave at midnight cause they gotta get up for church Sunday mornings." Jazz laughed when Willa's mouth formed a wide circle. "Your Aunt Ametrine would be up in here spraying holy oil if she knew. Bet I could name some of her church members."

"I'd pay to see online videos of church deacons jammin', a drink in one hand," Cedric said with a laugh.

"Humph, you don't have typical nights anymore. Half dead enemies show up. Evil ex-boss pops in like the devil." Willa walked over to the screen and stared as if looking for suspects.

"Typical for this part of town," Jazz joked as she joined MiMi in dancing.

"Impressive indeed ." Willa picked up the remote, lightly tapped a key and the music stopped.

"Hey, I just got my groove going good," MiMi complained loudly.

"Tell me again what Lorraine had to say." Willa sat down.

"Basically she admitted setting me up," Jazz replied. She fanned her face as she sat down as well.

"She dropped enough hints to make it clear, but nothing you could report to the police," Cedric put in.

"Yeah. You're on notice to deliver what she wants or else." Willa wore a frown of anxiety. "We've got to stop her."

Jazz pointed a forefinger at each of them in turn. "You, you, or you won't do anything. I'm handling Lorraine and her crap."

"Let's review then. With your fancy security cameras she waltzed her ass in here and caught you by surprise," Willa deadpanned.

"We had a busy night. I was reviewing the receipts, invoices, and a half dozen other details." Still Jazz avoided returning Willa's gaze.

"Not to mention you're going on trial for *murder*. Please describe to us how you're 'handling Lorraine'? Or maybe you want us to believe this is all according to your grand plan." Willa crossed her arms.

"I, uh, well. Um." Jazz sighed. "Okay, for once you have a point. But the fact that she showed up says something."

"Yeah, that she's gloating because you're about to go down for a murder you didn't do," Willa shot back. "The bonus is she'll get her grimy hands on your property."

"Ouch." MiMi winced at Willa's sharpened point.

Cedric switched his attention from admiring the security monitors and back to the conversation. "Wait a minute. I agree with Jazz to some degree. Lorraine didn't come to just gloat. She came over to make Jazz an offer. Why would she do that if Jazz going to prison is a done deal?"

"Because I have something she wants. Not my property," Jazz said fast when Willa opened her mouth to comment.

"Hmm." Cedric stood, legs apart. He frowned as he rubbed his hands together. " Yeah. The city is trying to shut you down. Seems like all Lorraine has to do is wait until you go to prison and make a bid for it again. So why go to the trouble of trying to cut a deal?"

"Willa's right. She's a bitch enjoying your misery," MiMi tossed out casually. She glanced at her fingernails. "I need a manicure bad. But I have to economize since *somebody* won't help us find our cash."

"You won't need manicures if thugs cut off your fingers, right?" Willa replied and grinned when MiMi let out a squeak.

MiMi clasped her hands together. "You're so mean."

Jazz gazed at the monitors with a frown. "Maybe.

Nah, I don't see it."

"What?" Cedric sat down in a chair.

"MiMi may not be the only one hot to find Filipe's missing money," Jazz said.

"You mean my fiancé's missing money," MiMi piped up.

Jazz flipped a hand at MiMi's comment as though brushing away an annoying gnat. "But Lorraine definitely wasn't in Filipe's gang, so how could she know? Much less think she had a right to it."

"Didn't they hang out at Candy Girls back in the day? Filipe used to come here when Lorraine owned the place. That's how y'all met," Willa said.

"She chatted him up like she did most customers dropping a bunch of money. Him and his boys would drink her best liquor, get the private room and tipped well. Real well." Jazz smiled.

" Guys stuffed a bunch of bills in your g-string, huh? Shoot, the way my finances are going, I may have to do a bump and grind soon." MiMi looked at her fingernails again.

"Ah the good old days," Jazz quipped. "You don't want the down sides of working the pole, sweetie. Trust me."

"Where's your private room?" MiMi asked. She seemed not to have heard Jazz's warning.

"I used that extra floor space for a DJ, and made my office bigger. My girls didn't want to do private dances. Guys tended to expect more than dancing, and they'd want to do drugs. Not in my place."

"Aunt Ametrine would be pleased to hear it," Willa joked with a crooked grin. Her fiercely church-going aunt still preached at Jazz from time to time.

"Yeah, at least I'm cutting down on the number of

sins I'm committing," Jazz replied with a laugh.

"So Lorraine wasn't in Filipe's gang. Did she get drugs from him for the customers in that private room?" Cedric asked.

"Nah, I would have known. Most of those folks brought their own." Jazz rocked her leather executive chair back and forth a few times. A thought, really a memory, hit her. "Lorraine has three sons. Well she had four. One got killed back in 2010, shot on the street. One is locked up in New York State, death row. The other one is in Hunt Correctional, convicted in 2012 maybe, and got twenty-five years."

"You said four. What about the other one?" Willa said.

"He lives straight from what I hear. Got a family and a good job in Dallas. He doesn't come to visit. Too much drama I guess," Jazz replied.

"So one or all of the three bad boys could have been a member of Filipe's gang." Cedric frowned again. "But you would know that, too."

"I didn't meet every thug Filipe did business with. He had a close circle of guys around him, but he had some loose associates as well." Jazz gazed at Cedric. "Can you do some research?"

"Hey, you've got that fine detective sweating after you. Put him on the case," MiMi said with a wink.

"I don't want Don gettin' caught up. He could lose everything behind this shit," Jazz said with force.

MiMi raised an eyebrow as she cut a glance at Willa. "Well, well, well. Sounds like you care a whole lot about Detective Feel Good. How long have y'all been a couple, may I ask?"

Jazz lit a cigarillo. "No, you may not ask cause it's none of your damn business."

"I believe that's the answer." MiMi wore a satisfied smirk.

"Humph, from gangstas to a policeman," Willa murmured with a shake of her head.

"Back to the subject of why Lorraine came here," Cedric put in before a battle could pick up steam.

"Thank you, Cedric. Women always focus on getting up in other people's private life." Jazz gave Willa and MiMi a sour look. "Okay, so let's go with the theory that at least one of Lorraine's evil kids was in Filipe's gang. I'd bet on the Jay-Jay. The oldest has been out of state too long."

Cedric took out his four inch wide smart phone. "Give me full names and anything else you know. Would be nice if you knew his birth date, last known address."

"J'Derrick Taylor. He lived in New York with his older brother for a while, but came home in 2006 when big bro got locked up. He's only a year or two older than me. Or maybe younger." Jazz squinted in an effort to remember more.

"With an unusual first name and a general date range for his year of birth, I should be able to get information. I'll look up Lorraine's old addresses." Cedric nodded with satisfaction. "Yeah, this should be enough."

"Lorraine didn't move around much after 2007. Her mama died and left her house to Lorraine. Her and her two sisters got into it hot and heavy over it, too. She's still living there. Guess she kept up the taxes over there at least," Jazz retorted. She wrote down the address on a sheet of note paper and handed it to Cedric.

"I'm on it. Hold on a minute." Cedric walked to a corner as he tapped the screen of his phone.

"You're lucky to have such a hard-working man so *close* by all the time," MiMi whispered to Willa and winked at her. She pressed her lips together to smother a giggle before it escaped.

"Don't even start," Willa hissed low. She glanced over her shoulder at Cedric.

"We know you've done a sleep over at his place at least once," Jazz added with a sly grin.

"Who told you..." Willa stopped. She stared at Jazz, eyes lit with fire.

"Bam! You just did. I played a hunch and hit the lotto." Jazz hooted with laughter. She jumped to her feet and shared a fist bump with MiMi.

"Well played," MiMi chirped with glee.

Willa squinted at them. "I'm going to slap you both in about a minute."

"At least y'all got somebody." MiMi slumped again in misery over the state of her romantic life.

"Yeah, he's ten steps up from your late ex-husband," Jazz retorted.

"Hey, watch it. Jack is my baby's father and he was a good guy. Well, most of the time,"

Cedric came back. "Okay, so I started doing some checking around on Lorraine. Willa told me the woman doesn't like you much."

"Try hates her with a burning passion," Willa broke in.

"Obviously, since it's a good bet she helped set Jazz up. Anyway, I wondered about the tax situation and how she let it get out of hand," Cedric said.

"She's triflin' and dumb," Jazz blurted out.

"Maybe." Cedric grinned at her blunt assessment. "But she didn't get any delinquent tax notices for about six years straight. An investigation into local government offices led to three people being fired and pleading guilty to a string of charges. They were taking kick backs . Forms were falsified showing notices had gone out and payments made."

"When did they get arrested?"

"Eight months before all Lorraine's tax troubles started." Cedric nodded when Jazz snapped her fingers.

"Bingo. The end of 2012, right? Her kid Jay-Jay got convicted around that time." Jazz whistled.

"I can look, but so far I don't see a connection to Filipe's gang or any other of the small time Baton Rouge gangs operating at the time.

"Yeah, but that doesn't mean if we dig enough we won't find it," Jazz said.

Willa sucked in air and then exhaled. "Y'all are going way out there looking for conspiracies. Look Jazz, you've got a rich guy who wants this property. Sell and start over. It doesn't matter who did what or why. Let Lorraine think she's won. Pocket your money and ditch all this crap from the past."

"Lorraine, Cleavon, or somebody is serious about finding out what I know. *Dead* serious. They're not going to stop coming after me because I walk away from all this." Jazz swept a hand around. "Even if I wanted to, which I don't."

"I didn't say give up on having your own business. There is nothing special about Candy Girls or even this neighborhood. And please don't try to tell me you have some sentimental attachment to the place," Willa insisted.

Jazz folded her arms. "You didn't know shit about running Crown Protection. Jack died and Cedric offered to buy the business. So why didn't you sell?"

"Ha, she's got you," MiMi blurted out. She snapped

her lips shut when Willa glared at her.

"That was different .I have two kids and... I mean their father's legacy was under attack," Willa said.
"

"I happen to agree with Jazz. Lorraine might be satisfied, but what about Cleavon? Something of value is motivating them. I don't think it's just about the property for Lorraine." Cedric gazed at Willa as though sending her a silent message.

"Thank you. Somebody got some sense up in here besides me," Jazz said. She gave Willa a satisfied smirk. "You're just trying to get me out of Candy Girls so you won't be embarrassed in front of your bourgie family and sorority sisters. You don't care if I lose something I care about."

"That's not true. 'Keepin' it real' and staying close to street life has gotten you shot at and a murder charge. Give me the protection of boring bourgie life any day," Willa shot back with heat.

Jazz gave a loud grunt of scorn. "There's plenty of dirt on that side of town, sweetie. Being bourgie sure as hell didn't protect Jack."

MiMi stood up, both hands on her hips. "Okay, that's enough," she shouted.

"Screw it, I'm going home. Glad we came in separate cars. I just hope mine is still on the parking lot." Willa slung her purse over one shoulder. She marched to the office door.

"Willa," Cedric tried to put a hand on her arm, but she moved too fast.

"I'll see you later," Willa said over her shoulder and was gone before he or the others moved.

When MiMi and Cedric turned back to Jazz with twin frowns of judgment, she threw up both hands.

"What?"

"You went too far, that's what. And you know it," MiMi barked at her. "Willa works hard to have a better life for the kids. And by the way, for a while Willa blamed herself for Jack's death. She still cared about him even after the way he treated her."

"But--"

"Willa is just as scared of losing you, but you're too hard-headed to take that into consideration," MiMi pressed on. She met Jazz's glowering expression with resolution.

Several seconds of silence, heavy with unspoken arguments, went by. Jazz lit a cigarillo. "Okay, so I maybe crossed a line."

"You definitely crossed a line," MiMi replied. Then her severe expression eased into one of sympathy. "Look, you cool down. Let her cool down, and then apologize."

"I don't know about no apology," Jazz mumbled. Still, guilt stabbed into her gut at the hurt she'd seen in Willa's eyes.

"Great advice," Cedric said calmly. "Y'all take a deep breath and then talk. Meanwhile, I'll start doing research on Lorraine and her son. If it's okay with you, I'll contact your lawyer to let him know. We work for law firms, mostly on civil matters. But I'm sure he'll be glad to have an investigator gathering information for your defense."

"Sure, you can call him. Thanks, Cedric. I'm going to pay you like any other client." Jazz gave him a brief sisterly hug.

Cedric blushed. "Hey, don't worry about it. Friends back each other up, right?"

"Right," Jazz said softly. She swallowed hard

against the emotional lump in her throat.

"See? We're all family." MiMi beamed at them.

"I'm going to get on this right away. Talk to y'all later." Cedric hurried out.

"He's not going to start investigating right way. First he's going to call Willa, then maybe he'll buy takeout for her and the kids." MiMi heaved a sigh. "He's going to make a wonderful brother-in-law."

"Yeah, with me and you always in some kind of trouble, we need a professional private investigator in the family," Jazz said dryly. She went back and flopped down into her executive chair. "What a damn mess."

"Don't get all discouraged. We're going to figure out what's going on, just like we did when Jack was killed," MiMi said as she put an arm around Jazz's shoulder.

"I sure hope you're right," Jazz said with a smile.

"But you may have to let Detective Addison give you an alibi if Cedric can't dig up some reasonable doubt," MiMi said, her voice pitch low by the gravity of Jazz's predicament.

Jazz's smile vanished. "As a down to the wire, back against the wall last resort, MiMi. I swear."

Chapter 13

Monday morning dawned as dreary as Jazz's mood. Saturday night's receipts from the club were the cause. Not even the restaurant and take-out food orders had made up for the few paying customers in Candy Girls. When Jazz looked at spreadsheets, the downward trend jumped out at her. Rain came down in a steady grim beat. The water and gray skies made the neighborhood look more unattractive than usual. As she stared past the security grill of her office window, Jazz wondered what potential her investor saw now. The local news media had begun a series of reports on criminal activity in the area. Business pundits speculated on whether development would be affected. Jazz saw her chances of cashing in going down the storm drain like the dirty rain water falling outside.

She left the window and went to her desk. The spreadsheet stared back at her with cold indifference. Jazz hit the keyboard, closing the depressing reminder of less money coming in. One screen was on showing a morning talk show, but Jazz had the sound on mute. A knock on the door startled her.

"It's me," Byron rumbled through the door.

"Come on in. I forgot you were here. You didn't need to come in early again," Jazz said, glad to see him despite her words.

"The soft drinks, beer, and stuff was being delivered. You can't stack them heavy boxes by yourself." Byron grinned. "Anyway, I'm a manager now so I got to set an example for the employees."

Jazz laughed. "I like the way you see a silver lining in all these clouds."

"You mean the weekend receipts? Yeah, it's down some. But I'm thinkin' that's gone be temporary. We got core customers that will stick with us."

Byron crossed over to a tall metal filing cabinet. He opened a drawer, stuffed the invoice in a folder, and closed it. Without asking, he turned Jazz's computer to face him. He entered figures in the inventory application they'd bought. Jazz watched him work with a listless feeling.

"Core customers, huh? You learning a lot from that online business class."

"Yeah, and to think mama had to practically call the police to make me go to school when I was a kid." Byron wore a crooked grin. "Okay, our inventory tracking is updated."

"Working on a degree and talking like a big time business school graduate already," Jazz replied, her mood lifting a little. "Making mama proud."

"She almost dropped her pot of gumbo at Sunday dinner when I told her. Hugged me like I'd just announced I was mayor or something," Byron said with a hearty laugh. "Good to see she got reason to smile instead of cry because of me."

"You should be proud of yourself. I just hope my

troubles don't screw with your plans." Jazz's mood swung low again. "We might not have a need for software, security systems, or any of my fancy ideas."

"Hey, don't get down on yourself. We have to be ready when things turn around," Byron said.

Jazz sighed and lit a cigarillo. "I'm facing facts, Byron. Once again my choices are bringing grief to people around me. I could have passed on buying Lorraine's property. Sure I wanted something of my own, but I knew it would piss her off."

"Mission accomplished," Byron said dryly.

"Hell yeah. I never would have guessed she'd go so far as to frame me for murder. I knew she was tough, but damn."

Byron heaved his tall, burly frame from the chair. "It's like Cedric said, there's somethin' else goin' on. We gonna figure it out."

"Hope we figure it out before I go to prison for life." Jazz took a pull on the cigarillo. Puffing out a stream of smoke relaxed her a little.

"Look, the indictment and arraignment happened fast, but the trial is months away. We got you on this, boss."

"Thanks, and I mean that. You and the others have been great." Jazz held out a hand and Byron gave it a firm shake. "Team JV Enterprises."

Byron let go of her hand and snapped his fingers. "Hey, we oughta have T-shirts. I'll get my cousin to come up with some designs. She's studying art. A brand is very important for a business."

"Go to it manager," Jazz said. Despite her Monday blues, she had to grin at his enthusiasm. The buzzer announced someone at one of the entrance doors.

"I'll get it." Byron strode out and five minutes later

came back with Cedric and Willa.

Willa put down a large white paper bag. "Sure you won't stay and have some, Byron."

Cedric placed a shallow cardboard box with five cups of coffee on the small side table in Jazz's office. "We have plenty. Wasn't sure who would be in at this hour."

"No thanks. I got to get home. I have a class assignment due. Then I'm gonna get some sleep before I work tonight. See you tonight, boss lady." Byron gave Jazz a playful salute.

"If you don't quit calling me boss or boss lady..." Jazz said in a mock threatening tone.

Byron merely laughed and waved at her. "I'm out."

"Bye," Willa called to him. Cedric followed to walk with him to the door. "He was an excellent hiring decision."

Jazz stubbed out the cigarillo so her sister wouldn't whine about the smoke. "Glad you think so."

Willa opened the bag. The smell of hot biscuits and bacon floated up. "Can't wait to dig into this food. Crazy morning already and it's just nine-thirty."

"That right?" Jazz watched Willa sniff the biscuit like a connoisseur sniffing fine wine.

"Hmm." Willa stuffed two slices of bacon into the fluffy treat. With a sigh she bit into it. After chewing for a few moments, she nodded. "Anthony pitched in and took Mikayla to school for me. You were right. Helping him buy a car wasn't a disaster."

"You're welcome," Jazz tossed back.

"Then we had a seven-thirty meeting with a potential client." Willa got a cup of coffee. She dumped sugar and creamer into it.

"Damn, you gonna run business away making

people come that early to talk." Jazz waved away her offer of a biscuit.

"Mr. Barilla has a growing wholesale produce business. He wanted to meet at seven-thirty because he's used to working before sunrise. I think he was testing us. You know, seeing if we were his kind of people." Willa grabbed a napkin before she sat down.

"I hope you get a contract after getting up with the chickens for the guy."

"I think so. He'll call us by Wednesday at the latest, so we'll need to hire." Willa chewed more bacon and biscuit. "This is so good. Have one, girl."

"No thanks. Since you're impressed with Byron, keep him in mind for a job. He might be needing one," Jazz said with a grimace.

"Stop that kind of talk," Willa replied.

"What kind of talk," Cedric said as he came in. He retrieved a cup of coffee.

"Jazz is being pessimistic way too soon. Besides, we have news." Willa wiped her mouth with dainty dabs.

"Good news I hope," Jazz retorted.

"Well, I'd call it interesting news for sure," Cedric said. He took a sip of black coffee.

Willa put down her half-eaten breakfast. "Okay, remember the city employees that were caught up in a scandal three years ago?"

"One of them ended up getting jail time for taking bribes," Cedric added.

"I wasn't watching the news much back in the day. Now that I'm a main topic, I'm keeping up more." Jazz grunted.

"Cedric, tell her the rest. This is *good*."

"One woman worked in the Clerk of Court's office collecting business taxes. The other one worked in the

Sheriff's department tax section. They would 'lose' or falsify documents so these businesses would pay less or no taxes. That was just one of their schemes. Guess who was one business owner who benefitted for at least three years," Cedric said.

"Oh man. I should have known. Lorraine wasn't stupid enough to let those taxes slide, not that she wasn't a sloppy record keeper," Jazz replied. "She knew all about the city auctions downtown where you go pay taxes on property to own it. Now it makes sense. Her tax problems started after those folks got caught."

"Yes. The city parish did audits. Eight months later tax notices went out. They didn't have enough to indict Lorraine. Her lawyer claimed she was charged 'fees', and she didn't know the employees were doing anything illegal. But the city wanted their money," Cedric said.

"And she couldn't pay the interest and penalties," Jazz added.

"Plus she paid a fine for the overdue taxes and a fine for falsifying public documents. She had to admit not reporting all of her business income, too." Willa picked up her biscuit sandwich again. "She squeaked by with only misdemeanor criminal charges."

"All I remember was her complaining about crooked politicians stuffing their pockets while the little guys got screwed." Jazz rocked back in her chair considering this new twist.

"I suspect Lorraine thinks you knew all about it," Willa said.

"If you recall, I was distracted with my own worries," Jazz replied, raising an eyebrow at her sister.

Willa's no good ex-husband had been murdered and her son had been one of the suspects. Jack Crown managed to get into business that included Filipe's gang. Jack didn't know about the drug and gun smuggling part at first. But greed had made him too stupid to check out his new partners. At least the Scar Face clone hadn't figured out Jazz helped solve Jack's murder, which in the process put the police onto Filipe's lucrative game—yet.

"Thanks for taking the risks for us, but don't do it again," Willa added, pointing a finger at Jazz.

Jazz affected a fake sugary smile. "You're so welcome, sweetie. See how easily she reverts to being a woman of the street, Cedric? You've been warned."

"Duly noted," Cedric said with a chuckle despite the dark look Willa gave him.

"Y'all both getting on my nerves," Willa muttered and ate the rest of her biscuit.

"So Lorraine and Cleavon threatened to send word to Filipe that you stabbed him in the back?" Cedric said to Jazz.

"Yeah. How'd you figure that one out?" Jazz liked this guy. Willa could do a lot worse, and had.

"Logical since they know about you and Filipe, and how you stood by Willa when Jack was murdered." Cedric frowned. "I don't know. Something's missing."

"Did you find out about Lorraine's son? He could be the missing link," Jazz said.

Cedric stood. "Nothing solid yet, but I'm still tracking down street gossip about all three of her sons."

Willa glanced at her fancy wristwatch and stood as well. "In the meantime, you need to eat regular meals. I know how you get when times get rough. You can go two days without anything much in your stomach."

"Yes, mama. I promise to eat my veggies," Jazz said in a childish sing-song voice.

"Smart ass. Speaking of, have you heard from Vivienne lately?" Willa asked, grimacing at the mere mention of their biological mother's name.

"No, and no news is good news," Jazz replied with the old phrase they always used when their mother went MIA on them.

"Yeah. You know Lorraine reminds me of her a lot. Anyway, watch your back and front." Willa crossed around the desk and gave Jazz a hug before she could object.

"Yeah, whatever. See ya, Cedric." Jazz tried not to look pleased at Willa's big sister affection.

"Bye." Cedric gave the two siblings an amused look as he followed Willa out.

Seconds later, Willa burst through the door again. She pointed a magenta polished forefinger at Jazz. "Don't try to do any investigation about Lorraine's thuggish offspring. Let us do the sniffing out."

"Stop worrying about nothing," Jazz said. "Now get to work so you can make some money."

Willa squinted at her but said no more. Jazz rocked and thought. And rocked some more. Answers to the riddle banging around in her head seemed as elusive as the smoke from her cigarillo.

* * *

Monday sped by as Jazz tied up details at Candy Girls. By four o'clock in the afternoon she'd given Rochelle instructions. Lilly had come in insisting she should dance to bring in more money. Plus the blunt young woman missed the tips. So much for her ambitions to get off the pole, Jazz mused. She left Lilly and Tyretta working on a poster to advertise Lilly's upcoming Thursday night performance. Chyna had come in by five o'clock to help Rochelle in the kitchen. By six thirty, few men had drifted in. Lilly had gone home, and Rochelle's brother was in the kitchen. Tyretta and Rochelle assured Jazz they could hold things down.

"Go up to your place and rest. Stop thinking about the business and all the drama and stuff," Tyretta insisted.

"Yeah, we got this. Not much goin' on here anyways," Rochelle agreed.

Jazz grimaced as she glanced around at two customers warming seats. "Thanks for reminding me."

"Mondays are always slow," Rochelle replied. She patted Jazz on the arm as she headed back to the kitchen. "Take it easy."

"Call my cell if y'all need me," Jazz said.

Tyretta waved at her to leave. "Uh-huh, now go."

Jazz glanced over her shoulder once as she headed through the side entrance. They were right. Sitting around a slow night didn't make sense. But she had no desire to lounge around watching dumb television shows or listening to music. Jazz went home and changed clothes. She let her hair hang down her back. Two inch silver hoops decorated her ear lobes. Jazz turned left to right checking her look in the full length mirror in her bedroom. A gray knit blouse with silvery threads over black leggings fit the ready to party image she wanted. Jazz added a pair of Luichiny Hot Seat ankle boots to finish the look. Deep red lipstick added the final touch. She stuffed her driver's license, some cash, and knife in the pocket of her suede jacket. The only item in her small cross body bag was a small .38

pistol. She smiled at the reaction Don would have to her bad habit of carrying weapons.

"What you don't know..." Jazz murmured as she walked out.

Twenty minutes later she was perched at the bar of Grown Folks. For a good thirty minutes Jazz chatted with a middle-aged man determined to get her into his Lexus SUV. She played along to blend in with the other customers. Willa would scream that Jazz was nuts to be at a club only five blocks away from Lorraine's new place. But this was ripe territory to pick up street buzz.

Jazz bobbed her head to the music. A mixture of music blared, including tunes from the eighties. Grown Folks catered to an older, less volatile crowd than the twenty-something and younger bar flies. To her surprise, Jazz liked the way the new owner had transformed the place. The decor had a sophisticated look. The club looked shady from the outside, but inside, the muted gray, green and blue tones classed the place up.

"I have one of those new apartments downtown. Nice view of the bridge even. I'm on the eleventh floor," the man said, leaning closer to stare down Jazz's blouse.

"Sounds expensive," Jazz replied with a flirty smile. She knew the game. Lawrence had dangled the hint that he had money.

Lawrence shrugged. "I like it until I build a house somewhere."

Jazz glanced around looking for a familiar face as he droned on about his big plans. Two women kept shooting hungry glances at Lawrence. About ten years older than Jazz, they seemed ready to pounce if she gave up the prize. She switched her attention past them to a group that entered the lounge. An insistent tug on her harm pulled her back to Lawrence.

"Hey beautiful, you want another glass of bourbon?" he said, voice pitched low in an attempt to be sexy.

"Sure. Hit me again."

Jazz turned around and acted like his every word fascinated her. Yet she kept the newcomers in her sights. Two of the guys were wannabe players who hit the Baton Rouge club scene hard regularly. She'd let them get settled before ditching Lawrence to strike a conversation with them. Before she could make her move, a surprise plum appeared. Kelli Granger joined the male bartender to handle the onslaught of customers. Kelli had worked for Lorraine on and off for over five years. Now they were definitely off since Lorraine fired her a year ago.

"Don't you slip away, sweet thing. I have to pay the water bill," Lawrence said with a wink.

She somehow managed not to roll her eyes at the outdated cutesy reference to his need to pee. "Okay," Jazz said with a smile.

Kelli came over with the drinks. She blinked hard at Jazz and then boomed out a laugh. They slapped palms by way of a greeting and shared a brief hug across the bar.

"Girl, you up in here checking out the competition?" Kelli leaned against the polished wood.

"What competition?" Jazz wisecracked. "How the hell you been?"

"Great these days. Getting fired turned out to be my blessing in disguise. Lorraine is asshat crazy. But I don't need to tell you." Kelli gave a grunt. "Hey, you need me?"

"Nah, I got it. Visit with your fine ass friend." The

bartender gave Jazz a broad grin.

"Real smooth, Derrick" Kelli said. She turned back to Jazz. "And he thinks you'll melt all over him because of that crude compliment."

"Other than him, you like it here?" Jazz snapped her fingers to the beat of Kanye West music spitting from the speakers.

"He's alright. It's just these desperate women got men spoiled. They don't even have to be polished or polite. Just say any kind of stupid shit." Kelli started to say more, but she gazed past Jazz. "Oh no. Lawrence done latched on to you? Lawd have mercy."

"He's not half bad," Jazz replied and giggled at Kelli's grimace.

"Dude hasn't had game since the eighties, if he had any back then," Kelli said low. Then she straightened up to beam at him. "Hey Lawrence. What up?"

"Spending quality time with the prettiest woman up in here. I..." Lawrence frowned at the sound of his cell phone during a lull in the music. He glanced at the caller ID. "Excuse me a minute."

Kelli watched him leave the club, cell phone in hand. "His wife."

"He's got an apartment downtown he said."

"His friend has an apartment downtown that he uses when the guy is traveling on business. Lawrence has been married for a long time. He and wifey got two teenagers. Plus, his girlfriend has his six year old little girl. He looks good, and he's got money, but he's trouble."

"So am I," Jazz reminded her.

Kelli laughed hard. "You gonna play him? Please, let me watch."

"I'm not in the game no more, girl. I'm a business

woman," Jazz said with a wink. "Still, if he keeps bragging about his money..."

"He ain't lyin' either. His family has real estate. He owns an insurance franchise and a couple of sandwich shops. He's overdue to get played the way he's been playin' women for years." Kelli said. "Shh, here he comes. Lookin' whipped, too."

"I've got some urgent international business to take care of, you know time zones different over there. Can I call you sometime?" Lawrence stood close to Jazz with a hand on the bar.

"I hear you got a wife, Lawrence," Jazz drawled.

He shot a grimace at Kelli. "I thought we were friends."

"I'm her friend," Kellie replied with a grin.

"When were you going to tell me about being a family man?" Jazz put in.

"Look, we lead separate lives and... No, no, as corny as it sounds, I'm telling you the truth." Lawrence had nerve enough to place a palm over his heart as if swearing an oath.

"I like you, but I don't know," Jazz said, putting just enough indecision in her tone to give him hope. Bingo.

"Look, look, I have a gorgeous apartment downtown like I said. I can offer you good times with no drama. I travel to Atlanta, New York and San Francisco a lot. Sometimes I go to Hawaii. Here's my card. We can have beautiful times together. Promise you'll call."

Jazz gazed at the white business card with gold embossed lettering. "You gave out about ten of those in the last month I'll bet."

"I've been looking for the right one, and here she is. Please Monesha, give me a chance." Lawrence put on a sincere serious expression.

Kelli's mouth flew open. She cleared her throat and turned away. "Let me go catch this customer."

"Okay," Jazz said with a smile. She took the card and tucked it into her jacket pocket. "I'd love to see New York again."

"You will, baby girl. The best hotels, restaurants and more. Now don't lose that ticket to paradise."

Before she could duck, he planted a kiss on her right cheek. Jazz managed not to punch him. "Yeah, sure."

Kelli watched him leave before she joined Jazz again. "What the fuck? Monesha. Warn me next time. I almost lost it."

"I wasn't going to give that fool my real name," Jazz said.

They both burst out laughing. After a few more jokes at Lawrence's expense, they exchanged chitchat to catch up. As usual Kelli had complaints about her grouchy mother and latest no-good man. She took breaks from talking to Jazz to serve up drinks. The other bartender worked alone while Kelli took a break. "Okay, so instead of being at your club holding it down, you're here. Checking up on Lorraine is my guess," Kelli said as she glanced around.

"How come I can't just be takin' a night off to relax?"

Kelli grunted. "Uh-huh."

"You nailed me. Damn, I need to be less obvious." Jazz studied the crowd to see if anyone was paying too much attention to her.

"Don't worry. I haven't spotted any of her crew up in here," Kelli said, reading Jazz's mind.

"Yeah, but you haven't worked for her in a while either," Jazz retorted and kept looking.

"True. I hear Lorraine has changed, and not in a good way. Bitch," Kelli hissed. She clenched a fist.

"She was never sweet and cuddly, Kelli. How the hell could she get worse?"

"Lorraine got paranoid to the point of being a nut after her son got killed. The kid was a terror, so nobody was surprised when he got taken out."

Kelli walked off and wiped a spill on the polished bar surface. The customer wanted another drink. The male bartender nodded to Kelli, and she rejoined Jazz.

"Yeah, he started fights everywhere he went," Jazz said, taking up where they'd left off.

"Needed his ass kicked, not that I'm saying somebody should have killed him. Anyway, Lorraine started goin' off on all kinds of shit. Then she accused me of stealing liquor and money from the register. I told her she needed to look at her son and nephew. That heffa exploded and took a swing at me." Kelli's hands clenched.

"Lorraine was lucky you didn't swing back. She must have lost her mind knowing how you moved in the ring." Jazz looked at her friend. Kelli had boxed from the age of sixteen and during her short stint in the Navy.

"Yeah, well her six foot four inch thug son and two of his gangstas stood nearby. I was pissed, but not as crazy as *her*," Kelli retorted. "But like my grandmamma always said, rest her soul, God ain't sleep. Lorraine lost the club, buried a son, and saw another off to prison."

Jazz grinned. "You think the Big Guy delivered payback just for you?"

"Nah, they done a whole lot worse to other people. I just enjoyed watchin' though. Anyway, her old regulars have been coming here lately. They say a bunch of serious gangstas hang out at her new place. A couple of 'em are known hit men still in their teens."

"I hope you know what they look like." Jazz tried to look casual as she turned to lean against the bar. She sipped from her glass as she scanned the crowd. The door swung open and she muttered a curse word.

"He's fine. If he ain't yours, introduce us," Kelli smoothed down her cute short cut bob. She stood straight to give the world a view of her ample cleavage.

"I don't own nobody" Jazz kept her expression blank as Don strolled in. Yet irritation boiled toward full blow anger. He had the nerve to smile at her.

"Hey, I lucked up when I walked in and found two beautiful women waitin' for me." Don spoke in a sing-song voice typical of a player showing off his charm. He wore baggy jeans and a designer red knit sweater that hugged his muscular body. He put swagger in his step the closer he got to them. "Hit me with a private room and set up of Cristal. Both y'all can join me."

"That simple, huh? All roads lead to you I guess," Jazz shot back with attitude. When he slid onto the barstool next to her, she lowered her voice. "You got hella nerve following me. I don't need a baby sitter."

"Apparently you do because coming here was a stupid bad idea," Don replied softly. Then he winked at Kelli and spoke loudly. "C'mon, let's get this party started. Three's company."

"I can't drink, sorry. But I'm ready to serve you up the best, man." Kelli's lips smiled, but her gaze darted around nervously. "Tell me what's goin' on, Jazz."

"Nothin' except a dude stickin' his nose where it don't belong," Jazz replied. She looked straight ahead and pointedly avoided looking at Don.

"You shouldn't be this close to Lorraine's territory," Don whispered to her.

"Humph, Lorraine doesn't have territory," Jazz shot back with a snort. Then her mocking grin froze. "Unless you know something I don't."

"If she had a part in what happened to Kyeisha like we think, then Lorraine is in something deep." Don kept up the appearance of a man trying to get laid. His easy smile covered the serious theory he'd just shared.

"Shit, they messed her up bad and then..." Kelli pressed a wet dish cloth to her neck. "Look, y'all need to get outta here like ten minutes ago."

"You two scared little kids need to calm the hell down." Jazz stopped when three laughing men came through the club's front door.

"What?" Don said at the same time as Kelli.

Two squat but well built men stood on either side of a tall man. All three were various shades of brown, with the taller man being the color of light caramel. He wore a long sleeved white t-shirt rolled up to expose forearms covered with tattoos. His friends wore open collared shirts under denim jackets. They had tattoos on their necks. One of them was bald with a tattoo on one side of his head. Jazz didn't know two of them, but the bald man sent a chill through her like jagged ice.

"We need to go, like now," Jazz said.

"You know them," Don murmured so low the music almost swept his words away.

"One of Filipe's guys used to ride with him as a bodyguard." Jazz turned her back to the club and faced the bar again. "Bald guy."

"He looks dumb and dumber," Don replied. Still he followed Jazz's lead. Instead he positioned his body sideways.

"Mateo is not stupid. He likes letting people assume he is, which makes him even more dangerous.

Kelli, I sure as hell hope a back way out is near that private room." Jazz spoke with the glass up to her face.

"This way." Kelli said. She moved stiffly with a tight smile on her face. She swung a small half door on hinges to come from behind the bar.

"Try not to look scared shitless, Kelli," Jazz mumbled.

"Screw you comin' in here draggin' trouble into my life," Kelli shot back low. Then she raised her voice to a normal level. "Yeah, y'all gonna have fun up in here."

Don placed a hand in the small of Jazz's back. "Move faster ladies. Baldy has separated himself and is moving to our left."

"Shit," Jazz and Kelli said at the same time.

Chapter 14

They kept walking and pretended not to notice Mateo moving parallel to them across the room. Then he was gone. Kelli led them down a hallway with muted lighting. The door to one of two private rooms had a keypad entry door. One glass wall showed the interior. A large black leather sectional sofa curved in a crescent shape. A round glass cocktail table sat in front of it. Around a corner down another hall was a door.

Kelli fumbled the code entry twice. She kept looking down the hall. "Damn it, what's the number?"

"Take a breath and slow down. We're okay," Don replied. He used his body to block her view of the way they'd come.

"Right." Kelli's third try resulted in a click. She pushed the door open.

"Hold on. We're only going in there if this room has a back exit," Jazz said.

"This is the assistant manager's office. It does have a back door. C'mon." Kelli led them in. Once she shut the door Kelli panted with anxiety.

"Thanks. Stay here for a minute. They'll go to the other side exit door looking for us." Don nodded for Jazz to follow.

"No problem. Hey," Kelli called before they pushed through the heavy steel door. When Jazz and Don stopped, she pointed at them. "Call me once you're driving off. If I don't hear from you in fifteen minutes, I'm calling the police."

"Check. Tell them officer in need of back-up," Don said.

"You're runnin' with a cop?" Kelli blurted out staring at Jazz in surprise.

Jazz shrugged . "Some days a girl needs protection."

"This one sure does. Let's move." Don pulled Jazz by one arm.

"We gotta have a talk for sure," Kelli called out before the door bumped shut.

"Everybody is a comedian," Jazz muttered.

She had sense enough to let Don continue in go first. They went down a narrow alley between Grown Folks and the building next door. A single flood light illuminated the way. Just like a low budget crime movie, a figure stood at the end of the alley. Don turned, pushing Jazz ahead of him. A high wooden fence stood about ten yards from the other building. They headed past a back door toward the side parking lot of the offices of a temporary labor company. Another figure, this one tall, waited for them.

"Hey Jazz, what's your hurry? Let's talk old times," Mateo called out.

"Don't stop," Don said.

"That's your plan? That thug ain't gonna just step aside cause you say, 'Excuse me, dude.'"

"Just follow my lead. We can't get boxed up here. He obviously wants to get information first. They could have shot us before now. Big man there will back up as we get closer. They'll circle us." Don pushed Jazz to move.

"Oh, so you're claustrophobic. You'd rather die in the open. Great," Jazz whispered.

"Yeah, come right this way," the tall man called out in good humor.

The second man followed them. Mateo emerged from the shadows of the back alley minutes after Jazz and Don. Jazz glanced around. They were in a parking lot. A side street with no traffic led to other businesses. All were closed.

"Hey, we just came out to have a good time. Sorry, but we drank up most of my money. The most I have is ten dollars." Don held his arms out.

The other short man snorted. "Dude, he thinks we wanna rob his pocket change."

Mateo laughed. "No, home. I'm just sayin' hello to my old pal right here. What is up, Jazz? Still lookin' all good and shit."

Don turned to Jazz with a scowl. "So I gotta deal with a jealous boyfriend. You told me you didn't have a man."

"I haven't seen this guy in almost three years, baby. I don't know why he's trippin'," Jazz said.

"Shit, we can't walk two steps in a club without stumblin' up on some guy you was with. Damn, girl. How many dudes you been bumpin'?" Don spat out waving his arms."

"Aw hell naw you ain't talkin' to *me* like that. Mutha, I'll kick your ass to several curbs if you don't watch it," Jazz shot back. She faced him with both hands on her hips.

"You ain't special. There's about ten of you waitin'

in the club. Another ten in the next club, too." Don gave a contemptuous grunt. He looked at Mateo. "She's all yours. I'm outta here and on to somethin' better."

"You ain't walkin' off after talkin' to me like I'm dirt," Jazz shrieked.

She leapt onto Don's back and pounded it with her fists. He attempted to shake her off while swinging in a circle. Jazz kept up a stream of cuss words, insulting Don and his parents. Obviously taken by surprise, the three men stood watching them. The tall man laughed until he bent at the waist.

"Aw man, you can't let her get away with this shit. Slap her ass down." The shorter man joined his companion in laughter.

"Hey you fools," Mateo yelled at the men. "Pull these other fools apart. This ain't no damn floor show."

Don and Jazz continued to tussle as the three men approached. Mateo looked angry and disgusted. His friends still laughed as they strode closer. They traded jokes about Jazz getting the upper hand on Don. Jazz prayed fifteen minutes would be up soon. Never had she hoped to see the police before in her life.

Mateo reached them first. "Break it the fuck up. I ain't got time to watch Divorce Court out here," he growled.

Before he could speak again Don landed a punch upside his head. Stunned, Mateo stumbled back. Don didn't give him time to recover. He hit him again. Jazz pulled out her pistol and shot twice over the heads of the other men. Both froze in the act of running. Don and Mateo traded blows, but Don's longer arms and weight gave him an advantage.

"Y'all must don't know 'bout me," Jazz shouted. "I don't bluff. You move, I'll shoot."

"You can't shoot us both at the same time," the tall man said, his gaze darting at Mateo's battle with Don.

"I can shoot one though. When he's down, I'll aim for the one still standing. This is an automatic. I'm good with it, too." Jazz moved away from the men as she spoke.

"We can take her, man. She's all talk," the tall man rasped aside to his buddy.

"Try me, muthafuckas," Jazz screamed. "My nerves bad from this drama. I might shoot you on general principle."

"Dude, this ain't even our fight," the shorter man said.

"You want Mateo lookin' for us cause we left him?" his friend replied with a frown. He glowered at Jazz. "You ain't got the guts."

Jazz pulled the trigger. The shorter man yelped and grabbed his thigh. "I meant to hit you in the stomach, bitch."

"Fuck this."

The tall man pulled a gun and fired at Jazz. Without hesitation Jazz shot twice more at both men. Don and Mateo hit the ground still locked in battle. Within seconds Mateo lay still on his stomach.

"Dumpster to your right," Don shouted to Jazz just as the sound of sirens cut through the air.

Jazz followed his voice running at top speed. The next five seconds became a blur of sounds. Gunfire mixed with sirens, running feet and shouting voices. She felt a punch on her shoulder but kept running. She barreled into Don's solid body. When she tried to keep going past him, Don wrapped her in a bear hug. Jazz couldn't hear his voice as she fought to get free. The powerful urge to flee drove her. Don lifted her until her boots dangled about a foot from the ground. He managed to twist her around until they were face to face. Then he shook her hard.

"Stop running. The cops will shoot you. They can't tell who's who out here," he said, his words a scratchy whisper.

She slumped against his chest, heaving in gulps of air. Don comforted her then gestured for Jazz to lean against the dumpster. He did hand signals that Jazz took to mean she should follow him. Before she could catch her breath, Don walked out from the relative safety of the dumpster into a flood of bright white light.

"Officer Don Addison. I'm going to reach for my wallet," he yelled.

"Keep walking with your hands up, sir," a deep voice replied. "Tell me which pocket and I'll get it."

Jazz slid to the ground, eyes squeezed closed. The voices of the other police officers sounded like white men . She shook so hard she was sure the dumpster would start to vibrate. Jazz felt tears rolling down her cheeks. "Do what they say, Don," she whispered.

"Look, just let me show you," Don started.

"What the hell. The police out here tryin' to kill more black men," an angry voice shouted.

The sound of a crowd from the club burst forth, a babble of about fifty outraged voices. Police officers ordered them to back away. The pop of breaking glass mixed with shouts.

"Wait a damn minute officers," Don yelled. A series of booms muffled the rest of his words.

Feet running away. Flashing blue lights crisscrossed the alleys. Jazz crawled in slow motion toward a prone tall figure. Red sweater. Blue jeans. She screamed his name twice before the nightmarish picture went black.

* * *

Jazz woke up in a hospital bed with a start, sitting straight up with a whimper. Two pairs of arms circled her instantly as she panted for breath. Her sister's familiar scent, an expensive perfume she wore daily, soothed Jazz.

"You're safe, honey. It's going to be okay," Willa said as she smoothed Jazz's tangled hair down with one hand.

"Yes, they have those criminals locked up in jail. That's where they should be." MiMi hugged her gently.

"Don," Jazz managed to gasp.

Willa's father seemed to appear out of nowhere. "He got shot, but it's not life threatening. Just a flesh wound. He was released this morning."

"Huh?" Jazz blinked at him.

"You've been here overnight, sweetie." Willa tried to say more, but got choked up. Willa covered her mouth as she sobbed.

"Come with me so you don't upset her." Mama Ruby led Willa out of the room.

Papa Elton fluffed the pillows on the bed. "Lay back now."

Jazz found herself sobbing against his chest two seconds later. He patted her and rumbled paternal words of comfort, something she wasn't used to at all. His solid embrace combined with his tenderness soon worked. She let him ease her back onto the pillows. Papa Elton wiped her face. Jazz even let him hold the tissue while she blew her nose.

"Thanks," she rasped, voice raw from crying like a baby. "Sorry I lost it. Hope I didn't get your shirt all wet and nasty."

"Ah forget it, baby. I've had my kids do worse on my shirt," Papa Elton said with a grin.

"No details please," Jazz joked back. She sighed and closed her eyes but they popped open again. "How is Don? Those damn thugs hurt him, I'm gonna--"

MiMi appeared to her left. "Hey, girl. You won't believe this, but a deputy shot Don. Thought he was one of the bad guys. Didn't give him time to show his ID and..."

"MiMi, not now," Papa Elton cut her off.

Jazz sat up again, but Papa Elton firmly pushed her against the pillows. "Raise the bed."

"You should go back to sleep," he said.

"I can't sleep until I know what happened to Don and how he's doing. He got hurt because of me and--" Jazz couldn't finish. Another crying jag threatened. She heaved deep breaths to shake it off.

"Okay, Okay. Let me work this thing." Papa Elton found the right button.

The bed rose so that Jazz could see more of the room. The obligatory white painted walls greeted her. To her left, a window with closed white blinds kept out the sunlight.

"Where am I?" Jazz looked at Papa Elton.

"Our Lady of the Lake Hospital. They've taken great care of you," he replied.

"I can't believe they let Don go home so soon. Somebody should check on him," Jazz said.

"Hmm." MiMi glanced at Papa Elton who cleared his throat. "His ex-wife took him to her house."

"She seems nice." Papa Elton shrugged when MiMi shot him a "What the hell?" kind of look.

Jazz sighed. "Okay, so he's not hurt that bad if they

let him go home. That's good."

"You're taking the news he went home with his ex well. I'd be jumping out of here to get my man," MiMi blurted. She shrugged when Papa Elton gave her a "Shut up" look. Not that MiMi cared. "I'm just sayin'."

"He's not 'my man', MiMi. We're... it's complicated. And no, I'm not gonna explain because it's none of your business," Jazz said before words came from MiMi's open mouth. "Who shot Don?"

"Girl, bullets were flying. They caught one of the guys that tried to attack y'all, the one that did the shooting. The other two got away." MiMi sat down in one of two chairs near the bed.

"They determined that the bullet that hit Don was police issue." Papa Elton frowned. "The local NAACP is having a field day talking about profiling. All three deputies were white."

"Humph, he needs to sue their butts off. So were you two just out on a date or were you tracking down clues? Channel 33 news reported that this might be a gang hit related to your murder trial and--"

"I said *not now*, MiMi," Papa Elton broke in. Before he could say more a deep voice came from the door."Excuse me folks. I'm Chief Detective Armand Miller with the Baton Rouge Police. This is Sergeant Evans." Miller held up his ID and nodded to his subordinate at the same time.

"Morning," Evans said. His gaze swept the room taking in details. He seemed most interested in MiMi's shapely legs extending from her blood red skirt.

"We need to talk to Ms. Vaughn. I checked with her doctor, and she's good with it," Miller added before Papa Elton could object.

"She's banged up and traumatized," MiMi spoke

instead, her smile aimed at Evans. "Maybe give her more time to recover. Jazz was very upset about Detective Addison. Cried her eyes out, poor thing."

"I'm fine, MiMi," Jazz said with force, glaring at her. "I'm not falling apart. Don can take care of himself."

"Sure," MiMi said with a sympathetic smile. She glanced at the two detectives as if to say "She's trying to be brave."

"After all she's been through, MiMi is right," Papa Elton advised.

"I'm up for it," Jazz said with determination.

"Good. I'm afraid we need to do this in private." Miller tilted his head to one side as he looked at Papa Elton and MiMi.

"She should have her lawyer here," MiMi said with a sideways glance at Papa Elton.

"We're interviewing you as a victim. This isn't connected to your pending case," Miller said smoothly. "Excuse us please."

Evans opened the door to reinforce the invitation to leave. Jazz saw Willa and Mama Ruby in the hallway. Both wore twin anxious expressions. She waved to reassure them. Under the circumstances she could muster up a smile. Papa Elton and MiMi left. Once the door whisked shut, Evans stood in front of it.

"You gonna tell the reporters which idiot cop shot one of his own? Y'all sure loved talking to the media about *me*," Jazz drawled.

Miller glanced at Evans seemingly as a warning. The younger man pressed his lips together. Then Miller turned his gaze back to Jazz. "Evans, go interview the family."

"Sir?" Evans blinked at him.

"Just do it," Miller said.

"Yes sir." Evans went out.

Miller turned back to Jazz. "Tell me everything, from the time you met Don for drinks until the shooting started."

"I didn't meet Detective Addison for drinks. He must have been following me as part of your investigation or something. I sure as hell didn't invite him," Jazz said evenly.

"So you had no idea he was going to show up at Grown Folks?" Miller took out a small notepad and pen.

"I just said so. I'm guessing those guys decided to rob him or something. He looked like an out of place bourgie guy looking for action." Jazz glanced at Miller. "The place was crowded but I spotted him. You better send him back to undercover school."

"Detective Addison wasn't undercover, Ms. Vaughn. Something I'm sure you know," Miller said dryly.

"Do I? He's your employee. Besides, don't ask me. Ask him." Jazz relaxed against the pillow.

"I plan to real soon," Miller shot back with a shade of annoyance in his voice.

"My friend says his ex-wife picked him up. Sounds like they're getting back together soon. Another kink in your story that he's hooked up with me," Jazz said mildly. "With all that home cooking and tender loving care, it will be like the old days."

"Nyla is a good woman, and a fine mother. That would be a good thing." Miller wrote on the pad without looking at her.

"Very sweet, but nothing to do with me. Anyway, I went out the back way to shake him. Hell, can't a girl hang out with friends these days. Pissed me off. These guys must have followed him out. That's all I know." Jazz looked at Miller with a "my story and I'm sticking to it" expression.

"You're saying those guys weren't after you? Funny coincidence," Miller drawled.

"Hilarious," Jazz said with a grunt.

Miller squinted at her as he shoved the notepad and pen into an inside pocket of his coat. "Truth time, Ms. Vaughn. Don and I go back a long way, so I know him well. He's trying to protect you for some crazy ass reason. . Don't pull him into danger if you care about him. Bad things seem to follow you. He's got kids, a career, and a future."

"And I'm climbing up from the gutter to drag him down, is that your point?" Jazz looked at him steadily.

"Cops get hooked on the adrenaline rush of street life. You're sexy, smart, and you talk a good game. Light years away from the steady type of life Nyla could give him. He understands you and your world. Nyla, well she can't connect to the dark crap we see every day on the job." Miller wore a stone face. "Leave him out of it."

"You want me to be noble. I should agree to step aside so him and sweet Nyla can ride into the sunset. Last time I checked, Don was a grown ass man who didn't need a nursemaid." Jazz raised an eyebrow at him. "Now if you'll excuse me, I need a nap."

"If this latest incident ties into the murder, I'll find out. If your gang banging ex-boyfriend, Filipe Perez, is helping you, I'll know about it. Soon." Miller fixed a laser stare on Jazz.

Jazz twisted around in the bed so that her backside was to him. She was sure he got the message to kiss her butt. "Goodbye, Chief of whatever."

"I'll be talking to you," Miller shot back.

"Not without my lawyer," Jazz said.

She listened to the clip-clip of his shoes on the polished linoleum floor and the whisk of the door opening. She turned onto her back once Miller was gone. Her sister walked in alone, a brittle smile in place.

"You okay?"

Jazz sighed as she arranged the sheets. "Yeah."

"He didn't just want to interview you as a victim I'm guessing." Willa took over smoothing the sheets until they were perfect. "The nerve of the man."

"He's doing his job." Jazz laughed. "I can't believe I just said that. I've been hanging around Don too much."

"Speaking of the detective..."

"No, we're not speaking of Don. I don't care what MiMi had to say," Jazz cut her off firmly.

Willa sat on the edge of the bed. "Sure you're not dizzy or nauseous? The nurse said those might be signs you have more serious injuries."

"I'm sore, but that's it. Well except for Miller grinding his heel on my last damn nerve." Jazz leaned against the pillows.

Willa gave a brief laugh and then cleared her throat. "At least Detective Addison protected you from being beaten. So far you don't have any signs of internal injury."

"No thanks to those punk ass thugs." Jazz closed her eyes.

"Since you're here, you could talk to the doctor about that surgery," Willa said softly. She stared down at her hands clenched together. "Maybe since you met Don, I mean, I can tell you care about him."

Jazz opened her eyes and sat up. "Stop it right there. Even if a doctor says I could have kids, I don't want any."

"At least let a doctor look. I've seen the way you look at Mikayla and Anthony, at little Sage when you think no one notices." Willa moved closer to Jazz. She reached for Jazz's hand, but Jazz pulled back. "I'm just saying."

"Look, I got over being raped by that sick bastard. The damn social workers forced me to go to counseling. I'm cured. Right as rain." Jazz looked away from Willa.

Jazz became preoccupied with sex, attracting male attention and being seductive. The social worker made her go back to the same therapist who'd treated when she'd become aggressive toward other children. The soft spoken woman had gently helped her understand the effects of being raped. From then on Jazz decided to be in complete charge of her body and her life as a whole. Doctors had explained the internal scarring might make her infertile later in life. Jazz didn't care. She told everyone. Kids were a pain that slowed a woman down. Men never stuck around to help anyway.

"I know, I know. You live on your own terms. Blah, blah, blah. But think about having a family," Willa pressed on.

"The world does not need another selfish, triflin' mother who can't or won't take care of her kids," Jazz retorted.

"You're not Vivienne."

"I'm not the bake cupcakes and attend PTA meetings type either."

"You think I am? Mama Ruby does my baking. I've gotten awards for NOT volunteering on PTA committees." Willa grinned at Jazz.

Jazz grinned back. "Don't think I didn't notice."

"Seriously, Jazz," Willa started but stopped when Jazz stopped smiling. "Fine. Subject closed."

Silence stretched between them. Jazz and Willa avoided looking at each other. Willa straightened the room. She put a fresh box of tissues on the table next to Jazz's hospital bed. Then she got a blanket and put it within easy reach in case Jazz got chilly. When she sat down gingerly on the bed again, Jazz grabbed her hand.

"Stop trying to fix things and forget that guilt trip Vivienne put on you. Protecting us was her, not yours. Jazz let her hand go. "Yeah. Mostly I know. I mean..." Willa's voice trailed off as she twisted her hands together.

When Willa sniffed a couple of times, Jazz reached for the box of tissues and handed them to her. They'd never discussed the, not in such direct terms. Jazz knew Willa felt guilty for years. At some point, in anger, Jazz had let her. More proof that Jazz had inherited more of Vivienne than she wanted. Yet distance and maturity helped Jazz grow past such bitterness.

"I wanted out of foster care and to live with Vivienne again. You wanted Miss Ruby and Mr. Elton to adopt you." Jazz could have added that unlike Willa, she'd held onto the fantasy that Vivienne would be a caring mother. "What we went through affected us in different ways. Let it go at that. Okay?"

"Yeah," Willa said, her voice muffled by a wad of tissues. She looked at Jazz as she dabbed her eyes.

"You want a big sloppy hug, don't you?"

Willa's bottom lip trembled. "Uh-huh."

"Let's get this outta your system." Jazz opened her arms.

Willa sniffed once and then wrapped Jazz in a tight embrace. She rocked Jazz from side to side. "Every time you get hurt, I hurt."

"Yeah, I know." The love radiating from Willa

comforted Jazz despite her rough exterior

Willa's parents peeped around the door. Both made cooing noises as they came in and joined in the hugging. Seconds later, MiMi came in to put her arms around as many of them all as possible.

"This is so wonderful," MiMi said in weepy voice.

After a while, Jazz extricated herself from the human clump of emotion. "I need some air y'all."

"Sorry, right. You're hurt." Willa stepped away along with the others.

"I'm so happy to see you girls getting along," Mama Ruby said between snuffles. She took a deep breath and let it out, one hand over her heart.

Papa Elton beamed at MiMi, Willa, and Jazz. "Yes, real nice. Don't give me that look, Jazzmonetta. Family is the most important thing any of us got."

"Yes sir," Jazz mumbled. She darted a warning glance at her when Willa started to smirk at her obedient response.

Godfrey Higgins pushed through the door. He paused when he saw Jazz wasn't alone. "Hello everyone. Sorry to intrude on family time. Jazz, I mean Ms. Vaughn, I need to discuss some business with you."

"Can't it wait? My sister has been through a bad few hours," Willa said ice in her voice.

"I think we should discuss it now. But if it might affect your health..." "If whatever you want to talk about brought you across town to my sick room, you better come in and spill it," Jazz said.

"Ahem, of course, if I didn't think it was important... By the way, I'm sorry you were hurt. Keith called me about this latest, um, incident." Higgins strode in, his leather portfolio under one arm.

"Ruby, we better get back to check on Jazz's club

and our place," Papa Elton said. He gave his wife a silent message with a slight nod.

Mama Ruby gazed steadily at the lawyer. "What?"

"I think we should be going now," Papa Elton said, putting more emphasis in his tone.

"Right, yeah." Mama Ruby blinked as though being pulled away didn't sit too well. Still she smiled at Jazz. "I'm going to check in with your employees this afternoon. I'm honored you trust me to handle your business."

"Hey, you've got a couple years more experience than me running a restaurant and lounge," Jazz replied. "Thanks for offering to help."

"Anytime, baby. Now if you need us, just holler," Mama Ruby answered. She shot a sharp glance at Higgins.

"Nice meeting you folks." Higgins tugged at his silk tie.

"Uh-huh," Mama Ruby said.

Papa Elton opened the door and caught his wife by the arm. His booming voice still carried even as he tried to whisper. "What was that about?"

Willa crossed her arms and waited. MiMi went around the bed to sit on the small sofa. Both women gazed at the lawyer with interest. Higgins adjusted his tie a second time and cleared his throat.

"This is about your night club, so maybe we should discuss this in private." Higgins spoke to Jazz, but glanced at Willa twice as he spoke.

"They know about the contract with Ames for investment money. Well mostly to get my ass out of jail. So what's goin' on?" Jazz said.

"Ames is concerned about the latest series of events. He's seeing a pattern that might affect the, er, value of his investment." Higgins stopped to let his words settle in.

"Yeah, but he signed on the line just like I did. So he's got to wear his big boy pants and deal with it," Jazz retorted.

"Of course the area is still very desirable. But he's not sure your name associated with the business isn't a liability. Ames has other business partners to consider, and they might get skittish given the media coverage of your exploits." Higgins sat straight.

"Skip the big build up and get to why you're here," Willa broke in.

Higgins didn't look at her, but focused on Jazz. "There are two relevant clauses in the contract about the current owner not harming the business. One includes putting Candy Girls at risk for civil liability. The other refers to criminal activity."

"Morality clauses in a contract with a strip? You got to be freaking kidding," Willa sputtered. She turned to Jazz. "I told you not to sign that damn thing."

"Let me freaking remind you, this is my damn business. I didn't plan to be accused of murder and I needed the money." Jazz slapped the bed sheet to get Higgins' nervous attention away from Willa and back to her. "What civil liability?"

Higgins pulled papers from his portfolio. "Ms. Lorraine Taylor is has filed a lawsuit because she was injured on your property and another one saying you defamed her. And a third one as well, a wrongful death action on behalf of the minor children of Ms. Kyeisha Lathers."

"I could strangle that..."

MiMi sprang up at light speed and clamped a hand over Jazz's mouth. "We're in enough trouble."

Chapter 15

Four hours later, Jazz, under much protest, had been installed in Willa's guest bedroom. She'd tried to fight back, but fatigue and muscle relaxers made Jazz less of a fighter. Plus the news Higgins had brought contributed to an overwhelming sense of defeat. Although Jazz felt she'd draw strength from being on her home turf, Willa's steel will won. MiMi sided with her big sister. When the nurse came in with the discharge instructions, Willa had taken them with smooth efficiency. MiMi packed up the few items Jazz had, her torn clothes from the night at Grown Folks. Dressed in comfortable sweat pants and a sweat shirt, Jazz was whisked into Willa's SUV and to her home. Jazz glanced around. The cool shades of green and pale yellow did sooth her nerves. But mostly, it was the drugs. Willa paced around setting an already perfect room in order.

"He knew. The slimy snake set you up so he and his buddy could get their greasy hands on your property," Willa fumed. She placed a basket of healthy snacks and bottled water in easy reach for Jazz.

"You need to calm down. Have some of my shit." Jazz grinned as she held up her bottle of pills.

"You sound like a drug dealer," Willa scolded. She took the bottle from Jazz and put them back on the night stand. "It wasn't a coincidence Ames took an interest in your business. Higgins watched the news and pounced." Willa slapped her hands causing Jazz to start.

"Standard clause, girl. Chill. Trying to protect his investment. Isn't that what your high powered attorney friend said?" Jazz reminded her. Brad had been Willa's employer before she left to take over Crown Protection.

Mikayla burst into the room without warning. She threw her back pack onto a chair and bounced on the bed next to Jazz. "Auntie Jazz, it's awesome having you down the hall from me."

Seconds later, Anthony strode in and gave Jazz a kiss on the forehead. "Glad you're okay."

"Thanks big man." Jazz patted her nephew's face before he stood straight again.

Mikayla wiggled closer to Jazz. "Are you going to live with us?"

"H... I mean, no sweetie. I'll just be here *overnight*," Jazz said and cut a glance at her sister.

"Aw, I was hoping you'd stay. You're fun even if you don't like kids." Mikayla giggled when Jazz tickled her in response to their inside joke.

"Lawd have mercy, but you're such a pain in the butt." Jazz pretended to scowl at her as they tussled.

"Little girl, get yourself off that bed. Jazz is still bruised up." Willa waved a hand motioning Mikayla to move.

"I'm fine. Besides, hugs from a favorite niece are better than any old medicine a doctor could give." Jazz smiled at Mikayla and took Anthony's large hand.

"Uh-huh. Don't think you'll get out of doing your homework, Mikayla. Go put your things away. I have snacks set out. In thirty minutes, you should have cleaned up, eaten, and have your head in a book," Willa ordered.

"But Mama, I'm in honors class. I'm always doing extra work and..." Mikayla stopped talking under the scrutiny of her mother.

"I have the list of your assignments," Willa said. She pointed to the door. "We'll see you at dinner."

"Yes, ma'am." Mikayla slid from the bed and grabbed her backpack. She left with a dejected end of the world expression.

"I'm going back to band practice. I just came to drop the sprout off since grandmamma couldn't pick her up. I should be back by dinner at six or six thirty. But first, I'll grab a snack to go." Anthony waved and strode out again.

"Bye, and be careful. He hardly waits to let me get it out," Willa complained.

"He's a man, and they don't like being babied." Jazz covered a yawn with the back of one hand. "And no, I'm not going to take a short nap."

"About our conversation at the hospital, I apologize. That was my clumsy attempt to... I don't know." Willa hung up a new soft terry cotton robe in a closet, also over Jazz's objection.

"Speaking of babying..." Jazz raised both arched eyebrows at her. "If you show up with any more clothes for me, we're going to fight."

Willa stopped fussing about the room. She faced Jazz. "You're right. I need to remember that you've been making your own decisions since you were fourteen. Anyway, like I was saying about back at the hospital."

"Stop with the guilt and trying too hard. I made my own life, which I kinda like by the way.

Well, minus the former acquaintances trying to kill me take everything I own, and send me to jail for murder . Other than that, life is fabulous," Jazz said with a snort.

"I wouldn't be surprised if Higgins isn't in on trying to snatch Candy Girls. I'm going to dig deep on him until we even know his great-granny's shoe size. Pisses me off so much I want to hit somebody." Willa scowled.

"Hey Anthony, your mama wants you," Jazz yelled. "Girl, I've been beat on enough in the past thirty-six hours, so don't look at me."

Willa burst into laughter. Soon they were both rolling on the bed giggling out the tension they'd both been under. Anthony and Mikayla had taken turns peeking into the room, shaking their heads, and then leaving.

"Damn, we used to have fun those times we'd go out." Willa wiped her eyes and fanned her face.

"Yeah, I know all your dirty secrets about being a bad, bad girl." Jazz wiggled her eyebrows at her big sister.

"I sure as hell couldn't keep up with you," Willa shot back and they started laughing again. "Seriously, we have to take care of Higgins."

"You know a hit man? Cause if you don't, I could..." Jazz used her right hand to point like a pistol.

Willa glanced over her shoulder sharply and jumped to her feet. She closed the bedroom door. "Shut up with the gangsta jokes. The kids might hear us and think you're for real.

"I'm only half joking. Yeah, I thought about him

coming to the jail with that contract. But to be honest, I had my back against a hard wall. I would have needed help eventually," Jazz added to head off Willa's complaint. "Putting your house and business on the line was a dumb idea."

"Gee, you're welcome. You must be getting better," Willa quipped. Then she frowned again. "I talked to Cedric, and he's sure your defense lawyer is legit. In fact, he's taking all the right actions to prepare for your trial."

"Well that's good to know. Saving Candy Girls won't help if I'm in prison until I'm seventy years old." Jazz rubbed her temples to ward off a headache.

"Nah, in your fifties if you get twenty-five years for second degree murder," Willa murmured as she gazed off in thought. Her paralegal training kicked in.

"Wonderful, I'll sure sleep better tonight." Jazz lay against the fluffy pillows Willa had piled up for her.

Anthony knocked and came in. "Moms, a cop is here to see Aunt Jazz."

"I'll take care of this." Willa stood with a scowl. She stomped past Anthony.

"Feeling sorry for the dude," Anthony joked. "See ya. I got to go."

Jazz blew him a kiss. "Bye sweetie."

Once Anthony withdrew, Jazz was tempted to go watch her sister in action. Where Jazz's temper was all fire, Willa turned cold as ice. She could tongue lash folks without a cuss word or raising her voice. Vivienne used to say Willa would get her butt kicked faster than Jazz ever would. Yet the comfy bed kept Jazz in place as if the memory foam mattress was a magnet. When the door eased open she was stunned to see Don. His left arm was in a sling. When he entered the room, his gait seemed stiff.

"Your sister made sure I knew this visit couldn't last longer than thirty minutes. Forty if I don't upset you."

He leaned down and gently kissed her on the lips. Jazz had no memory of lifting her face to accept it either. When she wrapped her arms around his neck, both sighed. T He pulled up the upholstered chair in the room until it was closer to the bed and sat down. He held both her hands in his.

"Thanks for coming. Wait a minute. I'm pretty sure you're not supposed to be driving," Jazz said.

"Nyla dropped me off. I'll get a cab home from here."

"Your ex-wife drives you to see another woman. Well I'll be damned. Thought I'd met some smooth operators, but you're in a class of your own, playa." Jazz raised an eyebrow at him.

"We're still friends, and not only because of the kids. We've known each other since high school. Nyla's a good person." Don wore a half-smile at the look Jazz gave him.

"So I keep hearing. Practically invented peace and love according to some sources," Jazz wisecracked. She fidgeted with the embroidered edge of the soft, green and beige pretty bedspread.

"We're not getting back together, Jazz. We work great as friends and parents. We're a ten car pile-up as husband and wife," Don said with a laugh.

"Hey, you don't owe me any explaining. None of my business," Jazz said and tried not to look as pleased as she felt. She heard the truth in her voice. A woman who was still hanging on wouldn't agree to drive her ex to see his current lover.

"I'm going to put Armand in a choke hold for talkin'

trash to you," Don said. "Don't bother to tell me. I can pretty much guess what he said."

"You got the lecture on staying away from me and how you should be with Nyla. Right?"

"He talked to Nyla, too. She said he looked so hurt when she started laughing at the idea. She told him, 'One bullet is no reason to ruin a good divorce'." Don burst out laughing. When Jazz giggled he squeezed her hand.

"So we're good?" Jazz squeezed back. "Nobody said we weren't."

His expression turned serious. "Shit is still goin' down. Byron says somebody tried to break in Candy Girls and your house twice. The alarms scared them off. He's got them on video, but their faces were covered." ."

"Any marks or tattoos?"

"Both wore long sleeves, but one had something on the back of a hand. Looked like roman numerals, but it's not real clear," Don said. "Mean something?"

"Yeah. Some Latin gangs get those in prison." Jazz frowned. Another link to Filipe's boys.

"Damn, you're right. I did a sketch. I'll get one of my buddies at the station to run it. These muscle relaxers must have my brain fuzzy."

"You would have put it together," Jazz said with a smile. She was getting used to thinking of them as a team. She had to decide if that was good or bad. Don's voice broke into more musing on the subject of them as a couple.

"I can't find any noise about Filipe pulling strings from behind bars. So this is one of his crew making a mark for himself maybe. But why break into your place? You'd tell me if there was more, right?" Don stared at her hard.

For a split second Jazz considered spilling about the missing money MiMi so desperately wanted to find. "I can't think of anything."

She didn't need to pull Don into anything more with Filipe. Besides, his good cop instinct might lead him to calling up the feds and leading a joint investigation. Anyway, it was technically MiMi's money to hear her tell it. Though Jazz felt she'd earned at least a few hundred thousand for putting up with Filipe's psycho ass.

"Okay." Don gazed off into space, his mind working.

Jazz didn't want him thinking too hard or long about her answer. After all, Don was no dummy. "Filipe was the brains, so I'll bet some of his guys are freelancing to make ends meet. Lorraine could have hired them."

"I don't get why though. And another thing, and don't get mad at him," Don said pointing a finger at Jazz.

"What?"

"Byron, um, entertained a pretty lady in the storeroom one night," Don said.

"I figure he's used that cot more than once. He's fixed up that room so it looks like a hook-up spot." Jazz chuckled.

"Compete with a compact player and soft lights. He's even got several boxes that he covers with a table cloth. Damned if it doesn't look like a coffee table," Don replied with a grin.

"His girlfriend will wring his neck one day. I'll talk to him. We don't need the drama right now."

"Here's the thing. Last night she showed up at the

club. As usual they ended up going to his spot. He went out to check on things, and when he got back, she was gone. He caught her searching your office," Don said.

"Trying to get in the safe?" Jazz frowned.

"When he walked in she was trying to pry open the file cabinet against the wall. Guess she didn't have time to find the safe."

Jazz stared into space, thinking. "Um."

"I guess Lorraine or Cleavon figure throwing everything they've got at you will work faster. When is your trial date?"

"Phillips says they've got more discovery and pre-trial hearings, but it could be in November." Jazz rose from the bed with help from Don. "I want some air. I've been cooped up in four walls too much lately."

"Sure babe."

He walked beside her until they got to Willa's large den. A sliding glass door opened onto a covered patio. Heat from the May afternoon sun beamed down, a taste of the scorching Louisiana heat that was to come. Willa's backyard was predictably well kept. A large magnolia tree shaded one corner of the lawn. The rest was grass suitable for kids to play without barriers. Several large potted plants decorated each end of the patio. Don helped Jazz settle into one of five chairs around a round glass table. Then he eased down in the one next to her.

"Nice day," he said.

"Did you have a house like this once with your wife?" Jazz looked at him.

"Not this big on our income. She stayed at home for a while, but we couldn't afford it after the second baby. But yeah, we had a yard in front and back." Don glanced around. The roofs of nearby houses could be seen over the wooden privacy fence. "Nice neighborhood."

"Right place to have a family. But I couldn't stand it for long. What I'm trying to say is..."

Don held up a palm. "I used to think white–picket-fenced suburbia would cleanse me after days on the job. Seeing the worst in people leaves a stain, ya know? I mean the blood, guts, downright brutality soaks in deep.. Nyla couldn't take the darkness and, I couldn't leave it at the door like she wanted. So if you're asking if I'm going to regret replacing that life, the answer is no."

"I kinda know what you mean. Certain things change you in ways you might not like, but... it is what it is." Jazz gave a short laugh. "Something is seriously wrong with us, man."

"Nyla says some people are dumped into bad stuff, and some, like me, deal with it to hold back the night. As long as a person doesn't become the darkness, then they'll be okay. Always understand the line between living with it and *being* it."

Don and Jazz gazed at the lovely normal life like tourists in a place other than home. Both sat content to let the only sound be the breeze rustling leaves. Jazz put on a lopsided grin. She playfully tapped him on his massive bicep.

"Damn, you're gonna make me like your ex-wife. As if I'm not screwed up enough," Jazz wisecracked.

Don laughed hard until he winced in pain. Willa joined, and a minor tug of war ensued. Don surrendered to Willa's logic that calling a cab was a waste when she could drive him home. Once they were gone, Jazz continued to sort through the puzzle that her life had become.

"Lorraine has somebody trying to break in? That

doesn't make any sense," Jazz murmured as she dozed off.

* * *

The next day Jazz woke up in hell. Willa had flat out refused to drive her home, insisting that Jazz stay and be taken care of properly. When Willa's aunt came into the guest bedroom with a tray of breakfast, Jazz tried shrinking under the covers. It didn't work. Aunt Ametrine knew she was still there. The fastidious church lady was in full force.

"I made you a bowl of grits, fried an egg the way you like it, and buttered up some whole wheat toast. Willa says you like coffee strong enough to make the spoon stand up in the cup." Aunt Ametrine set the tray down on the chaise lounge across from the bed. "Let me help you into the bathroom so you can wash up. I set clean underwear and another sweat suit out for you."

Jazz blinked at her in horror. She waved away the sturdy hand offered to her. "I can take care of myself."

"Nonsense, you might fall. The most deadly accidents happen in the bathroom. I read that in a magazine just the other day." Aunt Ametrine expertly helped Jazz walk across the hardwood floor to the pretty tile of the bathroom. "But I understand. Don't try to stand in that shower too long."

"Thanks," Jazz managed to get out.

Aunt Ametrine kept up a stream of advice through the closed door. The sound of the shower didn't deter her. After five "Are you okay in there?" shouts, Jazz gave up the notion she'd leave. She got dressed in the fresh clothes and went back to the bedroom.

"The food is still hot. This is a warming tray. See? I

just unplug it and now I can put it across your lap. Oh, it won't burn you," Aunt Ametrine said the second Jazz reappeared.

She explained the wonders of the tray she brought from home. Then she went on to tell Jazz more than she wanted to know about her husband's surgery. Of course being the good Christian wife she was, Aunt Ametrine nursed him to a full recovery. Jazz wondered if the poor dude was still sane. When Willa showed up, Jazz wanted to hug her neck and beg to be rescued. Her older sister's eyes gleamed with suppressed mirth.

"You feeling okay this morning?" Willa pursed her lips at the look Jazz gave her.

Aunt Amtetrine piped up. "She's moving around real good. A bit slow, but no wonder after being beat like rug. Bless her heart."

"Yeah, wonderful," Jazz replied in a dry tone.

When Aunt Ametrine stared at her and then the plate for several seconds, Jazz picked up the fork. She pushed it into her mouth. Buttery goodness warmed her tongue. The grits tasted delicious. For the first time, Jazz realized how hungry she was. As Aunt Ametrine had said, the egg was cooked the way she liked it. When Jazz sipped the coffee, the rich taste made her sigh with pleasure.

"I'm glad you like it. Now Willa, if you have work at the office, I can stay here with Jazz all day." Aunt Ametrine turned to Jazz. "I retired six months ago. Thirty years working for the state as an administrative assistant. My last boss was the Assistant Secretary of..."

"Thanks, but Willa's taking me home on her way to the office," Jazz broke in before she got Aunt Ametrine's full career history.

"No I'm not," Willa replied.

Jazz glared at her. "We agreed I only needed to stay overnight."

"I have to agree with Willa, baby." Aunt Ametrine vanished into the bathroom. She emerged with Jazz's dirty clothes and towels. "I'm going to put fresh towels in. Be right back."

The second her solid steps moved down the hall, Jazz blurted, "Get me outta here."

"Don't be silly. Aunt Ametrine loves taking care of people." Willa sat down on the chair. "Seriously, she's a kind-hearted person. You have to admit she can cook."

Jazz remembered the food and tasted more egg. After savoring rich flavor chased down by the best coffee she'd had in a long time, Jazz sighed. "Damn, I can't argue with you on that. Now if she'd just stick some of this in her mouth and shut up."

Willa burst out laughing and then covered her mouth. "Stop it, she might hear you."

"Once I finish eating you *will* take me home." Jazz scooped up more buttery grits.

"Cedric is holding down the office, so I don't need to be there this morning. You should stay another night, but listen." Willa wore her familiar determined expression. "We need to get onto this contract business."

"I signed the thing of my own free will. End of discussion. There's nothing I can do." Jazz wiped her mouth with the checked cotton napkin on the tray.

"I've gone over the clauses and done research. Brad says we have several options to make Ames back off." Jazz soaked up the last bit of runny yolk with toast. After she'd swallowed it and more coffee, she put down the cup. "You want to go after Higgins and Ames on this, don't ya?"

"Sister, this is my kind of fight. Sitting across a desk or in the courtroom, punch and jab with the facts until they're dizzy." Willa wore a fierce smile.

"Then do your thing," Jazz said "Wish we had more ammunition on my criminal case."

Aunt Ametrine bustled in. "I started a load of laundry. I can give the floor a sound dust mopping while it goes through the cycle. Ah, so you ate breakfast. Good girl."

"That was some real good cooking, ma'am," Jazz said.

"Thank you. And stop this 'ma'am' nonsense. I'm Aunt Ametrine," she replied briskly with a smile. "I was listening to the news. They brought up the investigation into Kyeisha Lathers' murder."

"Aunt Ametrine--" Willa frowned at her aunt.

Aunt Ametrine faced Willa sharply. "You don't have to tell me Jazz didn't kill her. Jazz has her faults. Like shaking her half-naked backside in front of men for money, or having criminals for boyfriends. But murder? Nonsense! Now don't you worry, sugar. I have you on the prayer list at my church. We're gonna pray old Satan back to hell."

Jazz gazed at her slack-jawed and dumbfounded before she found her voice. "I, uh, I don't know what to say."

Aunt Ametrine beamed at her. "You're welcome, darlin'. Now, I'll let you two talk. Back in a little while to get that tray." She left humming a tune. By the time she made it to the kitchen, Aunt Ametrine was singing a gospel song at full volume.

"I need to get outta here," Jazz blurted out.

Willa cleared the dishes from the tray. "Oh keep quiet and listen. I drew up this letter firing Higgins. You can't trust him to act in your interest. And here is a letter you should send to Ames disputing his grab for your property."

Jazz signed both. "I can't pay back the money Ames put up."

"You don't have to. Nothing in the contract says his investment has to be repaid. What is an investment? A risk the investor takes on a venture," Willa said, answering her question before Jazz could speak.

"Makes sense, I guess."

Willa slipped the signed letters into an envelope. "I'll happily deliver the letter to Higgins personally this morning. Now, is it okay if Brad's associate Zachary Miles becomes your new lawyer?"

"You asked first. Usually you just order me around."

"Of course you should make the decision. We're talking about a business you sacrificed to build. I think you should fight, but it's your call." Willa nodded.

"So this Miles has experience representing ex-strippers who are charged with murder, and who signed a contract for bail money but didn't read the fine print?" Jazz raised both eyebrows.

"Absolutely," Willa replied with a grin. "Seriously, I wouldn't recommend Zach if he wasn't good."

"Then let's do it," Jazz said. "Now about the murder charge..."

"I set up a meeting with Phillips for tomorrow. It's time for an update face to face. Over the phone isn't enough. I want to set eyes on the guy, read his body language." Willa stood. "Mama Ruby says your place is running like a top. She's impressed with Byron. No so much with Tyretta. How good a friend is she?"

Jazz got out of bed with stiff movements. She

crossed to the plate and grabbed the last corner of buttered toast. "We go back a ways. Why?"

"Mama Ruby says something is off about her. I trust Mama's instincts. Maybe we need to run a check on her." Willa tapped the envelope in her right hand against one thigh.

"Don't be doing backgrounds on my friends. We all have a past, so you could be tied up a while," Jazz said with a laugh.

"If you say so. Anyway, I'm headed to the office." Willa turned to leave.

"You ain't leaving me here with the church lady on steroids." Jazz started to say more when a burst of "He's An On Time God" echoed down the hall.

"You need at least another day of rest. If I take you home, you'll be in the club working the minute I drive off. Byron has things under control.." Willa tucked the envelop under one arm.

Before Jazz could protest, a wave of dizziness hit. She stumbled a little. Sore spots all over reminded her she'd hit the pavement hard. Willa grabbed her by one arm and guided Jazz until she sat down in the chair.

"Must be those pain pills," Jazz said.

"Uh-huh. Look, you don't have to stay in bed all day. But you should relax. Let us wait on you for another day at least." Willa put the tray on the dresser. Then she straightened up the bed linens until it was neatly made. "I'll be home about four o'clock."

"No, come get me at lunch time. I'll be fine by then," Jazz insisted.

Willa leaned down and kissed her cheek. She handed Jazz the remote for a twenty-five inch flat screen in the bedroom. "Watch some television. I'll see you later."

Jazz wanted to debate the topic of her staying longer, but Willa hustled out too fast. Besides, the cushiony soft chair caressed Jazz's aching body. She turned on the television, but her eyes soon drifted closed. Aunt Ametrine started a second gospel song with just as much energy.

"Willa is gonna pay for this," Jazz murmured with her eyes still closed. "She's got a good voice though."

Chapter 16

The next day, Wednesday, dawned bright and cheery. The view outside her defense attorney's window framed blue skies and the tops of oak trees. Keith Phillips had an office with three other attorneys downtown. The stone building was nestled in a historic neighborhood called Beauregard Town. They waited for Phillips seated in dark green leather chairs around along oval conference table of highly polished dark wood Sunshine and a chic decor clashed with the reason Jazz was there.

"Y'all have a seat. We have coffee set up." The efficient blonde legal secretary gave them a professional smile before she vanished.

"Thanks," Willa said to thin air. "She moves fast that one."

"She's a pro, didn't stare at me. I'm sure she's read my file. Must be novel having a black stripper accused of murder in these fancy walls." Jazz got up and went to the carafe on an equally polished credenza against one wall. She poured the strong brew into a china cup.

"Have some. Smells like the good stuff."

"No thanks. Phillips represented that white socialite who shot her ex-husband in the shower. Then she drove to New Orleans for a cocktail party. Turned out she didn't take talk of divorce kindly. Next, he represented the man who set fire to his gay lover's house. The lover was asleep inside with another younger man." Willa snorted. "That's not the half of it. So I'm pretty sure his secretary is shock proof."

"Damn," Jazz whispered. Jazz took a sip of coffee and was rewarded with rich flavor.

Phillips strode in. He put down the folder he carried and shook hands with them . "Good morning, Ms. Vaughn, Mrs. Crown. I see Leslie has coffee available. Excellent."

"Colombian blend. Very nice," Jazz said with a nod.

"Glad you like it. Let's get down to it ladies. I have excellent news. Our pretrial motions have gone well. The judge ruled that the prosecution can't bring up Filipe Perez or the murder investigation of your late husband, Mrs. Crown."

"My late *ex*-husband," Willa corrected him.

"Right. Unfortunately, they can introduce evidence of your past conflicts with the victim." Phillips gazed at Jazz expectantly.

"My motive. Except I got the club, so why would I need to kill Kyeisha? That doesn't make sense." Jazz frowned at him.

"Yeah, and juries want the motive to make sense. You had nothing to gain by killing her. Ms. Lathers remained loyal to Lorraine Taylor. Both were furious you ended up with the property on McClelland too. But, they have a back-up theory of the crime." Phillips wore a serious expression.

"Which is?"

"She had knowledge that could cause you trouble. The assistant DA hasn't fleshed out the theory yet. They're still digging. What I need from you is anything from your past they can use against us." Phillips folded his hands, a platinum wedding band glistened in the light. "This isn't the time to be embarrassed or secretive."

Jazz looked at Willa. Her sister cleared her throat. "I wasn't involved in any kind of crimes if that's what you're asking. I wouldn't have trusted Kyeisha if I had been. She has, had, a big mouth. Plus, I knew she was tight with Lorraine."

Phillips turned his razor sharp attention to Willa. Clearly, like any good attorney, he read body language very well. "Mrs. Crown, you'd like to add something?"

"Well there's..."

Jazz cut her off. "Lorraine used to let shady stuff go on at the bar when she had it. Maybe Kyeisha assumed I kept it going."

"I see." Phillips continued to study Willa.

"We should tell him about the money," Willa said.

"Don't get stupid," Jazz hissed under her breath.

"I'm not going into a case with one hand tied behind my back. Make up your mind, ladies. Tell me everything or find another lawyer." Phillips relaxed in his chair as if to say he was fine either way.

"There's talk on the street that Filipe has hidden money," Willa said. She glanced at Jazz.

Jazz sighed. "Shit. It could be money, drugs, guns, or all three. Some think I know Filipe's secrets."

"But there's also chatter that Jazz may have stolen his property," Willa added. She squinted at Jazz. "Don't give me that look. Sounds to me like the DA's investigators or the police have heard something."

"Mrs. Crown is on target. Did Kyeisha Lathers threaten you, Ms. Vaughn?" Phillips pulled a legal note pad to him and started writing.

"She pretended to know more than she did. I could tell she was fishing the first night she came to see me. I told her I didn't know what the hell she was talking about, which is the truth. Not that anybody seems to care. My guess? Cleavon sent her. He thought they could scare the information out of me," Jazz said.

"Cleavon..." Phillips glanced up at her.

"Bennett, her latest boyfriend. He was a murder suspect himself until recently. The next time Kyeisha showed up was that night at the club. She was begging me to help her, which is crazy. We weren't buddies for sure. Somebody did a number on her, and she was trying to get away."

"Does Cleavon Bennett have gang connections?" Phillips looked from Jazz to Willa.

"That's like asking if Louisiana has mosquitoes. He's a thug from way back," Willa said.

"A family tradition. His daddy, uncles, brothers, cousins, you name it," Jazz added.

Phillips tapped the pen on the tablet. "So he could have some connection to Filipe Perez."

"We're checking right now," Willa put in before Jazz could reply.

"Give me everything you find. We need to build at least one credible alternative theory. Fortunately with Bennett's and Ms. Lather's histories, we've got something to work with."

"Cedric, my chief of operations, will be in touch soon," Willa replied. She looked at Jazz. "I never thought having shady friends would be an asset one day."

"See? All those lectures for nothin'," Jazz shot back.

"Now to another subject. Godfrey Higgins called me last night. Is firing him relate to your case?" Phillips raised an eyebrow at Jazz.

"Not unless your buddy wants you to either ditch me or throw me to the dogs." Jazz stared at him steadily.

"Godfrey Higgins and I aren't 'buddies'. We've networked at local social functions. He's referred several cases to me over the past four years or so."

Jazz's eyes narrowed. "What did he want then?"

"He wanted me to talk you into reconsidering terminating his services. I told him that was not my concern. Your business with him will not affect how I represent you. I handle my cases as I see fit, for the good of my clients," Phillips said firmly.

Jazz exchanged a brief glance with her sister. She nodded. "Okay, let's keep goin' then."

They discussed details about possible defense strategies and a trial date. Thirty minutes later, Jazz and Willa were driving away. The Bluetooth connection in Willa's SUV buzzed. The caller ID on the dashboard flashed Cedric's name. She hit the button to talk hands free.

"Hi, babe. What's up?" Willa said.

"I've found some interesting information. Meet me at the office," Cedric replied.

"I'll be there in about forty minutes or so. I have to drop Jazz off first," Willa said.

"Okay, bye." His name vanished when Cedric ended the call.

"No, you'll be there a lot sooner. I'm not getting

out of this car. Save yourself time and aggravation. Keep driving." Jazz pressed against the leather seat to emphasize her determination.

"If somebody hadn't already done it, I'd beat your behind right now," Willa mumbled. She drove south to her office instead of to north Baton Rouge where Jazz lived.

* * *

Jazz wondered if they'd get a ticket or at least be pulled over. Willa drove through yellow traffic signals and exceeded the speed limit. She'd honked at least four times at silly drivers observing traffic laws. Jazz glanced at her, but said nothing. Fifteen minutes later they arrived at Willa's building. They went straight to the conference room of her office suite. Cedric was already there with a mug of coffee and his android tablet. Ten minutes into his summary, Willa blinked hard at him.

"Let me get this straight, Lorraine's son in Angola has ties to Filipe?"

"At some point, most of the local thugs did business with Filipe," Cedric said with a shrug. "So it's logical to conclude they knew each other."

"Filipe hung out at Candy Girls. It's where we met, remember," Jazz said. She drummed her tapered fingernails on the table's smooth wooden surface.

"Yeah, but all kinds of gangsters and crooks hung out there. I still don't get the connection." Willa frowned in concentration.

"Cleavon grew up with Lorraine's kids. He even use to date her daughter," Cedric said.

"Even I didn't know that much. Of course, I've been

too busy staying alive to investigate," Jazz joked. "Good work."

"Hey, it's what I do. Your friend the bartender at Grown Folks gave me the best lead. I talked to this girl who was friends with Lorraine's daughter in high school. Next best thing since I couldn't find the daughter," Cedric said with a frown. "Netta lost track of her."

"She went to nursing school in Houston. Never came back. She married a fellow student and they moved to San Antonio," Jazz said. "Lorraine and her youngest son used to talk trash about her. Said she got educated and uppity."

"Or maybe she wanted a different kind of life," Willa replied.

"I used to agree with her. I thought it was terrible she just dumped her family that way." Jazz shrugged when Willa glanced at her. "What?"

"Sometimes you have to cut ties to save your own life, Jazz." Willa looked at her hard.

Jazz knew Willa wasn't talking about Lorraine or her daughter. They'd had this argument about their own mother. Jazz clung to her despite all Vivienne had put them through. "Hell, she could at least call on holidays."

"Yeah, and when you keep in touch, they want something. But do they ever show any kind of concern for you? No. It's all about them, what they need or want." Willa balled both hands into fists.

Cedric reached over to cover them with one of his large hands. "Have some coffee."

"Right. This isn't about my mama issues," Willa said softly.

"So this friend remembers Cleavon and Lorraine's sons were buddies," Jazz put in to take them back to the subject.

"They were kids in the old neighborhood together. Zion City is still a rough place," Cedric continued. "As teenagers they got in trouble together. This friend didn't know much else. She went to community college and got out like Lorraine's daughter."

"Cleavon hung around the club. Lorraine used to let her boys drink before they were legal. Yeah, model parent," Jazz said when Willa grimaced. They all fell silent. "Okay, try on this theory. Baton Rouge has these neighborhood gangs, disorganized. Then Filipe comes to town."

"Filipe is from California by way of Mexico, right? He knows about running a gang with structure. He's the man with the plan. But he's always smart. He doesn't go to war with the locals. He shows them how to make more money." Cedric nodded. "Naturally there's still some resentment that simmers."

"Filipe goes to prison. Lorraine's oldest two end up in prison, the youngest dead. Cleavon decides he can make his move to become the next kingpin?" Jazz barked scornful laugher. "He doesn't have the brains. But then, neither did Lorraine's sons. Or I read them wrong."

"They could have had more power in Filipe's hierarchy than you realized. Think back. Did Filipe have many meetings at Candy Girls?" Cedric asked.

"Nah, it was mostly pleasure not business." Jazz winked at them.

"No details. Please," Willa said and rolled her eyes.

"I don't kiss and tell," Jazz wisecracked. Then she grew serious. "Filipe's closest boys were Latino, two of his cousins. Their meetings weren't at Candy Girls. He may have let one of Lorraine's boys think they were important. That sounds like Filipe. He's always ten steps ahead of anyone else."

"Lorraine's sons figure out they're small fry in the big picture?" Cedric rubbed his chin in thought.

"Here's another question." Willa sat forward, both elbows on the table. "Is it a coincidence that one son wound up dead and the other in prison?"

"You mean they might have started showing signs of taking on Filipe. Is it a coincidence Filipe ended up in prison?" Jazz looked from Willa to Cedric.

"Damn, that's going deep." Cedric fell back in his chair.

Willa glanced over her shoulder even though the door was closed. "But you nudged him into that position, right? I mean when we were trying to figure out who killed Jack a couple of years ago."

"All I did was place some nuggets out there for Don and Miller to follow-up on. I told them enough to get him picked up. I figured two days tops he'd be in. He always carried a gun," Jazz said.

"He's a felon in possession of a weapon," Cedric put in.

"But then some dude rolled on him. The police got onto one or two of his business ventures." Jazz looked at them. "I told Miller the truth when he questioned me. I never knew or wanted to know details of Filipe's operation."

"You're saying Cleavon or maybe Lorraine's sons seized an opportunity? That might explain some things," Cedric said.

"But one son is dead. The other one is locked up for a long time. Why do any of them care about Jazz?" Willa frowned.

"A criminal enterprise is like any business. If

Cleavon wants to take over, he could use assets to establish his own operation. Most street crooks are small time, but he has bigger ambitions. And that's where you come in," Cedric said to Jazz.

"Cleavon thinks I know where Filipe has a stash of valuables. What a dumbass," Jazz retorted. She massaged the back of her neck. "I'm getting a damn headache thinking about these muthas."

"I told you to let me take you home. Okay, enough theories for one day." Willa stood. She raised a palm when Jazz opened her mouth. "Yes, I'll take you to your place. I got the message that you can't stand being around us for too long."

Jazz stood slowly. "The guilt trip won't work, so stuff it." Not that her sister listened. The price of a free ride courtesy was another lecture. Jazz didn't get pissed off though. She recognized the nervous energy beneath her sister's nagging. When Willa pulled up the short driveway leading to Jazz's apartment, she sighed.

"Try not to get punched, shot at, or accused of another murder until I see you again," Willa said.

"You never let me have any fun, mom." Jazz stuck her lip out in an exaggerated pout. She laughed when hissed a cuss word. "Hey, I'm gonna be okay. Byron will take over smothering me the minute you drive off."

"I already talked to him," Willa replied with a satisfied sniff.

As though he'd heard his name, Byron came out to the car. He and Tyretta helped Jazz climb the stairs to her apartment. Her fridge had food. A comfy fluffy robe and slippers were waiting for her.

"You guys are the best," Jazz said with a satisfied yawn. She went to her bedroom, changed and lay on the sofa.

"Me and Rochelle got some of your favorites. Nothing heavy," Byron said when Jazz started to speak. "Chyna whipped up some Chinese dishes. Rochelle made a big meatloaf. What you don't eat I will. Now all you gotta do is watch the movies I got set up for you. Lots of action adventure stuff you're gonna enjoy."

"Deal." Jazz rested her head. "Y'all don't have to hover. Go on back downstairs to the club. I'm good."

"Yeah. So what happened? I bet the cops picked up Lorraine. Those must have been her thugs." Tyretta chattered at high speed with more questions. She helped herself to a bowl of nuts. When she reached for the glass of iced tea Byron had set on the table, he scowled at her.

"What's wrong with you?" Byron rumbled.

"The salt in these cashews made me thirsty." Tyretta hissed at him through her teeth.

"You can have it. I'll get another," Jazz replied. She got up and went to the kitchen. She found a bottle of spring water. "Y'all sure taking care of me."

Jazz turned around. Byron stood looking at Tyretta. He wore a deceptively blank expression on his face. Tyretta continued a steady stream of commentary. Jazz honed reading people. Decoding body language had become a survival tool. At that moment, Byron radiated dislike for Tyretta.

"Go down and help out Rochelle, Tyretta," Jazz said.

"She doin' fine. Chyna is helping her." Tyretta stuffed another handful of cashews in her mouth.

Byron kept his tone casual as he turned away. He pressed buttons on Jazz's remote. "We got our usual good Thursday crowd again. The city closed down The Sweet Spot. Guess that's why. Anyway, she could use the help."

"I'm on a break. Got to catch up with my girl," Tyretta said, still chewing. "You're the big time second in command. You go help."

"You started breaking almost an hour ago. Sitting at the bar on your cell phone," Byron tossed over his shoulder.

"S'cuse me, she's my pal from way, way back. You been around for nothin' but a minute. Hell, I should be the assistant manager any damn way," Tyretta mumbled, but not so Jazz didn't hear her. When Jazz came around the sofa again, Tyretta had a friendly smile plastered on her face.

"He's right, Tyretta. Happy customers come back and spend more money. We sure as hell need the business," Jazz said mildly. She gave Tyretta a friendly tap on the shoulder. "We'll talk later. Promise."

"Okay, I'm leaving cause *you* asked me." Tyretta tossed a glare at Byron. When he seemed not to notice, she left in a huff.

Byron put the remote on the sofa. "I got you lined up with some good on-demand stuff for the next four hours. But the TV will be watching you. Bet you're worn out."

Jazz settled against the sofa cushions. She pulled a soft throw around her but didn't touch the remote. "Thanks. You wanna tell me what's up with you and Tyretta?"

"You know how she's always mouthin' off. Plus she's always lookin' to get outta work," Byron replied with a frown on his dark brown face.

"I know she can be a pain, but Tyretta stuck by me. She's one of the few that did after I got Candy Girls." Jazz eyed him. "Well?"

"I mean she's your good friend and all." Byron cleared his throat.

"Byron, I'm not gonna jump you for talkin' real about Tyretta. Like you said, I've known her a long time. I know what she can be like." Jazz grinned at him. "Tell it all."

"I don't know." Byron rubbed his jaw. "Now don't get mad. It's more than her mouth."

Jazz's gut instinct kicked in. She put down the bottle of spring water and sat at attention. "Meaning what?"

"A couple of times she left the back door open. She had volunteered to lock up, right? She played it off, but her excuse didn't sound real. One of those times is when somebody tried to break in. Maybe the other time, too. I don't remember because I wasn't thinkin' about it then."

"Could be a coincidence," Jazz's gut nudged her as if to say "Don't be stupid!"

"It's like she's watchin' and waitin' for something." Byron scratched his thick dark curls. "I don't know. Maybe I'm paranoid because of all the crap goin' down lately."

Jazz mentally shook free of his line of reasoning. Tyretta and she had been friends a long, long time. Their friendship had been tested by the split with Lorraine and her crew. "Tyretta isn't all that steady a worker on a good day. I'm thinking the stress is making her more of a pain. Maybe she's on guard for the same reason you are, Byron. She'll back down if you don't let her get away with shit."

"Yeah, you right. My damn nerves on edge. I sure as hell hope we get clear of all this drama soon." Byron put both hands on his waist.

"And make some money, if we can keep the thieves from stealing us dry," Jazz retorted. She relaxed again. "I keep asking myself, what are they looking for in here?"

"Lorraine's got to be behind it boss. It's all too neat that she's after us and we got break-ins." Byron blew out a breath and sat down to help her theorize.

"The street knows business was slow. I don't see her thinking her boys would take a big haul." Jazz sipped water absently.

"We got some nice sound equipment in here they could pawn. Then there's the liquor. Hell, she'd do anything to pay you back for owning what used to be hers." Byron grabbed a handful of nuts and munched. He turned on the television, but kept the volume low.

"Lorraine has been making big time moves against me. A murder set up, and getting the city to come after Candy Girls. Hiring crack heads to break in is penny ante shit for her now." Jazz started to sip from the bottle again, but paused to consider what she'd just said.

Byron glanced at her. "What you thinkin'?"

"Lorraine isn't acting like Lorraine," Jazz said softly.

"Huh?"

"The old Lorraine would have shown up here and called me out for a street fight. For real." Jazz sat up again. "I was wrong about her losing these properties because she was dumb. Lorraine had a plan. She's different now."

"Humph, I'm surprised she hasn't set the place on fire," Byron said with a grunt before throwing more nuts into his mouth.

"No way. Lorraine doesn't want the buildings burned down. Somebody tried to break in my house, and then tried to break in the club."

"Fools," Byron grumbled around chews.

"She wants, no she's desperate, to get at something around here somewhere. First, the health inspectors. That didn't work, she called the city on me. But that's gonna take too long. Next I get set up for killing Kyeisha. She's turning up the heat hoping I'll get out of this damn kitchen. That's gotta be it." Jazz stood up fast and started pacing. For the first time Jazz saw her way clear to a theory that made sense.

"Hey, hey, you better watch yourself. You ain't long out the hospital." Byron frowned at her with concern.

She winced at the pains from her bruises. The facts sank into mud, buried again. When she eased back onto the sofa, Byron sighed with relief. Lightheaded, Jazz pressed the still cold bottle of spring water to her throat. When he tried to her to eat something, Jazz waved him away.

"No food." She swallowed hard against the queasy feeling in her stomach.

"You lie down and stop thinking. I got your favorite video game set up if you get bored with the movies." Byron pointed to the wireless controller.

"Lorraine wants something in the club or here. You said that woman was searching my file cabinets," Jazz said faintly. She leaned her head against the sofa back.

"Lorraine's boy might think you have Filipe's stash." Byron clumped to the kitchen, his heavy black athletic shoes defying even her soft carpeting. He came back with a bottle of beer. "And none of this for you."

"Don't worry, I wasn't going to ask," Jazz replied. "Anyway, Filipe wouldn't have left anything with me. He's old school when it comes to letting women in his business. If his old gang thought he had, they'd have taken this place apart by now."

"Lorraine didn't know him like that. Lots of folks still talk about how y'all was so tight for a minute." Byron shrugged when Jazz squinted at him. "I'm just telling you the street gossip. Tyretta runnin' her mouth as much as anybody."

Jazz grimaced. "Maybe, but it sounds weak."

"Maybe Lorraine left something of value that belongs to her. It's something she don't want you to know is here," Byron tossed out with a wave of the beer bottle. Then he focused on the television again. One of his favorite Anime television series episodes had come on.

"She left a bunch of junk behind." Jazz slapped the sofa in frustration. "Damn it. I shouldn't have thrown away all her stuff. It's at the bottom of the landfill."

The furniture in the club and surplus crammed into the building that became Jazz's home was old. Most of it was either rickety or outright broken. Mounds of sloppily kept paperwork had been scattered around as well. Jazz not only didn't want was left behind, she didn't need reminders of a seedy past. The neighborhood was changing, and Jazz was ready to change with it.

Jazz's eyes drifted shut. The dull aches from her bruising came back. Even the effort to get her pain medication seemed too much, yet fatigue pulled at her more. She would rest for a moment and then get up.

"I didn't throw it all away," Byron said. He reached for a bowl filled with white cheddar popcorn.

Jazz's hand shot out to stop him from stuffing his mouth. "What did you say?"

"My mama says don't throw out no records unless you sure, never know when you might need 'em," Byron said. He cleared his throat the longer Jazz gazed at him.

"You kept stuff I told you to trash? Where is it?" Jazz squeezed his thick wrist.

"Now don't get mad. The first month was free, and it's just nineteen dollars a month. I pay for it with some other invoices outta the receipts. I was gonna tell you about it if we had to cut expenses, I mean, with business slowin' down in the past few weeks. But then that rich guy kicked in some cash and--"

"A storage unit," Jazz said and blinked at him. "You put a bunch of Lorraine's old files in storage."

Byron looked uneasy. "Boxed it up and tried to arrange it in some kinda order. She had old ledger books, but like you said it was all messed up. Listen, I can stop payin' and throw it all away like you told me to."

Jazz ignored her aches and jumped to her feet to do a little dance. "Like hell you'll stop paying. In fact you better call to make sure our contract is not about to expire."

Chapter 17

The following Monday, Jazz sat in her defense attorney's fancy conference room again. Willa and MiMi had come along. For once Jazz didn't mind having someone with her for support. The upcoming hearing made her murder trial all too real.

MiMi stood examining one of three framed prints on the wall. She nodded approval and sat down at the polished table. "Elegant decor and real leather, good signs. Your lawyer represents people with money. You're in good hands."

"Why don't you take out a magnifying glass and give us an estimated retail value of everything?" Willa rolled her eyes.

"Ah, yes. The working class argument that money isn't everything. Well that theory has been disproved umpteen times." MiMi sniffed. She rummaged in her designer leather handbag as if to prove her point. "Money does equal quality. So get over it."

"I won't bring up some of your fancy friends or even your family as counterpoint," Willa said with a smirk.

"I guess your posse from 'Da Hood' is proof you

can count on them. Remind me again who recommended Higgins." MiMi raised an eyebrow at Willa.

"Oh shut it," Willa snapped. "Speaking of which, Brad got Ames to back off once he laid it on the line. Ames pretty much implied that Higgins suggested he enforce the fine print. Higgins wants to build his own little real estate empire."

"Really?" Jazz tapped a fist on the smooth polished wood surface of the conference table.

"It's not unusual. Desperate people with no cash sign over property to lawyers as payment. Higgins just got a little too slick," Willa said. "Your friend Tyretta knew him long?"

Jazz gazed out of the window. Chic drapes the color of cream had been pulled back to let in the light. A dogwood tree with white flowers bloomed outside, but Jazz wasn't thinking about the pretty scenery. She turned to her sister.

"I'm not sure. Maybe I should ask her. You know?"

"Tyretta doesn't impress me as a planner or a brain. I don't see her helping Higgins craft such a scheme," Willa said.

MiMi scrolled through text messages on her Smartphone. " In my experience, shady lawyers don't need help coming up with ways to screw people. Damn it, these people at work keep bothering me."

"You better stop taking off. We've been listening to you whine about needing money for months," Willa replied in a dry tone.

"I'm their top buyer and merchandise manager. My schedule is flexible, plus I work from home a lot. Thank God I found an excellent daycare for Sage." MiMi sighed. "Those folks should be lifting holy hands to the

Lord they have me."

"Yeah, right." Willa shot a glance at Jazz and rolled her eyes. "Back to Tyretta"

Jazz added the fact that Tyretta hooked her up with Higgins to Byron's observations. "You can't dig using those fancy databases to find out what I need to know."

"What's your plan then?" Willa crossed her arms.

"First, I'm gonna search through a bunch of crap Lorraine left behind in the club. I've got an idea there might be some clues in there. I think she's trying to find something *inside* my house or Candy Girls."

"You mean the break-ins? She hired some street criminals to break in. But she wouldn't trust them with something valuable," Willa said. "Hell, she's not going to tell them it's valuable. Or maybe she promised them a cut of the money." Jazz waved a hand. "All I know is she wants in bad."

"I thought you threw away most her junk," Willa replied.

"I told Byron to, but he's a pack rat. For once I'm glad he ignored me." Jazz grinned. "He put old file cabinets and papers in a storage unit on Foster Dr. We're going to search it this afternoon. Mondays are slow."

MiMi lost interest in her text messages. Eyes wide with excitement, she dropped the phone into her purse. "You could be right. Like a treasure hunt."

Willa squinted at Jazz. "Be careful who you tell and don't take anymore crazy risks."

Before Jazz could reply, the lawyer came into the conference room followed by another younger man. Both wore expensive suits, one gray and the other navy blue. The young lawyer introduced himself as Chad

Blanchard, a junior associate. He had blonde hair and hazel eyes. His boyish handsome face made him look like a member of a popular teen pop idol. Phillips got right to business.

"Morning ladies. We have an evidentiary hearing scheduled. I filed a motion to dismiss based on lack of any evidence directly connecting you to the injuries that resulted in the victim's death. I argued that the fact she came, apparently of her own free will, implies she thought you could help her. The DA's case is still built on circumstantial evidence. I'm going to argue that at least three other people had motive and opportunity to harm Ms. Lathers." Phillips straightened his silk tie like he was before the judge already.

"Excellent strategy," MiMi interjected with a smile directed at the handsome junior lawyer.

"Says the expert on legal matters," Willa muttered. Her comment earned her a sour look from MiMi.

"Thank you," Phillips replied with an amused glint in his blue eyes.

The man smiled back at MiMi, but turned to Jazz. "Ms. Vaughn, did Ms. Lathers say anything about Cleavon Bennett or Brandon Wilks?"

"She didn't lay Brandon's murder on Cleavon if that's what you mean. But she was there when it went down," Jazz replied.

"To wit, it's entirely plausible she could have been a threat to Bennett. He's not entirely clear as a suspect in that murder by the way." Phillips glanced through his files. "Also, her ex-husband was released from prison two months before her murder. He was on record as wanting to harm her."

"Kyeisha ended up selling everything he owned when he went to jail, and she started sleeping with one of his friends," Jazz said.

"The police went on numerous domestic disturbance calls to their home," Phillips nodded to his associate to go on.

"Her oldest sister pulled a gun on her a year earlier. A dispute over family property became very heated." Blanchard's dark blonde eyebrows went up.

"Humph, that's a nice way of describing it. All four sisters, their kids, and boyfriends got into a brawl in the street one night."

"Her sister pulled a gun? My goodness." MiMi shook her head.

"Plenty of motive to go around," Phillips replied with a pleased expression. "Therefore the judge scheduled an evidentiary hearing. Witnesses will testify to support the DA's case."

"But you'll be able to present these theories, right?" Jazz tensed.

"No, we can't mount a defense during the evidentiary hearing, but..." Phillips raised a hand to forestall Jazz's worried protest. "I can cross examine the witnesses. I'll take care not to give too much of my defense away though."

"Okay." Jazz didn't feel okay at all. Her heart hammered. The prospect of listening to people give reasons she should go to prison for life made her sick.

"I think we have a good shot at knocking holes in the DA's circumstantial evidence. Ms. Lather's led a pretty... colorful life," Phillips said. "I'd tell you if there was reason to worry."

"The recent attack on you adds weight to our alternative theories. Bennett could be behind that as well," Blanchard put in.

Jazz barked a short laugh. "Gee, glad I could help."

"No, I didn't mean you getting attacked was a good thing," Blanchard stammered, turning a shade of bright pink.

"Don't worry, she knows. Jazz has a dry sense of humor. How long have you been at this firm?" MiMi beamed at him, batting her long eyelashes.

"Three years," Blanchard said, his face going to a darker shade of pink. He gazed at the curve of MiMi's breasts beneath the clingy royal blue sweater she wore.

"Ahem, back to my case," Jazz cut in. She eyed MiMi, who blinked innocently but said no more.

"The hearing is in three weeks. Lorraine Taylor, Bennett, and several others are listed as witnesses," Phillips said as he neatly arranged his file on Jazz's case.

"Great, I get to see those liars in full effect," Jazz retorted with a grimace.

"On to another topic which might seem unrelated, but isn't. Have you resolved this issue with Higgins representing you? The DA knows about it. He could try to somehow connect it to a motive to kill Kyeisha Lathers." Phillips glanced from Jazz to Willa and back again.

"I'll bet Lorraine filled him in," Jazz said.

"How would she know?" MiMi blinked at her.

"Yes, how would she know details about your business deal with Ames?" Willa raised an arched eyebrow at Jazz.

Jazz stared straight ahead as if someone not in the room stood in front of her. "Yeah, a good damn question."

* * *

Byron and Jazz timed leaving for the storage unit

after the lunch rush. Rochelle happily served up the last late orders by one thirty that afternoon. Chyna and Lilly would come in to work at four o'clock to get ready for evening business. Tyretta had the day off, which eliminated the problem of explaining anything to her. Monday was Byron's day off as well, but he volunteered without hesitation to help with the hunt.

When Jazz swung open the side door of the club, the Louisiana hot and humid air hit her. "Damn, I hope this storage unit you rented is climate controlled."

"Yeah. Since there was paperwork and all. some of it I sealed in big plastic bags to keep 'em dry and the bugs out." Byron settled behind the wheel of his old Chevy Tahoe.

"You're gonna be a big time business man one day, Byron." Jazz climbed into the passenger side.

Just as she was about to pull the door shut, MiMi's Enclave pulled into the driveway in front of Jazz's apartment. She parked next to Jazz's Explorer and jumped out of her car. The lights flashed as she armed the alarm. She was dressed in casual clothes. Still, her jeans, long-sleeve t-shirt, and sneakers looked stylish. She carried a tote bag. Waving at them with a big grin, MiMi trotted to the Tahoe. She opened a back door and jumped in the passenger seat behind Byron.

"Hey y'all. Whew, got here just in time. I thought I was going to have to meet y'all over there." MiMi fanned her face.

Jazz twisted around to glare at her. "S'cuse me, but what the hell?"

"Oh don't worry about work. I put in early hours. Auntie Beryl is going to pick Sage up from daycare in case we run later than six o'clock. Girl, they charge ten bucks for every five minutes you're late." MiMi rummaged around in her tote bag as she talked.

"I didn't ask you to come with us, MiMi, so you need to hop your lil' bold ass outta this vehicle," Jazz snapped.

"Look, I'm trying to *help* you, so don't take that tone with me. The longer we sit here arguing, the later it gets. Plus we'll attract attention." MiMi sat back in her seat to signal she wasn't going anywhere.

Just as Jazz wound up to cuss her out, Byron spoke up. "She's right, boss lady. There's a crap load of stuff in that unit. Three of us will make the search go faster. We don't wanna be out there too late after dark."

"Don't forget the part about attracting attention," MiMi put in. "Lorraine or that gang member whets-his-face have eyes on you."

"Another solid point," Byron rumbled, his voice solemn as he glanced around.

Jazz hissed in frustration. "Fine let's get moving."

Byron started the engine, and they drove on for twenty minutes in silence. Red Stick Storage was in the southern part of East Baton Rouge Parish. The remote location was part of the reason the rates were so reasonable. After stop and go traffic, they hit Airline Highway. A billboard advertising the storage facility told them they were five minutes away.

"My buddy manages this one and two others. They bought that billboard," Byron said. "We're taking management classes together. He was my cellmate back in the day."

"That's wonderful. I don't mean that you two were in jail," MiMi added. She gazed out of the window at passing businesses.

"Humph." Jazz cast a hot glance at MiMi over her shoulder before facing front again.

"I know what you meant." Byron smiled at MiMi in the rearview mirror. He gave Jazz an amused side look. "I put labels on boxes, but just general like 'Receipts'. I didn't search through it all. Didn't seem necessary at the time."

"I'm just glad you ignored my orders, but don't make it a habit," Jazz added and pointed at him. "Unless you know better."

Byron chuckled softly. "Yes ma'am. I got it."

"And you, follow orders and keep quiet," Jazz said to MiMi without looking at her.

"Yes ma'am. I got it, too," MiMi chirped and gave a sharp salute.

Jazz started to say more, but decided not to waste her breath. MiMi on a mission didn't listen to anyone. Byron turned onto a side street. A variety of businesses lined both sides of a wide four lane street. Other streets branched off with more. Interline Boulevard was one of several light industrial sections of the city. A big red and white sign to their left announced they'd arrived at Red Stick Storage. A driveway led down the center of one long row of connected metal buildings on either side. More rows stretched behind these. Street signs were posted at intersecting driveways.

"Just up here. We're on Sesame Street," Byron said.

"You've got to be shitting me," Jazz replied, gaping at him.

"Cool. Cookie Monster is my fave." MiMi laughed when Jazz threw another angry glare her way.

"If you start singing that song, I'll strangle you and stuff your body in one of these storage units," Jazz grumbled.

MiMi giggled. "You're the grouchy monster."

"You owe Baby Sage a lot. If I didn't want to orphan that child..."

Byron stopped the Tahoe. "Here we go. Unit number thirty-six, that's yours."

Jazz got out of the SUV and stopped MiMi from exiting. "Let's get one thing straight, MiMi. Don't get your hopes up you'll find a treasure map leading to money Jack hid. Lorraine didn't even know Jack that well. He just hung out at Candy Girls a minute."

"Okay, okay." MiMi looked around.

"You need to listen to me," Jazz warned as she shook a forefinger at MiMi.

"I heard you for goodness sakes. But finders' keepers," MiMi replied in a sing-song voice as she pushed the door open.

Jazz jumped back to get out of the way. "Girl, you gonna earn a butt kicking' yet."

"Here we go. I knew oiling this lock and these hinges was a good idea." Byron had ignored their dramatic play and opened the storage unit.

"We love you Byron," MiMi breathed as she scurried past him into the open unit. "Now what?" her voice echoed back.

"Now, I turn on the lights and you wait for me to tell you where to search." Byron found the switch. A florescent bulb spread white light over the contents.

"Whoa, there's a big pile of stuff up in here." MiMi picked up a lamp with an orange and pink shade. "Ugly stuff."

Jazz squinted as her eyes adjusted from the sunlight. She took off her sunglasses. "Lorraine is not known for her sense of style. Damn, Byron. You could have thrown that away for sure."

"We could have a garage sale. Bet somebody

would buy it," Byron replied matter-of-factly.

"One woman's junk is another woman's treasure. I'm sure there are more than enough people with tacky taste buy this mess." MiMi sniffed at a purple stuffed chair.

"We're looking for files or old papers," Jazz said as she stared at a stack of boxes.

Byron pointed to the right. "Then look along that wall. Six boxes."

"Six isn't too bad." MiMi started for them, but Jazz yanked her back.

"You're taking orders, remember?" Jazz frowned at her.

"Sheesh, I get it. You don't have to pull my arm out of its socket." MiMi rubbed her shoulder.

Jazz walked over to the stack of boxes. They were made of sturdy cardboard She grunted with the effort to pick one up. "This thing weighs a ton."

"Lorraine might have been messy, but she kept records. Sure you want to dig through it? All of them boxes are stuffed like that one." Byron scratched his head as he looked around. "

"Let's get started. We'll each take a box. Look for anything that doesn't look routine," Jazz said.

"Routine like what?" MiMi asked.

Byron cleared a space by stacking smaller items on others. He talked as he worked. "Old receipts for food or liquor, or invoices for stuff they bought like tables. I'm guessing you want to look for bookkeeping ledgers."

"Yeah, or anything that looks out of place. Names of people, anything odd." Jazz fanned her face.

"Don't worry, the air will kick on soon. This place is high tech, too. Forty percent of the cooling is with a heat pump system. That cuts cost. I'm considering a franchise myself," Byron said.

"If I had money, I'd invest," MiMi complained. She glanced at Jazz.

"Don't start with the whining." Jazz tugged open the box with effort.

Byron put two more boxes on the floor. "You can sit on that chair. Boss, here's a small stool. I'll sit on this old trunk."

MiMi's eyes lit up as she circled the old fashioned box. "A trunk! Now talk about possibilities."

"Don't bother cause there ain't much in it. Nothing but old fake jewelry, clothes from the fifties and sixties. I think it must have belonged to Lorraine's mother," Byron said. He opened the other two boxes.

"Sit your ass down and start looking through these papers," Jazz barked.

"Fine." MiMi huffed, but she followed orders as promised. "I can't believe Lorraine left her family keepsakes behind."

"The Taylors ain't sentimental," Jazz retorted. She gazed at the boxes. "Might as well get started."

For the next three hours they burrowed into the mounds of paper. Jazz kept glancing at MiMi. She expected the diva to lose her enthusiasm for the hunt. Instead MiMi seemed to have endless hope that some intriguing clue would be discovered. Jazz began to think they were wasting time. By almost five o'clock they'd stacked up a pile of papers Jazz decided she needed to keep.

"Byron, you're a true packrat like you said. I think we can trash most of this stuff." Jazz slapped dust from her hands and the front of her shirt. A coughing fit was her reward.

"Okay boss lady. I was hoping it wasn't a bunch of worthless paper. Nothing in those old notebooks either, huh?" Byron started packing one of the empty boxes he'd brought along with.

"What notebooks?" MiMi spoke up before Jazz could draw a breath to ask.

"Hmm, I musta forgot a box or something. Let me see." Byron started rooting around another corner with more boxes.

"At this point, I don't care. I want a shower, a hot meal, and my bunny slippers," Jazz mumbled. She cursed as a tiny spider crawled up the leg of her jeans. "Damn bugs."

"Don't kill it," MiMi squealed. "They're good luck!"

"You must be out of your ever lovin' mind," Jazz shot back, but MiMi caught her hand to stop her from squashing it.

MiMi brushed the spider to the floor like it was a beloved pet. "There you go little guy. Just hide in another corner. Jazzy is scared of the itty bitty spider."

"When his three feet wide mama shows up, I want to hear you sweet talk then," Jazz said. "C'mon Byron. The creepy crawlies are comin' out. Time to leave for damn sure."

"Nah, this place has pest control. Nothin' big gets in here or lives long." Byron's voice came from behind a pile of furniture. "Ha, I must not have been paying attention. The box is next to some old Christmas decorations."

"First thing, you do an inventory and dump a bunch of this crap," Jazz mumbled.

"I stored it all in case Lorraine might show up claiming we stole her belongings. I guess the law can consider it abandoned after so long." Byron breathed heavily as he climbed over a small table with the last box. He dropped it at Jazz's feet.

Jazz heaved a deeply annoyed sigh, but pulled open the taped top. "I hope this is the last one."

"Definitely. I checked since I was back there." Byron mopped his face with the wad of paper towels he brought along. He sat down on a table with a grunt.

Jazz lifted out two ledgers. Another stack of spiral notebooks shifted and slid to the side. MiMi peered over her shoulder until Jazz scowled at her. "Back the hell off me."

"Oh shush and hand me a stack," MiMi replied without moving one inch.

Jazz shoved two old notebooks into MiMi's hand. "Here. Sit. Shut up."

"I'll take two or three myself." Byron accepted them from Jazz and flipped through the pages.

Shadows lengthened outside as the sun began to set. The only sound was the rustle of paper as each of them continued to read. Jazz tossed an old ledger book back into the box. She glanced outside to see some of the lights coming on as sunshine faded.

"Nothing. A waste of time." Jazz stood and massaged the small of her back.

"There are about eight more of 'em." Byron picked up the notebook Jazz had thrown down. He took a marker and wrote on it. "I'm marking the ones we looked at already."

"I say we all get cleaned up and get some dinner. My treat," Jazz said. She tapped her on the shoulder when MiMi didn't reply. "Hey, you must not have heard me. I'm paying for your meal at a nice restaurant."

"Umm-hum," MiMi answered, her eyes still on the page of a ledger.

"Something is wrong. She jumps up at the sound of somebody picking up the tab," Jazz wisecracked to Byron. He chuckled in response.

"I know you said Lorraine isn't very bright, but it's strange she had so many records." MiMi looked up at Jazz.

"Lorraine isn't educated, but she's definitely smart, streetwise at least." Jazz squinted. "I was wrong to think she was dumb. Look how she set me up."

"She musta stayed up nights plotting." Byron reached for another notebook.

"Yeah." Jazz felt gloom descending on her like the dark outside. "My lawyer seems to think he can fight the evidence, but lots of folks go to prison on less than what they have on me."

"Hey, you gotta stay positive," Byron replied.

"Hush, I'm concentrating." MiMi waved a hand at him before he could go on.

"S'cuse us. You need to be nice cause he's your ride outta here," Jazz muttered.

Byron shrugged and whispered, "Maybe she's on to something."

He laughed when Jazz made a face. Byron got to work. He carried the box of loose papers Jazz wanted to keep to the Tahoe. Jazz scanned the last few notebooks without much interest. When Byron returned, he and Jazz whispered about what he could throw out. Byron marked items for a yard sale. He moved between the SUV and the storage area. Jazz almost fell when MiMi whooped.

"Lorraine or somebody came up with a code and a cipher. Look, these look like simple phrases about beer and stuff, but there's a pattern. And, on the inside back cover is another code. It's written in tiny letters so anybody glancing wouldn't notice. But I did." MiMi flashed a big grin of victory.

"What? Give me that." Jazz took the grease stained notebook MiMi waved at her. "This is about frozen onion rings for happy hour. She used to have it on Wednesday to get more business."

MiMi grabbed another notebook from the box. "No, no, no. There is a definite pattern. Each one has a list of numbers, then maybe three paragraphs after them."

"What I see is a bunch of bad handwriting about appetizers or invoices she has to pay and who owes her money," Jazz replied. Still she gazed at the pages intently. "Lorraine had the sense to create a code?"

"Wrong question, girl. *Why* did she use a code?" MiMi said.

Jazz was about to answer when they heard Byron talking loudly. He kept up a steady stream of banter. As his voice got closer, Jazz realized he wasn't talking on his cell phone. She heard another voice. Byron came in and put a finger to his lips seconds before Tyretta followed. She jogged to keep up with his long-legged stride.

"Look who showed up to help us clean out the storage unit," Byron boomed. His gaze shifted to MiMi. He gave her a slight nod.

"Hey, Rochelle said something about y'all coming over here to look around." Tyretta scanned the inside of the unit. Then she looked at Byron. "I thought it was your day off. Damn, you racking up brownie points with the boss, huh?"

Chapter 18

"Well we..." MiMi started but blinked in surprise when Jazz stepped in front of her.

Jazz put both hands on her hips. "That's more than I can say about you. Hell, these days I'm surprised you show up when you're supposed to."

"There you go gettin' all smart when I'm being nice. Hell it's almost dark. Must be something important." Tyretta started to go in the storage unit, but was blocked when Byron pushed a large rocker in front of her.

"Nothin' but some fancy decorations we decided to keep. We're gonna have a yard sale. You want this rocker and that table?" Byron said.

"Huh?" Tyretta wore a puzzled frown. She glanced around the interior.

"They're just dusty is all. I got a cousin who could refinish 'em for you cheap," Byron said. He went on to point out other items.

"I'm gonna load these New Year's Eve decorations. Some of this stuff is pretty nice. Right, MiMi? Come on;

help me. This box isn't heavy," Jazz said as she gave MiMi the eye.

"Wha... I mean, yeah, for once Lorraine showed some taste," MiMi replied, her voice almost too loud to be credible.

Jazz had taped up the box containing the notebooks. She motioned for MiMi to hide the one she held under an arm. Byron distracted Tyretta, though she kept trying to glance at Jazz and MiMi. Once Jazz and MiMi got to Byron's SUV, MiMi seemed about to burst with questions.

"You're suspicious of her? But she's been your bestie for years," MiMi whispered as she glanced over her shoulder.

"We'll talk later," Jazz whispered back. Tyretta's voice got closer. She shoved the boxes back into the SUV so that they weren't easily visible. Then she used an old blanket to cover them.

Byron walked ahead of Tyretta carrying a small round table. "I got plenty of room in the SUV. I'll bring this to your house tomorrow if you want."

"Yeah, okay. Sure you don't need me to help unpack when you get to Candy Girls? I don't have to hurry home." Tyretta looked from Jazz to MiMi, then at Byron, then back to Jazz.

" I'm too tired to look through dusty old knick-knacks tonight. But thanks anyway." Jazz leaned against a stack of boxes.

"Maybe I'll just hang with y'all a minute." Tyretta wore a slight frown as she gazed at them.

"I'm going to drop them off and go home," Byron replied.

"I have to run, too." MiMi waved goodbye at Tyretta and got into the Tahoe.

Jazz yawned as she got in the front passenger seat. "I'm gonna lay on my sofa and not move until morning. See you later, Ty." Byron was already behind the wheel. "It's dark out here and ain't nobody around. We'll wait 'til you get in your car. Can't be too careful."

Tyretta blinked at them. "Yeah. Right. Okay."

She glanced at them over her shoulder as she walked to her Ford Fusion. Tyretta got in, waved, and drove off. Jazz watched her nervously, sure Tyretta would follow them. Instead, the Ford eventually left the four lane street heading away from their direction. Byron and MiMi sighed at the same time Jazz did.

"How did she know to come here?" Jazz blurted out.

"There's some cooking equipment in a couple of boxes Rochelle helped me sort through. She knows I rented the unit." Byron hunched his shoulders. "Sorry, boss. I didn't think it needed to be a secret back then."

"Neither would I if I'd known." Jazz chewed a fingernail.

"Stop messing up your manicure," MiMi said absentmindedly. "I'm confused. Why are you suspicious of Tyretta again?"

"Byron thinks she's acting funny. I was skeptical, but then she showed up." Jazz rubbed her forehead. The thud of a stress headache took root.

MiMi reached across the seat and placed a hand on Jazz's shoulder. "You've got us."

"Damn right," Byron rumbled without taking his eyes from the road.

Jazz blinked back tears and lifted her head. "Thanks."

* * *

At ten o'clock the next morning, Jazz sat in Willa's office. Cedric would join them later because of a meeting across town with a client. Phillips joined them via video conference. His solemn expression on Willa's twenty-five inch computer monitor did not reassure them. Jazz felt as if her body would fly into pieces from the tension building in her muscles. Her fingernails pressed into the leather on the chair's arms.

"Is it good or bad that the judge insists on moving the hearing date up?" Willa asked. She gazed steadily at Jazz with concern reflected in her brown eyes.

"It's a scheduling shuffle. Don't read anything into it. But I have a bigger concern. The DA has a witness that you assaulted and tied up Ms. Lathers less than a week before she was murdered. True or not?" Phillips shot the words out.

"They left the part out about her bringing a gun and pointing it at me," Jazz said. "Tell me what happened blow by blow. Don't leave out anything," he replied curtly.

Jazz shifted in her chair feeling like it was a literal hot seat. Still she told him everything, including giving Kyeisha pills to make her sleepy. When she finished, there was silence.

"It was self-defense," Jazz said in her loud grumpy tone.

"I'll argue it's hearsay. Lorraine Taylor says an employee at her bar claims Ms. Lather's told her. Ms. Taylor never got a chance to ask her about it."

"Well that's something," Willa replied. Yet her frown of worry didn't go away.

"I don't like surprises, Ms. Vaughn." Phillips'

frowned at them.

"There's nothing more. We promise," Willa answered before Jazz spoke.

After they discussed more details about the upcoming court hearing, the lawyer ended the conference . Willa rocked back and forth in her executive chair. Kay, her executive assistance, came in with a box of donuts. She checked that they had fresh coffee. Noticing the grim expressions of the sisters, she made as little sound as possible and left.

"He didn't say it was all bad," Willa said.

"Only if the judge rules it's hearsay. We need to find out who beat and tortured her." "How much sleep did you get last night?" Willa got up and poured a cup of coffee.

Jazz waved it away when Willa offered it to her. "Two hours. Maybe. I Three of my friends turned into enemies overnight. Shit."

Willa nodded, but didn't respond. She put a donut on a large paper napkin and sat down again. She ate, sipped, and ate more donut. Minutes ticked by as they both settled on thinking through facts. For a time, only the distant ringing of the office phones broke the silence.

"Listen, I..."

"Don't say it," Jazz broke in.

"Say what?" Willa licked donut glaze from one thumb.

"They weren't my friends. You tried to warn me about the kind of people I was running with, etc." Jazz looked at the coffee pot, but didn't move at first. Then she got up and poured the strong brew into a mug. "What the hell. One more cup won't make a difference. This isn't what's keeping me awake anyway."

"You're grown, girl. I wasn't going to lecture you," Willa said.

"That's never stopped you before," Jazz retorted.

Her big sister ignored the dig. "Besides, not everyone in your crowd is the same. Look at Rochelle, Chyna, and Lilly. Byron is tops. I'd hire him any day of the week."

Jazz wagged a forefinger at her. "Hands off my second in command."

After more seconds of silence, Jazz got up to walk around the office. She gazed out of the fourth floor window at traffic on the busy city street below. Then she sat back down again. Not that she paid attention to her surroundings. Jazz continued to mentally turn over facts in her head. She snapped her fingers causing Willa to jump.

"When Kyeisha came to my house," Jazz said.

"You mean the time you tied her up?" "She had a gun. Everybody seems to forget she had a damn *gun on me*," Jazz snarled.

"You drugged her and used a disabled man's wheelchair to dump her over at Lorraine's place," Willa continued mildly.

Jazz glowered at her. "Shut up and let me finish."

"Good thing she woke up confused and couldn't get her story straight. But finish your thought," Willa said.

"What if Kyeisha wanted to make a deal with me? She kinda implied that she would cut Cleavon out of any money we made. What if that included Lorraine's gangsta sons?" Jazz blinked at Willa waiting for her reaction.

Willa frowned as she seemed to work through her theory. "But the youngest was killed, and the older two are in prison for a long time to come."

"Lots of guys continue to operate while on the inside," Jazz countered. "Lorraine could be holding things down, keeping him and his gang informed. Lorraine or Cleavon found out. If they think I told her something..." Jazz snapped her fingers again.

"They tried torturing her into talking. But... Good Lord, Jazz," Willa whispered and stared at Jazz wide-eye.

Jazz nodded. A chill went down her back. "She couldn't tell them anything because there was nothing to tell. Phillips said we could argue Kyeisha came to me for help. Maybe she did."

Willa went to her desk. "She sure didn't drive. I don't see her walking very far with those injuries."

" "What are you doing?"

Willa tapped the keys of her computer. "I'm pulling up a map around Candy Girls. I'll..."

"Good morning," Cedric said from the open door. He came in seconds later. "Y'all look quite intense."

"Okay, here's my theory," Jazz blurted out. "Kyeisha wasn't brought to my place all beat up to frame me. She somehow got away after being tortured to warn me or hide. And I know what you're going to say. I'm thinking she had help."

Cedric rubbed his jaw. "I don't know who would have the nerve after what they did to her.".

"Maybe this person only made Kyeisha *think* he was helping her to get more information. He plans to get the information for himself," Jazz said.

"Cleavon," Jazz and Willa said at the same time gazing wide-eyed at each other.

"You two are scaring me," Cedric quipped. "Okay, but who called the police and why? Cleavon wouldn't have without getting the information he wanted."

"Maybe a suspicious neighbor," Willa offered. She looked at Cedric and shrugged when he gave a skeptical shake of his head.

Jazz paced as she spoke. "It had to be somebody close enough to know where she was and what was happening. Someone who had a reason to think they could profit from getting Kyeisha away from Lorraine."

"I'm dizzy just trying to sort out all that double crossing. Y'all been watching too many crime thrillers." Cedric looked from Jazz to Willa and back again.

"Like Willa always says, I know my shady crowd. Kyeisha would have sold her loyalty to me if I'd given her a chance. I can tell you stories with more twists than any movie written in Hollywood."

Cedric took a seat. "Okay, tell us what Kyeisha said both nights she showed up at your place."

"She talked about me knowing about Filipe's stash, and how we could make a killing. All I had to do was throw in with her. She said she hadn't told Cleavon or Lorraine. So, maybe she decided to dump them once she was at my place." Jazz sat down again.

"There was no blood trail like she walked or crawled for any distance. Not that I think she could have managed to in her condition. We figured somebody had to have brought her. I assumed they thought she was dead when they dumped her and then called the police to set you up," Cedric said.

"Yeah, but what if she convinced someone that they could get information out of Jazz," Willa said.

"Cleavon tortured Kyeisha until he believed she didn't know anything. Lorraine realizes they're gone and calls the cops?" Cedric rubbed his chin in thought. "I don't know."

"We don't have to know. We just have to make them *think* we know," Jazz said.

Cedric and Willa exchanged a glanced. Both started to shake their heads at the same time.

"Aw c'mon, Let me tell you what..." Jazz stopped when Willa held up a palm like a school crossing guard stopping traffic.

"I have a feeling you want us to do something stupid or dangerous," Willa said. "The answer is hell no."

"It's my ass on the line for murder. I could get convicted and locked up for twenty-five to life," Jazz said. She shuddered.

"Phillips says he can counter their evidence. He seems pretty confident," Willa argued.

"Men and women are sitting in prisons all over America because of circumstantial cases against them," Cedric said in a solemn tone.

"A little more help over here Cedric. *Please*," Willa hissed at him with a glare.

Cedric blinked at Willa. Then he cleared his throat. "Willa's right though. Let's take our information to the police."

Jazz jumped to her feet. "Now y'all gone to talkin' crazy. The police would throw a party if I got locked up. They're city employees, remember? And the city wants my club closed. I'm not feeling too confident about calling local authorities."

"Detective Addison believes you, and Miller values his opinion," Willa offered. She huffed a sigh at the frown Jazz gave her. Then she pressed on with her point. "Okay, Miller is not your biggest fan, and but he still respects Don as a friend and most importantly as a cop."

"I say we run our guesses by Don. He won't tell his colleagues if he thinks your theory is too out there. On the other hand he can convince Miller if what say makes sense," Cedric added.

"He's already put way too much on the line because of me." Jazz raked her long weave with one hand. "Don does not get involved. Period. No more discussion."

Willa got up and placed both hands on Jazz's shoulders. "You're always talking about how I should think of my family. That includes *you*. Promise you won't go up against Cleavon Bennett or his crew. Promise me on Road Runner's grave," Willa said, her voice cracking with emotion.

Jazz gazed into her sister's eyes. They were bright with the threat of tears. The fear in them was real. After several long moments Jazz gave her a quick hug then pushed free. She flipped a hand at Willa as she sat down again.

"Alright, alright. No need for all of the sappy soap opera drama. I promise to stay clear of Cleavon," Jazz said. She crossed her legs and dug into her purse until she found the make-up bag. Then she flipped open a mirror. With a frown she fixed her lipstick.

Cedric wore an amused, puzzled expression as he gazed at Willa. "What was all that about Road Runner's grave?"

Willa's tense expression eased. "He was our favorite cartoon when we were kids. Nothing that dumb coyote tried could take out lil' Road Runner. We loved that doggone thing. If we were serious about a promise, we'd swear on Road Runner's grave to keep it."

"Most people say 'I swear on my mother's grave'," Cedric replied with a laugh.

"Yeah, well, we put more value on the bird. He brought us more happiness than she ever did," Willa replied with grim humor.

Jazz stood and slung her purse over one shoulder. "I gotta run and take care of some business."

"Remember you promised," Willa said and pointed at her.

"Yeah, Yeah. Jeez, a little trust is too much to ask?" Jazz waved goodbye and left.

* * *

Later that day, a quiet Tuesday afternoon, Jazz sat in her office. Her door and windows were open. A sweet May breeze caused the gauzy beige curtains to billow in and out, managing to make it past the metal security grill. Smoke curled up from the neglected cigarillo resting in a large ceramic ashtray near her elbow. Byron strolled in with a white envelope in one hand.

"I signed for this certified letter the city," he said and handed it to her.

Jazz tore it open. "The hearing to shut me down is two days before my first trial date. Bastards like to pile it on."

"You got two good lawyers working for ya." Byron started to say more but stopped at the sound of approaching footsteps.

Seconds later Tyretta appeared at the open door. "Hey girl. How you doin'?"

"I'm goin' back up front to finish work." Byron brushed past Tyretta without looking at her.

"Yeah, make yourself useful. Actin' like he's hot shit." Tyretta pushed the door closed with one foot.

Then she sat on the edge of Jazz's desk.

"Byron looked up from street level to something higher. He's got goals," Jazz said mildly. She tugged at papers Tyretta had sat on causing her to get up.

"Well la-dee-fuckin'-da for him," Tyretta retorted as she slumped into one of the chairs.

"I didn't buy Candy Girls so I could run a hole in the wall for twenty-five or thirty years like Lorraine's mama or like Lorraine will end up doing." Jazz continued to sign checks for invoices. She stuffed, addressed, and stamped envelopes. "Look. Byron had all the invoices laid out for me. That's how a manager acts. He's helping me hold this place together."

"Uh-huh. So what's up with the city?" Tyretta seemed to avoid looking at the envelope on Jazz's desk.

"Nothing my new lawyer can't handle," Jazz said matter-of-factly. She went back to sorting through paperwork.

"Now that you mentioned it, Higgins told me you fired him. I'm surprised you wasn't satisfied. He helped me a lot with traffic tickets and stuff a couple of years ago or so."

"Hmm, wasn't that about the time of all those scandals with the city ? Tickets got fixed." Jazz looked up at her sharply, remembering Lorraine's hook-up to avoid city taxes. Dots connected. "Did he help out Lorraine, too?"

"Far as I know he never even met Lorraine. You know she too damn cheap to pay a decent lawyer." Tyretta gave a sharp laugh. "No, we went to court all legal and stuff. He wasn't caught up in that mess."

"I wouldn't call Higgins a decent anything. He tried to trip me up with that investment contract but it won't work." Jazz picked up the still burning cigarillo. She pulled on it, looking at Tyretta through the smoke.

"I hear you, girl. Keep fightin'. But you got a lot comin' at you. Course all that takes money. No wonder you sellin' things in storage. I didn't know you had so much of Lorraine's junk. Can't be worth much." Tyretta maintained her casual tone, as if discussing nothing important.

Jazz pretended to concentrate on the papers in front of her again. Anger, like a slow pressure, started at the base of her spine. Byron's instincts were spot on. Instead of wanting to explode, Jazz's emotions coalesced into icy resolve. She gave a slight shrug without looking up.

"The sheriff locked up the building before she could move everything I guess. You know, before they had the tax auction. I'm going to go through pick through the papers and notebooks tonight after we close. Who knows? Could be hidden treasure in a bunch of trash."

" I can look through 'em for ya," Tyretta said a bit too fast. Then she pulled back. "So you can run the business I mean."

"Thanks, but I need to do it myself. Besides, it's not that much."

"It'll go even faster with two of us lookin'," Tyretta said.

Jazz glanced up and tilted her head to one side. "I've never known you to volunteer to work longer hours."

Tyretta didn't miss a beat. She pulled a comical face. "I was bein' polite, girl. You know I'ma run outta here when my shift is over. I ain't gonna fight to stay late."

"That's what I thought." Jazz gave a grunt and went

back to looking at the paperwork again. More silence.

"Maybe you'll find something in Lorraine's old papers that will help you fight the city or somethin'." Tyretta brushed at the fabric of one pant leg.

"Doubt it. ," Jazz said.

"Oh. Like I said, what went down with Higgins don't seem like him."

"People do a lot of nasty stuff for money. You know what I mean." Jazz looked at her steadily.

"I hear ya." Tyretta stood and stretched. "Let me get back to work before Byron comes in here with an attitude."

"Yeah," Jazz replied calmly. She watched her leave. Then Jazz sent Byron a text message.

Chapter 19

By ten o'clock that night, the base from the club's sound system thumped the walls of Candy Girls. More customers than expected had turned out for a Tuesday. About ten construction workers from a nearby site sat scattered around the club. Some enjoyed a late supper. Others traded jokes with Tyretta and Chyna as they served. Jazz enjoyed walking the floor to join in the banter. Byron watched over it all with an impassive expression. He didn't make it obvious, but Byron kept an eye on Tyretta. By eleven, the number of customers had dwindled to a handful of hold-outs determined to close the place down. Still smiling at a flirtatious plumber, Jazz motioned to Byron. He crossed the floor in long strides. One look at him and the plumber decided to call it a night. The man was gone before Byron got to them.

"What's up?" Byron said.

"You scared the poor man outta here," Jazz said with a laugh. "I could have dealt with him easy, that's not why I called you over."

Byron grunted as he glanced around the club floor. "Yeah, he looked pretty harmless. But he was about to get a little too friendly. I could tell."

Jazz nodded at a short, but strong looking swarthy white man. His gaze followed Chyna around the room. "No more liquor that dude at table eight. Make sure he's not driving or getting too free with his hands. I think he's going to be trouble."

"I'll handle it," Byron said. "Might give him a word of warning before it goes that far."

"Yeah," Jazz replied.

"Listen, about your plan..." Byron turned his back so Tyretta couldn't see his face. She was across the club behind the bar. He'd complained because Jazz had prodded Tyretta without warning him.

"Cleavon must be pretty desperate by now, boss lady. I don't like it." "Has she made any phone calls that you could tell?" Jazz pretended not to notice Tyretta stealing glances at them.

"Not that I saw. No tellin' what they might do."

"What who might do?" Don said. Hidden by Byron's bulk, neither of them had seen him come into the club. His left arm was no longer in a sling. A portion of a bandage showed from his rolled back long sleeved shirt.

"Hey sweetie. We're just talking about these horny construction guys. Byron's about to clear the house. First, he's gonna walk the girls to their cars. Right, Byron?" Jazz reached up to clap the big man's large left shoulder.

"Right. Glad to see you on the mend detective." Byron nodded at Don with a smile then walked away. He looked at Jazz one last time as he left.

"Thanks, man." Don turned to Jazz again. "Nice try, but I can tell you weren't talking about your customers."

"You should still be home with the wifey resting, man. You know, eating nutritious meals and getting the royal treatment." Jazz tugged him until he walked beside her to the office.

"Stop dropping hints about my ex. We're *not* getting back together, and don't try to distract me. I'm not going to bite," Don said firmly. He opened the door and let Jazz go in first. Then he closed it.

"Okay, okay. I tried being matchmaker, but if you insist. Let's see how creative we can be around those injuries." Jazz stood on tiptoe to kiss him. She slid a finger inside the waistband of his pants.

"Soon enough," Don replied. Still he pulled her close to deepen their kiss.

"Wow, you don't need two hands, baby. I can deliver some hot buttered medicine that will heal all your aches and pains," Jazz whispered.

"I know you will. But first tell me what you're up to." Don stepped back to gaze at her steadily.

"Stop being such a... cop," Jazz retorted. She stomped over to her small bar area. She poured cold cream soda soft drink into a mug. Then she fixed herself a vodka and orange juice. "No alcohol for you, young man. You're still healing."

Don accepted the mug from her. He waited until Jazz had her drink and they were both on the sofa before he spoke. "Byron told me he doesn't trust Tyretta. Seems she's been acting shady. I gotta wonder why she's still working here."

Jazz stifled a curse word. Showing she was irritated with Byron for talking would be a quick giveaway. She covered her expression with the heavy crystal tumbler as she drank. Then she shrugged. "Byron and Tyretta have always gotten on each other's nerves."

"So nothing specific?" Don followed her lead and drank from his mug as well. His tone sounded casual.

Jazz wasn't fooled. Don's lie detector scanned her despite his laid back expression. "Look, Tyretta has a big mouth. Byron thought she's been talkin' too much, which explains how Lorraine got wind of some of my business."

"So Byron's dislike for Tyretta is coloring his judgment? You could be right." Don's unwavering dark-eyed gaze stayed on Jazz's every move.

"To satisfy Byron I told him to keep an eye on her. Like I figured, he came up with nothin'." Jazz finished off her drink. "We've been tight for a long time. I know her better than Byron. She can be a bitch, but the same can be said of me."

"No comment," Don replied.

`"Hey, you come in here insulting the owner and you'll pay the price."

Don grimaced dramatically. "Oww-wee, careful. I'm still a wounded warrior."

"Big baby. I thought you said your injuries weren't that bad. And how'd you get over here anyway? I doubt you're supposed to be driving this soon."

Don's grimace melted into an impish smile. "Lady doc. I charmed her into letting me drive short distances a couple of times a week. I just don't take those strong pain pills."

"You're straight up nuts, Detective Addison. Following medical advice is a smart move.," Jazz said with a frown.

"Nuts is right. Staying inside day in and out is definitely driving me crazy. This is my one and only trip today."

"I can't complain because you came to see me, I'm

glad." Jazz snuggled close and kissed his smoothly shaved cheek. "But you should be in bed, late as it is."

"You could tuck me," Don murmured and placed a large hand on her thigh. "Like you said, it's late. Let's go up to your place. Byron can shut the club."

Jazz stopped planting kisses on his neck. "I wish, but I gotta be here awhile. Lots of bills to make out and juggle since our daily take dropped. With all the drama the last two weeks, things have piled up. I can't keep putting it off. And besides, you'd rest better alone."

"No I wouldn't." Don bent down to brush his lips against her mouth as an argument. He flinched and grunted when Jazz hugged him.

Jazz stood and took the mug from him. " You can't handle me yet, Detective Addison. I'll work, you'll go home to sleep."

"You're not trying to get rid of me for some reason?" Don said.

"Sure I am. So you can heal faster. I'm missing that hard body." Jazz winked at him with a grin. She placed the mug and her tumbler on a table.

Don watched her. "Jazz, I..."

A loud knock was followed by Byron opening the door, a brown folder in one hand. "S'cuse me y'all. I apologize for interruptin' but I forgot some invoices need signin'. I want to mail those checks first thing in the morning. The beer and chip distributors are restless 'bout gettin' paid."

"Yeah, I know. See what I'm dealin' with, honey?" Jazz shook her head.

"Alright, alright. I'll let you two take care of business this time. Call me tomorrow." Don stood.

"I will. Promise." Jazz walked to him and accepted his goodbye kiss.

"Keep her out of trouble my man," Don said.

"Always," Byron replied with a grin.

With a final wave, Don walked stiffly out of the office. When Byron moved to close the door, Jazz gestured for him to stop. The sound of Don's heavy footsteps faded. Seconds later, they heard him calling out to the staff. Byron left and came back moments later.

"He's gone." Byron closed the door.

"You've got what they call perfect timing, Byron. If Don had stuck around any longer he'd have known something was up." Jazz heaved a deep sigh. She went to her desk and sat down.

"Yeah, well maybe him stayin' wouldn't have been a bad thing. We don't know what might happen tonight," Byron said, a frown creasing his brow.

"If Tyretta creeps in here to snoop, I'll whip her ass myself. I don't need no police to handle her." Jazz signed the invoices and wrote out two checks as she spoke.

Byron went to the windows. He pushed aside the curtains and looked down the alley. "Tyretta ain't dumb enough to try somethin' herself. Nah, I'm worried about who shows up because she snitched."

"Stop being so jittery. Tyretta will play it cool. If she thinks the place is empty, she'll let herself in and search it. If she finds me in here, she'll act like she left something or come up with another lie, and then pump me for information. Then she'll take call Lorraine. When the fake information comes back, we'll know for sure she's a rat." Jazz handed him the papers.

"You sound real sure she's gonna follow that script." Byron accepted the invoices and checks.

Jazz lit another cigarillo and reclined against the

executive chair back. "Yeah, because that's what she did to Lorraine."

Byron's head snapped up. "Say what?"

"Back when I was working at Candy Girls, business started going down. Lorraine let her thug sons, their friends, and Filipe's gang members ruin the place. There was drug dealing, guns being sold out back. There was a shooting and fights. Pretty soon paying customers stayed away, workers at the plants, solid blue collar guys that make good money. We even had white collar clients. They didn't want their names or faces on the news when cops raided. Let alone end up getting killed. You know how crazy those thugs get. And that's when they ain't drinkin' and druggin'."

"Right, bad situation," Byron said with a nod.

"You ain't lyin'. Tyretta and me was friends. Lorraine started being evil to just about everybody, just like her mama was. I used to talk to Tyretta about wanting to run my own place, but finding the right building would be tough. Tyretta tipped me off to the tax auction, and that Lorraine was facing legal trouble." Jazz raised an eyebrow at Byron as he rubbed his chin, deep in thought. "I never told anybody that until now. I didn't want Lorraine or her sons to find out."

"They would have put some hurt on her for sure. Now you're in trouble and Tyretta is on Lorraine's team again. Damn, that's cold-blooded."

Jazz shrugged and took a pull on the cigarillo. She blew out curls of smoke. "We both could be wrong, and she won't show up."

Byron stood. "I hope you're right. It's a helluva tough world, and true blue friends are even tougher to find."

"So I'm finding out, Byron," Jazz said softly. She

swung her chair around to gaze at the closed circuit television images. "We'd spot any strangers. She knows the system is working. Tyretta will know a way to slip in."

"The outside attempts didn't work, so now it's gotta be an inside job." Byron scowled. "Always worse when the hand holdin' the knife stuck in your back is somebody you shoulda been able to trust."

"You just dropped some straight heavy truth," Jazz replied. The heat of anger burned through her sentimentality. "So I'm gonna be waiting right here tonight and tomorrow night. It won't take long. Like you said, Lorraine is desperate."

"I'll leave like I'm goin' home. Then I'll double back and keep an eye on the place," Byron said.

"Only Tyretta will show and I can deal with her alone, but I'm not going to waste time arguing. You'll just do it anyway."

"We got some time. Rochelle and her brother are still cleaning up. Chyna is gettin' tables cleared off and the bar set up again. It's after midnight. We'll shut down in a minute." Byron glanced at the monitor. "I'll shove that last guy out the door. Then I'll lock up after the ladies are gone."

"Okay." Jazz brushed back her hair. She gazed at the pile of work on her desk. "Might as well knock this stuff out since I'm gonna be here anyway."

"Boss, if you don't mind..." Byron rubbed his jaw.

"Spit it out. You've earned the right to speak your mind." Jazz gave him a half-grin.

"Let me in your place. I can watch surveillance feed on the monitors up there. Beats prowling around outside."

After the burglaries, Byron had purchased more

electronic equipment. A friend of his had connected the cameras to monitors in Jazz's apartment. Without hesitation Jazz took out a set of spare keys from a desk drawer. She tossed them and Byron caught them with one large hand.

"If you want to sit up there bored instead of going home, be my guest," Jazz said. "At least I won't be worried you're going to get jumped in a dark alley."

"My grandmamma used to say better to watch your back than pull a knife outta it later," Byron said with a grin.

Jazz laughed. "Your grandmamma must have lived an interesting life. I'll have to hear about her later."

"You got it." Byron saluted Jazz and left like a man with a serious mission.

"Dude is on his job for sure." Jazz smiled at the image of Byron moving through the dark like a ninja .

Between sorting through paperwork Jazz glanced at the television screens showing the inside and outside of the club. As he'd said, around twelve-thirty Byron put the last straggler out and locked the front entrance. Tyretta left first, loudly calling out farewells to all. Jazz's eyes narrowed as Tyretta made it a point to saying she was going straight home. Byron left at almost one o'clock. Jazz watched him lock the side door from the outside and stroll to his Tahoe. Moments later he drove away.

Despite her brave words to Byron earlier, the silence of the club unnerved Jazz after the first thirty minutes. Her gaze darted back to the monitor showing three views outside the club frequently. The digital time on both screens flashed one forty-five, and Jazz caught herself glancing at the security feed for the tenth time. She gave a grunt of frustration.

"I need to stop trippin'," Jazz said. "I let Byron rub off on me."

Jazz forced her gaze away from the security monitors, stood, and stretched her muscles. She turned on the sound system. Neo soul music turned low flowed from the speakers. Then she poured another drink, lit a cigarillo, and sat down again. A glance at the small business software on her computer confirmed they were breaking even, but just. Her profits had been up, down, and all over the place. What she needed was stability, or Higgins and the city would get their wish. She couldn't pay her employees and support herself long-term if that pattern kept up. In fact, the odds were high that the downward trend in cash flow would return. She'd soon be distracted by the trial and the hearings with the city. Sure, she trusted Byron. But she was the owner. No one else could work her dreams into reality. Jazz had developed clear goals in the past six months. She even had a written step-by-step plan to go beyond a strip club. Now her plan had way too many "ifs" written in the margins. The biggest uncertainly of all was the verdict in her looming trial. A twenty-five to life sentence for murder would blow up all of her ambitions.

After a life of hard-knocks, Jazz couldn't resist giving in to a morose mood. She rubbed her eyes and glanced at the clock on her computer. Two-twenty . The early morning hours always made life seem bleak. A couple of distant bumps in the night broke through deep thoughts of her hard childhood. Jazz blinked back to her all too real present and looked at the monitors. Both had gone blank.

"What the hell?"

Jazz shot to her feet. Her heart pounded so hard it

almost drowned out another bump. She sat alone in a locked club, blind, and with no back-up. Then she fought to control her fear.

"Byron," she whispered. Breathing hard she texted him. "C'mon, c'mon. Oh shit this is stupid."

She dialed his cell phone and got voice mail. Her heart rate speed up until blood rushed in her ears. A tidal wave of panic made it hard to breathe. The late hour and tension had to be playing tricks on her mind. No one could be in the club.

"He'll will text or call back in a minute," she mumbled in an attempt to reassure the scared voices in her head.

But minutes seemed like forever and still no reply from Byron. Jazz considered going into the club, but decided against it. Moving around alone would make her feel even more vulnerable. She'd imagine someone coming up behind her or hiding around a corner with every step. No, better to stay in the office. With a deep breath, Jazz took the Smith and Wesson .380 from a desk drawer and placed it in her lap. When the office door knob turned, Jazz remembered too late she hadn't bothered to lock it. As if to heighten her terror, the door cracked open and stopped. Anger spiked at the invasion of her hard won property and the intimidation tactic. Without standing, Jazz raised the gun and pointed.

"Bring your ass in here unless you want me to shoot through the damn door,. If you know me, you know I'm a good shot. I'm gone pull the trigger and put a hole in you.," Jazz said in a level voice.

Even as she gave the bold speech, Jazz's mind raced. Seconds ticked by as she wondered and worried about Byron. Questions popped in her head like blinding flashbulbs. Who? How? What did this unknown person plan? The door swung open. Jazz hissed in shock at the person standing before her.

Chapter 20

Lorraine wore a long-sleeved black t-shirt tucked into black slim jeans and carried a Glock pistol in her left hand as an accessory, though it was pointed down Hair pulled back into a single braid, she looked younger than her forty plus years.

"This bitch right here," Lorraine said.

Jazz recovered. Answers clicked into place like wooden puzzle pieces. "Bitch times ten."

"Got a gun I see." Lorraine's gaze darted left and then right in the split second before she looked at Jazz again.

Lorraine seemed to be surprised to find her armed. Jazz felt sure Tyretta searched the office for Jazz's gun, but didn't find it. For a good reason. Filipe had taught her useful gangsta skills, like how to hide a gun. Jazz felt a kind of calm settle over her. Seeing who she was up against didn't rattle her the way the unknown had moments before. This kind of danger she understood.

"You know me. I pack steel on the daily. Obviously I'm right cause you're carryin', too. So you were the brains all along. I was thinkin' your sons were runnin' the gang. They were just ordinary thugs with big ideas.

Easy enough to let everybody think they were in charge," Jazz said. "Nah, they didn't have the brains to make the moves you did."

"I have admit my boys ain't never been the brightest bulbs on the tree. So you think you got it all figured out, huh? Too smart for your own good."

"Kyeisha figured it out, too. So she had to go." Jazz reassessed how much danger she was in. Lorraine calculated every move. She wasn't just dumb and desperate.

"Humph, Kyeisha was greedy. That turned out to be hazardous to her health. She figured out you still had my property and tried to sell it to my son. Some damn nerve, huh? Charging me big bucks for my own shit." Wrath flickered in Lorraine's brown gaze for a second.

"Too bad for Kyeisha. Now I gotta ask why you dressed like a burglar and up in my place at two-thirty in the damn morning?"

Lorraine shrugged and gave an apologetic grin. "I know the timing of my visit is strange, but it's kinda urgent."

"You must not watch those forensic shows on TV. You don't write down your shit for people to find."

Lorraine's smile faltered before she plastered it back in place. "Nothin' but a bunch of old notebooks with receipts in them. I got tax troubles, so I need that stuff. I thought you threw it out. Now the tax man gonna say I lied."

"So instead of calllin' me like a normal human being, you decide to break in with a gun? C'mon, Lorraine. The lie is bad enough, but thinking I'm stupid is insultin'," Jazz smiled back, but let it freeze into a sneer. She lifted her gun slightly.

"None of it means anything to you, or ever will.

Look, just give me the notebooks and I'll call off the dogs," Lorraine forced out when Jazz didn't respond after fifteen long seconds of silence.

"Explain, but first relax while I come around the desk to hear you better." Jazz kept the gun pointed at Lorraine's chest.

"Okay."

Jazz continued to aim straight at her as Lorraine inched a few feet past the doorway. She glanced down at her cell phone hoping to see a text from Byron. The blank screen signaled bad news. "Explain in detail what call off the dogs means. This time I give you permission to assume I'm a slow learner."

"I can get the city to back off," Lorraine said.

"Your pals are all either fired or in jail for taking bribes," Jazz shot back bluntly.

Lorraine grimaced for a second, then her expression eased. "I can make sure plenty of folks around the neighborhood testify for you. They'll say this place ain't as bad as others say. They'll say you feed the homeless and hungry kids."

"Why would they listen to your pals? You got a dirty record when it comes to obeying the law," Jazz replied.

"Friends of friends with no criminal records. I put some layers between them and me. There's a least a couple of city employees left who won't scratch the surface," Lorraine said.

"You spread around some cash, huh? Okay, but the city closing me down is the least of my worries. What about the murder charge? Only right you fix that since you set me up," Jazz said matter-of-factly with a shrug.

"Hmm, maybe I can find some witnesses that saw Kyeisha with unknown guys that night." Lorraine glanced into the office warily. "I've heard talk she got in with a bad crowd."

"What? Oh, you think I'm recording our little social visit or something. Look around. I'm not dumb enough to have a camera in here, even I was expectin' company." Jazz nodded an invitation for Lorraine to check again.

"These days cameras can be anywhere and look like anything." Despite her words, Lorraine's gaze darted from the walls, the desk, and back to Jazz several times. A full minute ticked by.

"You're not into computers, which is why you had those nice notebooks for me to find." Jazz smiled at Lorraine.

Only the slight tightening of her jaw gave away Lorraine's fury. Then she smiled back at Jazz easily. "You won't get anything out of the notebooks."

Jazz started to say more when the screen of her cell phone lit up to display caller ID. MiMi's grin looked back at her. What the hell did she want? "Why don't we let the police decide if they're useful or not."

Lorraine stared hard at Jazz. "I can help you out a lot more than the police. Including that cute cop you been screwin'. The rest of his cop friends want to see you go down for Kyeisha's killin'."

"Maybe so. But this is still my property. You're trespassin' and armed. In Louisiana I could shoot you and claim self-defense," Jazz said.

"I'm tired of playin' this silly ass game. I didn't come here without back-up. And why you think that fancy security system ain't workin', huh? Why your boy Byron ain't textin' you back? Cause he's *my* boy, that's why. " Lorraine gestured with her head toward Jazz's desk. "Go on, check your phone. Nothin'."

"You're lyin'."

Lorraine laughed with genuine amusement in her voice. "You sure?"

Jazz felt a stab of cold fear. Her words rang with truth, setting off more alarms bells in her head. Tyretta didn't know the security system or cameras, but Byron worked with the installer. Byron hadn't known the significance of the old papers until Jazz told him. He could have been feeding Lorraine inside information instead of Tyretta. Or maybe it was both of them. Jazz's mind swirled with the effort to sort through truth, lies, and deceptions. Every conversation, suggestion, or gesture for months took on a new meaning. "I know you've had a shock. Let's call it a draw with the guns, alright? You show me where in here you got the notebooks. I take them and leave. Sure I got help, but they can't get in. I came inside alone." Lorraine spoke like she was negotiating an everyday business deal.

"How'd you get in here? I saw Byron lock the doors. The cameras were still working," Jazz said.

"You couldn't watch every door every minute. While you were busy, I slipped in. I hid in the storeroom until everybody was gone. Kinda comfy in there. I had water and some wings. Taste good, too. All I had to do was wait." Lorraine seemed relaxed now. "Like I said, you can't figure out what's in my old tablets. Just some scribblin'."

Jazz glanced at her cell phone. MiMi, chatty even in text, had kept tapping away on her end. "You mean the code with names of your son's drug and illegal guns customers? Filipe won't be happy to know you decided to write a book that includes him. I'll bet some of your other business partners won't be happy either."

"You're lyin', bitch," Lorraine hissed. She started to

move.

"I wouldn't if I was you," Jazz warned. "I may be so upset I just start shootin'. You got a problem. I'm not the only one that knows about the notebooks."

"What are you sayin'?" Lorraine asked, but from the way her brown face turned gray it was clear she already knew.

"If my back-up doesn't hear from me, she'll start sending e-mails to Crime Stoppers, the police, and the DA's office. No tellin' how creative my crew will get. They love spreadin' juicy news."

"I should have killed your ass back when you stole my property. Let's put down our guns and fight it out. Shooting you won't be as satisfyin' as stompin' in your damn head until I see your brains," Lorraine shouted.

"I ain't into hand-to-hand combat, fool. A bullet in your head will do me just fine," Jazz retorted. "I didn't have to steal your property. You practically *gave* it to me, and thanks by the way. You should have had sense enough to keep cash on hand to pay the taxes."

"Shut the fuck up," Lorraine snarled. She gripped the gun tighter, but didn't raise it.

"Yeah, the truth hurts like a mutha, don't it? Wait a minute. You hid your cash away, or maybe your punk ass son stole it. That's why you didn't have the money. Damn, I thought you woulda planned better." Jazz laughed as Lorraine breathed out in angry puffs like an enraged cow.

"Shuttin' your big mouth for good is worth any price." "Uh-huh. You're back-up is runnin' late," Jazz said, putting as much taunt in her tone as possible. "You can't seem to control your crew. Ding, more points off."

Lorraine started to speak again, but instead she darted a look at the window. Then she stared at Jazz again. A slow smile pulled up her full lips. The tinkle of broken glass alerted Jazz and she ducked. A pop followed a split second later. Lorraine fired a shot at her. Jazz felt a punch to her shoulder, but she managed to scramble behind her desk.

"Byron ain't comin' like I said, bitch. Here's the deal. You're going to get killed by a burglar. Naturally he'll never get caught. Tomorrow your employees won't be able to get into the club. Maybe a day or so will go by before your sister finds your body. But tonight we'll have plenty of time to find my notebooks and disappear like ghosts," Lorraine called out.

When she peeked around the desk corner, Jazz saw Lorraine still stood outside in the hallway. "You been watchin' too many cop shows, Lorraine. Byron wasn't my only back-up. My sister knows I'm here."

"Bullshit. She'd have shown up by now," Lorraine said.

"I think she's hit. You want me to come in? I can shoot the lock off the door." A female voice came from the window.

"Don't be so damn stupid. That might take three or four shots. Neighbors would call the police," Lorraine yelled.

"I didn't know you were so handy with a gun, Tyretta," Jazz shouted as she shifted position. She winced at a burning pain in her right shoulder. Her right arm started to feel weak, and blood made her sleeve stick to it.

"Shit," Lorraine hissed.

Jazz had been distracted, but then she heard the sound. Sirens whining in the distance got closer. Help on the way. She fought against the dizzy feeling that threatened to leave her helpless.

"You lied, huh? If Byron was with you Tyretta would already be inside. He's got keys." Jazz forced confidence into her voice. She fired a round into the ceiling to scare them, and in hopes it would be heard outside.

"I'm gone get outta here," Tyretta screeched through the broken window.

"You leave, and I'll hunt your ass down. Get your shit together and shoot through the back door," Lorraine shouted back.

"I thought you said..."

"Shut the fuck up and do it," Lorraine screamed.

Jazz laughed and fired again. "Will she make it before I put a hole in you?"

"Shit!"

Feet pounded down the hallway as Lorraine abandoned her position in favor of escape. Jazz forgot about being hurt as she raced after her. Two muffled pops came from the direction of the steel reinforced back door. She couldn't see Lorraine though. Police sirens blocked out other noise and then went silent.

"I know you in here. Won't take 'em long to get in, Lorraine. You're outnumbered and out gunned," Jazz yelled, but kept her head down. She decided not to risk going into the club. Instead she crouched in the hallway.

"Fine, I'll catch a charge. You're still going to trial for a killing," Lorraine shouted back.

"They've got Tyretta by now. A hundred bucks says she tells 'em everything within the first two hours," Jazz replied. She laughed loudly.

Lorraine let fly a string of curse words. "I don't give a shit no more."

Gunfire hit the walls outside the hallway. As Jazz scrambled away intense pain brought back the dizziness. Lorraine kept firing and cussing. Jazz fired back in a desperate attempt to hold her off. But Lorraine seemed enraged to the point of insanity. Voices filled the club, then more shots. Nauseated, Jazz crawled along the floor toward her office. Boots thumped against the floor behind her. She shuddered in anticipation of a bullet to her head, but spun to face the attack with gun in hand.

"Jazz, stop!" A tall silhouette loomed against the dim light. "It's over."

"I know," she whispered and blacked out.

* * *

Sirens. Blurred lights and the sensation of movement roused Jazz from a deep sleep. She blinked hard at a strange white face.

"Good thing you ran out of rounds," a deep male voice rumbled.

She turned her head toward it. Byron's brown eyes stretched wide with fear. Perspiration beaded on his forehead. His face looked odd, one side larger than the other. A hand stretched out to him, and Byron accepted a towel. He dabbed his forehead.

"We let you ride to keep her calm. But you have to sanitize yourself," the EMT said softly.

"Yeah, don't let that funky sweat drip on me," Jazz mumbled.

"Smart ass." Byron grinned at her, relief easing the furrows in his brow.

"I sign your checks," she said, her voice came out low and scratchy. "What happened to you?"

"Dudes jumped me and..."

"No talking for now," the EMT ordered.

Jazz didn't protest because she couldn't. A soft darkness pulled her in a hole as her eyes closed. When she woke again, Willa and Don leaned over her from opposite sides. Willa gently touched her arm seconds later. Don's taught expression relaxed in relief. Jazz tried to talk around the cotton in her mouth, realized it was her tongue and grimaced. A cup with a straw appeared in Willa's hand and Jazz drank.

"Unless we at the funeral home, I think y'all oughta look a bit happier," Jazz managed.

"Ten minutes only, please," a crisp voice said and the door whisked shut.

"The nurse," Willa replied to the questioning gaze Jazz shot at her.

"Byron?" Jazz looked from Willa to Don.

"He's fine. Two guys jumped him on the way back for his little stake out. He fought them off for a good ten minutes before we showed," Don rumbled. "You two need a good long lecture on playing cop."

"Oh she'll be hearing from me," Willa put in firmly. She kissed Jazz's forehead.

"Lorraine?"

"You managed to plug her shooting wild. Well, we'll find out for sure once we do the ballistic. I don't think she was hit by one of the officers though," Don said.

Jazz raised her head, but Willa pushed her back. "Is she..."

"Not dead. She's in critical but stable condition. She'll make it to trial," he replied.

Willa gently tucked a blanket around Jazz. "Tyretta is talking non-stop. She's trying to get a deal. Girl, Lorraine..."

"Is the top gangsta," Jazz broke in. "Lorraine kept

that nice and quiet. I'll bet anyone who found out ended up dead."

"We're gonna clean up the trash, get those thugs off the streets. We're rounding up her crew now. I'll bet we solve some drive-bys and more." Don gave a satisfied grunt at the solid police work ahead, the reason he loved his job.

Jazz looked at him. "There'll be plenty of young dudes ready to take their place. I bet some guy is makin' moves to be the next leader right now."

"Yeah, but I'll worry about them later."

Willa smiled down at her. "Hey, let's get to the good news. Phillips says the charges will likely be dropped in the next few days. The police have to submit the results of their investigation of course but with Tyretta being so very cooperative, you're in the clear."

"The city is backing off closing you down, too. Your big time suspect is linked to the complaints they got. They don't want the publicity." Don's grin indicated he played a role.

"Since you didn't get yourself killed, I won't fuss too much about the chances you took," Willa added with a scowl. "Okay, before time is up, I'm going to let Mikayla and Anthony set eyes on you. They imagined the worst."

"Okay," Jazz said with a sigh as she watched Willa hurry out. "I hate the kids being scared like that."

Don leaned his long frame down and kissed her softly on the lips. He drew back to stare into her eyes. "Promise me you're gonna become a regular boring girlfriend from now on."

Jazz blinked at him in a rare moment of speechlessness. All she could get out was a weak, "Okay."

"I'm consider that a sworn oath. Now I gotta move. I'm on desk duty, but they need me to help with the investigation. Oh, you'll be happy to know Armand decided I'm not throwing my career down the toilet. Y'all might be pals in a minute." Don gave a deep hearty laugh at the expression Jazz put on.

"Not sure I wanna be his buddy," Jazz wisecracked. She accepted a goodbye kiss with a smile.

Anthony and Mikayla came in looking just as terrified as Willa had said they were. Her nephew tried to look brave, but Jazz saw him examining her bandages. Mikayla looked on the verge of tears as she approached the hospital bed. Soon they were smiling as Jazz joked around to show them she wasn't headed for the grave. The nurse came in to politely but firmly usher them out. She allowed Willa a few minutes longer.

"You're coming to my house," Willa said. "I don't want to hear it."

"Please ask your aunt not to sing so loud this time," Jazz retorted with a roll of her eyes. Then she smiled with affection at her big sister.

With her family reassured and gone, Jazz settled against the surprisingly comfortable hospital pillows. The television set high over her was on a bland nature show, the sound muted. Her eyes drifted shut in the cushioned quiet enforced by nurses. She started when the door eased open.

MiMi slipped in sideways like she was used to sneaking around hospitals. She sat down in a chair near the bed. "They can't keep me out."

"Damn, MiMi. I've gotten into enough trouble already. Don't get me kicked out of the hospital," Jazz blurted out. Then she laughed until it hurt. Literally. Still she couldn't help it. MiMi looked like a Black American

Princess burglar in designer clothes.

"Shh, keep it down. I just wanted to see how you were doing for myself. That stiff old nurse can't tell me what to do." MiMi sniffed. "So you're feeling better?"

"Oh yeah, since I'm off the hook for murder. Best freakin' medicine in the world." Jazz raised an eyebrow at her. "And?"

"Hmm, what do you mean 'and'? I came to check on my friend." MiMi brushed back her long hair. A few seconds went by as she examined her fingernails. "So those notebooks might tell us where Lorraine hid a lot of money or how much she stole from Filipe..."

Jazz managed to raise her uninjured arm and clap a hand over her eyes. "Oh, hell no. Here we go again."

* * * * *

If you enjoyed Devilish Details please let other readers in on the fun! Leave a review. Thanks!

Triple Trouble
Mystery Series:

BEST ENEMIES - Book 1

DEVILISH DETAILS - Book 2

PRETTY DANGEROUS - Book 3
(coming in 2015)

Visit www.lynnemery.com for more details and to watch trailers!

About the Author

Mix knowledge of voodoo, Louisiana politics and forensic social work with the dedication to write fiction while working each day as a clinical social worker, and you get a snapshot of author Lynn Emery. Lynn has been a contributing consultant to the magazine Today's Black Woman for three articles about contemporary relationships between black men and women. She sold her first novel in 1995 to Kensington publishing for their groundbreaking Arabesque line. **NIGHT MAGIC** went on to be recognized for Excellence in Romance Fiction by *Romantic Times Magazine*. Her third novel, **AFTER ALL**, became a movie produced by BET. Holly Robinson Peete stars as Michelle Toussaint, an investigative television reporter. In 2004 Lynn won three coveted Emma Awards. She was chosen Author of the Year and her novel **KISS LONLEY GOODBYE** won Best Novel and Favorite Hero. **GOOD WOMAN BLUES was nominated for the Romantic Times Best Mainstream Multicultural of 2005**

www.lynnemery.com

www.ingramcontent.com/pod-product-compliance
Lightning Source LLC
Chambersburg PA
CBHW021458110726

47899CB00001BA/205